TWIN CITIES

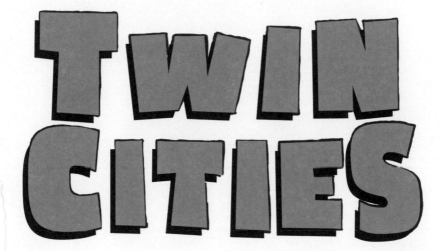

Also by Jose Pimienta

Suncatcher
Stars, Hide Your Fire (with Kel McDonald)
Soupy Leaves Home (with Cecil Castellucci)

JOSE PIMIENTA

RH
GRAPHIC

NEW YORK

Twin Cities was penciled and inked traditionally, and colored and lettered in Photoshop.

Text, cover art, and interior illustrations copyright © 2022 by Jose Pimienta

All rights reserved. Published in the United States by RH Graphic, an imprint of Random House Children's Books, a division of Penguin Random House LLC, New York.

RH Graphic with the book design is a trademark of Penguin Random House LLC.

Visit us on the web! RHKidsGraphic.com • @RHKidsGraphic

Educators and librarians, for a variety of teaching tools, visit us at RHTeachersLibrarians.com

Library of Congress Cataloging-in-Publication Data is available upon request.
ISBN 978-0-593-18063-1 (hardcover) — ISBN 978-0-593-18062-4 (paperback)
ISBN 978-0-593-18064-8 (lib. bdg.) — ISBN 978-0-593-18065-5 (ebook)

Designed by Patrick Crotty

MANUFACTURED IN CHINA
10 9 8 7 6 5 4 3 2 1
First Edition

A comic on every bookshelf.

To my siblings. I love you.

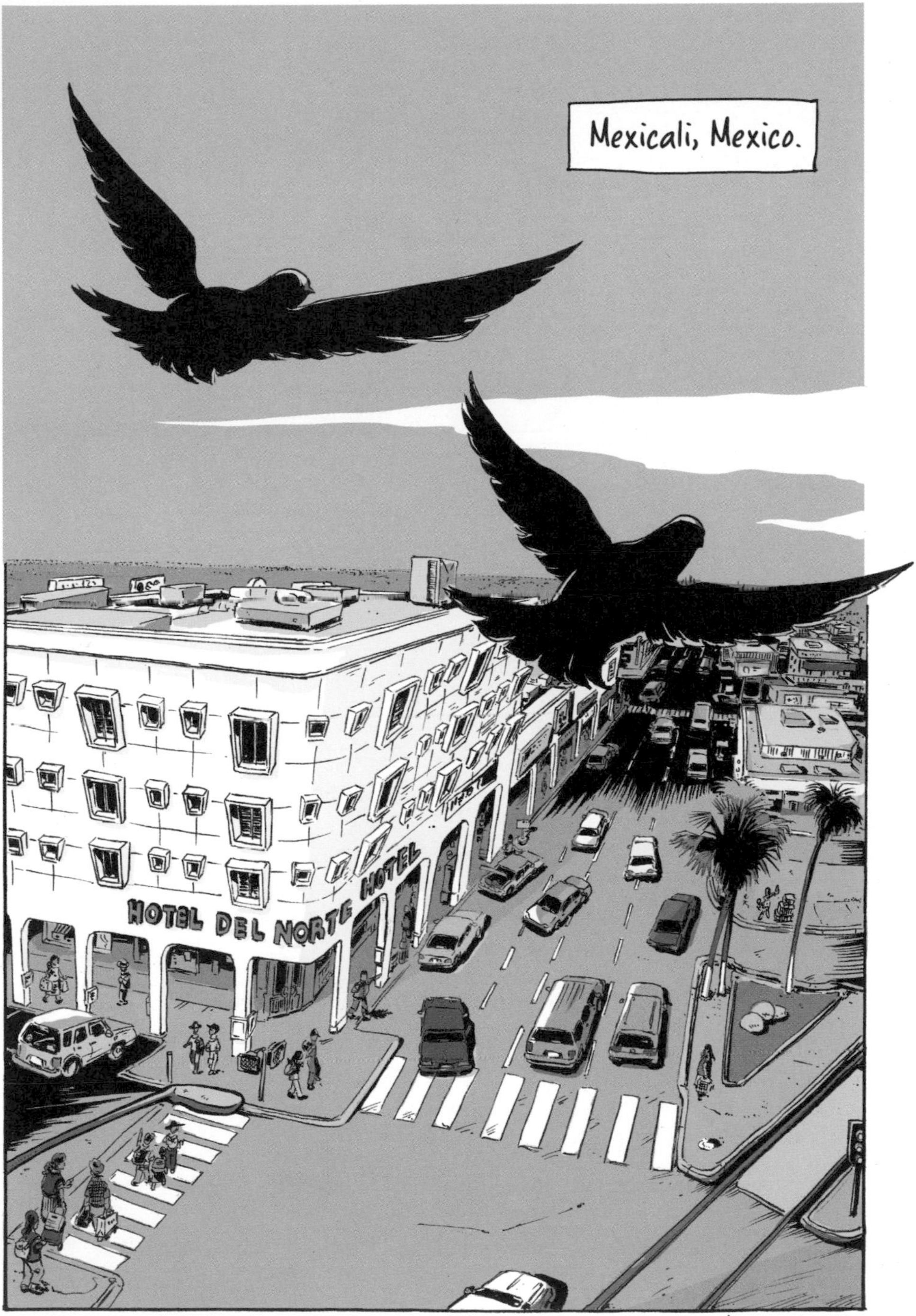
Mexicali, Mexico.
HOTEL DEL NORTE HOTEL

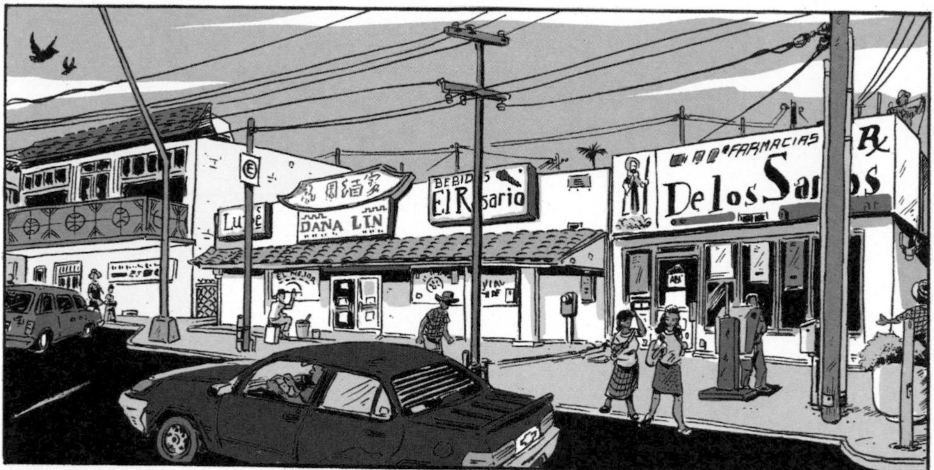
FARMACIAS
DANA LIN
EL MEJOR

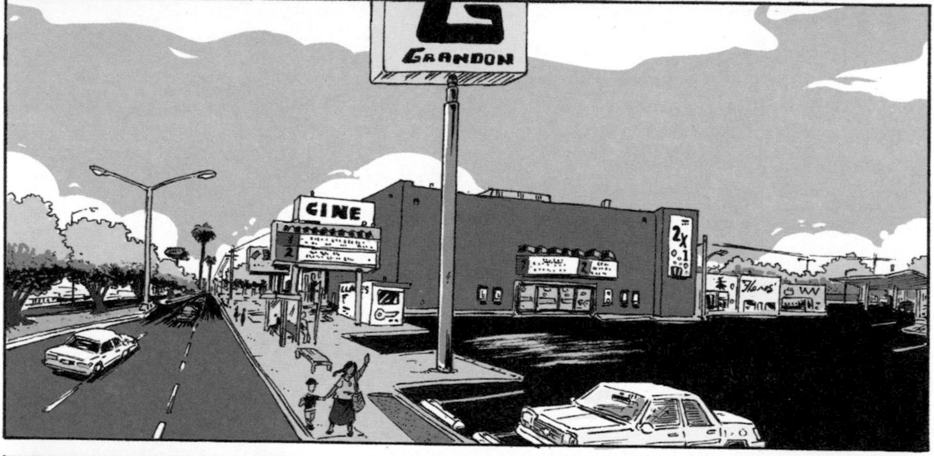
GRANDON
CINE
2x1

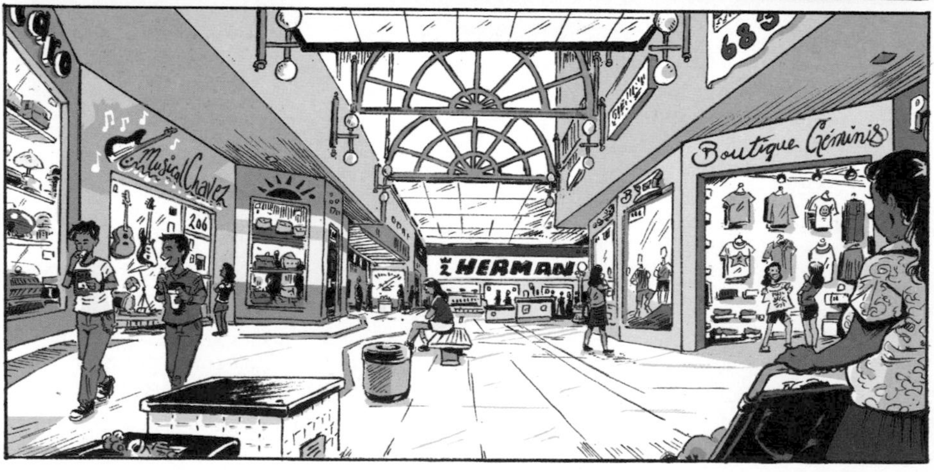
Musical Chavez
206
HERMAN
Boutique Géminis

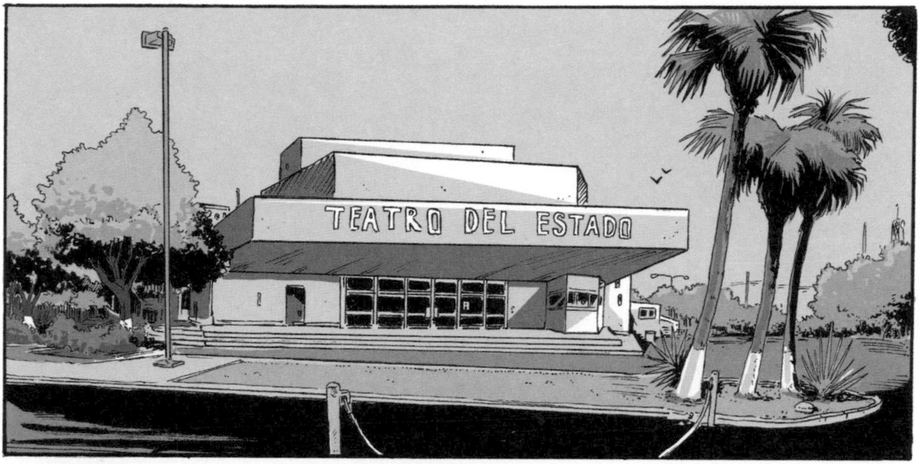
TEATRO DEL ESTADO

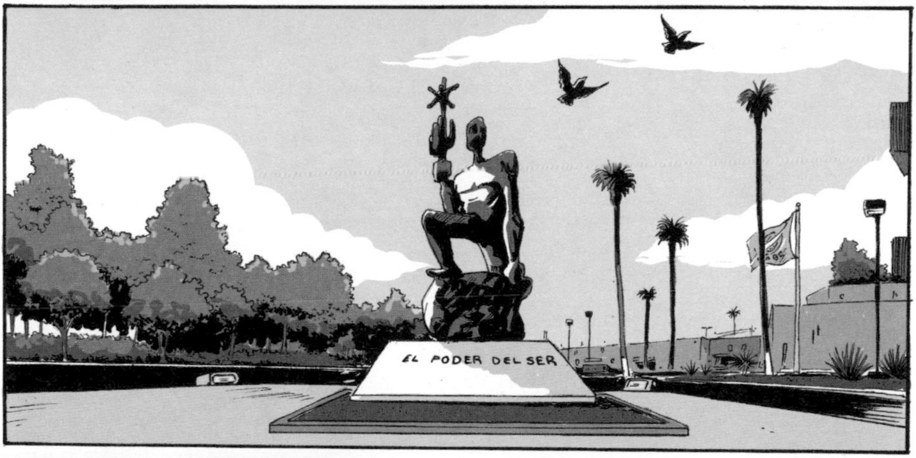
EL PODER DEL SER

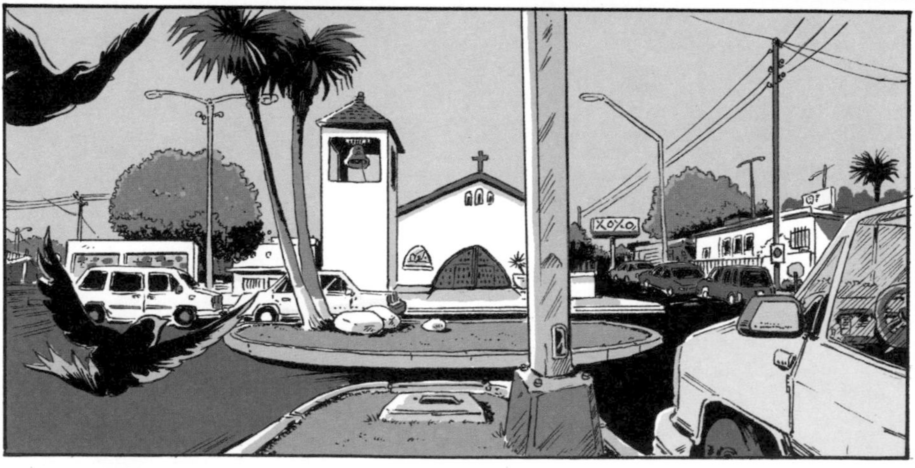
XOXO

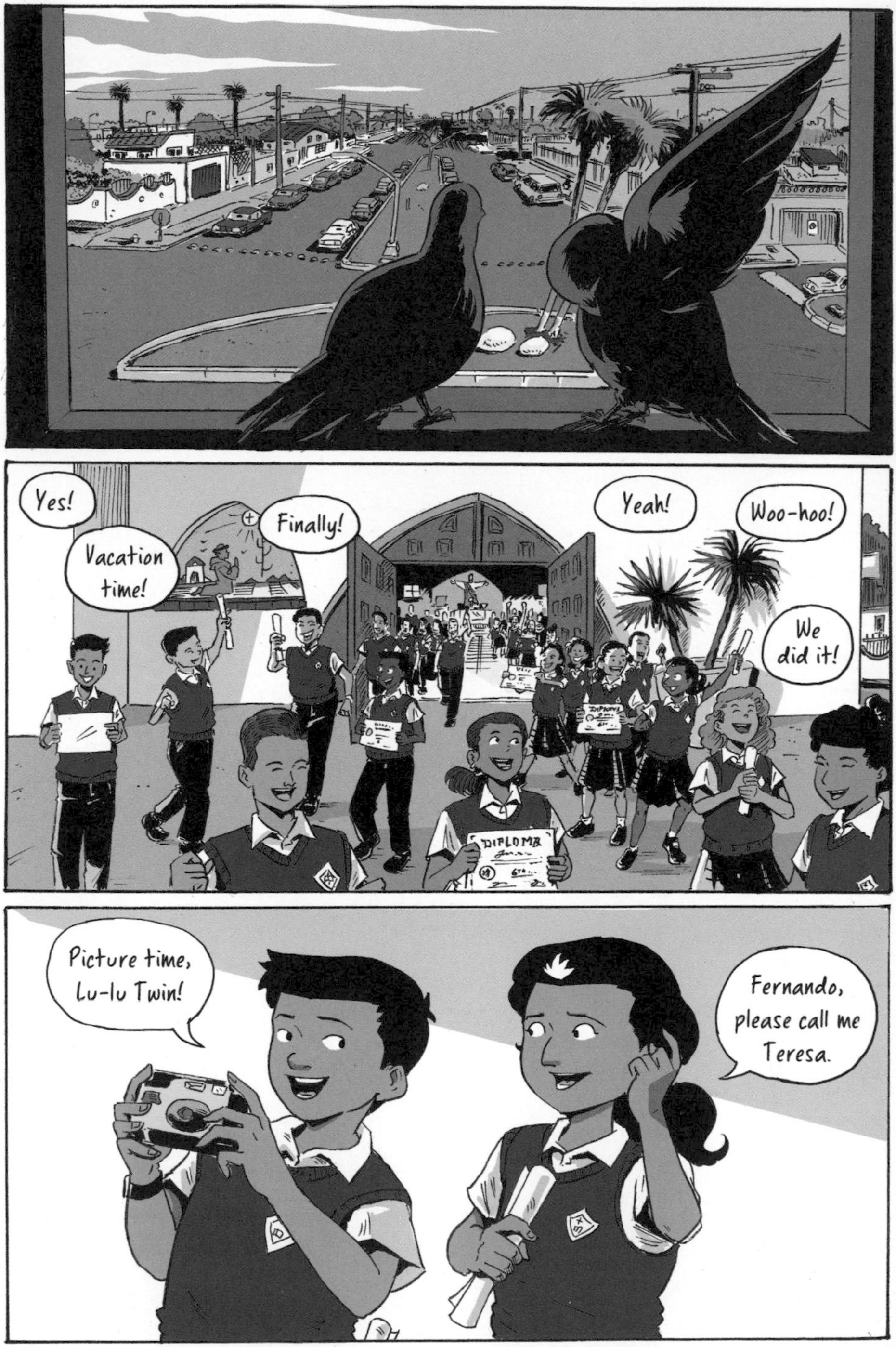
Yes!
Vacation time!
Finally!
Yeah!
Woo-hoo!
We did it!
DIPLOMA
Picture time, Lu-lu Twin!
Fernando, please call me Teresa.

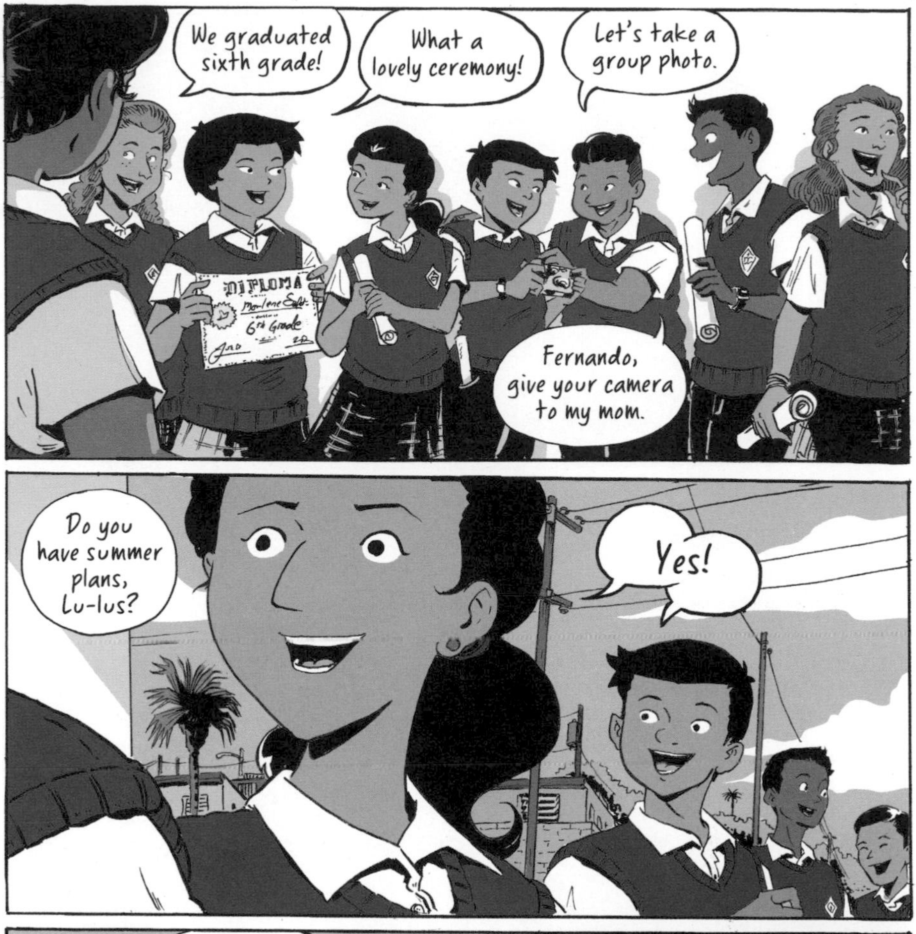
We graduated sixth grade!
What a lovely ceremony!
Let's take a group photo.
DIPLOMA
6th Grade
Fernando, give your camera to my mom.
Do you have summer plans, Lu-lus?
Yes!
Get together. This is the good one.
One, two, three.
SMILE!
DIPLOMA

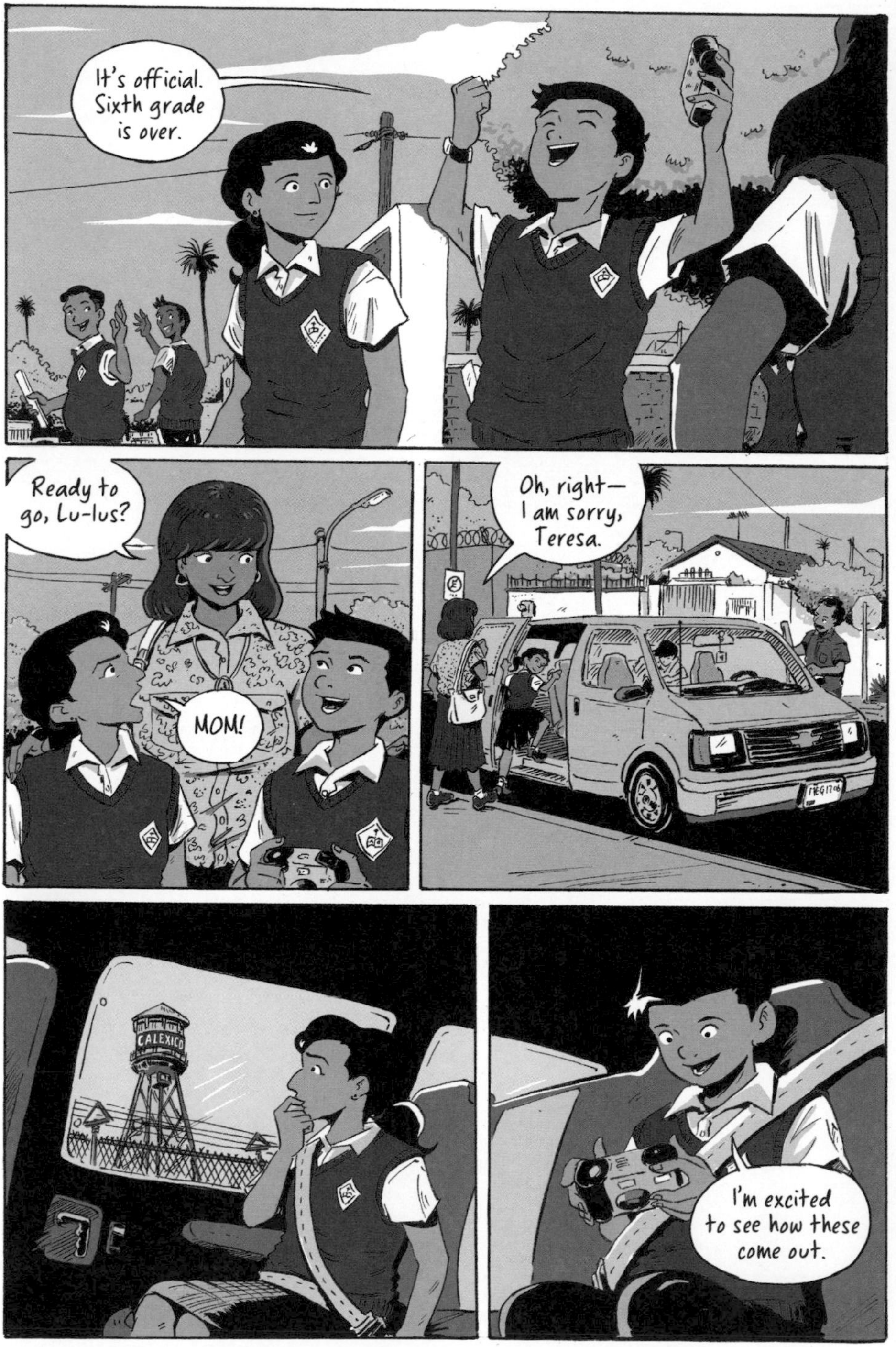
It's official. Sixth grade is over.
Ready to go, Lu-lus?
MOM!
Oh, right— I am sorry, Teresa.
CALEXICO
I'm excited to see how these come out.

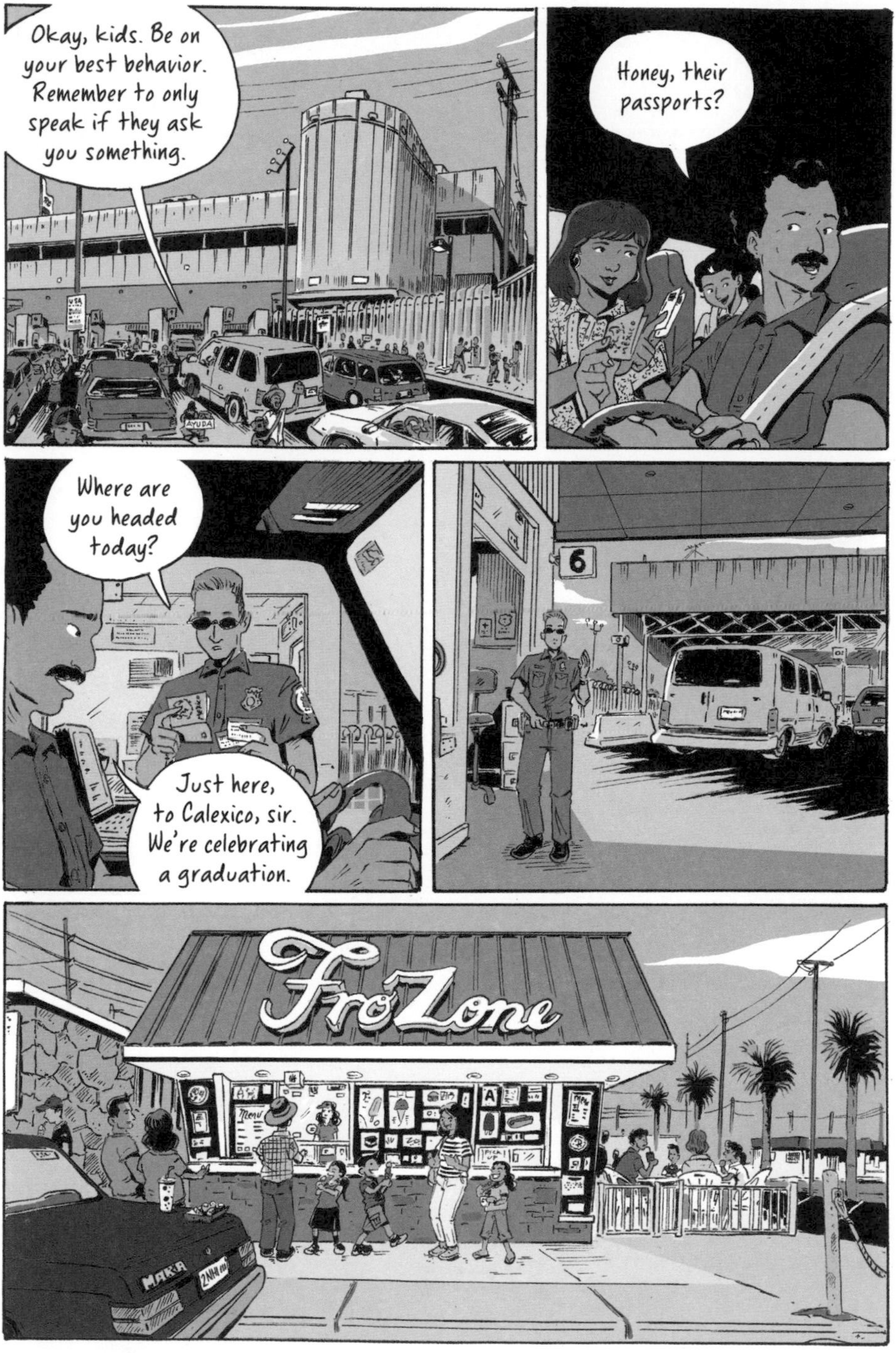
Okay, kids. Be on your best behavior. Remember to only speak if they ask you something.
AYUDA
Honey, their passports?
Where are you headed today?
Just here, to Calexico, sir. We're celebrating a graduation.
6
FroZone
Menu

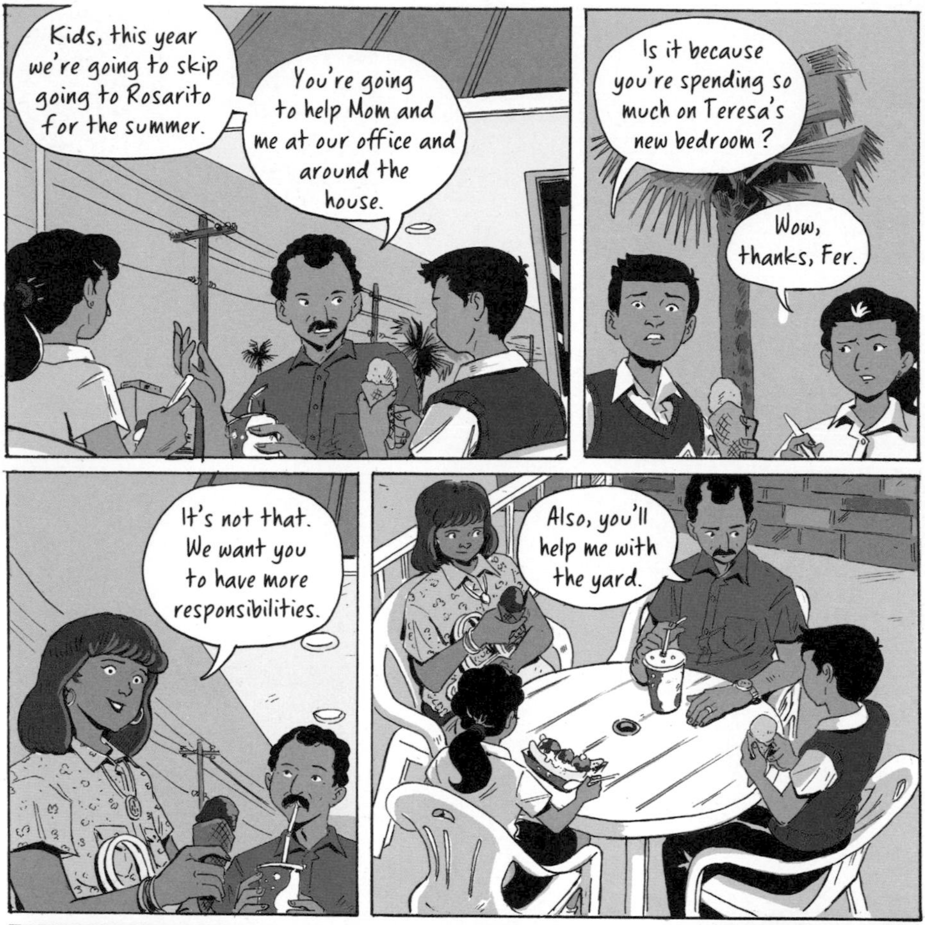
Kids, this year we're going to skip going to Rosarito for the summer.
You're going to help Mom and me at our office and around the house.
Is it because you're spending so much on Teresa's new bedroom?
Wow, thanks, Fer.
It's not that. We want you to have more responsibilities.
Also, you'll help me with the yard.
But we don't like gardening.
I like it okay—
I'm not interested in whether you like it or not.
You're going to help me.
AUTO

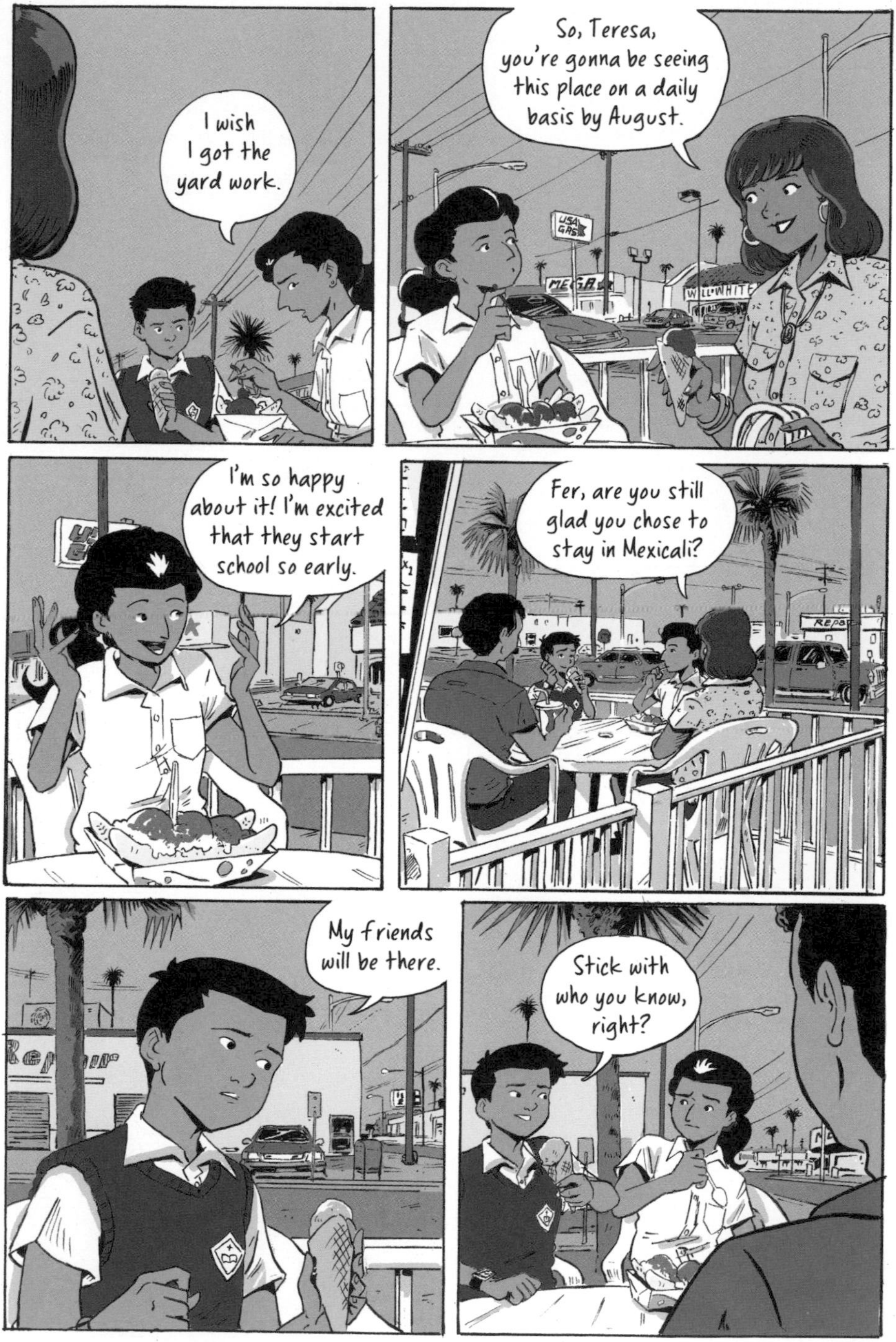
I wish I got the yard work.
So, Teresa, you're gonna be seeing this place on a daily basis by August.
USA GAS
MEGA
WILL WHITE
I'm so happy about it! I'm excited that they start school so early.
Fer, are you still glad you chose to stay in Mexicali?
My friends will be there.
Stick with who you know, right?

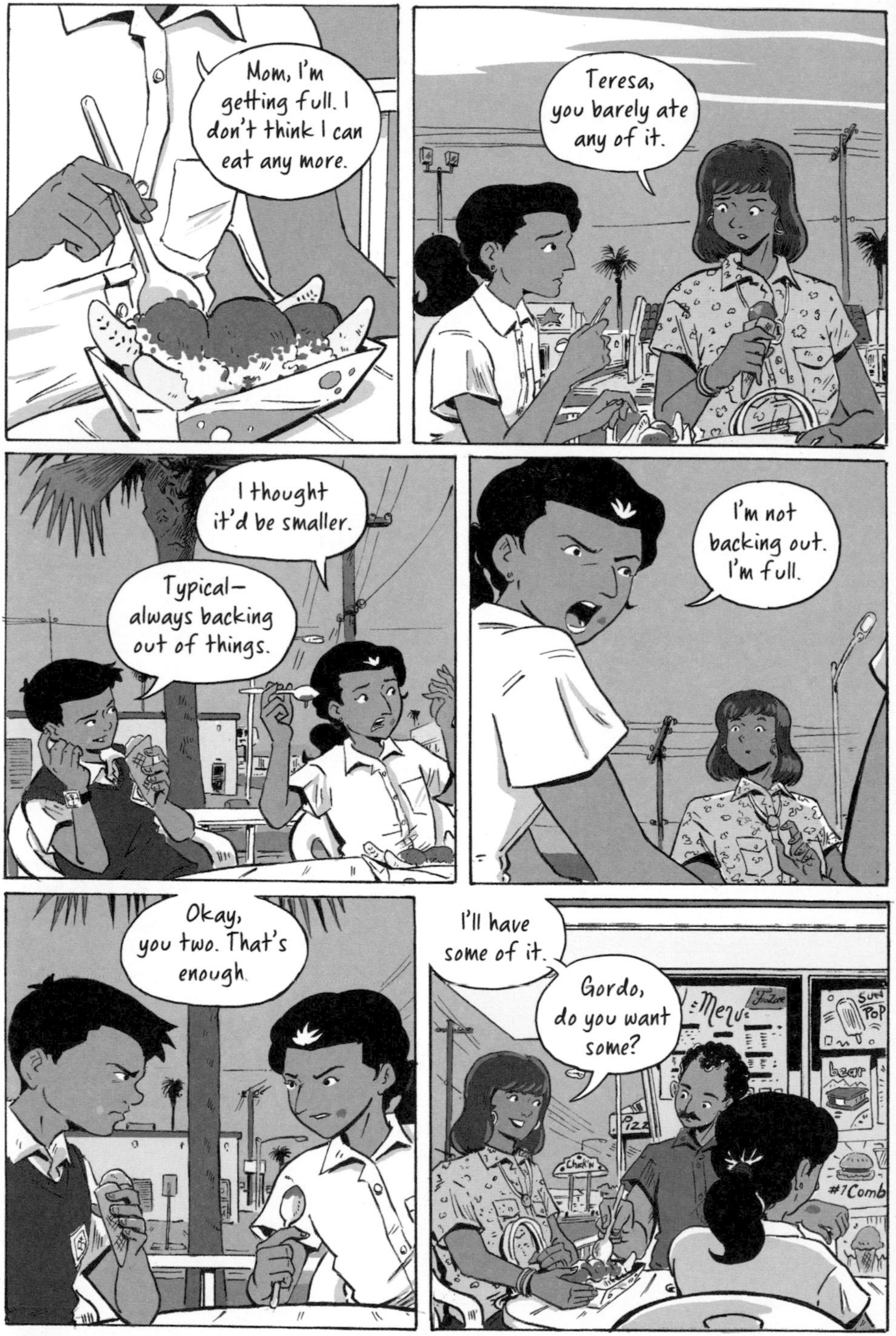

Mom, I'm getting full. I don't think I can eat any more.
Teresa, you barely ate any of it.
I thought it'd be smaller.
Typical—always backing out of things.
I'm not backing out. I'm full.
Okay, you two. That's enough.
I'll have some of it.
Gordo, do you want some?
Menu
SUN POP
bear
Pizz
Chick'n
#1Comb

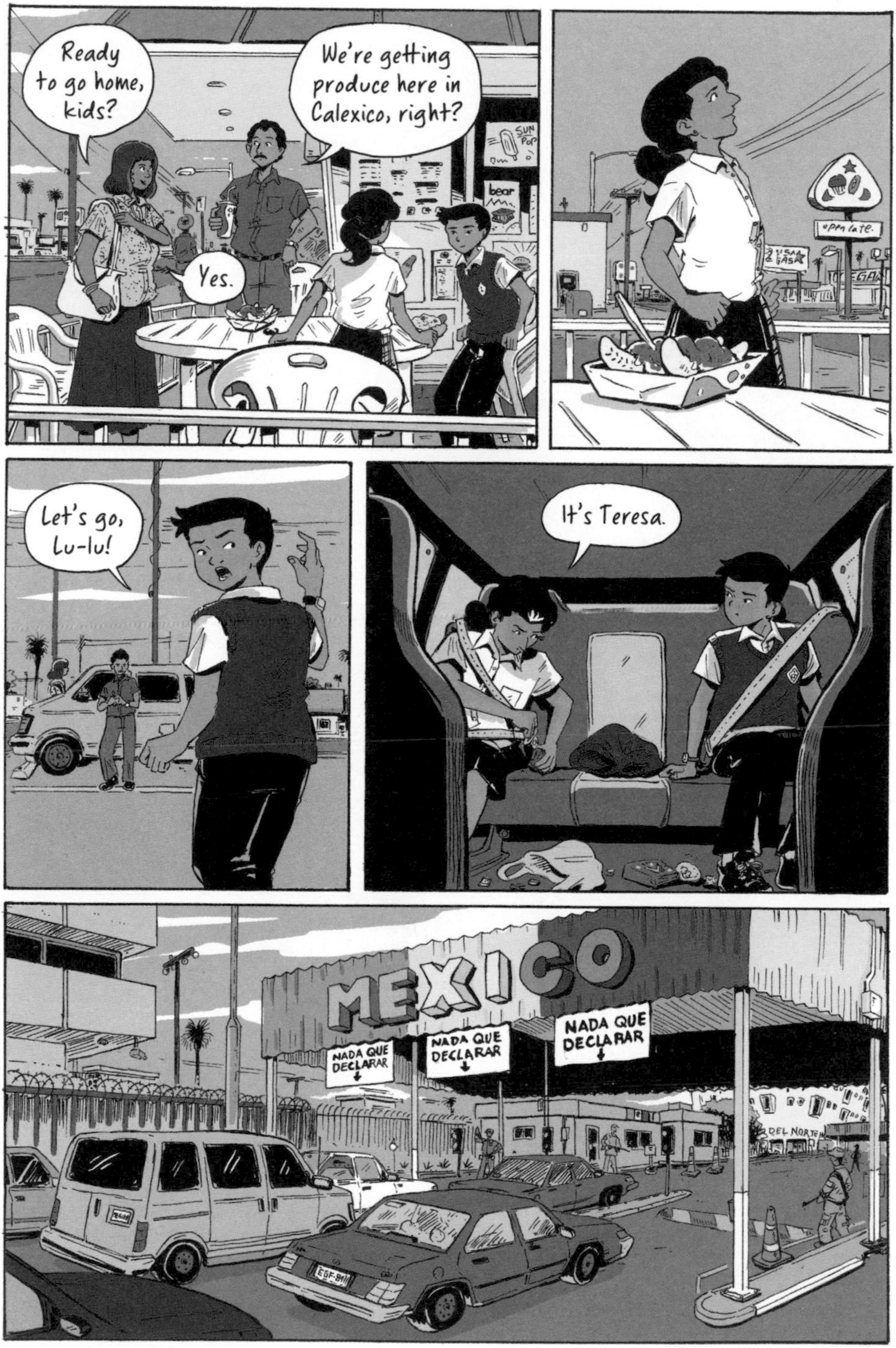
Ready to go home, kids?
We're getting produce here in Calexico, right?
SUN POP
bear
Yes.
open late
Let's go, Lu-lu!
It's Teresa.
MEXICO
NADA QUE DECLARAR
NADA QUE DECLARAR
NADA QUE DECLARAR
DEL NORTE

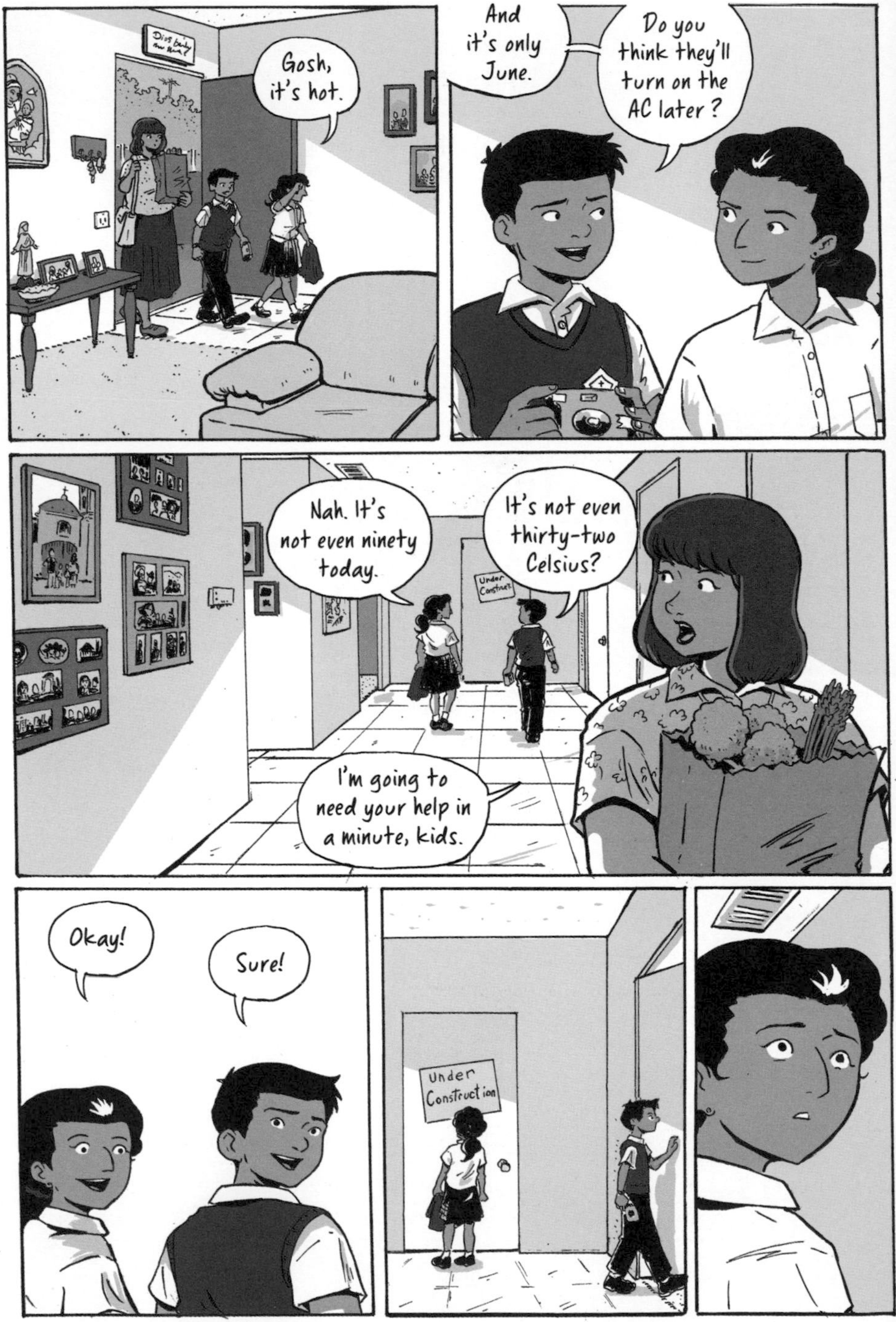
Gosh, it's hot.
And it's only June.
Do you think they'll turn on the AC later?
Nah. It's not even ninety today.
It's not even thirty-two Celsius?
I'm going to need your help in a minute, kids.
Okay!
Sure!
Under Construction

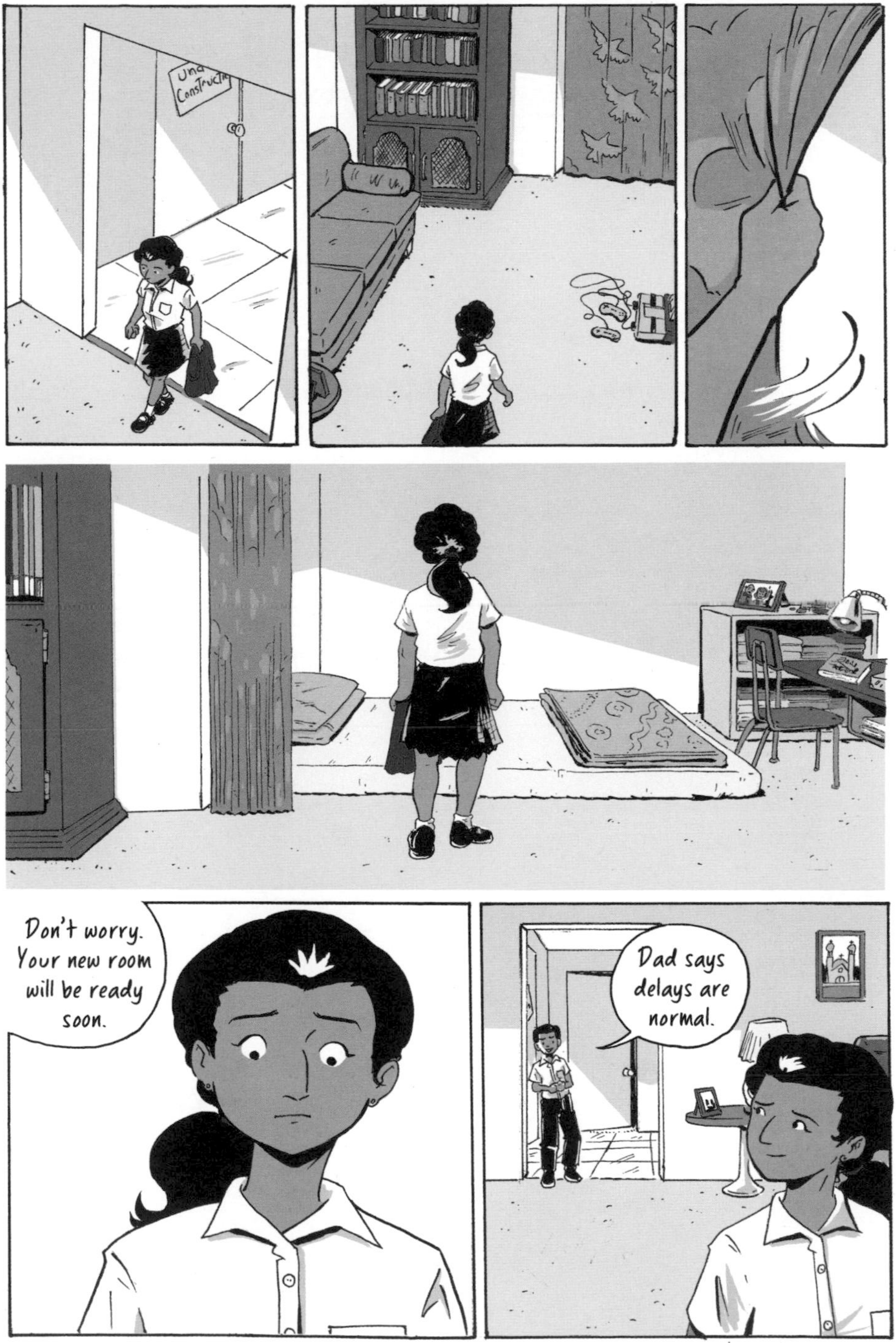
Under Construction
Don't worry. Your new room will be ready soon.
Dad says delays are normal.

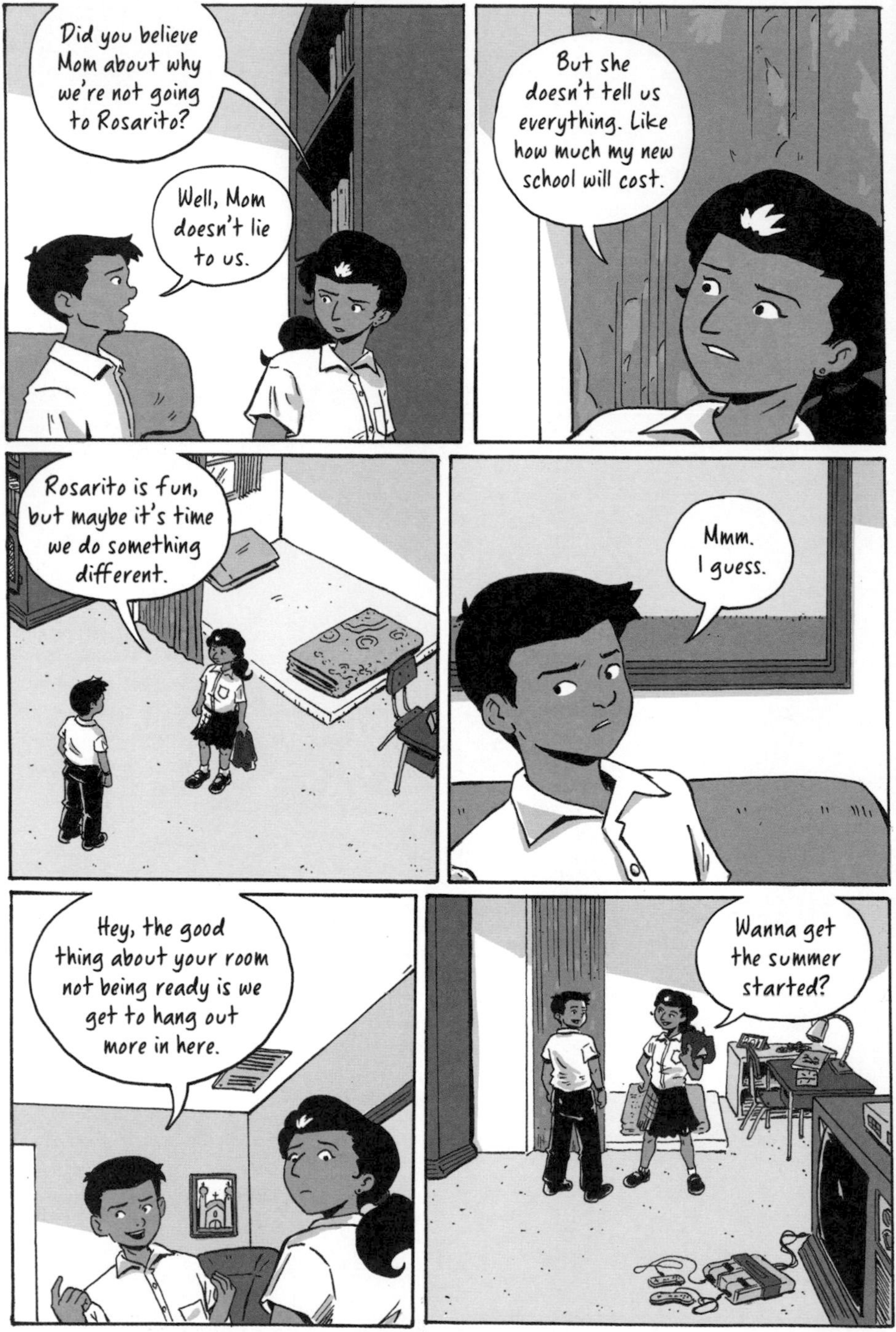
Did you believe Mom about why we're not going to Rosarito?
Well, Mom doesn't lie to us.
But she doesn't tell us everything. Like how much my new school will cost.
Rosarito is fun, but maybe it's time we do something different.
Mmm. I guess.
Hey, the good thing about your room not being ready is we get to hang out more in here.
Wanna get the summer started?

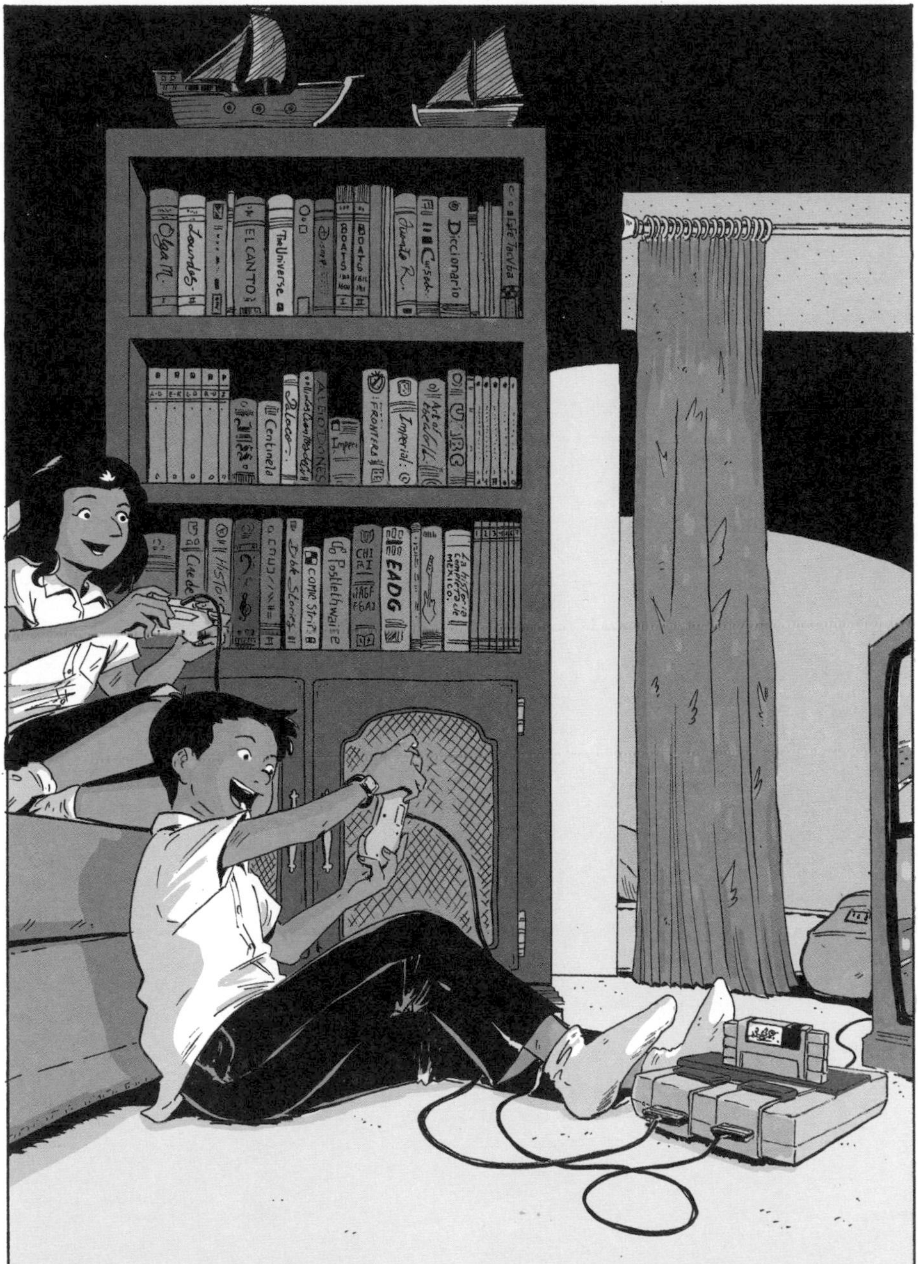
Diccionario
EL CANTO
The Universe
BOATS
Centinela
Imperial
EADG
Postlethwaite
comic strips

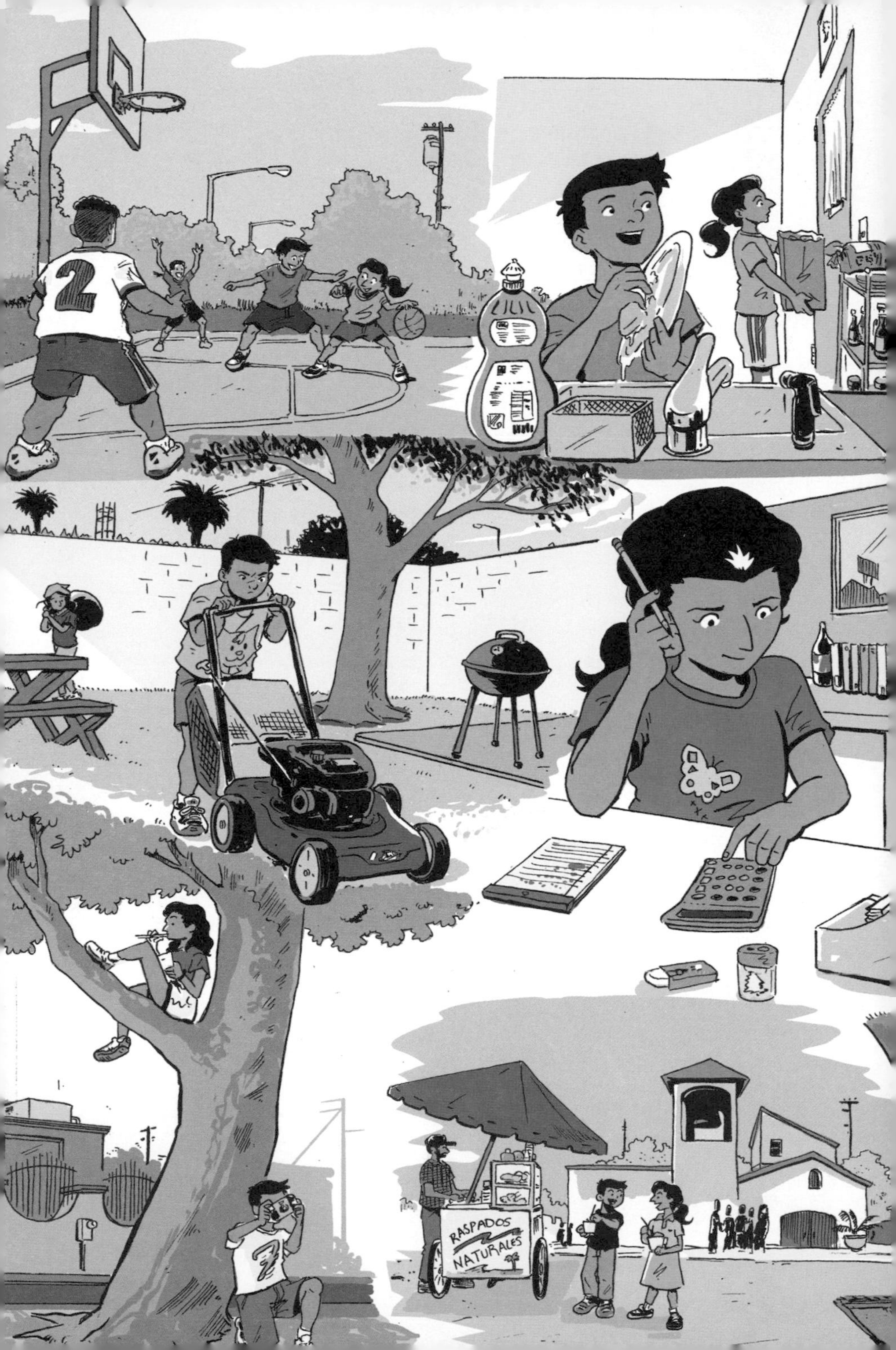
RASPADOS
NATURALES

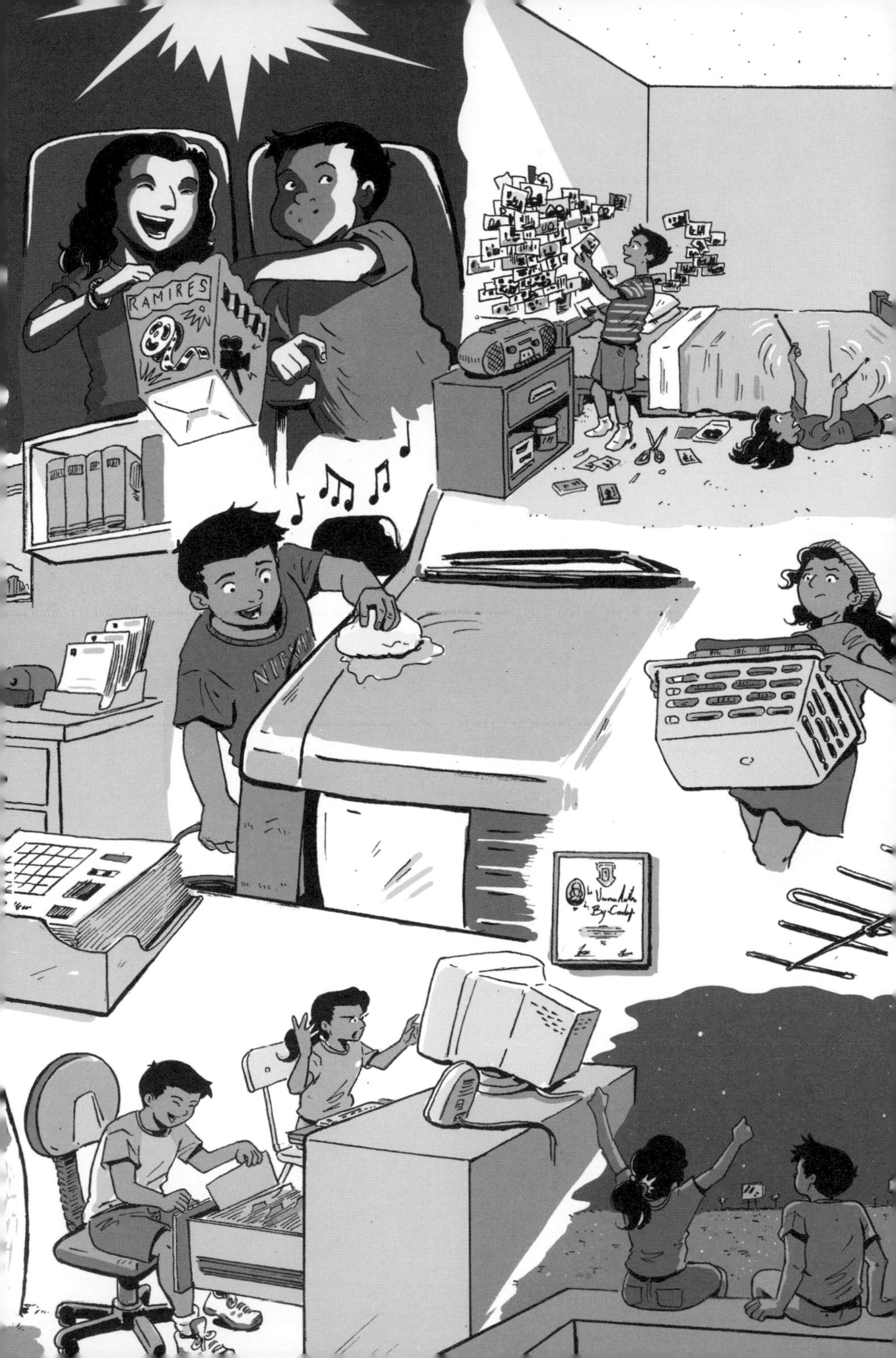
RAMIRES

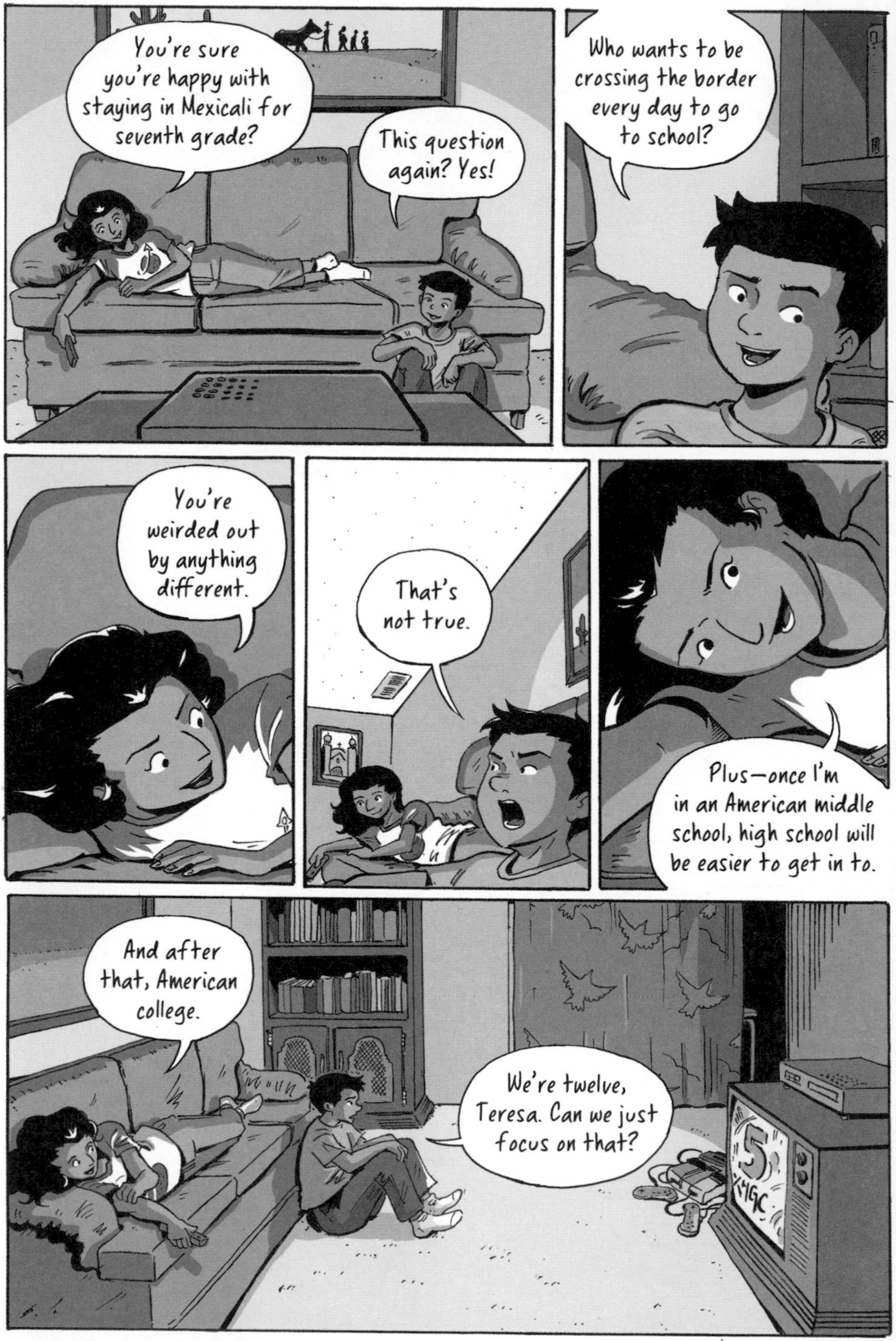
You're sure you're happy with staying in Mexicali for seventh grade?
This question again? Yes!
Who wants to be crossing the border every day to go to school?
You're weirded out by anything different.
That's not true.
Plus—once I'm in an American middle school, high school will be easier to get in to.
And after that, American college.
We're twelve, Teresa. Can we just focus on that?

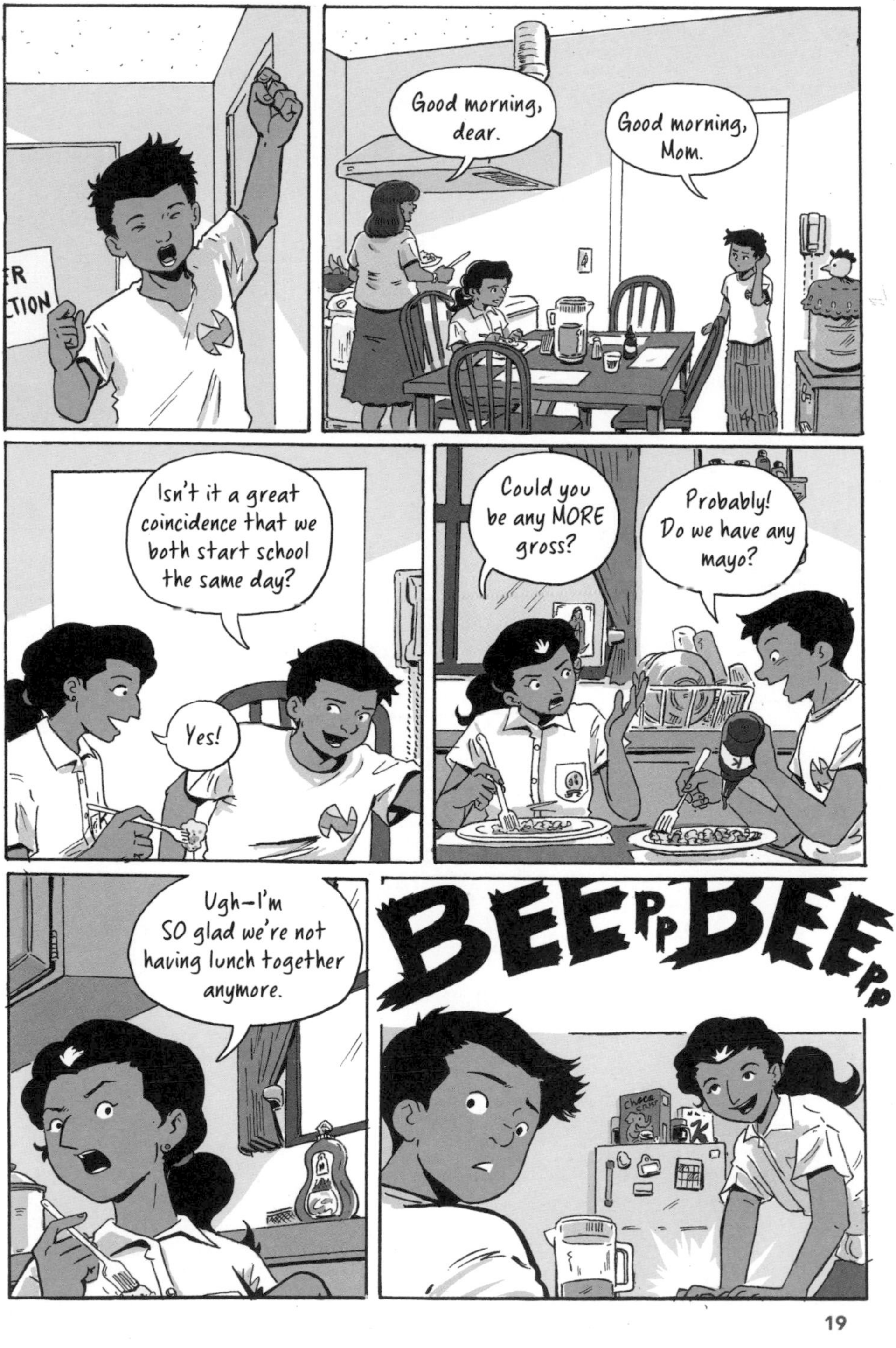
ER
CTION
Good morning, dear.
Good morning, Mom.
Isn't it a great coincidence that we both start school the same day?
Yes!
Could you be any MORE gross?
Probably! Do we have any mayo?
Ugh—I'm SO glad we're not having lunch together anymore.
BEEPP BEEPP

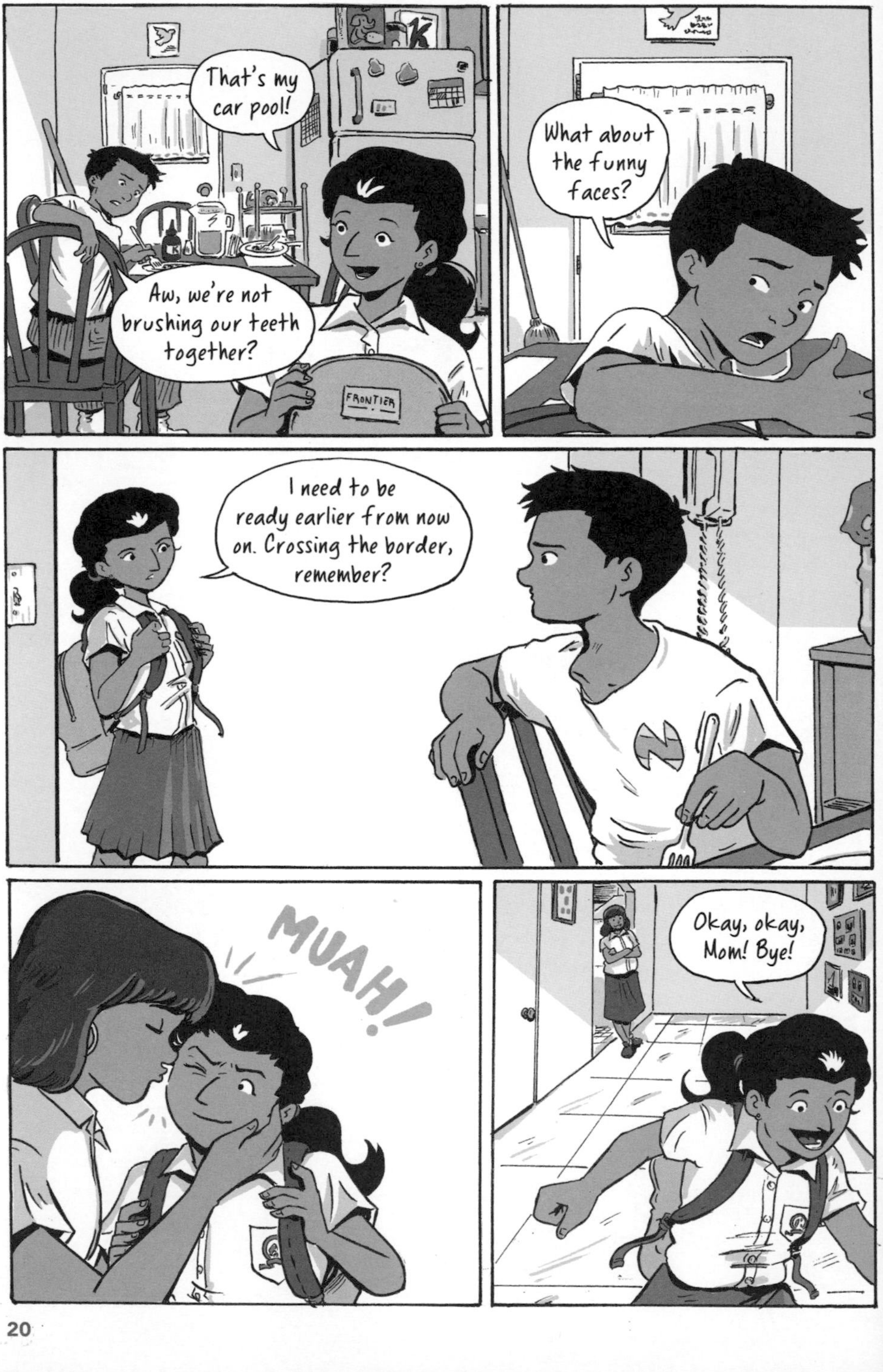
That's my car pool!
Aw, we're not brushing our teeth together?
FRONTIER
What about the funny faces?
I need to be ready earlier from now on. Crossing the border, remember?
MUAH!
Okay, okay, Mom! Bye!

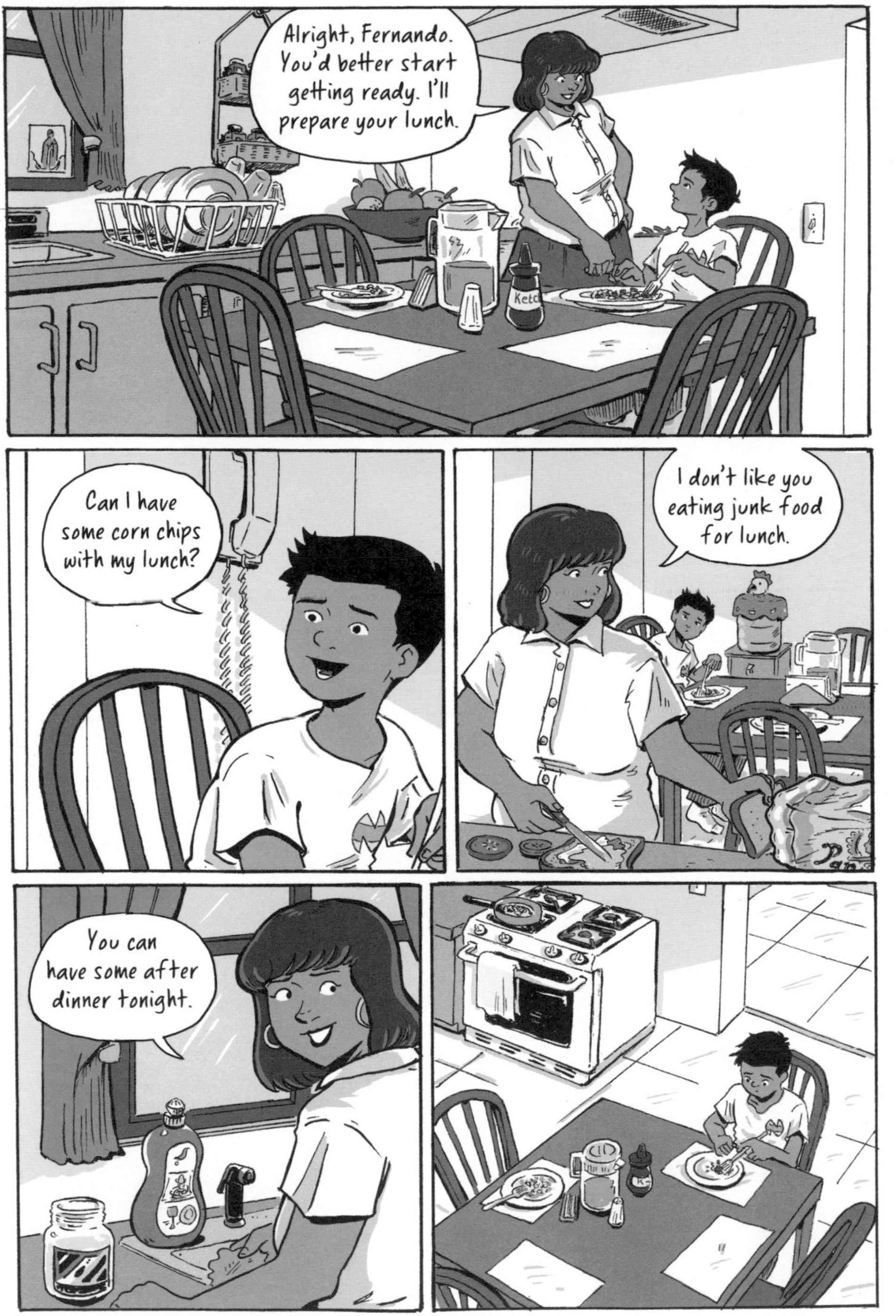
Alright, Fernando. You'd better start getting ready. I'll prepare your lunch.
Ketch
Can I have some corn chips with my lunch?
I don't like you eating junk food for lunch.
You can have some after dinner tonight.

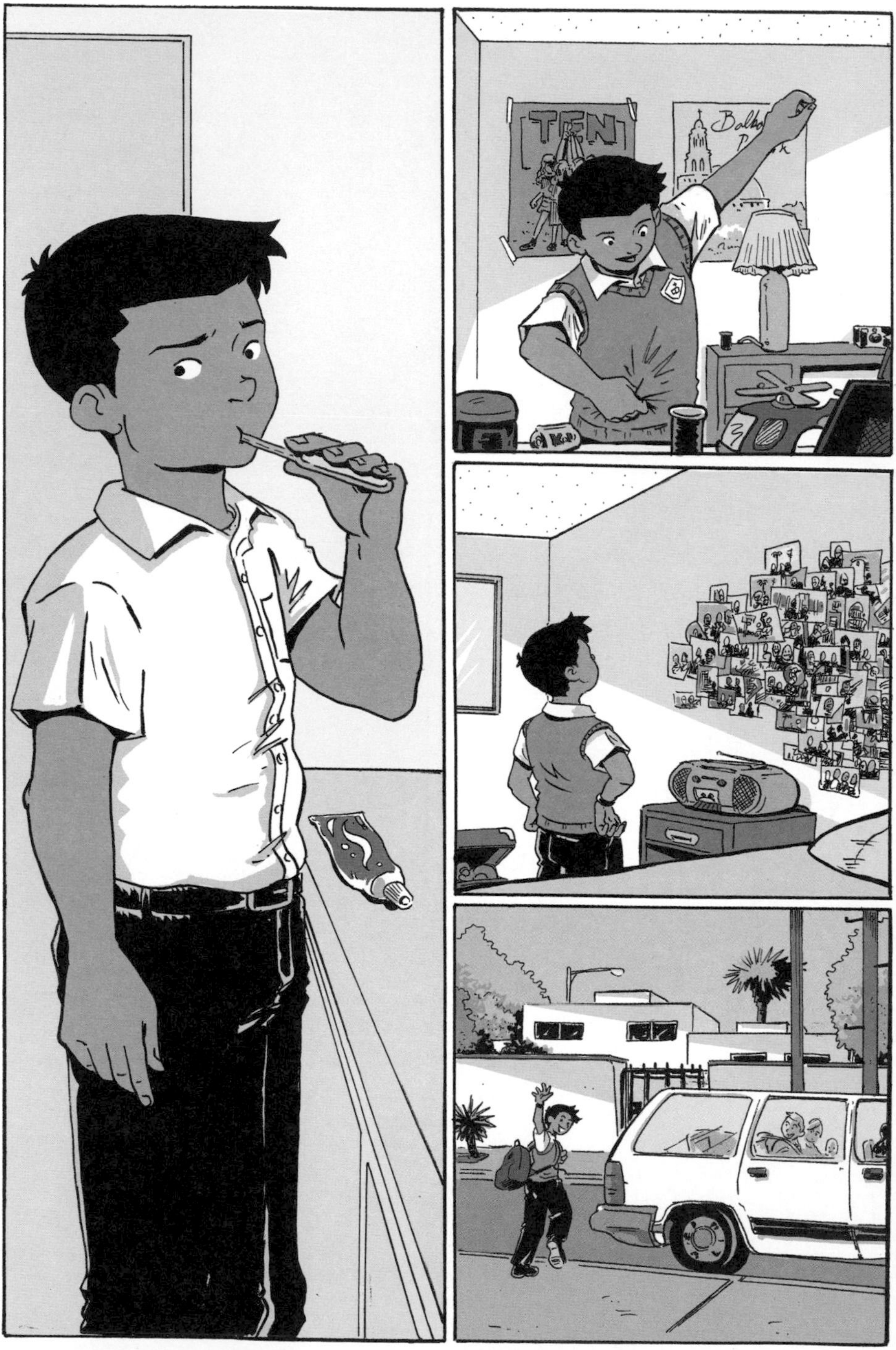
TEN

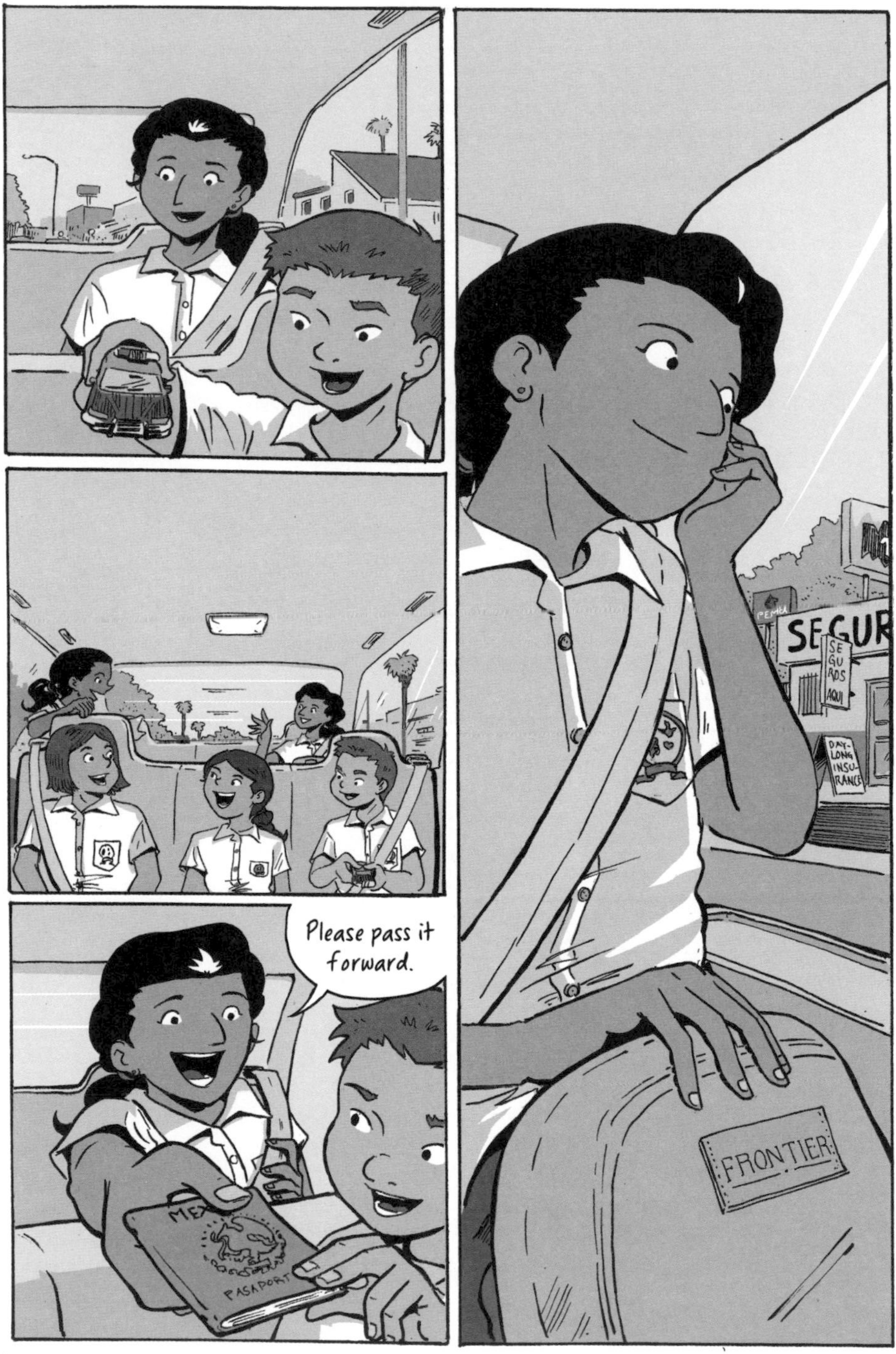

Please pass it forward.
SEGUR
DAY-LONG INSURANCE
FRONTIER
PASAPORT

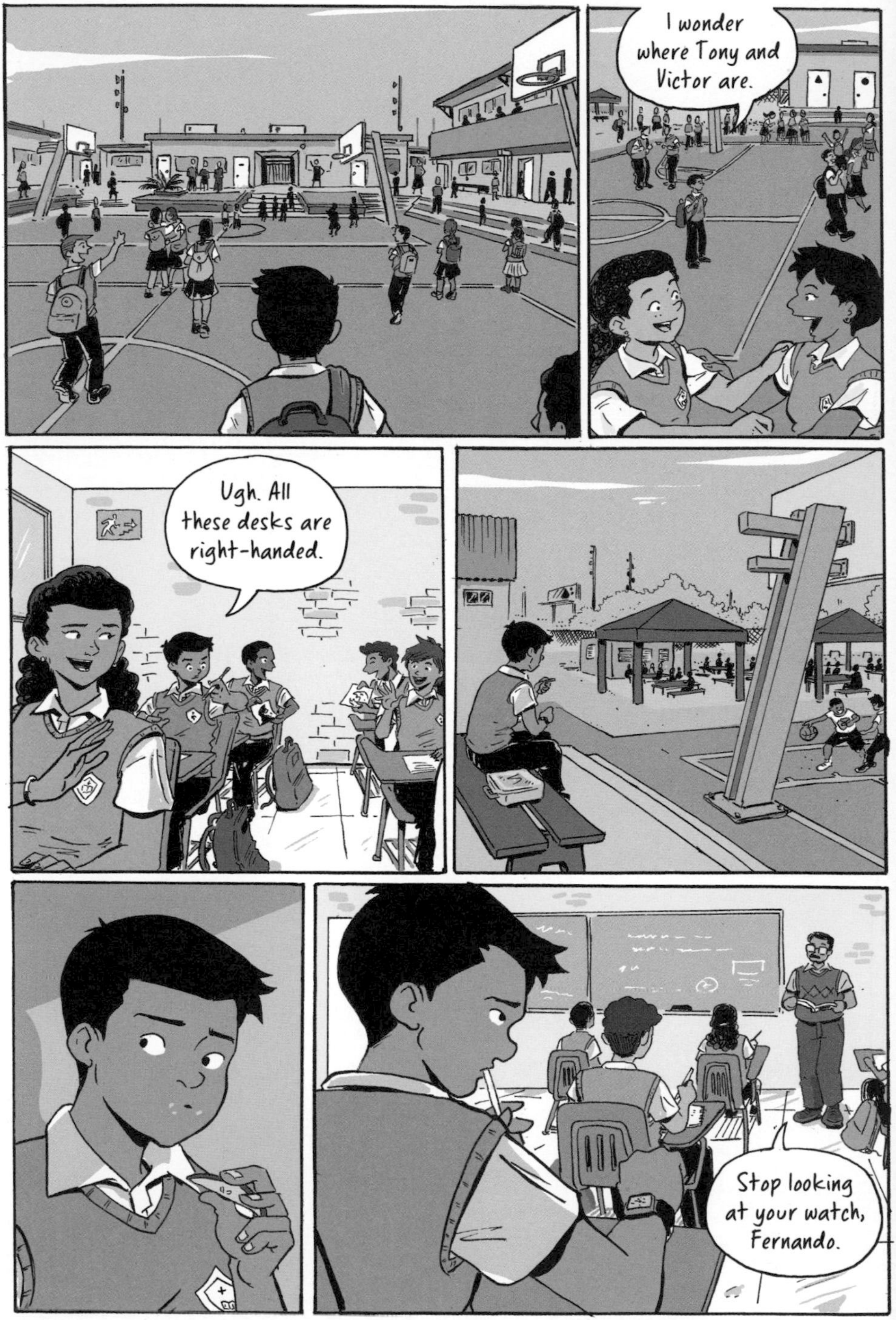
I wonder where Tony and Victor are.
Ugh. All these desks are right-handed.
Stop looking at your watch, Fernando.

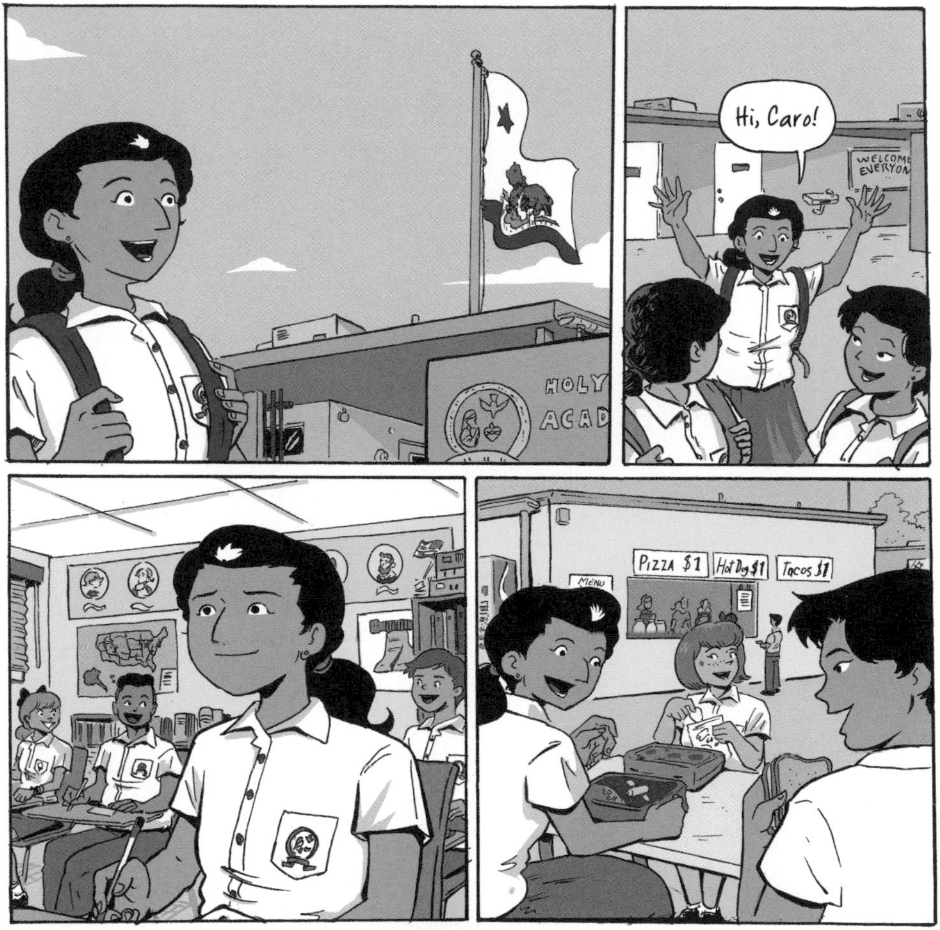
HOLY
ACAD
Hi, Caro!
WELCOM
EVERYON
PIZZA $1
Hot Dog $1
Tacos $1
MENU
Tell Fer we say hello!
You got it, Tony!
So take good notes, kids.

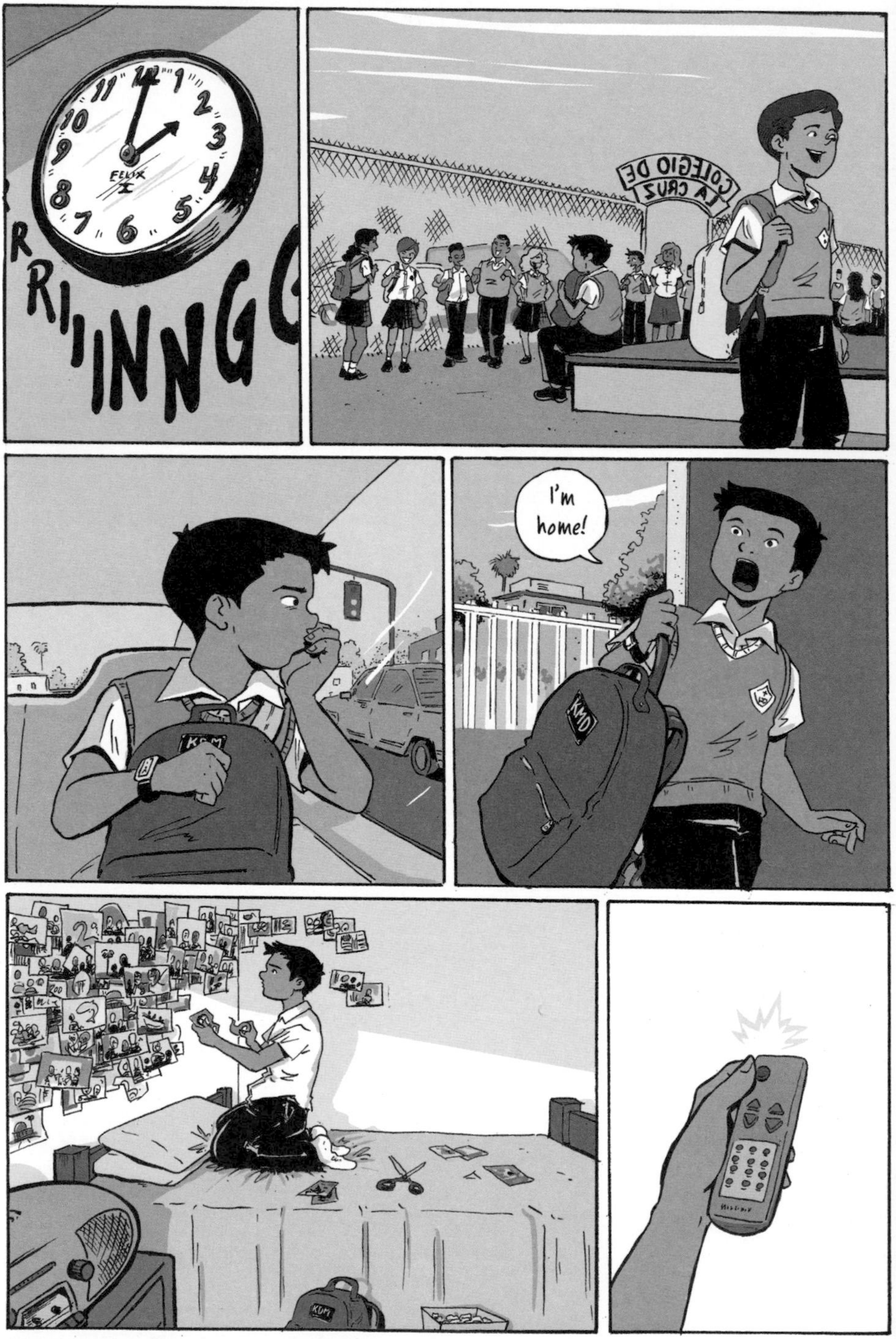
RRIIINNGG
COLEGIO DE LA CRUZ
I'm home!

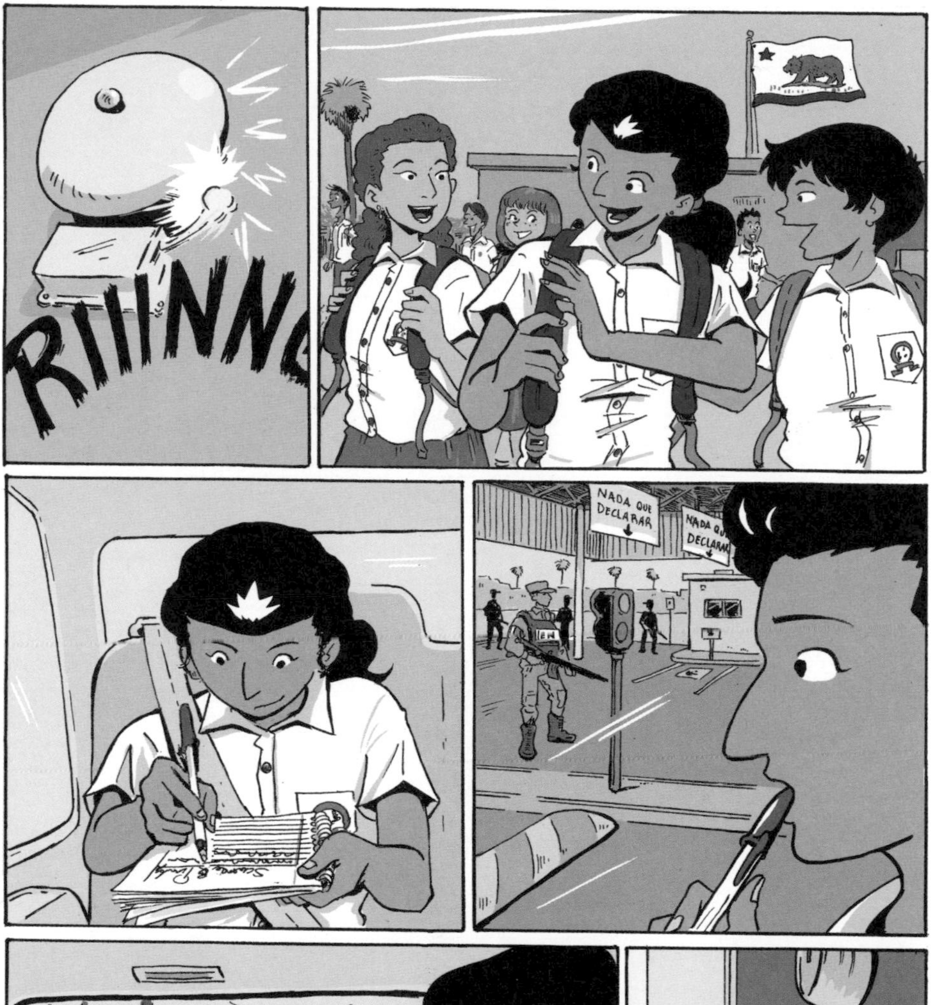
RIIINNG
NADA QUE DECLARAR
NADA QU DECLARAR
Dr. Vilchis
ARGENTINA
FARMACIA VERA 2000
DAVID
TAXI

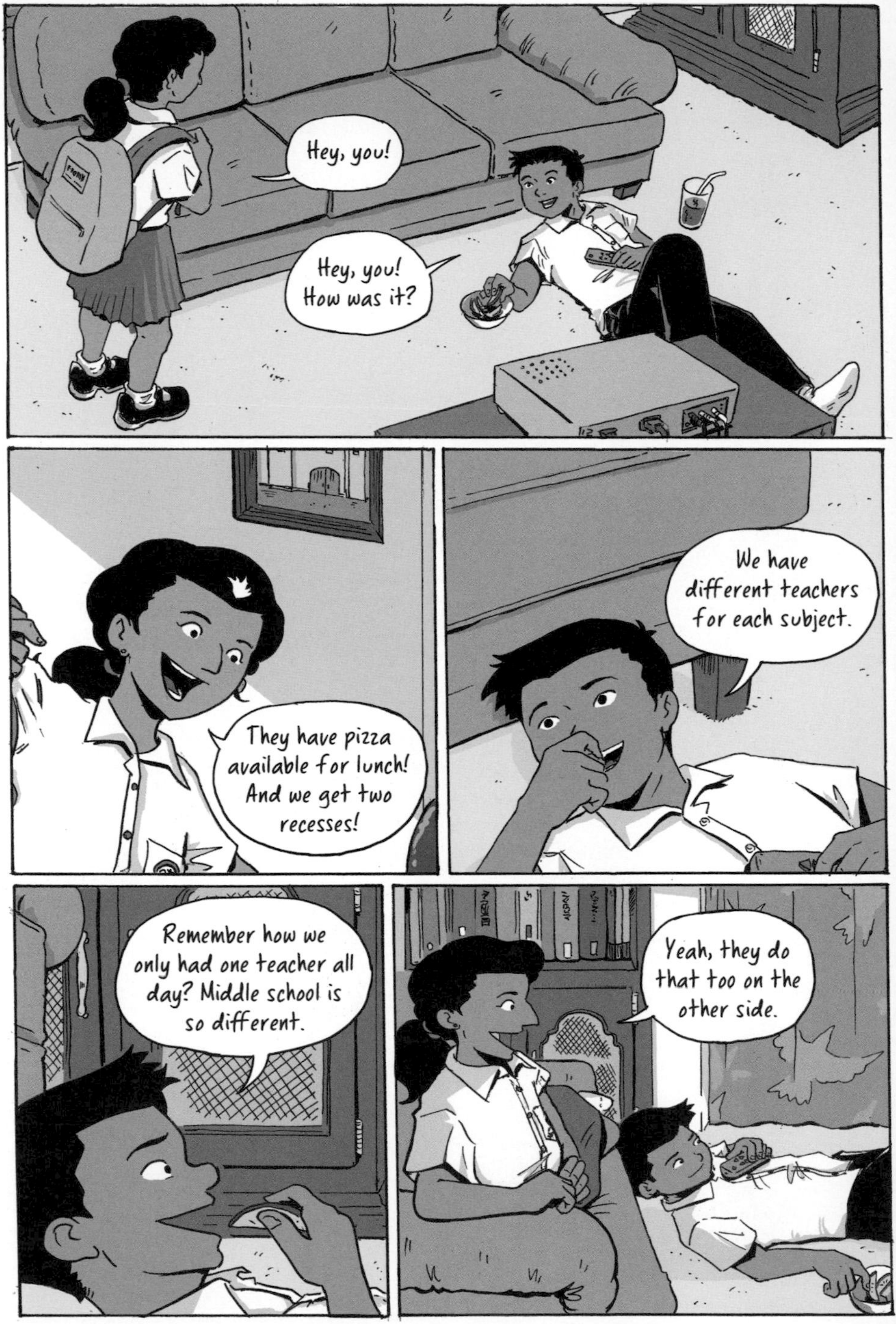
Hey, you!
Hey, you! How was it?
They have pizza available for lunch! And we get two recesses!
We have different teachers for each subject.
Remember how we only had one teacher all day? Middle school is so different.
Yeah, they do that too on the other side.

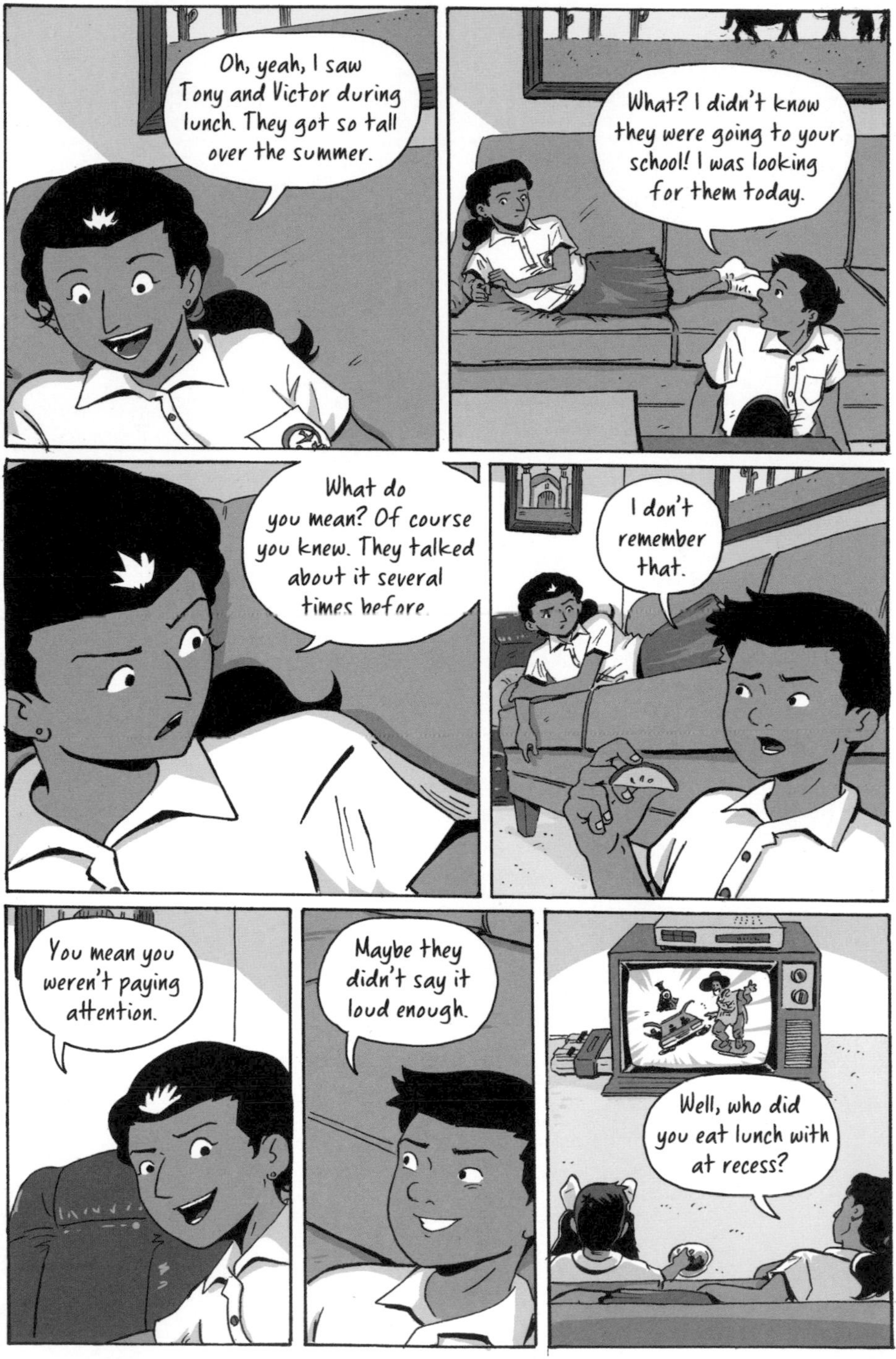
Oh, yeah, I saw Tony and Victor during lunch. They got so tall over the summer.
What? I didn't know they were going to your school! I was looking for them today.
What do you mean? Of course you knew. They talked about it several times before.
I don't remember that.
You mean you weren't paying attention.
Maybe they didn't say it loud enough.
Well, who did you eat lunch with at recess?

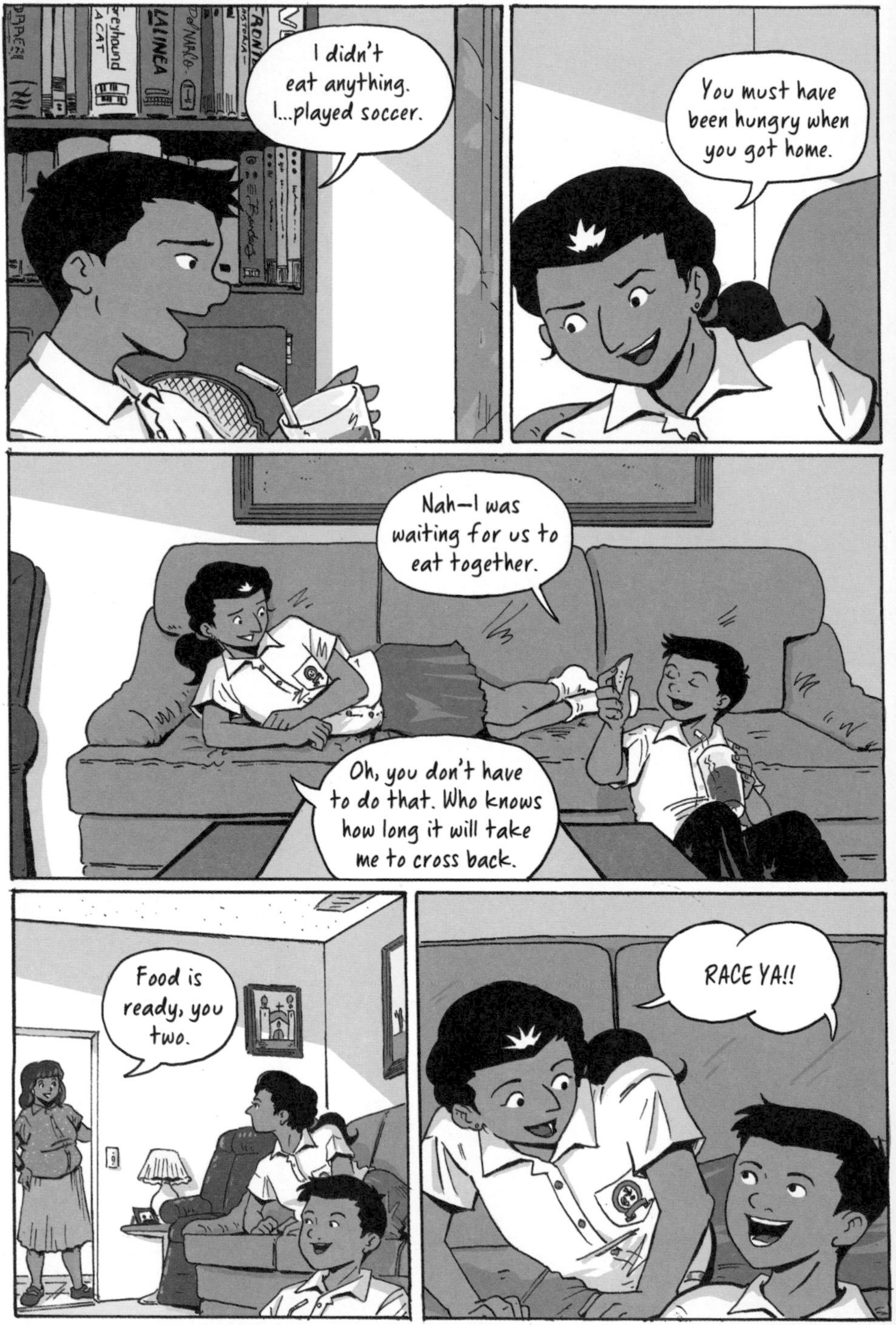
I didn't eat anything. I...played soccer.
You must have been hungry when you got home.
Nah—I was waiting for us to eat together.
Oh, you don't have to do that. Who knows how long it will take me to cross back.
Food is ready, you two.
RACE YA!!

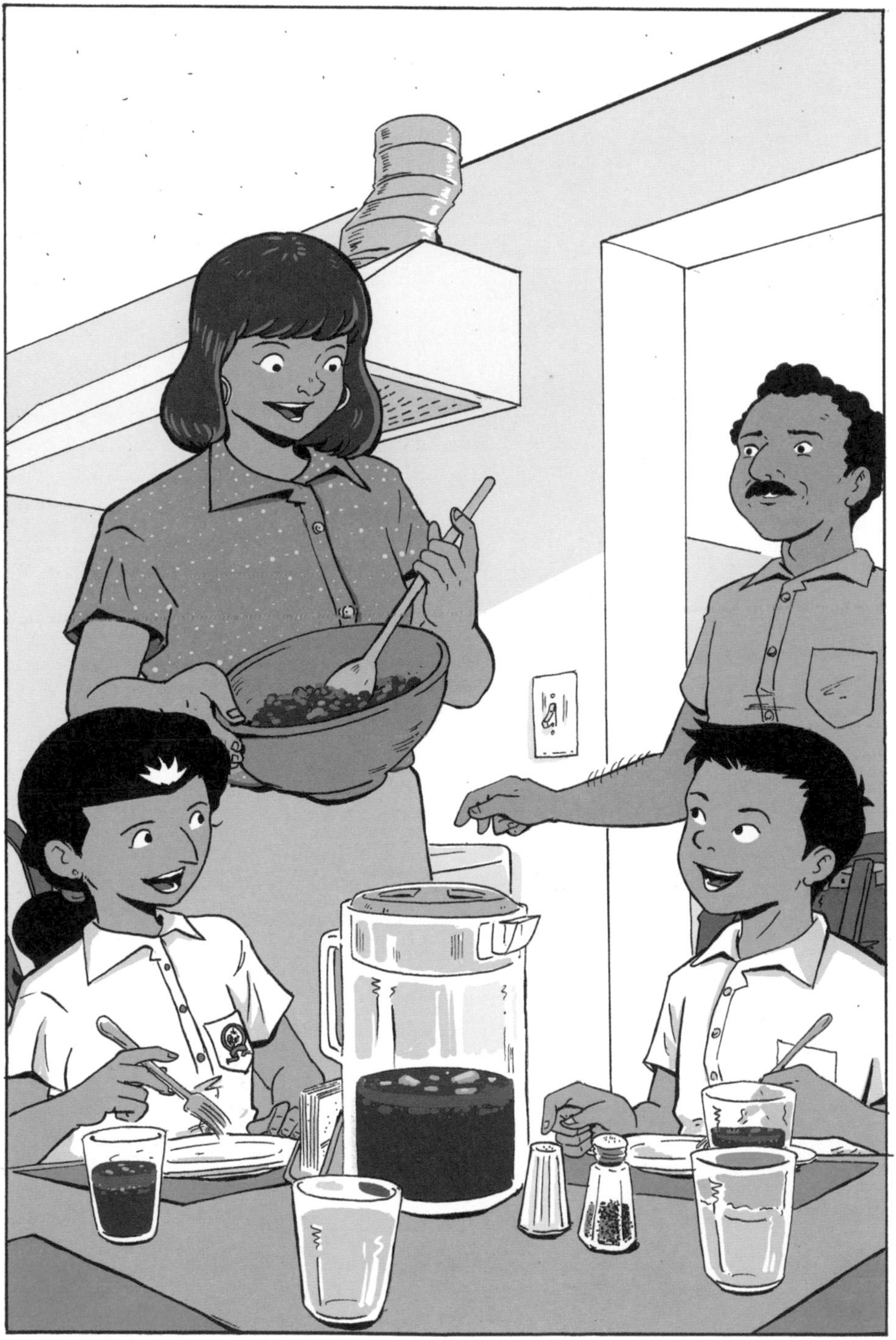

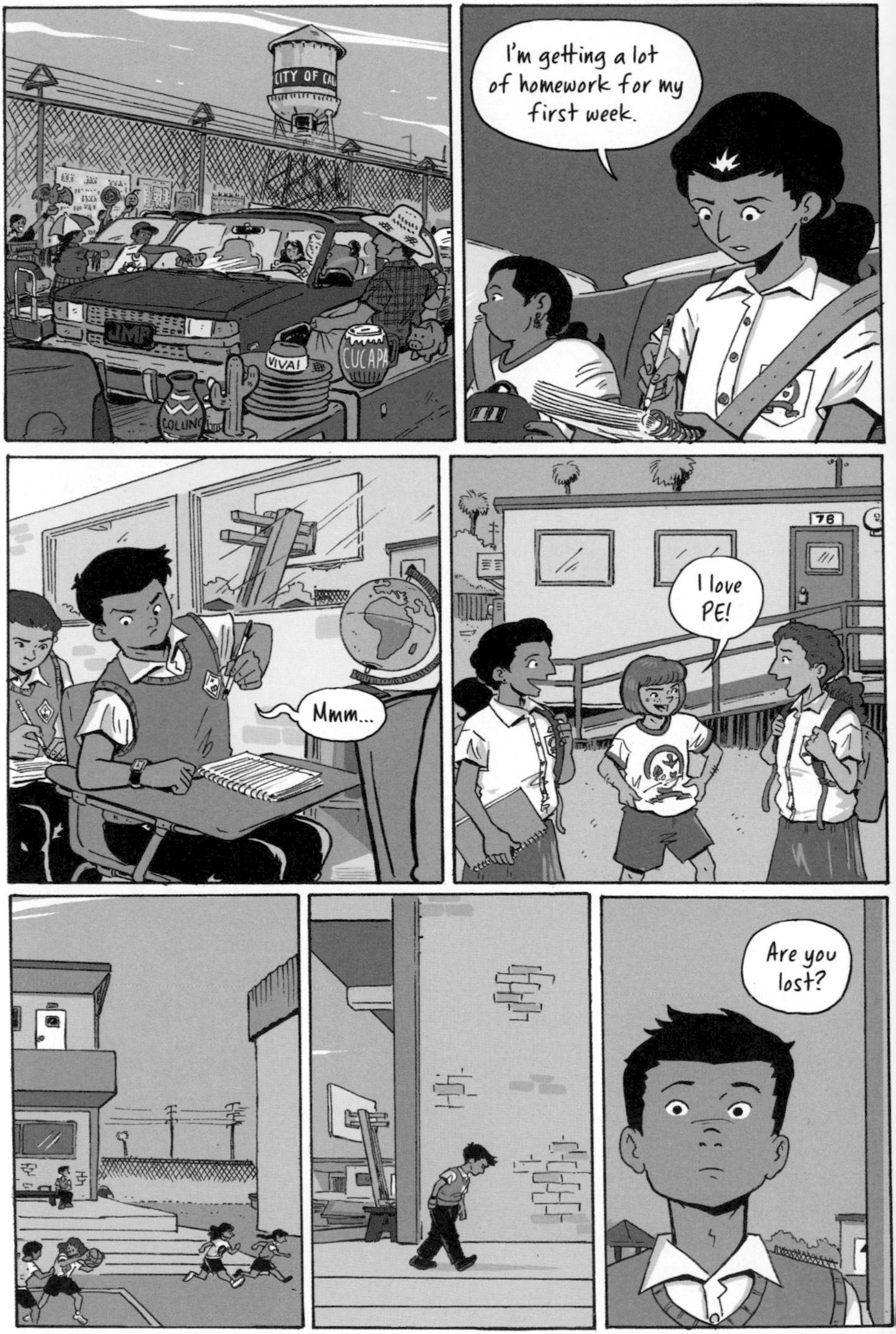
CITY OF CA
JMP
VIVA!
CUCAPA
COLUNG
I'm getting a lot of homework for my first week.
7B
Mmm...
I love PE!
Are you lost?

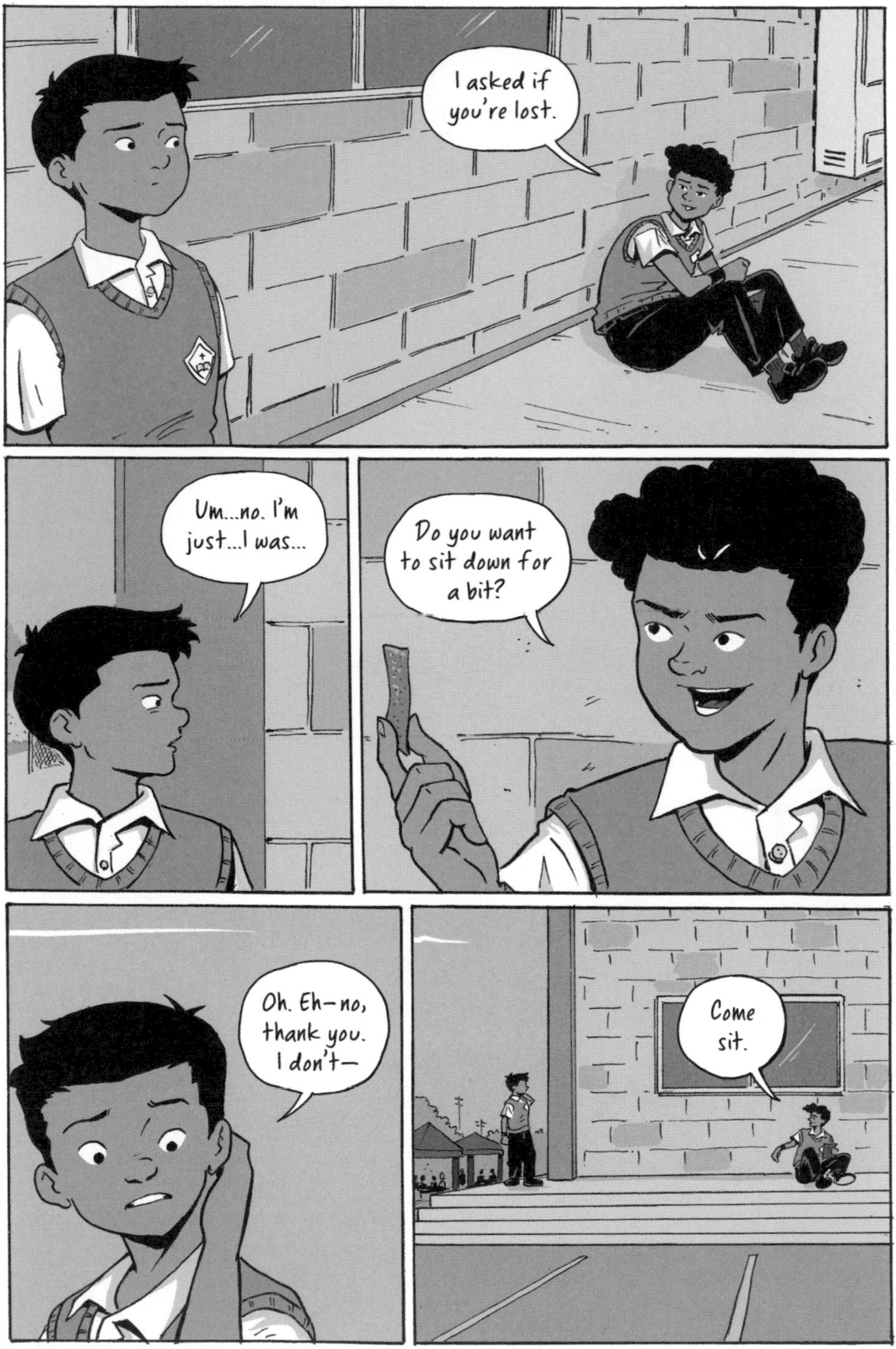
I asked if you're lost.
Um...no. I'm just...I was...
Do you want to sit down for a bit?
Oh. Eh—no, thank you. I don't—
Come sit.

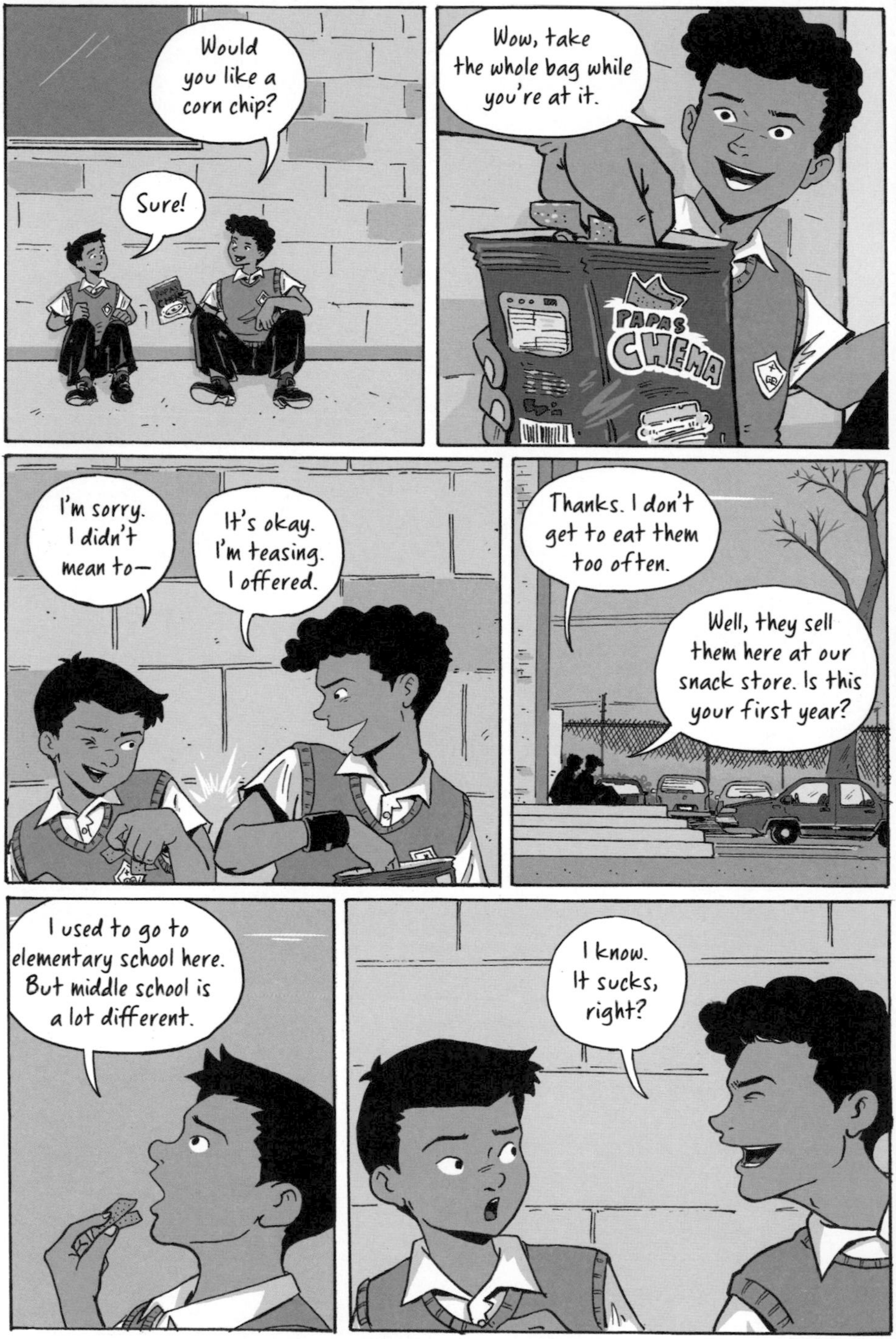
Would you like a corn chip?
Sure!
PAPAS CHEMA
Wow, take the whole bag while you're at it.
I'm sorry. I didn't mean to—
It's okay. I'm teasing. I offered.
Thanks. I don't get to eat them too often.
Well, they sell them here at our snack store. Is this your first year?
I used to go to elementary school here. But middle school is a lot different.
I know. It sucks, right?

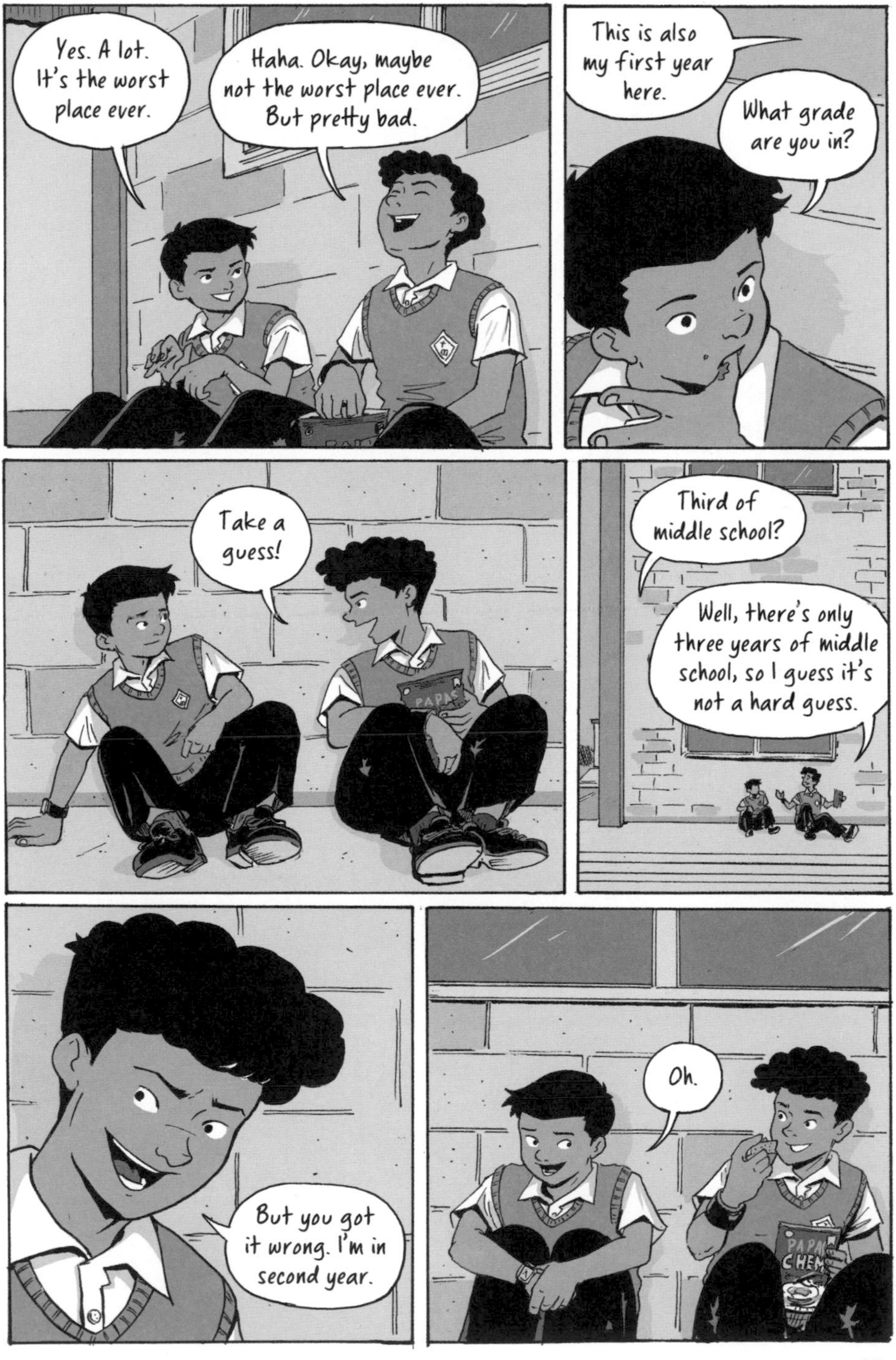
Yes. A lot. It's the worst place ever.
Haha. Okay, maybe not the worst place ever. But pretty bad.
This is also my first year here.
What grade are you in?
Take a guess!
Third of middle school?
Well, there's only three years of middle school, so I guess it's not a hard guess.
But you got it wrong. I'm in second year.
Oh.

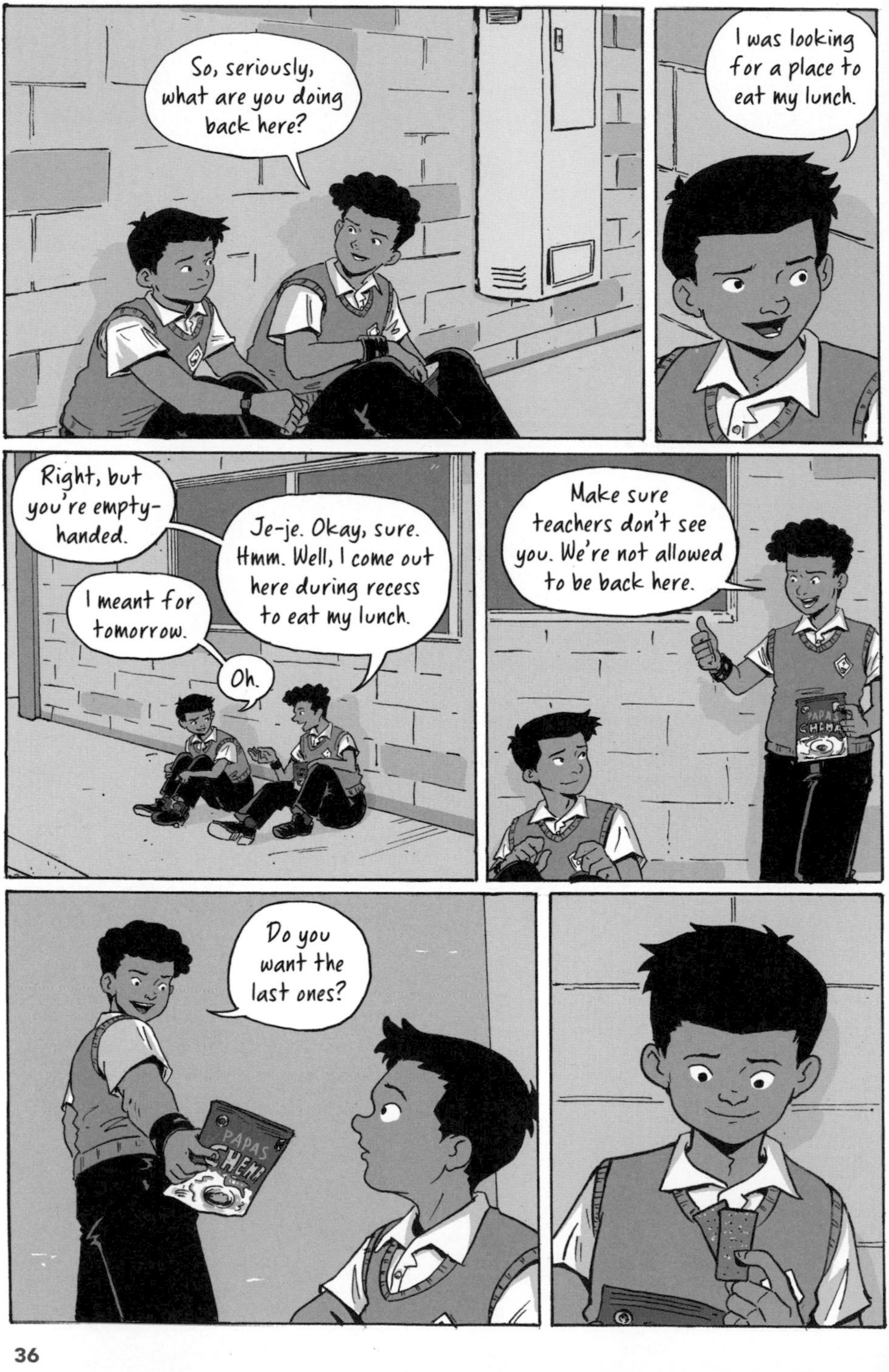
So, seriously, what are you doing back here?
I was looking for a place to eat my lunch.
Je-je. Okay, sure. Hmm. Well, I come out here during recess to eat my lunch.
Right, but you're empty-handed.
I meant for tomorrow.
Oh.
Make sure teachers don't see you. We're not allowed to be back here.
PAPAS CHEMA
Do you want the last ones?
PAPAS CHEMA

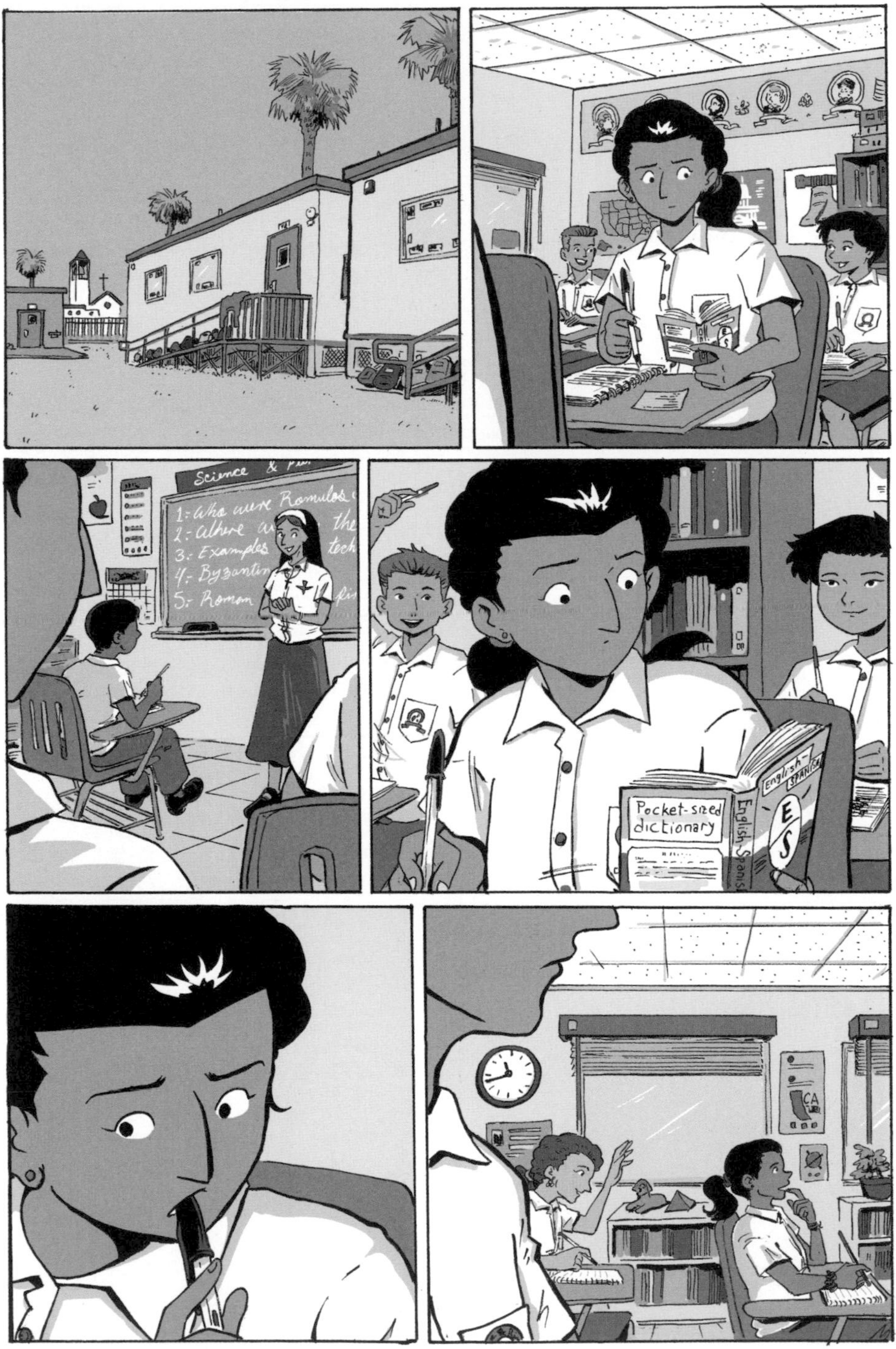
Science &
1:- Who were Romulus
2:- Where
3:- Examples
4:- Byzantin
5:- Roman
English-SPANISH
Pocket-sized dictionary
English Spanis
E S
CA

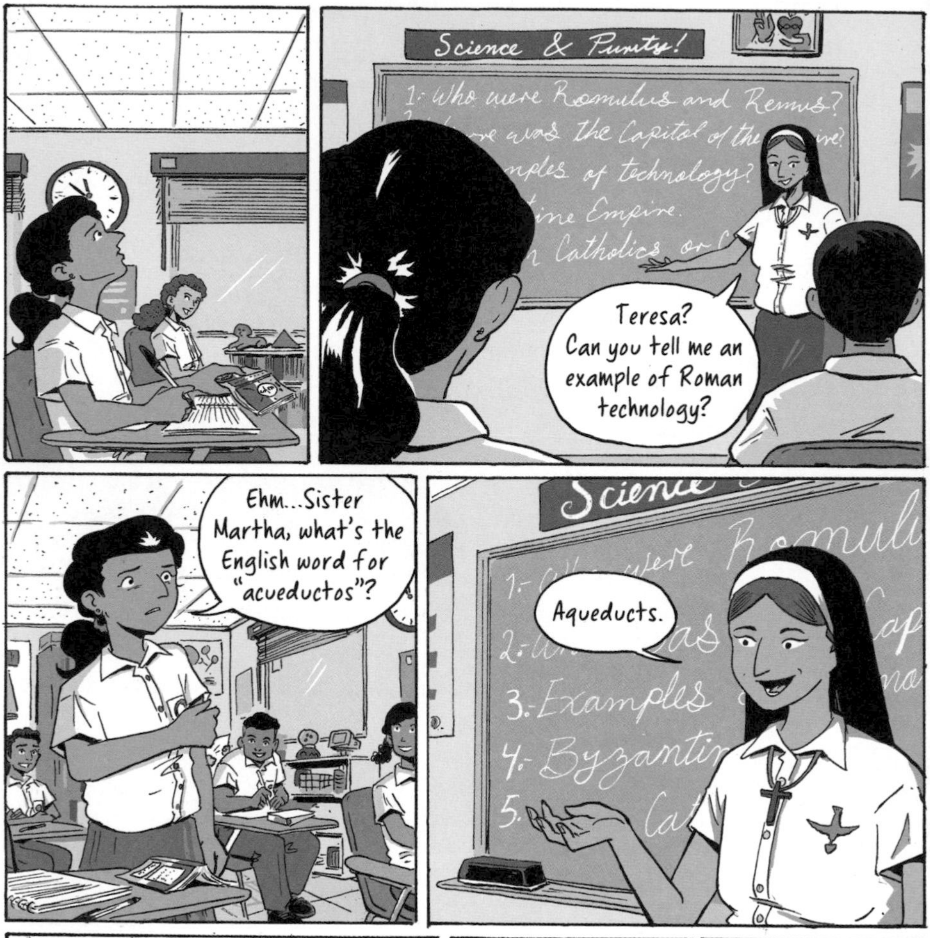
Science & Purity!
1: Who were Romulus and Remus?
Teresa? Can you tell me an example of Roman technology?
Ehm...Sister Martha, what's the English word for "acueductos"?
Aqueducts.
Oh, cool! Okay, then. Aqueducts.
Thank you, Teresa.

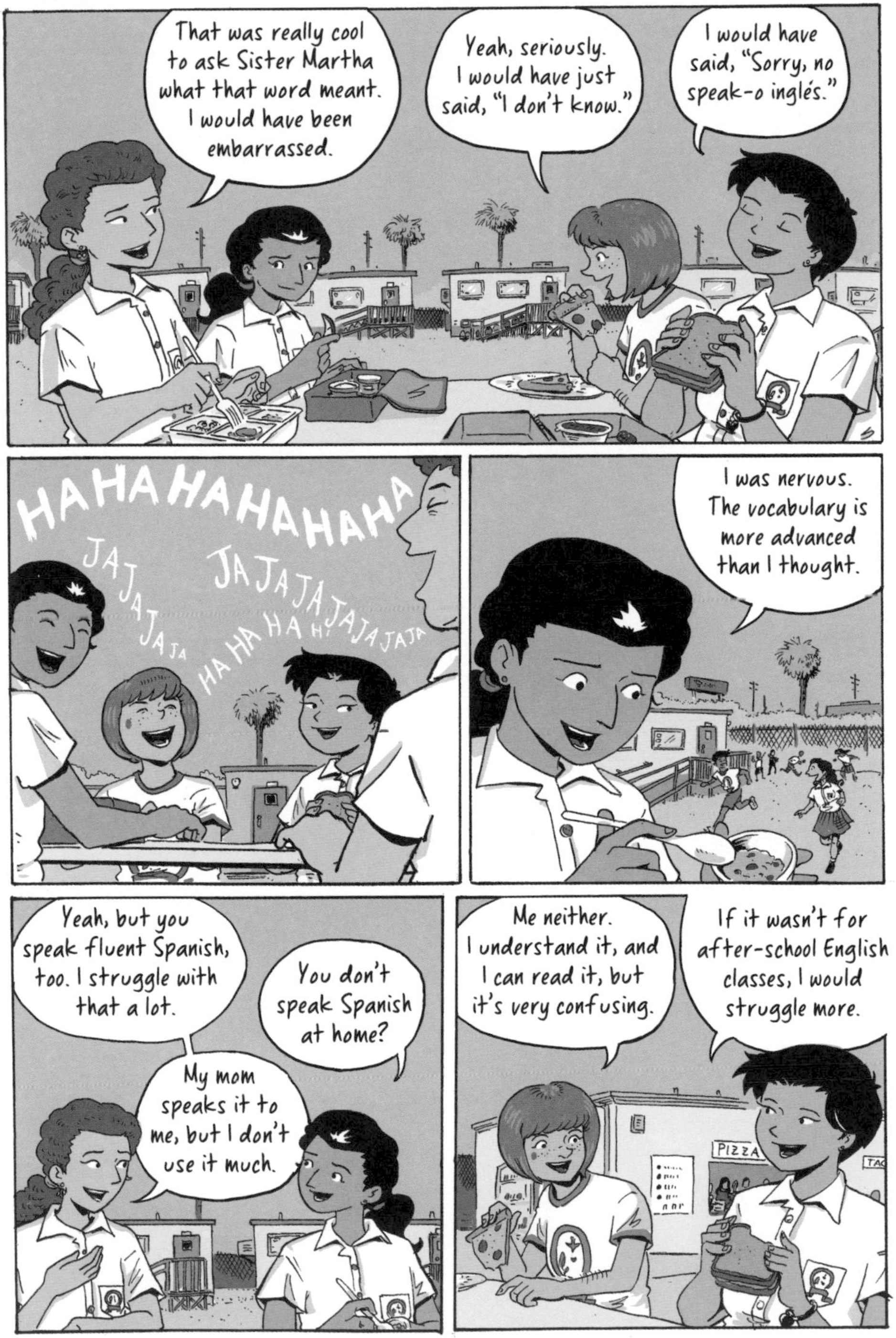
That was really cool to ask Sister Martha what that word meant. I would have been embarrassed.
Yeah, seriously. I would have just said, "I don't know."
I would have said, "Sorry, no speak-o inglés."
HAHAHAHAHAHAHA
JAJAJAJA
JAJAJAJAJAJAJAJA
HAHAHAHI
I was nervous. The vocabulary is more advanced than I thought.
Yeah, but you speak fluent Spanish, too. I struggle with that a lot.
You don't speak Spanish at home?
My mom speaks it to me, but I don't use it much.
Me neither. I understand it, and I can read it, but it's very confusing.
If it wasn't for after-school English classes, I would struggle more.
PIZZA

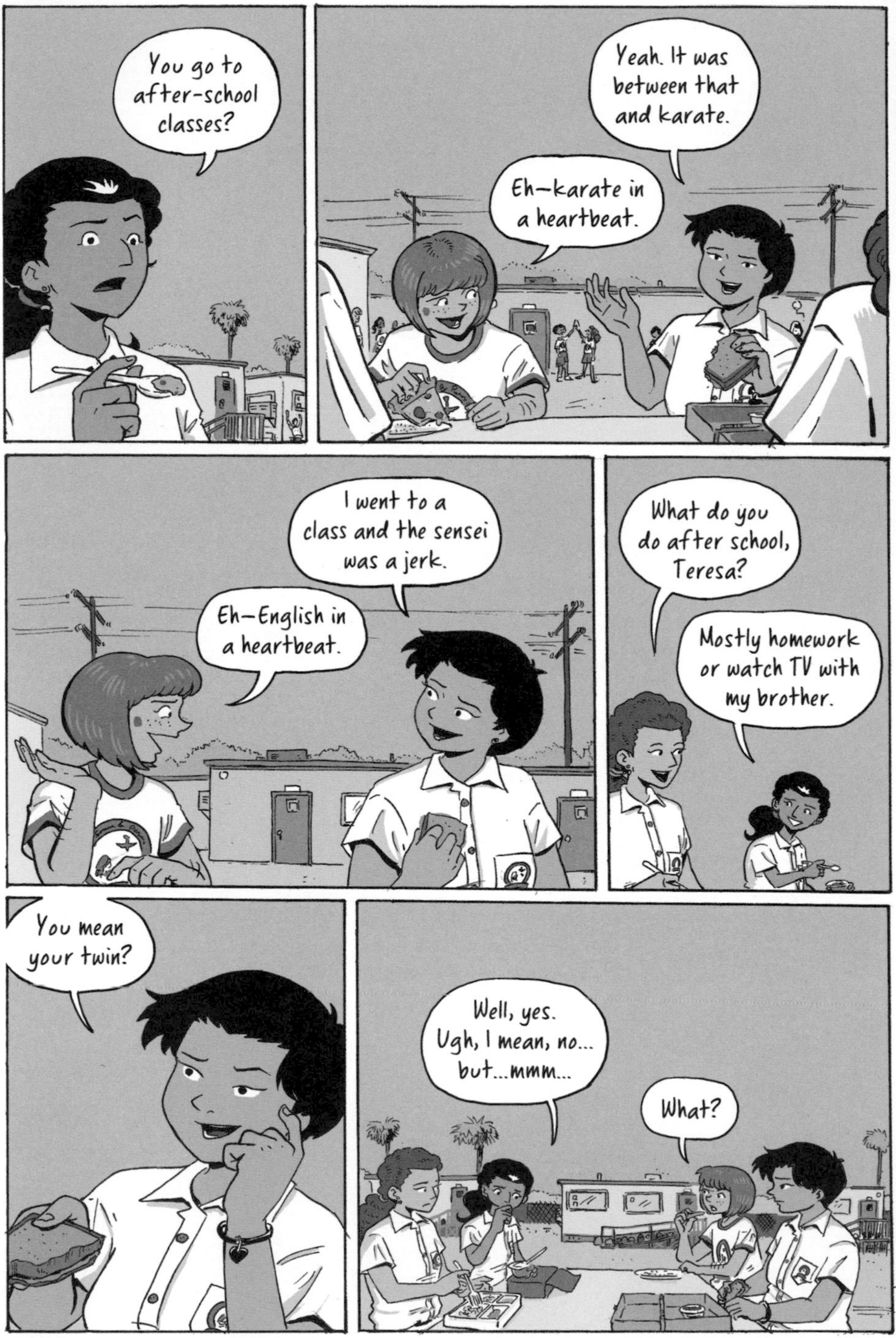
You go to after-school classes?
Yeah. It was between that and karate.
Eh—karate in a heartbeat.
I went to a class and the sensei was a jerk.
Eh—English in a heartbeat.
What do you do after school, Teresa?
Mostly homework or watch TV with my brother.
You mean your twin?
Well, yes. Ugh, I mean, no... but...mmm...
What?

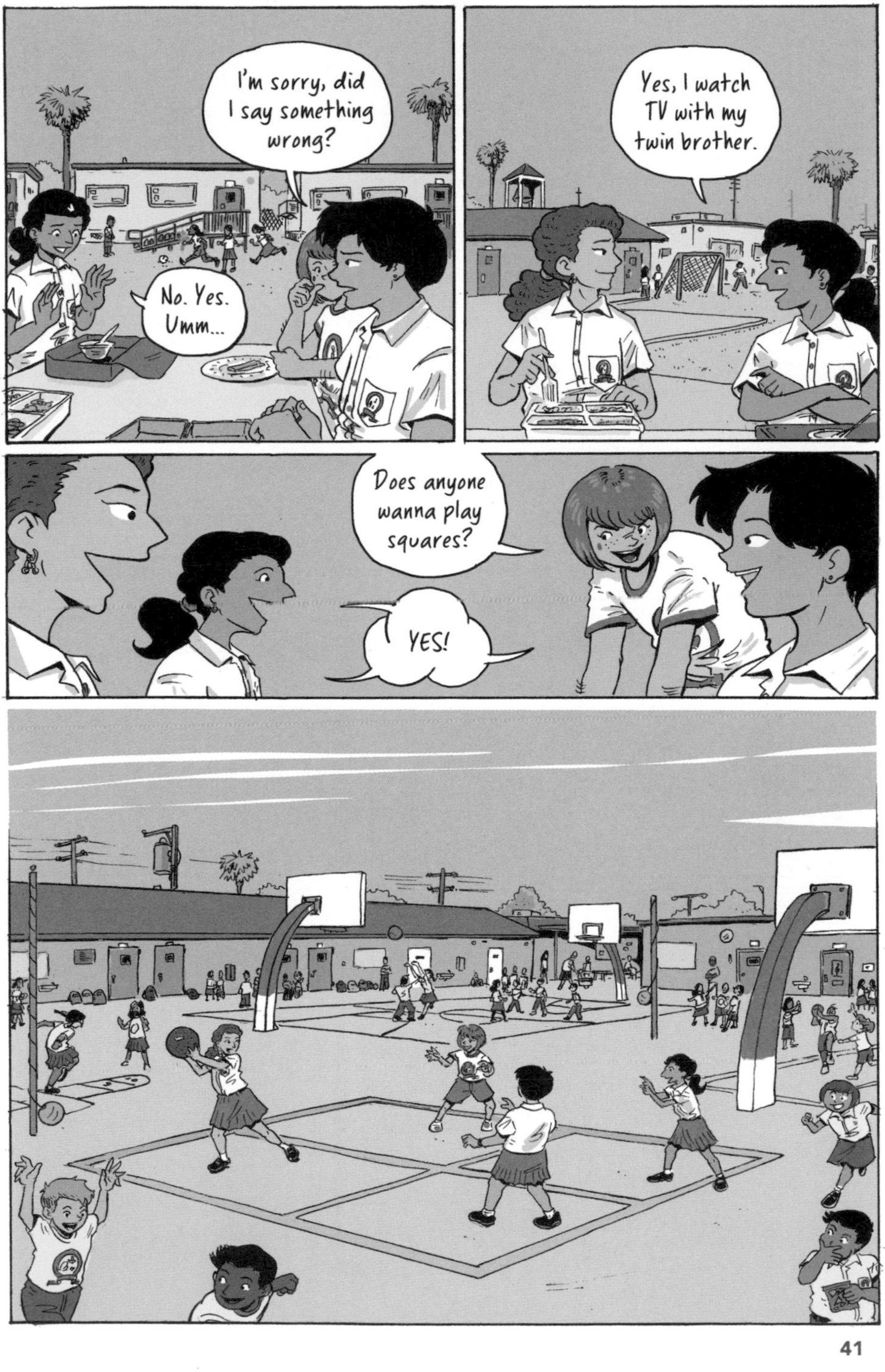
I'm sorry, did I say something wrong?
No. Yes. Umm...
Yes, I watch TV with my twin brother.
Does anyone wanna play squares?
YES!

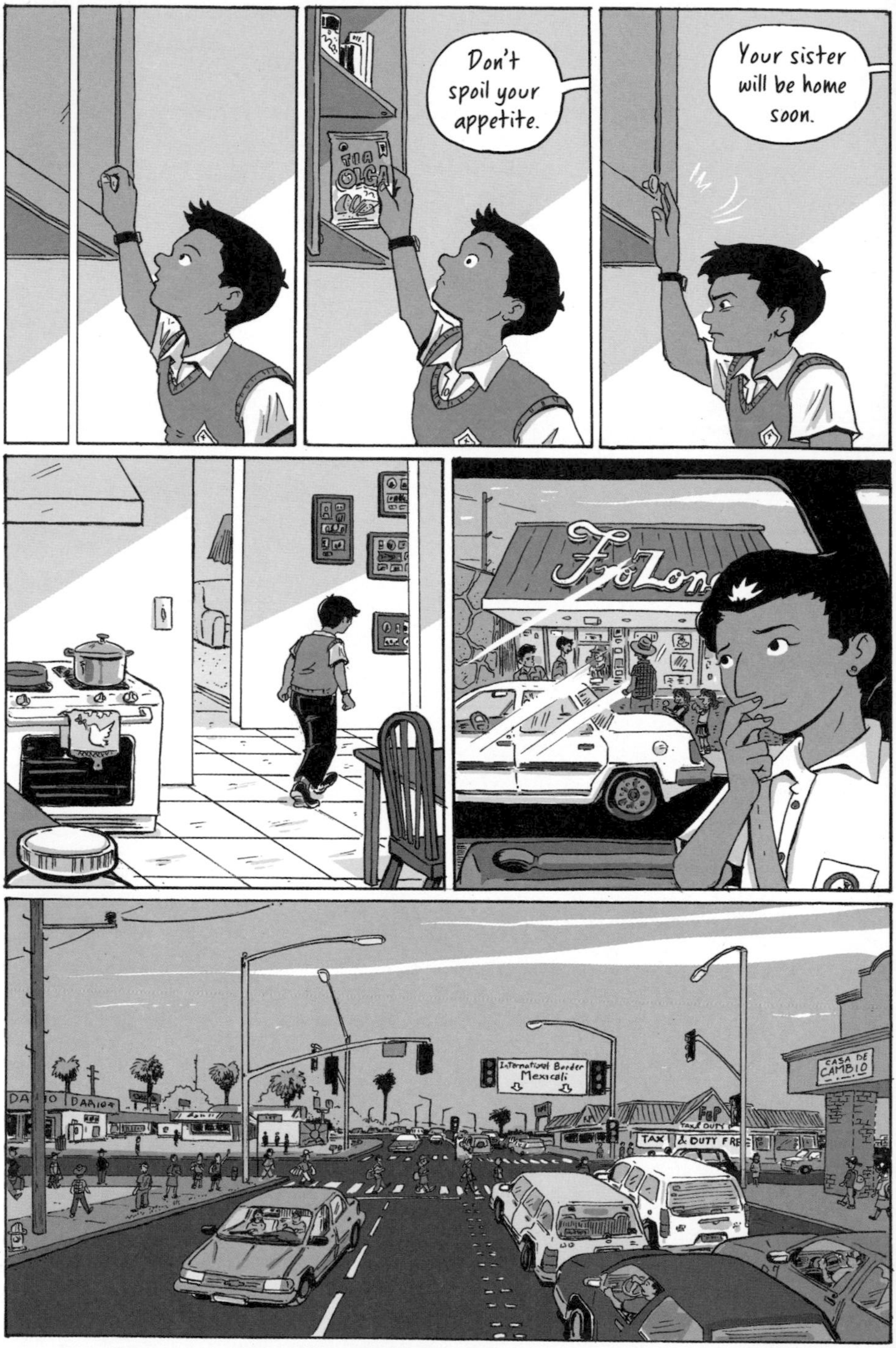
TIA
OLGA
Don't spoil your appetite.
Your sister will be home soon.
DARIO
International Border
Mexicali
CASA DE CAMBIO
TAX

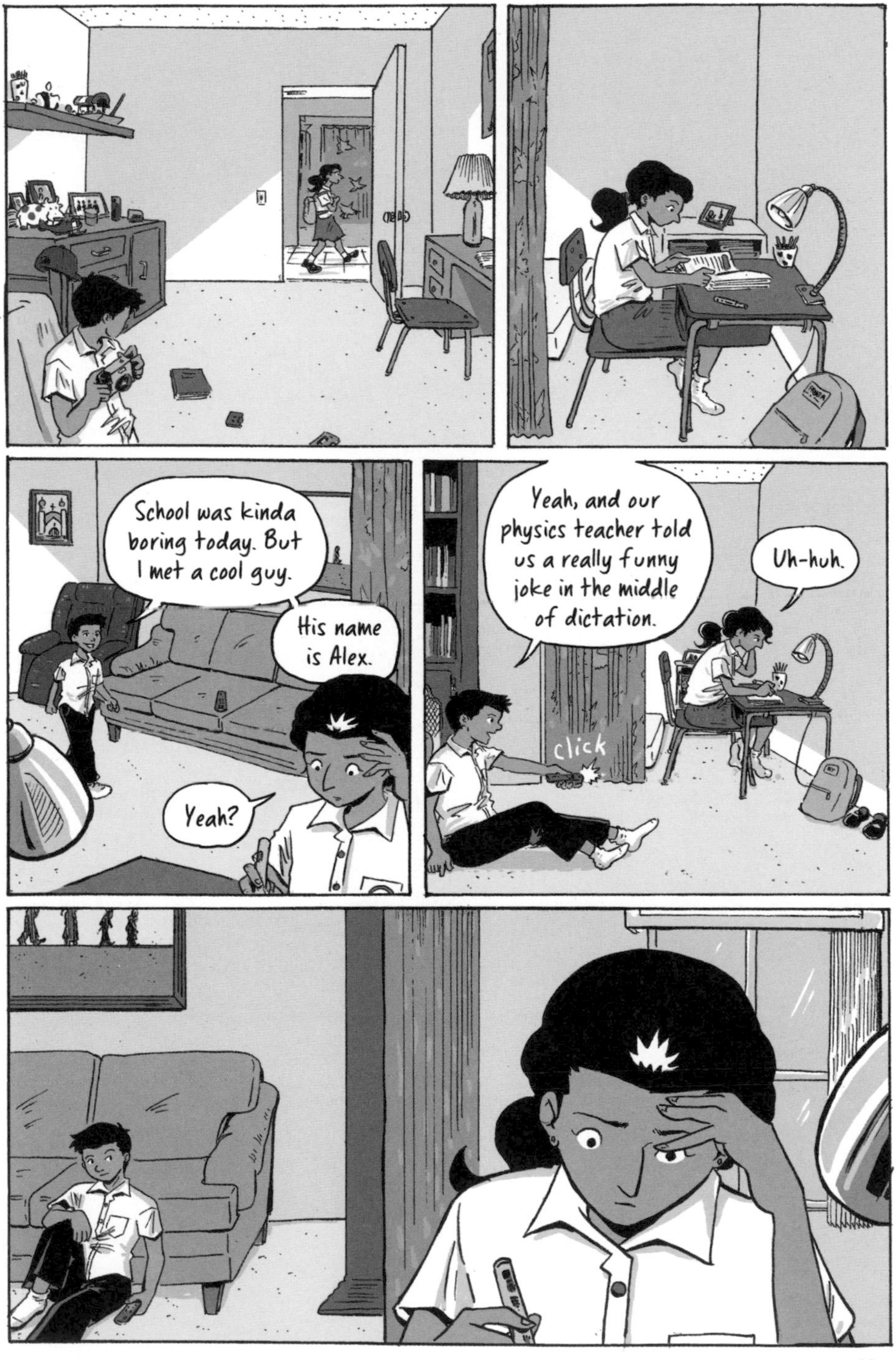
School was kinda boring today. But I met a cool guy.
His name is Alex.
Yeah?
Yeah, and our physics teacher told us a really funny joke in the middle of dictation.
Uh-huh.
click

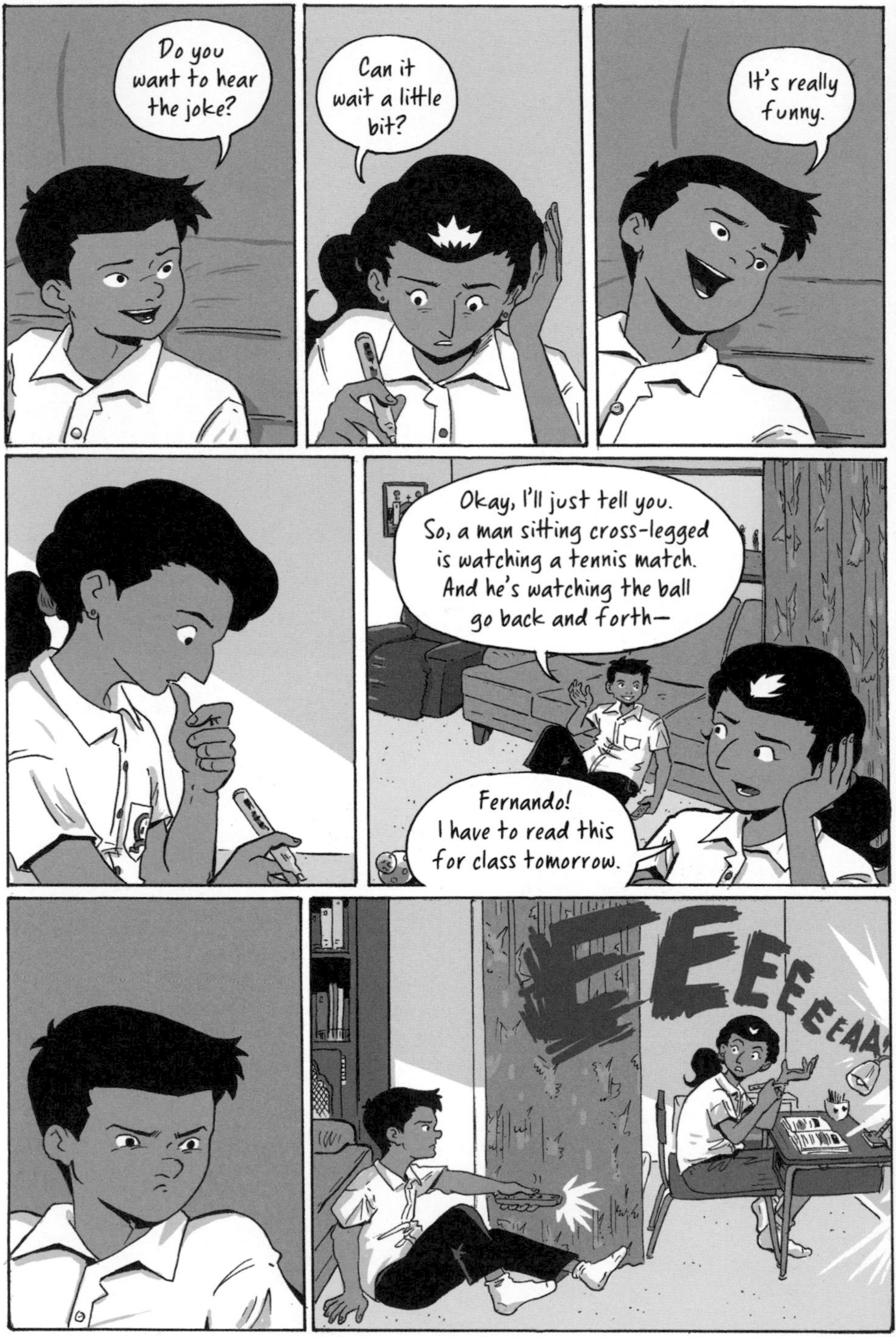
Do you want to hear the joke?
Can it wait a little bit?
It's really funny.
Okay, I'll just tell you. So, a man sitting cross-legged is watching a tennis match. And he's watching the ball go back and forth—
Fernando! I have to read this for class tomorrow.
EEEEEEAA

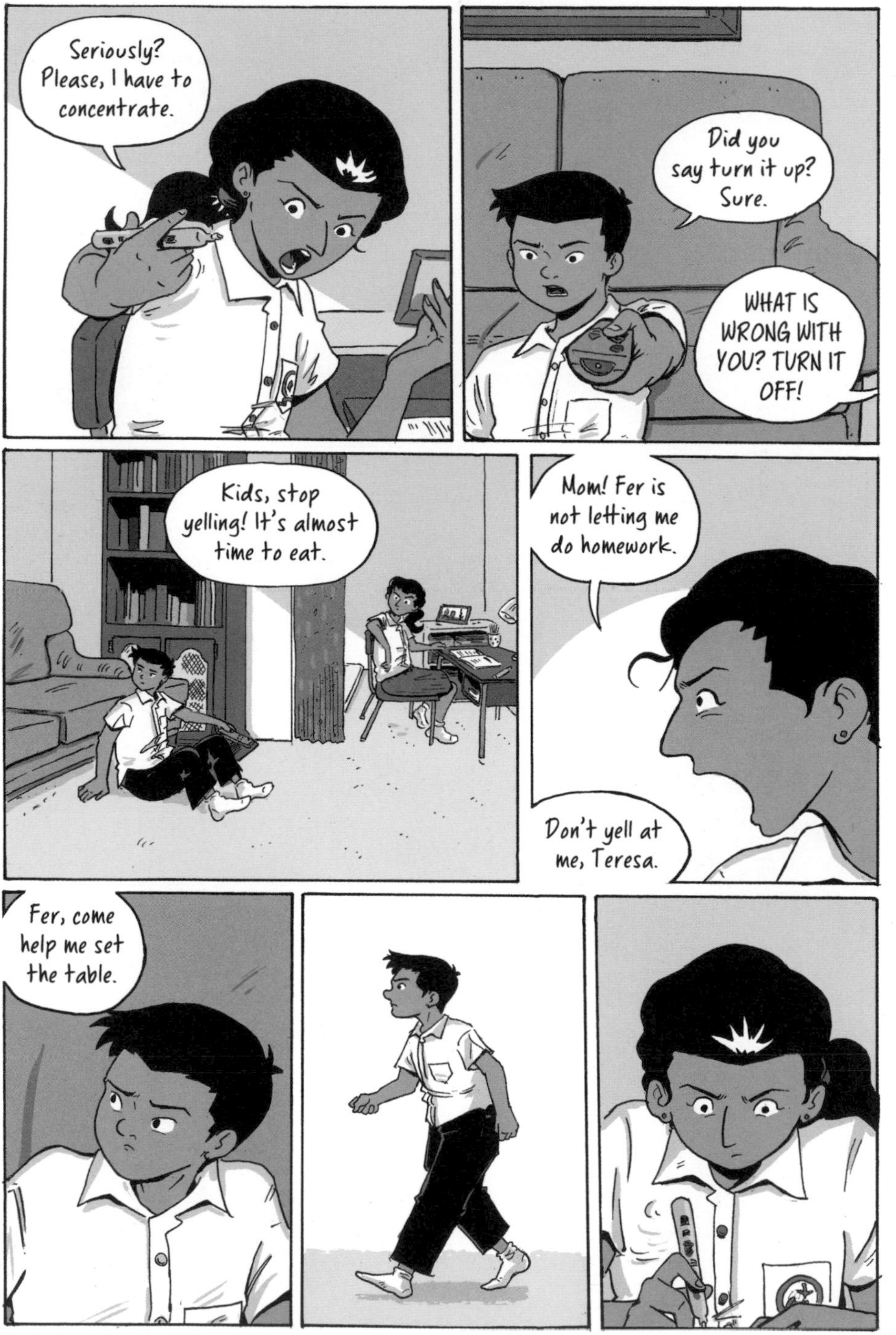
Seriously? Please, I have to concentrate.
Did you say turn it up? Sure.
WHAT IS WRONG WITH YOU? TURN IT OFF!
Kids, stop yelling! It's almost time to eat.
Mom! Fer is not letting me do homework.
Don't yell at me, Teresa.
Fer, come help me set the table.

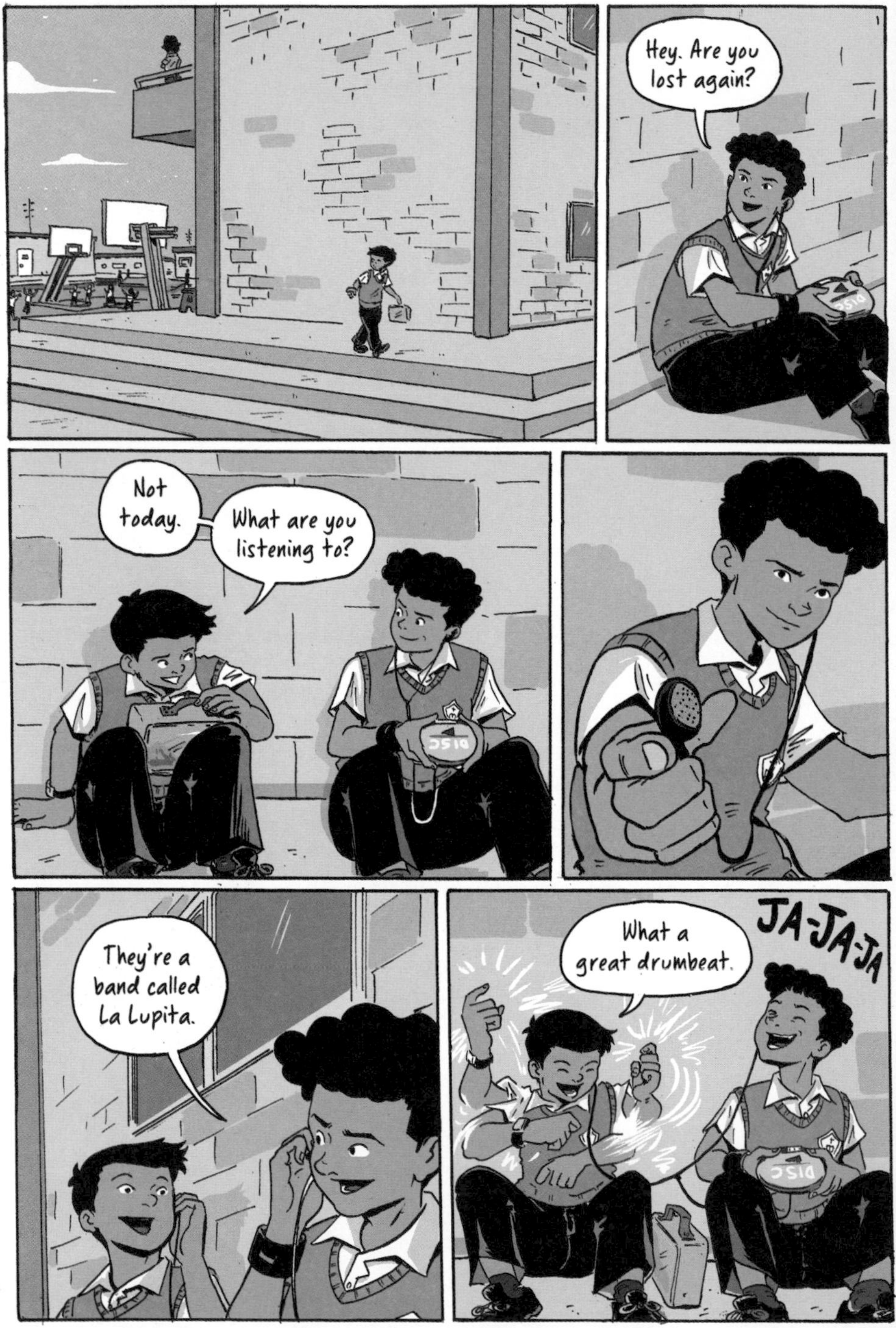
Hey. Are you lost again?
Not today.
What are you listening to?
They're a band called La Lupita.
What a great drumbeat.
JA-JA-JA

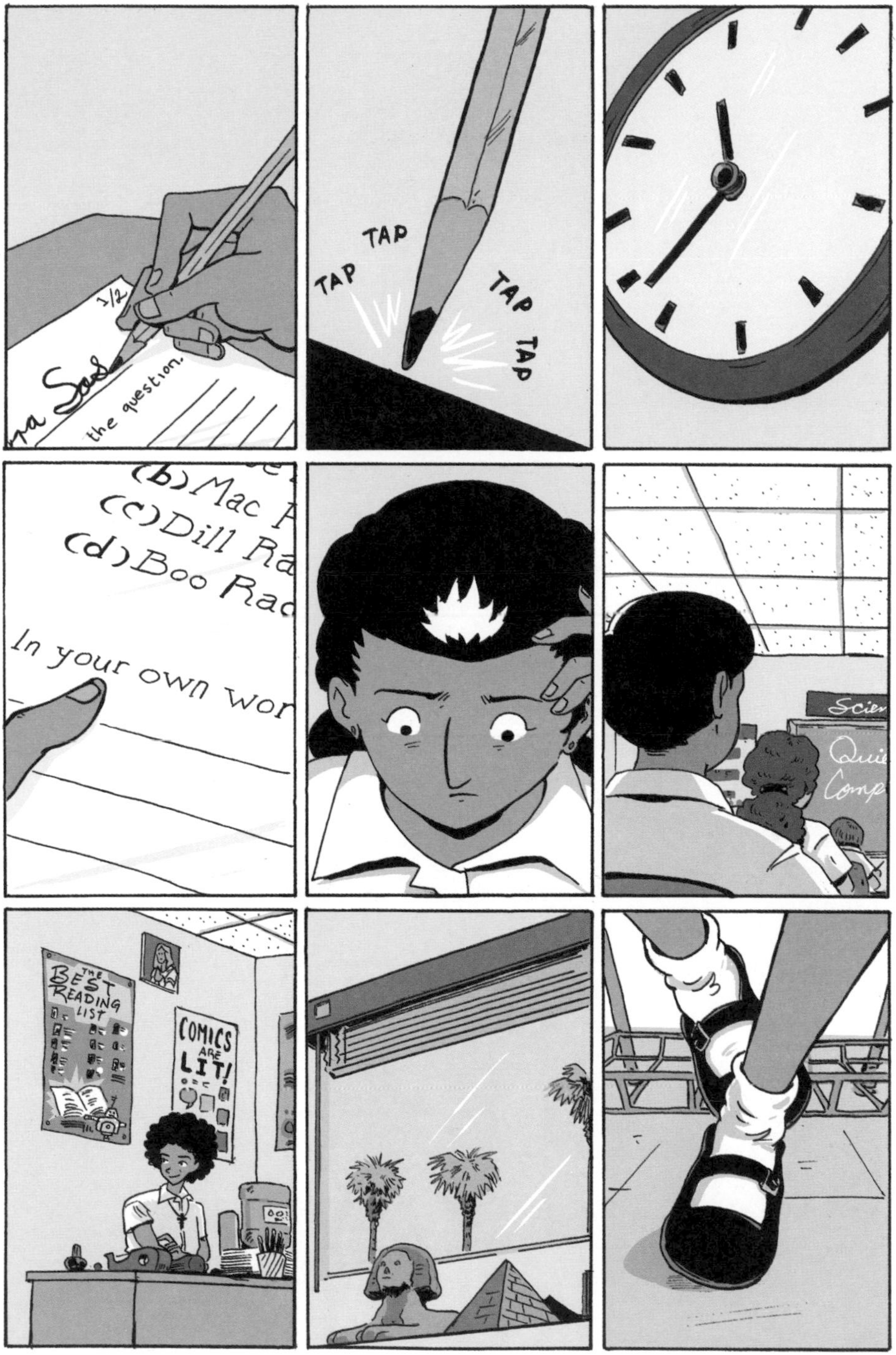
1/2
the question.
TAP
TAP
TAP
TAP
(b)Mac
(c)Dill
(d)Boo
In your own
THE BEST READING LIST
COMICS ARE LIT!

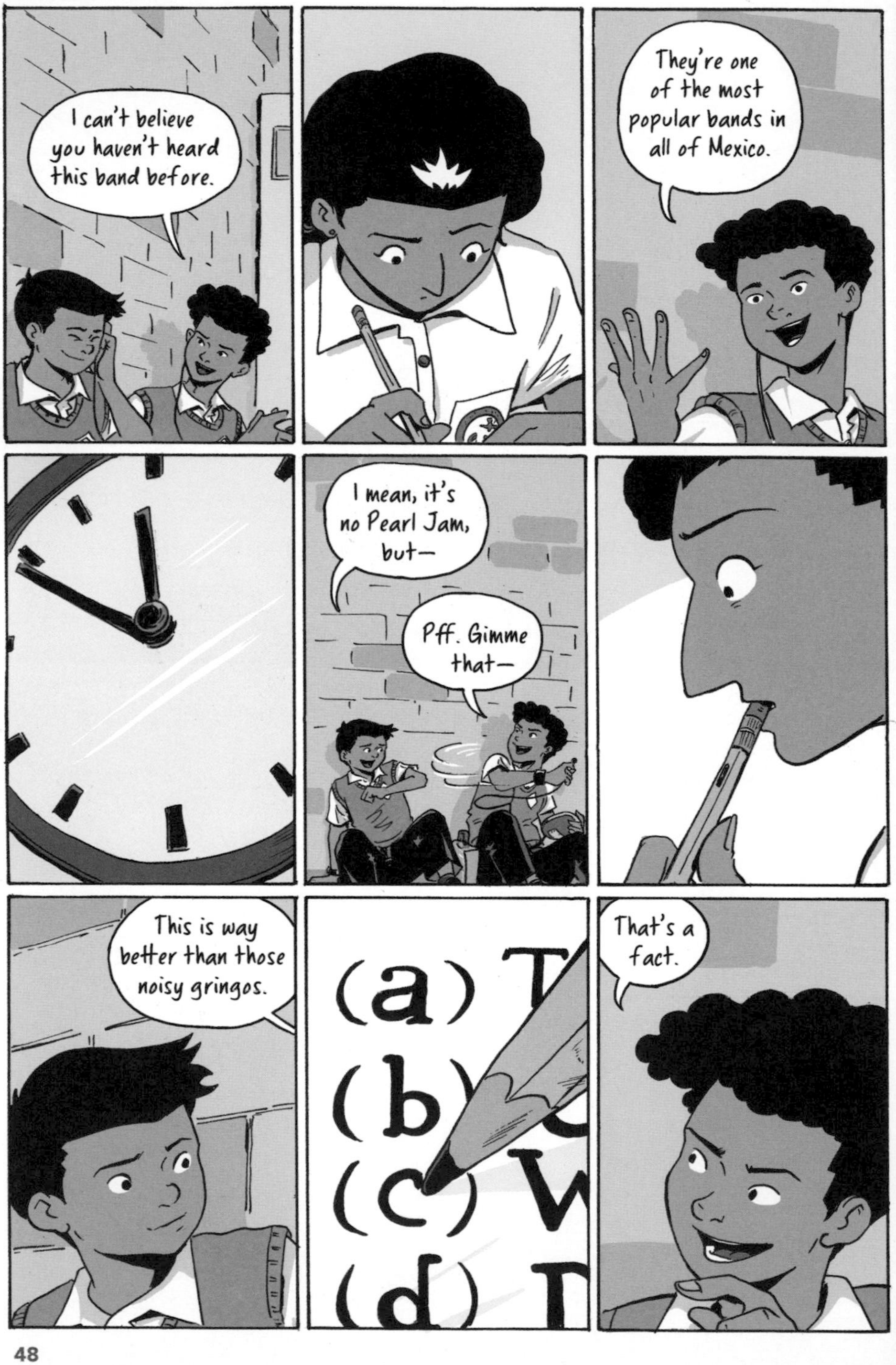
I can't believe you haven't heard this band before.
They're one of the most popular bands in all of Mexico.
I mean, it's no Pearl Jam, but—
Pff. Gimme that—
This is way better than those noisy gringos.
(a)
(b)
(c)
(d)
That's a fact.

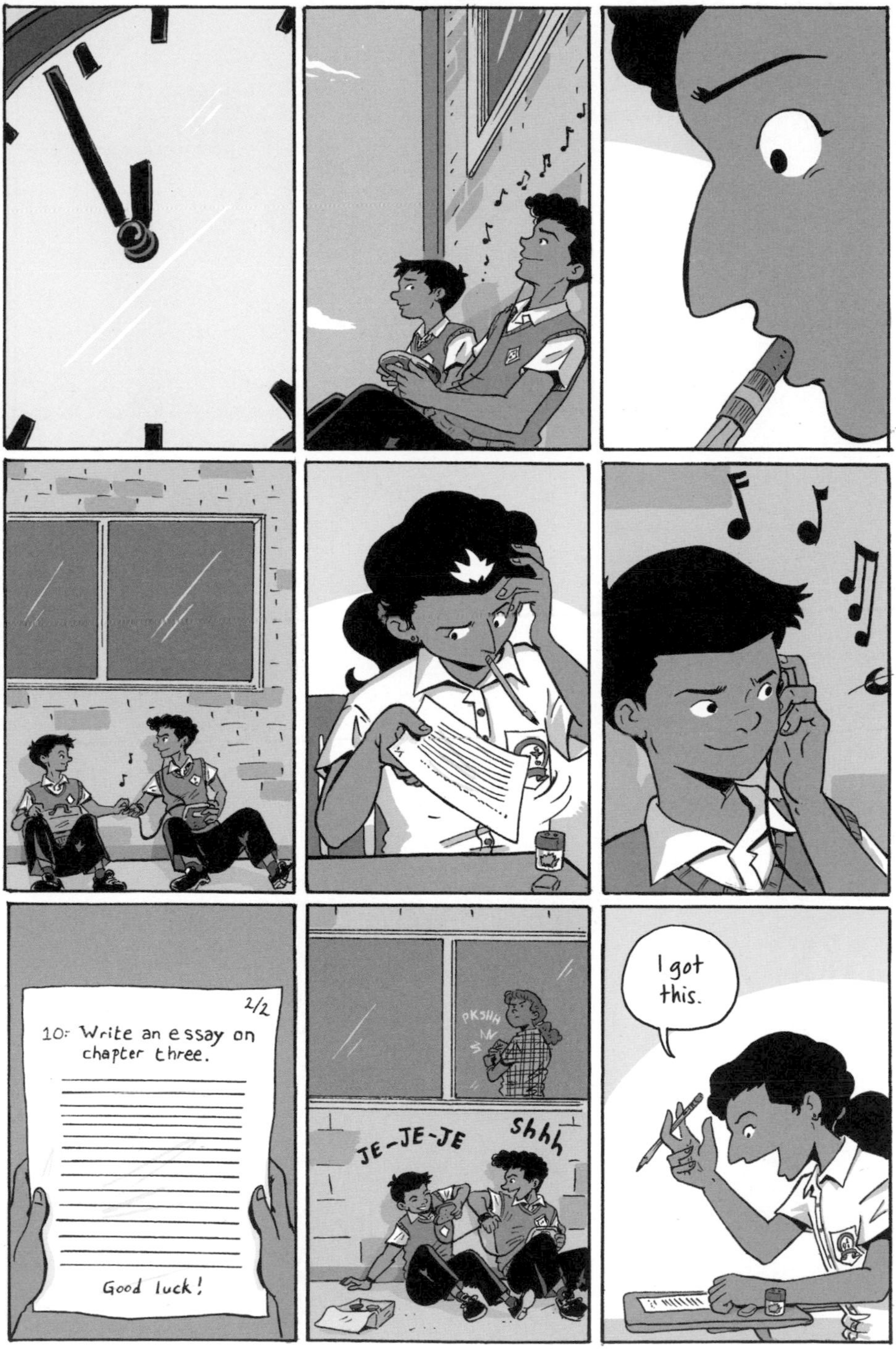
2/2
10: Write an essay on chapter three.
Good luck!
PKSHH
JE-JE-JE
Shhh
I got this.

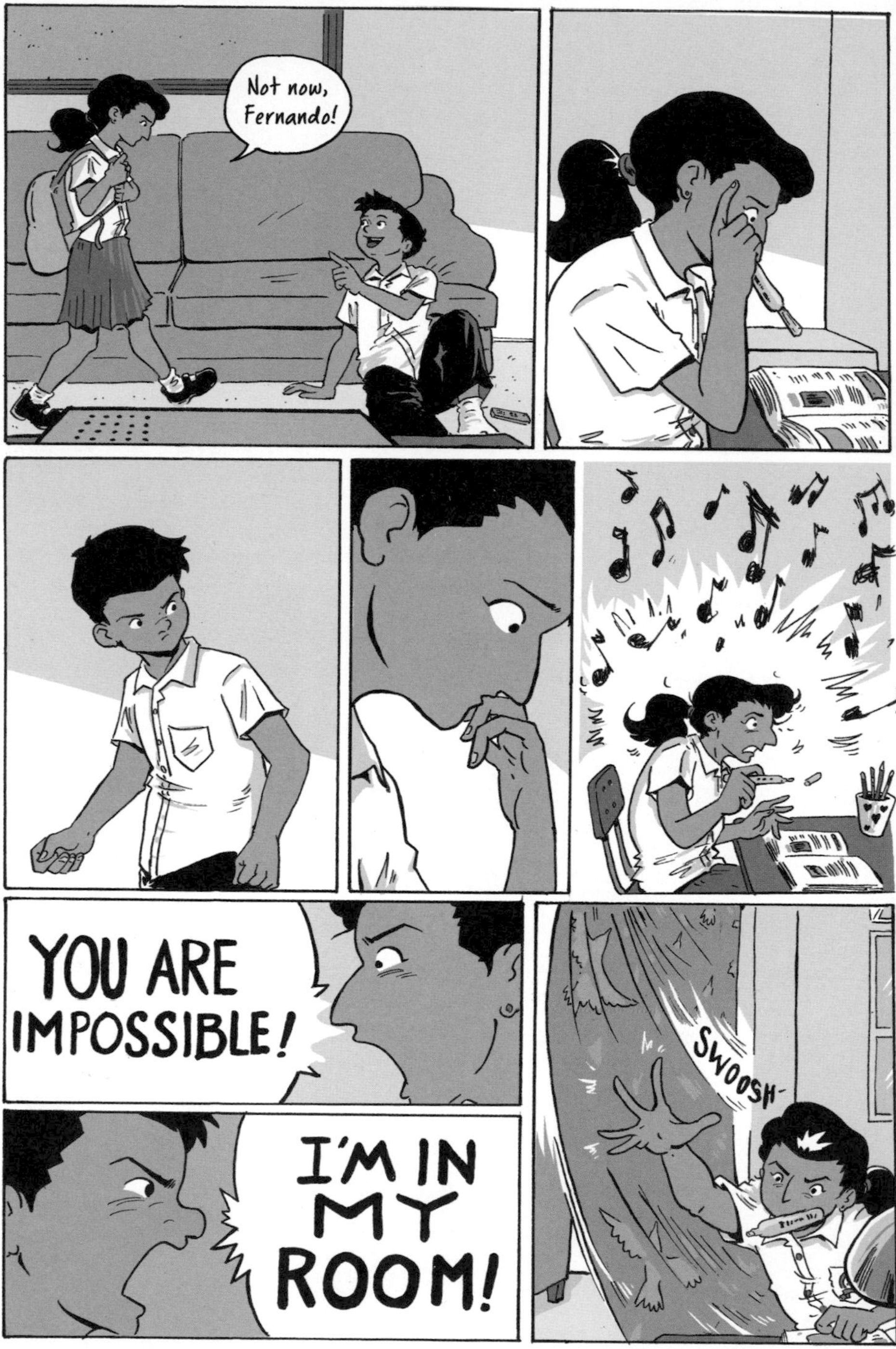
Not now, Fernando!
YOU ARE IMPOSSIBLE!
SWOOSH-
I'M IN MY ROOM!

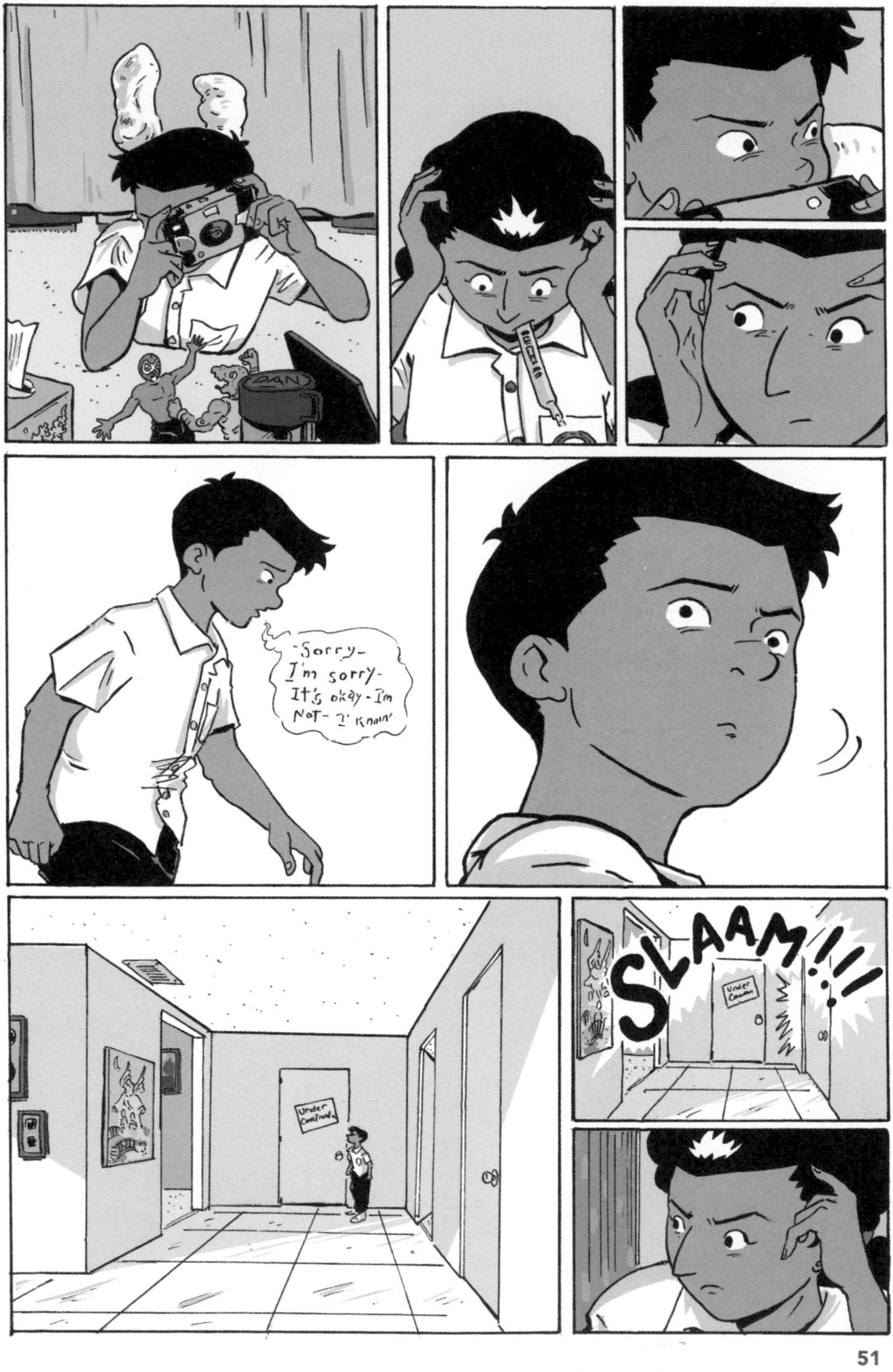
DAN
-Sorry-
I'm sorry-
It's okay - I'm
NOT - I' Knoin'
Under
SLAAM!!!
Under

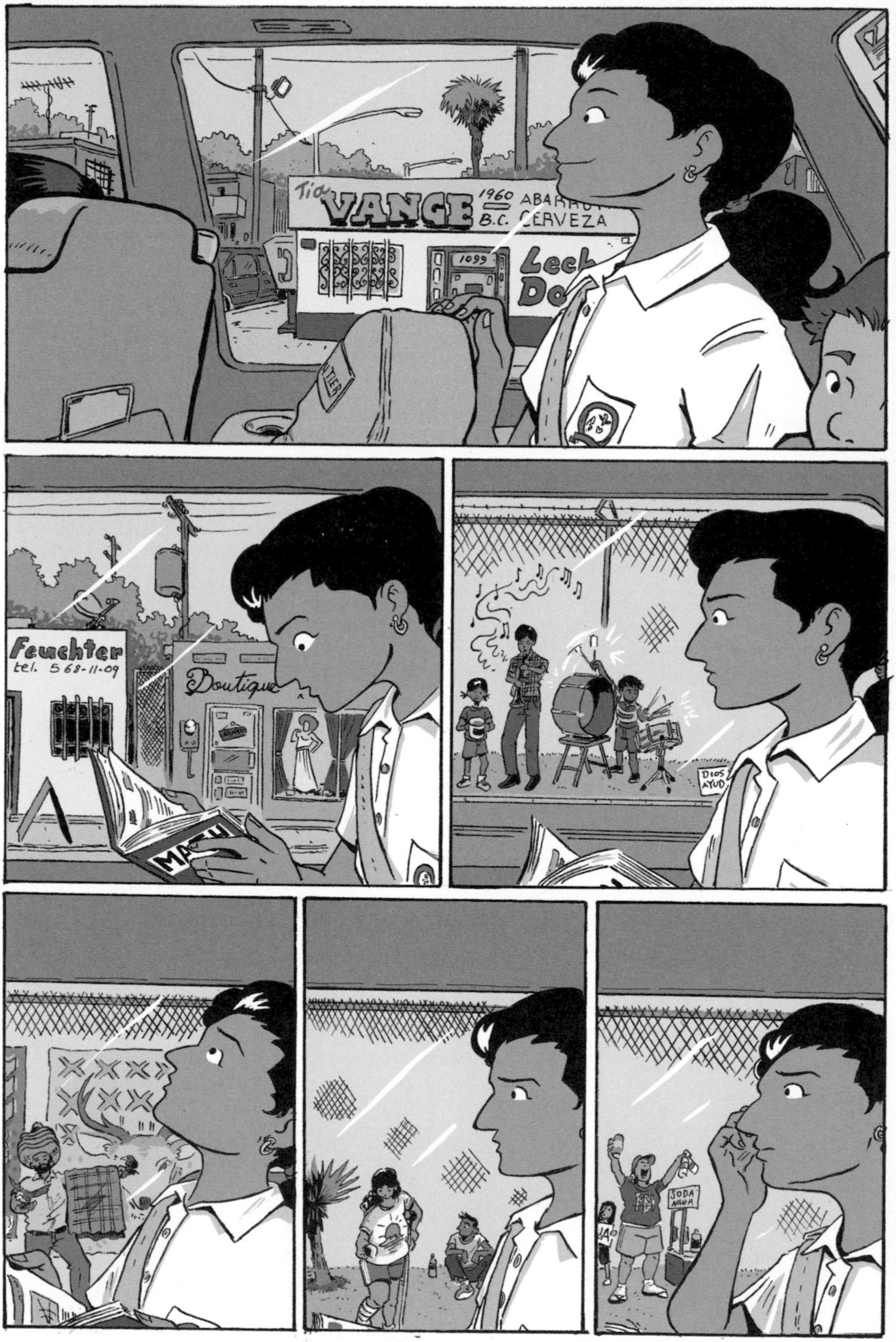
Tia
VANGE
1960
B.C. CERVEZA
1099
Feuchter
tel. 568-11-09
Boutique
MATH
DIOS AYUD
SODA AGUA

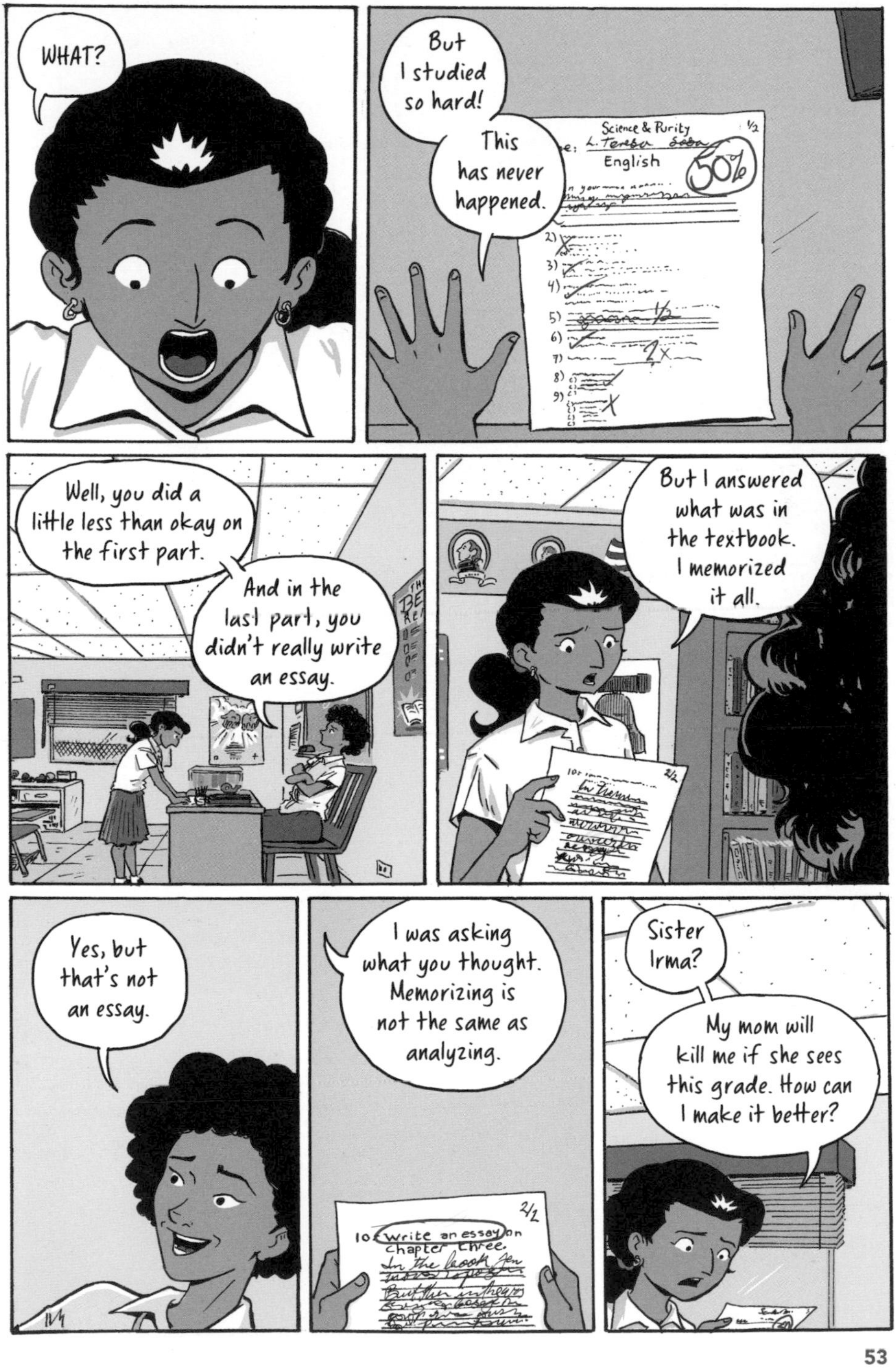
WHAT?
But I studied so hard!
This has never happened.
Science & Purity
English
50%
Well, you did a little less than okay on the first part.
And in the last part, you didn't really write an essay.
But I answered what was in the textbook. I memorized it all.
Yes, but that's not an essay.
I was asking what you thought. Memorizing is not the same as analyzing.
10. Write an essay on chapter three.
Sister Irma?
My mom will kill me if she sees this grade. How can I make it better?

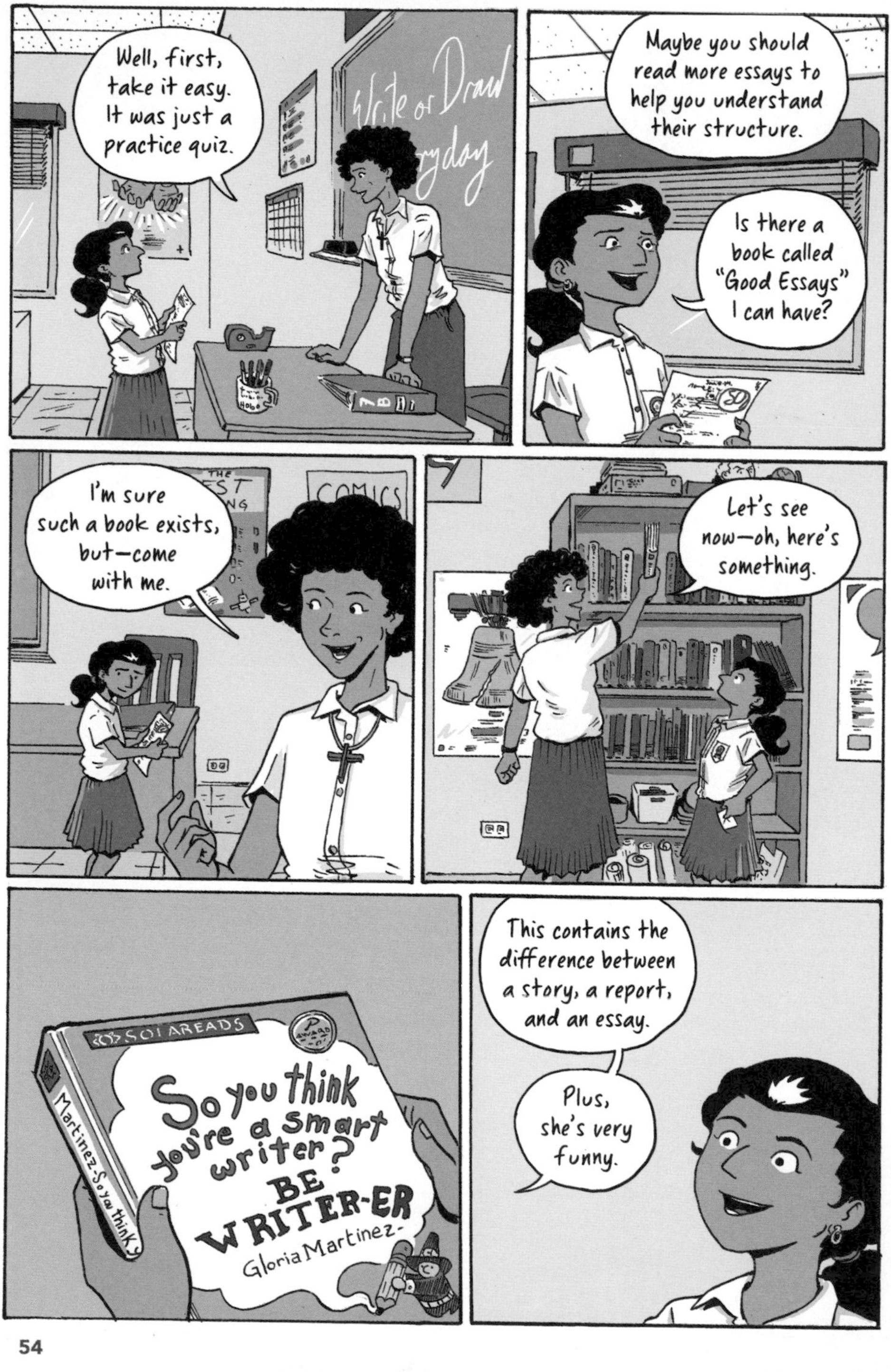
Well, first, take it easy. It was just a practice quiz.
Write or Draw
Maybe you should read more essays to help you understand their structure.
Is there a book called "Good Essays" I can have?
I'm sure such a book exists, but—come with me.
COMICS
Let's see now—oh, here's something.
SOIAREADS
So you think you're a smart writer? BE WRITER-ER
Gloria Martinez
Martinez-So you think
This contains the difference between a story, a report, and an essay.
Plus, she's very funny.

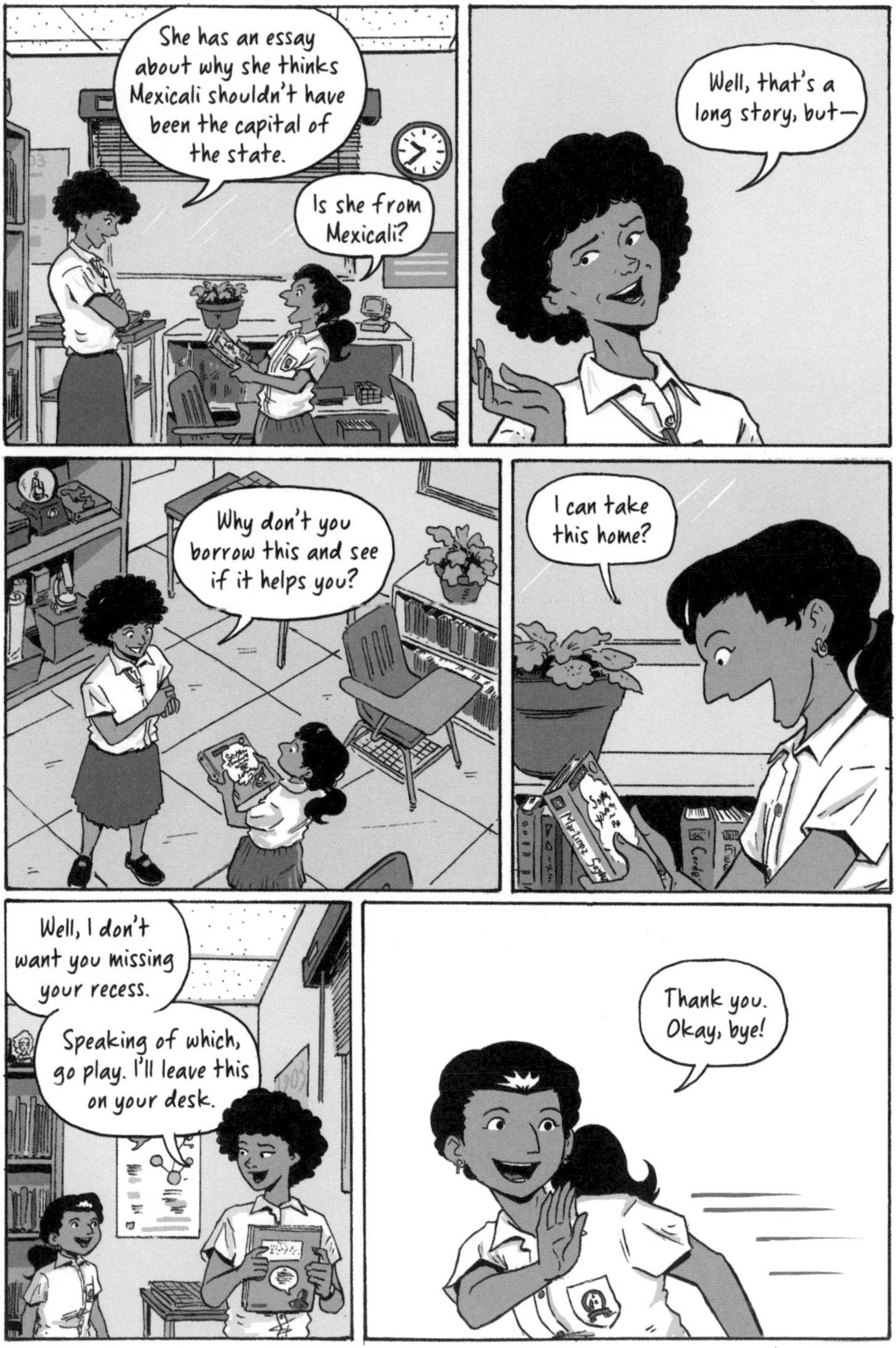
She has an essay about why she thinks Mexicali shouldn't have been the capital of the state.
Is she from Mexicali?
Well, that's a long story, but—
Why don't you borrow this and see if it helps you?
I can take this home?
Well, I don't want you missing your recess.
Speaking of which, go play. I'll leave this on your desk.
Thank you. Okay, bye!

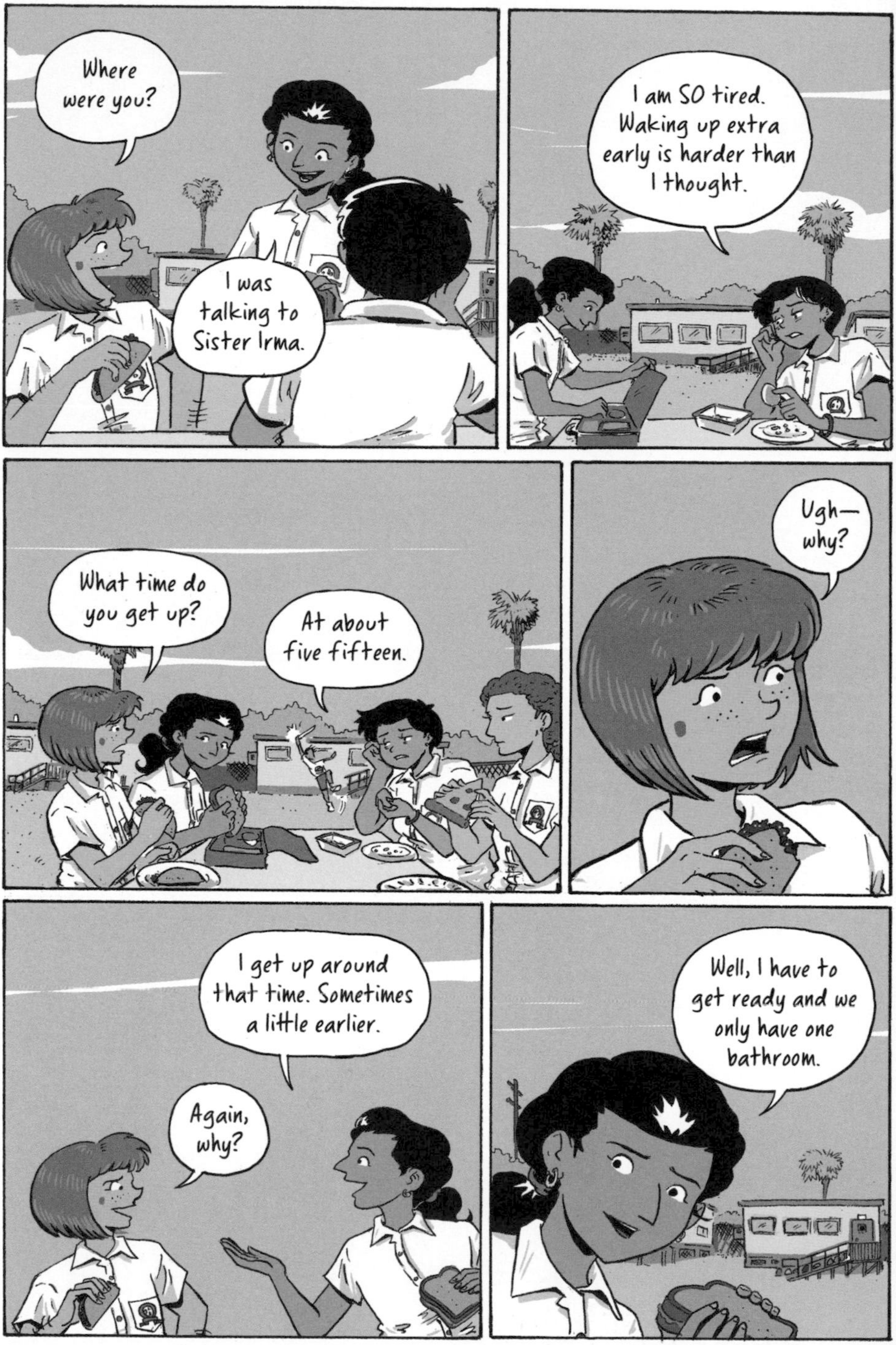
Where were you?
I was talking to Sister Irma.
I am SO tired. Waking up extra early is harder than I thought.
What time do you get up?
At about five fifteen.
Ugh— why?
I get up around that time. Sometimes a little earlier.
Again, why?
Well, I have to get ready and we only have one bathroom.

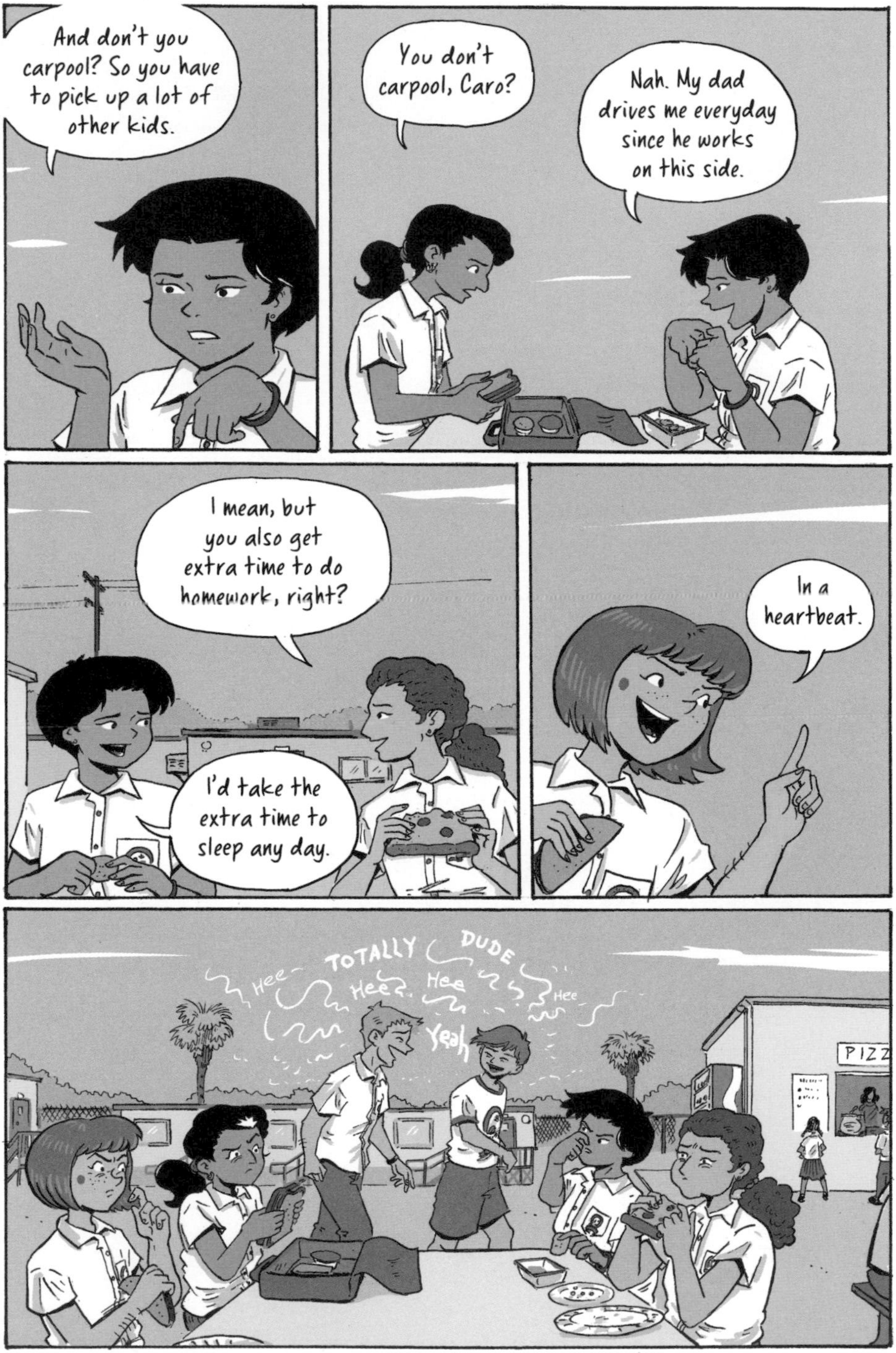

And don't you carpool? So you have to pick up a lot of other kids.
You don't carpool, Caro?
Nah. My dad drives me everyday since he works on this side.
I mean, but you also get extra time to do homework, right?
I'd take the extra time to sleep any day.
In a heartbeat.
TOTALLY
DUDE
Hee
Hee
Hee
Hee
Yeah
PIZZ

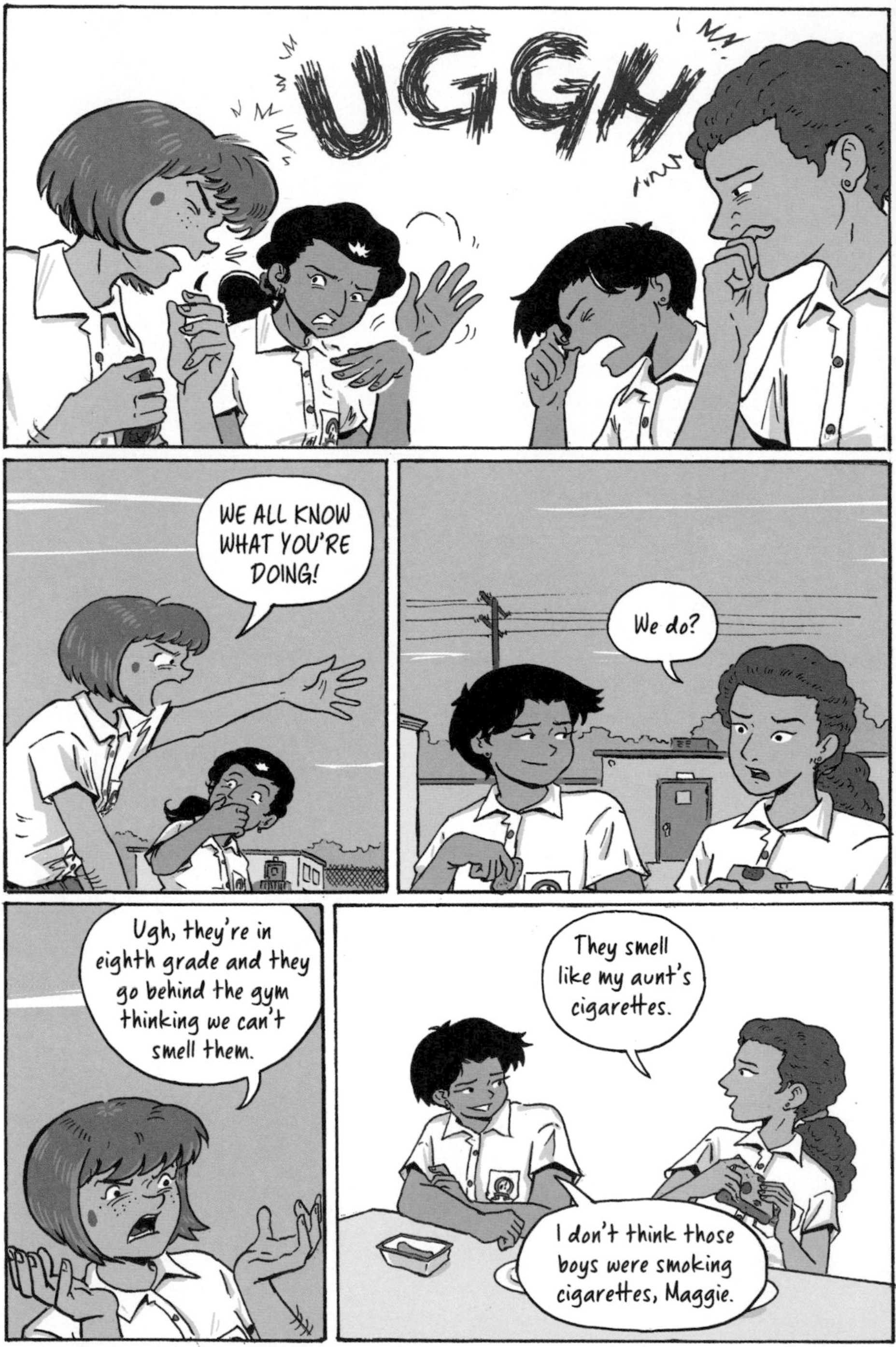
UGGH
WE ALL KNOW WHAT YOU'RE DOING!
We do?
Ugh, they're in eighth grade and they go behind the gym thinking we can't smell them.
They smell like my aunt's cigarettes.
I don't think those boys were smoking cigarettes, Maggie.

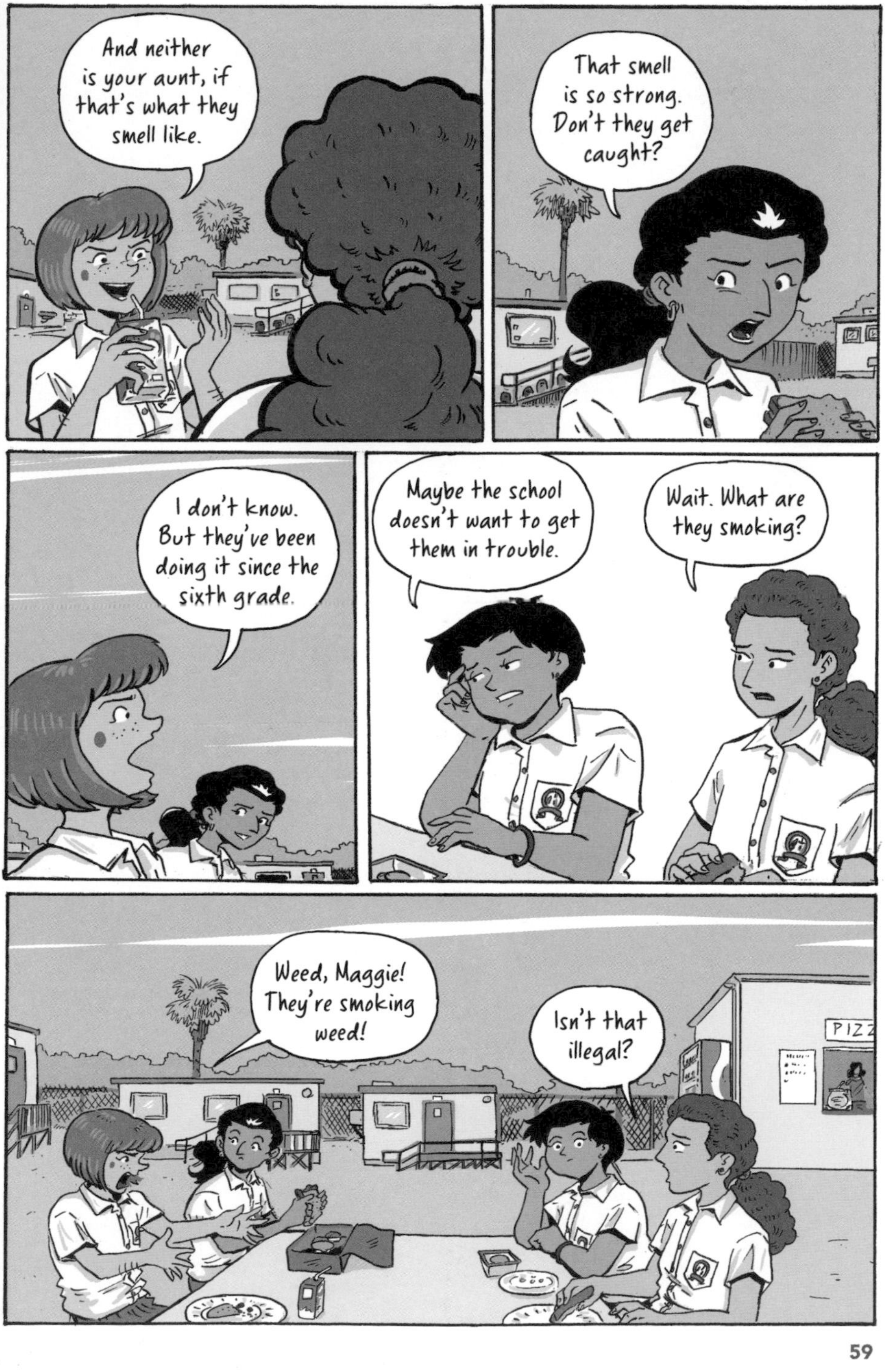

And neither is your aunt, if that's what they smell like.
That smell is so strong. Don't they get caught?
I don't know. But they've been doing it since the sixth grade.
Maybe the school doesn't want to get them in trouble.
Wait. What are they smoking?
Weed, Maggie! They're smoking weed!
Isn't that illegal?
PIZZ

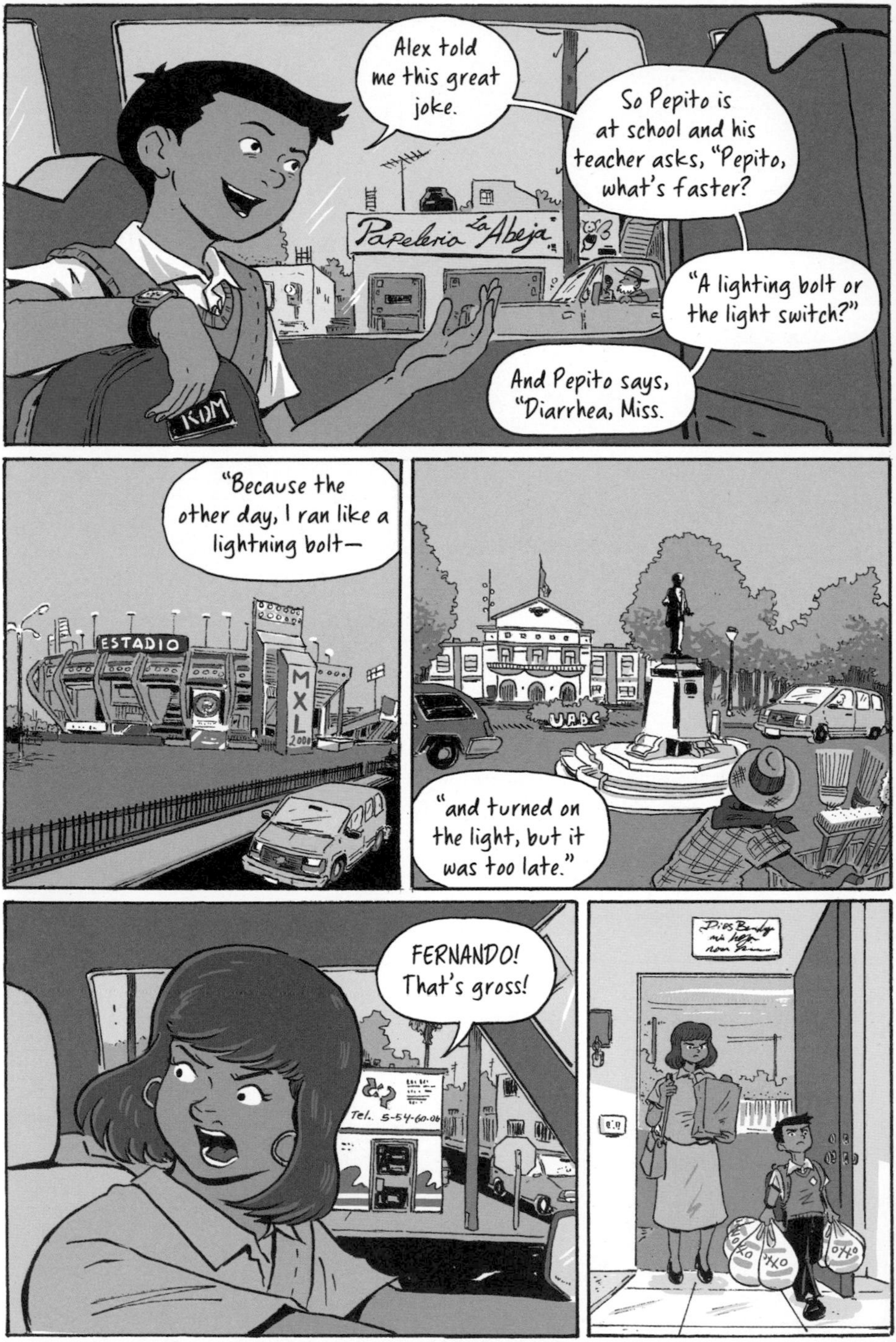
Alex told me this great joke.
So Pepito is at school and his teacher asks, "Pepito, what's faster?
"A lighting bolt or the light switch?"
And Pepito says, "Diarrhea, Miss.
Papeleria La Abeja
KDM
"Because the other day, I ran like a lightning bolt—
ESTADIO
MXL
UABC
"and turned on the light, but it was too late."
FERNANDO! That's gross!
Tel. 5-54-60-06

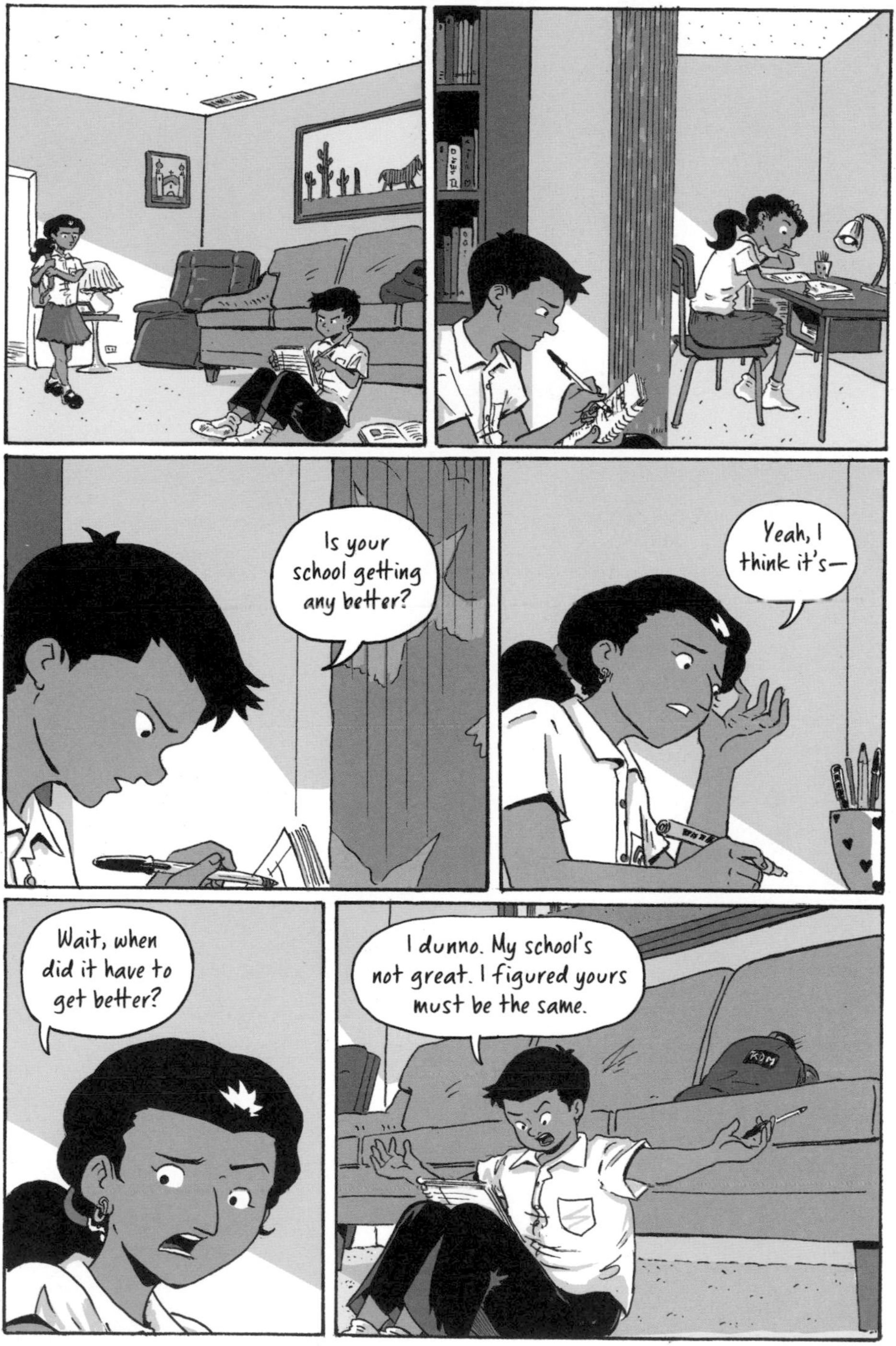
Is your school getting any better?
Yeah, I think it's—
Wait, when did it have to get better?
I dunno. My school's not great. I figured yours must be the same.

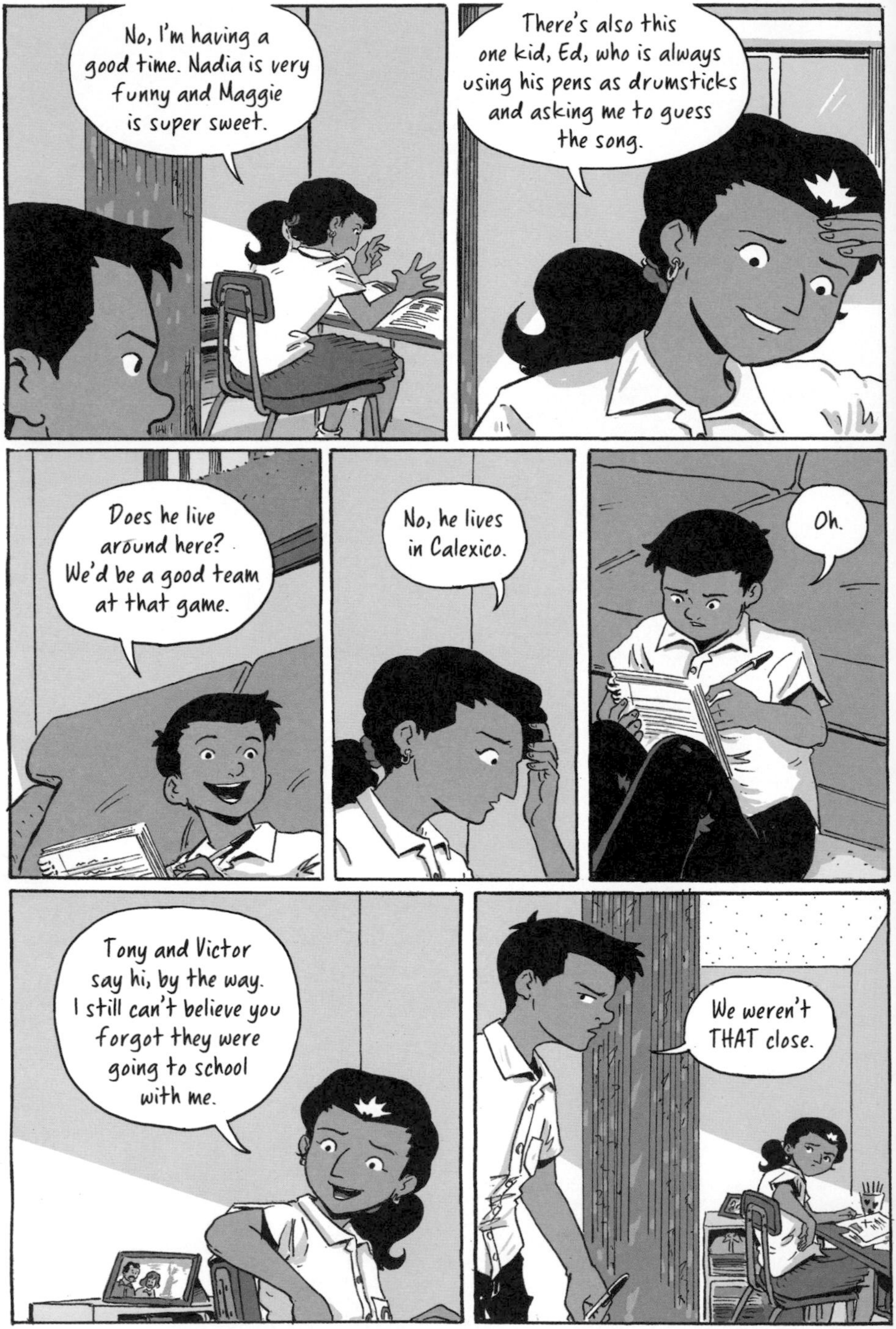
No, I'm having a good time. Nadia is very funny and Maggie is super sweet.
There's also this one kid, Ed, who is always using his pens as drumsticks and asking me to guess the song.
Does he live around here? We'd be a good team at that game.
No, he lives in Calexico.
Oh.
Tony and Victor say hi, by the way. I still can't believe you forgot they were going to school with me.
We weren't THAT close.

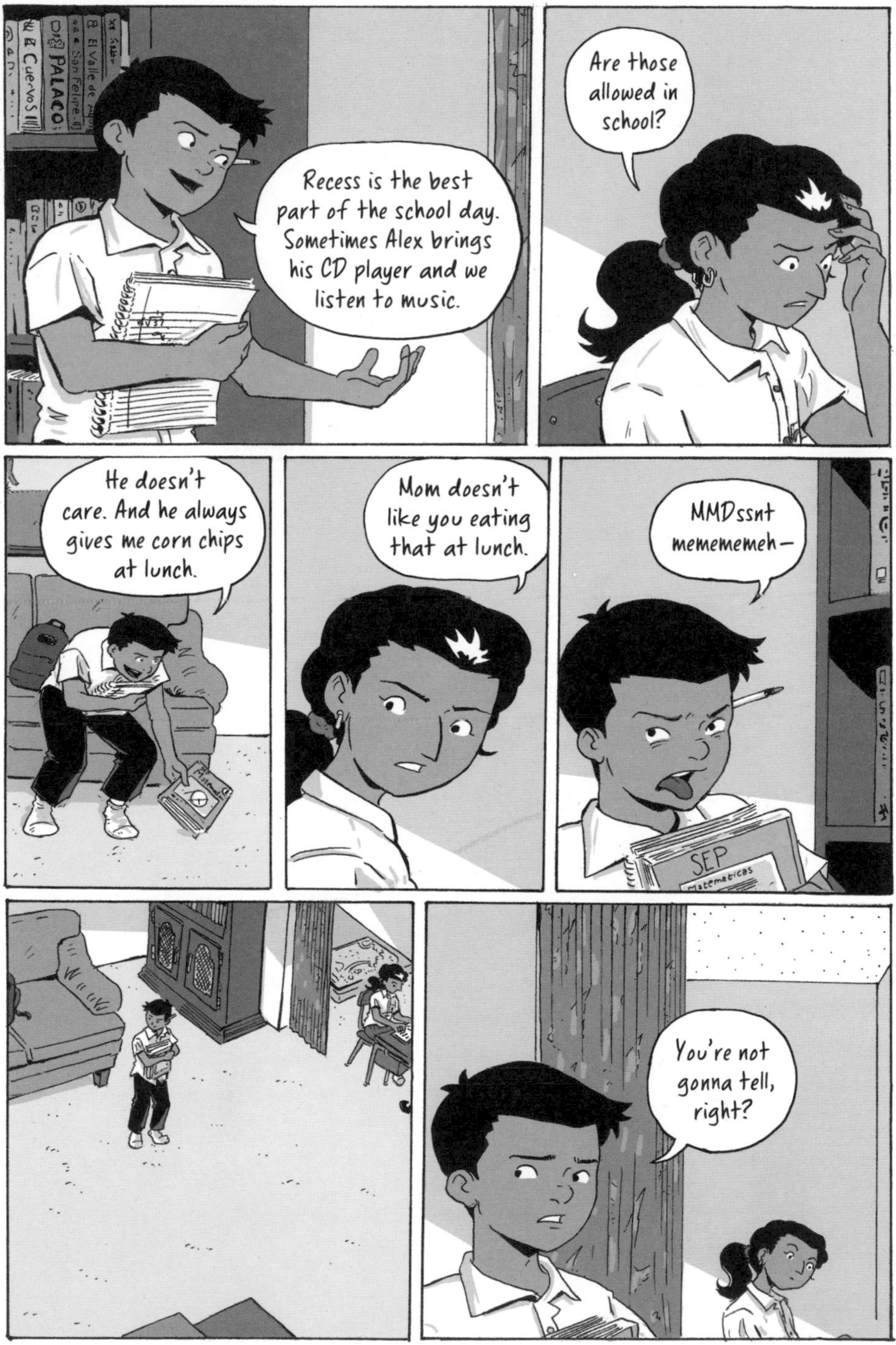
Recess is the best part of the school day. Sometimes Alex brings his CD player and we listen to music.
Are those allowed in school?
He doesn't care. And he always gives me corn chips at lunch.
Mom doesn't like you eating that at lunch.
MMDssnt mememememeh—
SEP
Matematicas
You're not gonna tell, right?

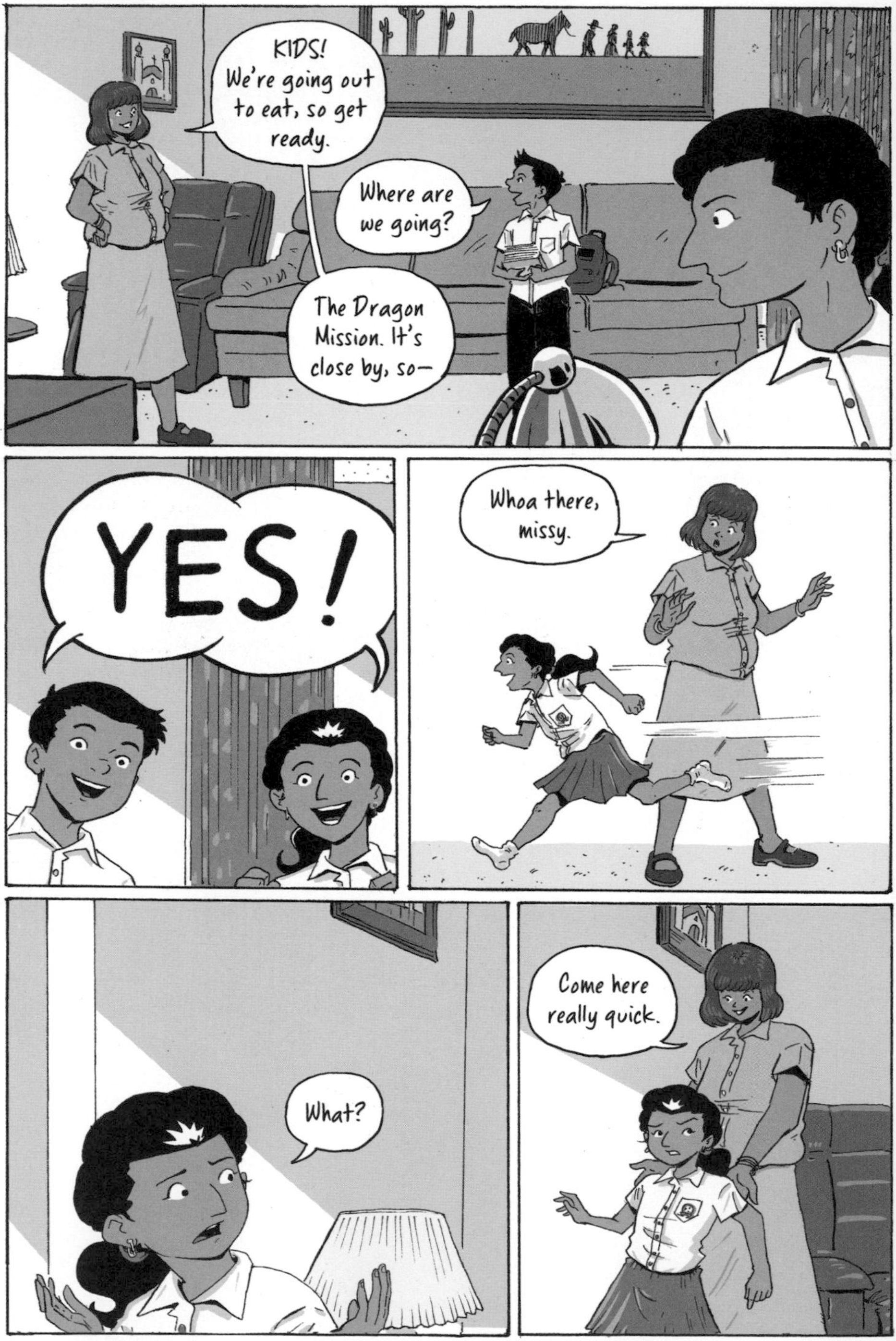
KIDS! We're going out to eat, so get ready.
Where are we going?
The Dragon Mission. It's close by, so—
YES!
Whoa there, missy.
What?
Come here really quick.

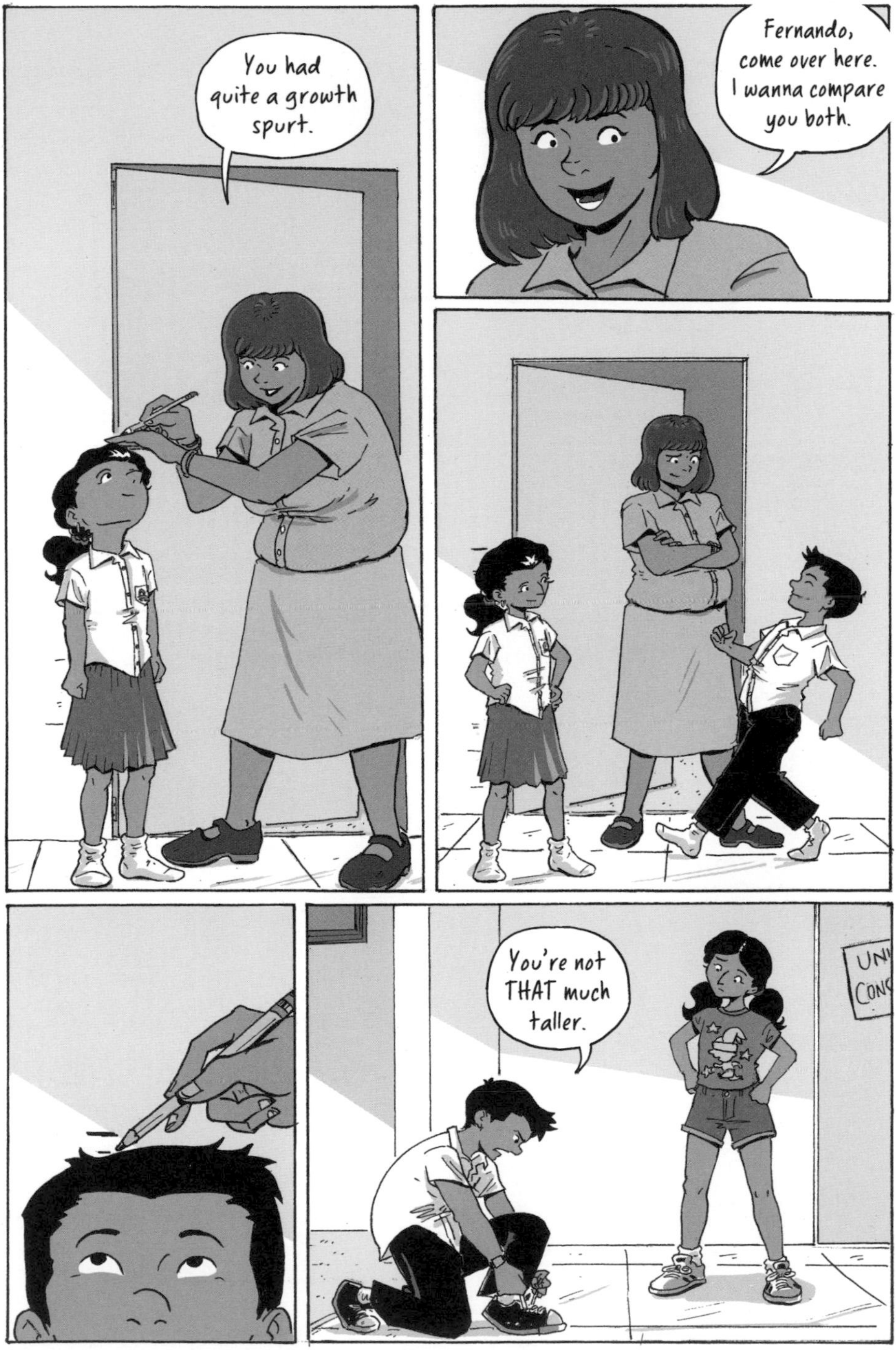
You had quite a growth spurt.
Fernando, come over here. I wanna compare you both.
You're not THAT much taller.

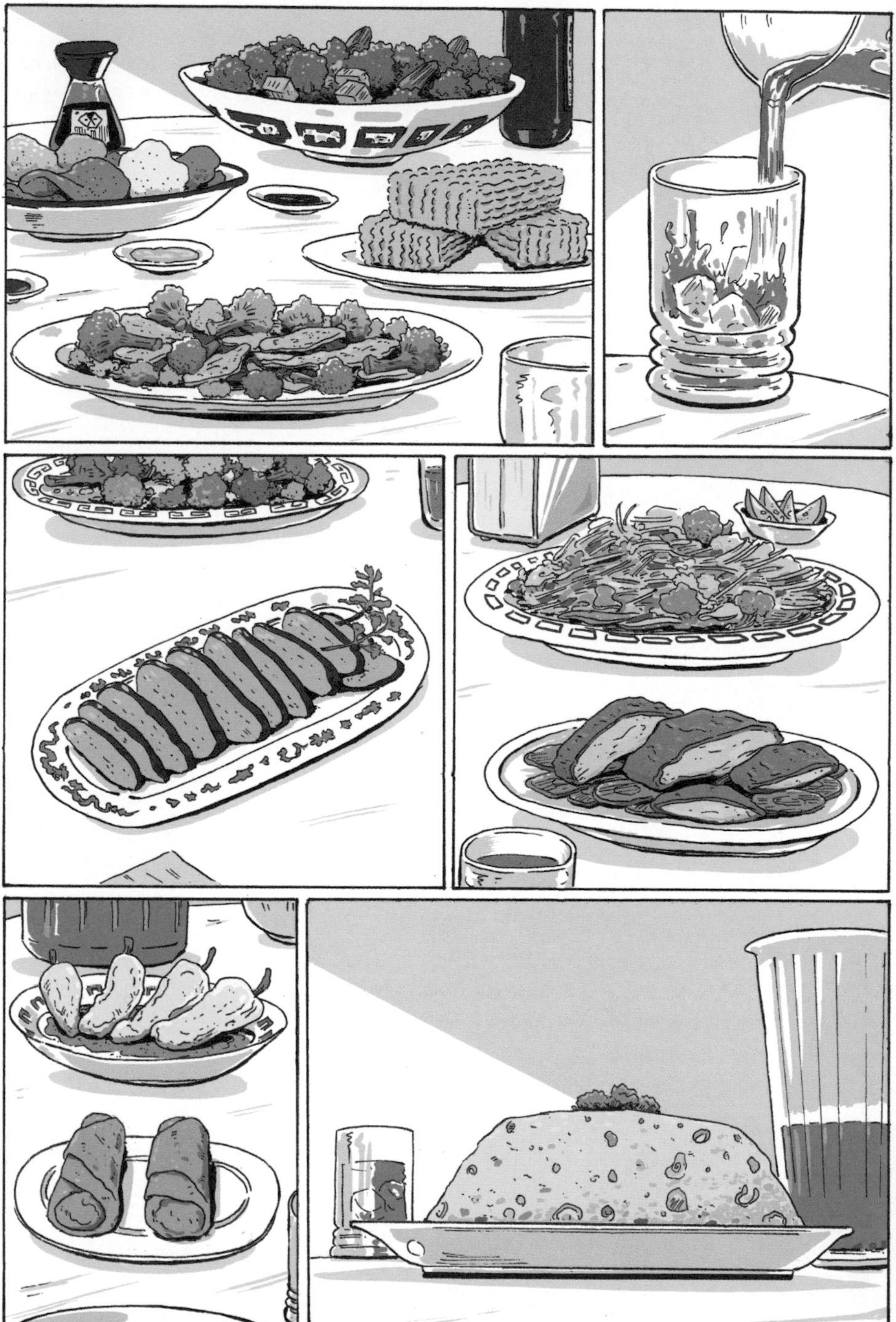

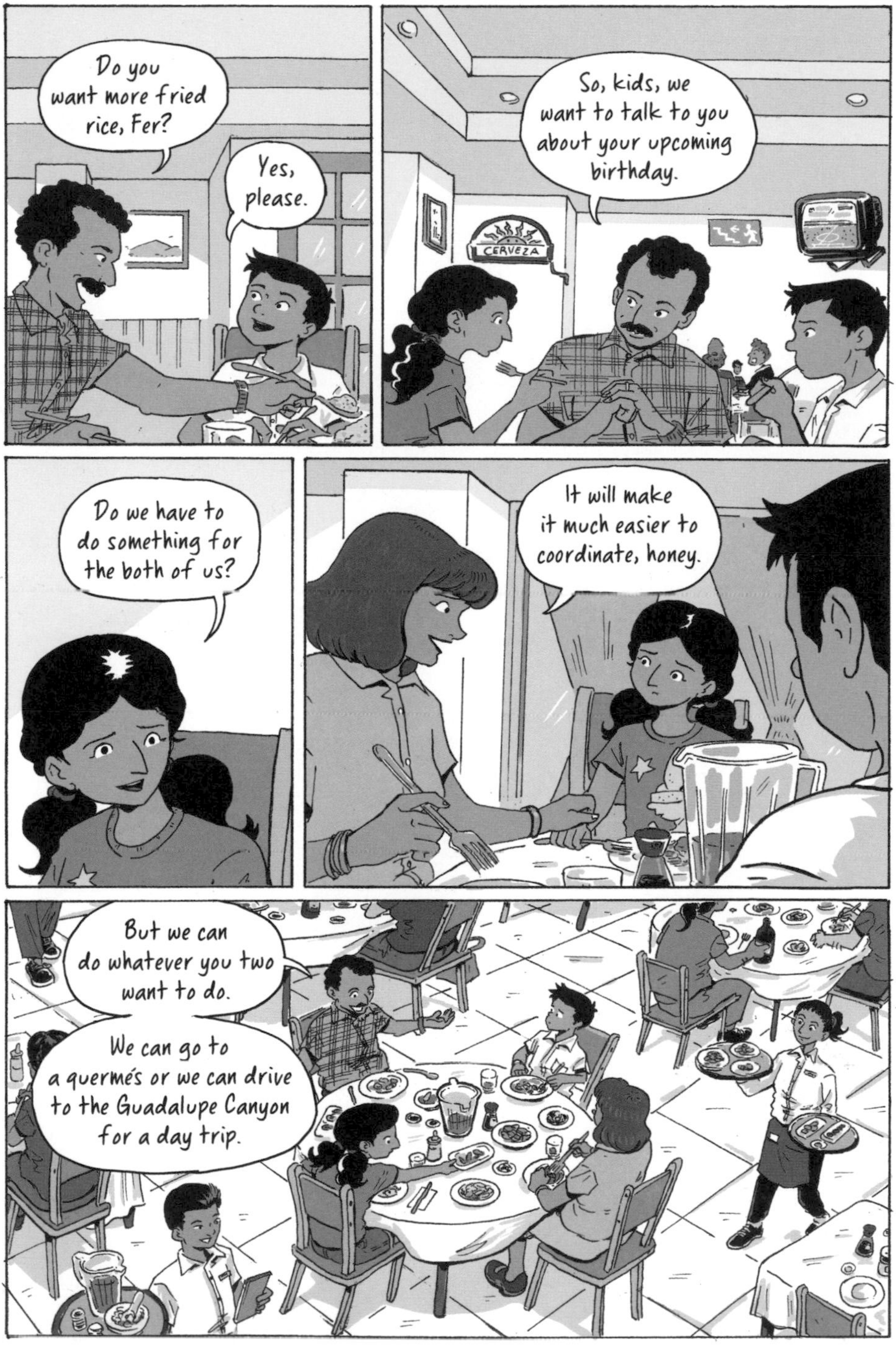

Do you want more fried rice, Fer?
Yes, please.
So, kids, we want to talk to you about your upcoming birthday.
CERVEZA
Do we have to do something for the both of us?
It will make it much easier to coordinate, honey.
But we can do whatever you two want to do.
We can go to a quermés or we can drive to the Guadalupe Canyon for a day trip.

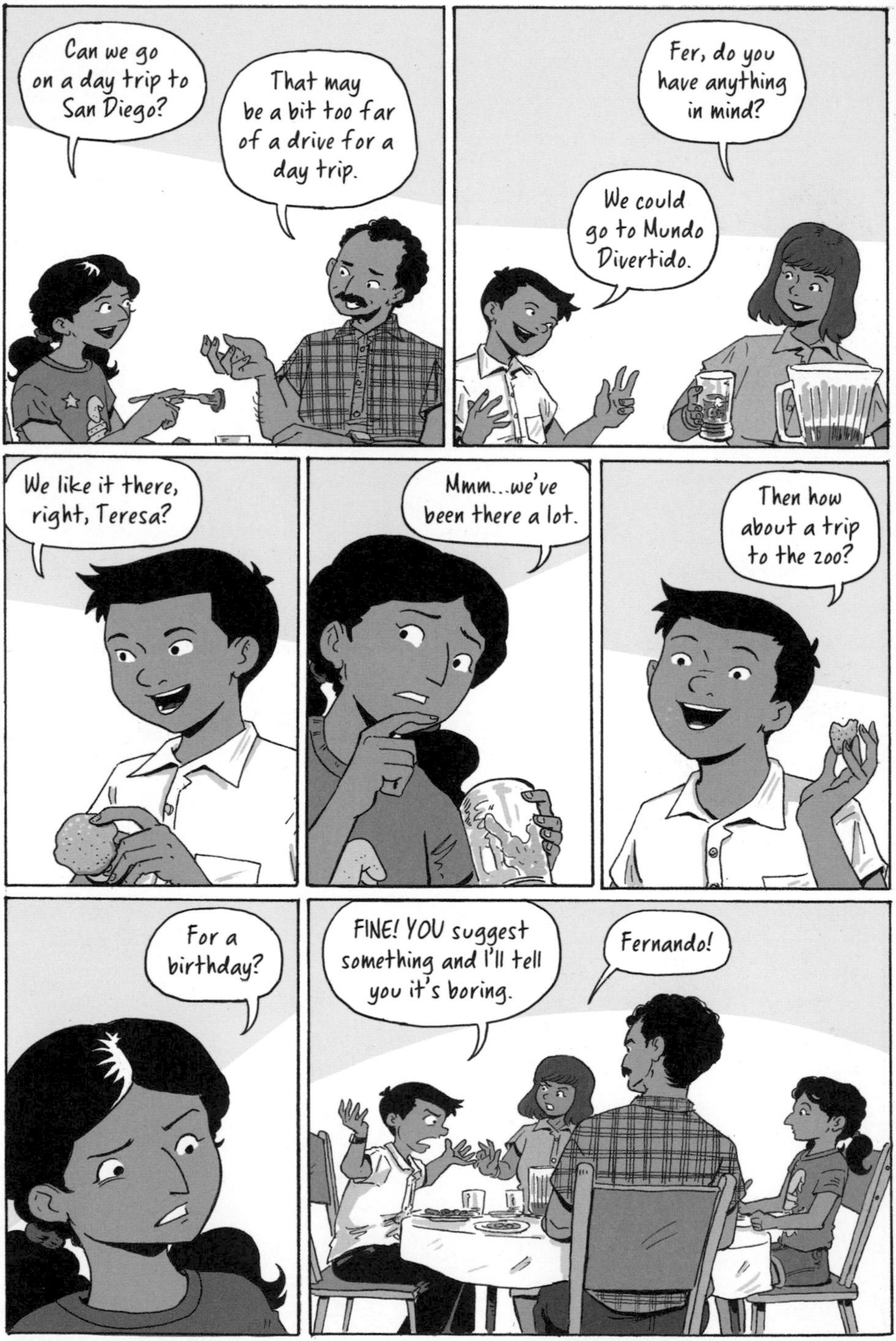
Can we go on a day trip to San Diego?
That may be a bit too far of a drive for a day trip.
Fer, do you have anything in mind?
We could go to Mundo Divertido.
We like it there, right, Teresa?
Mmm...we've been there a lot.
Then how about a trip to the zoo?
For a birthday?
FINE! YOU suggest something and I'll tell you it's boring.
Fernando!

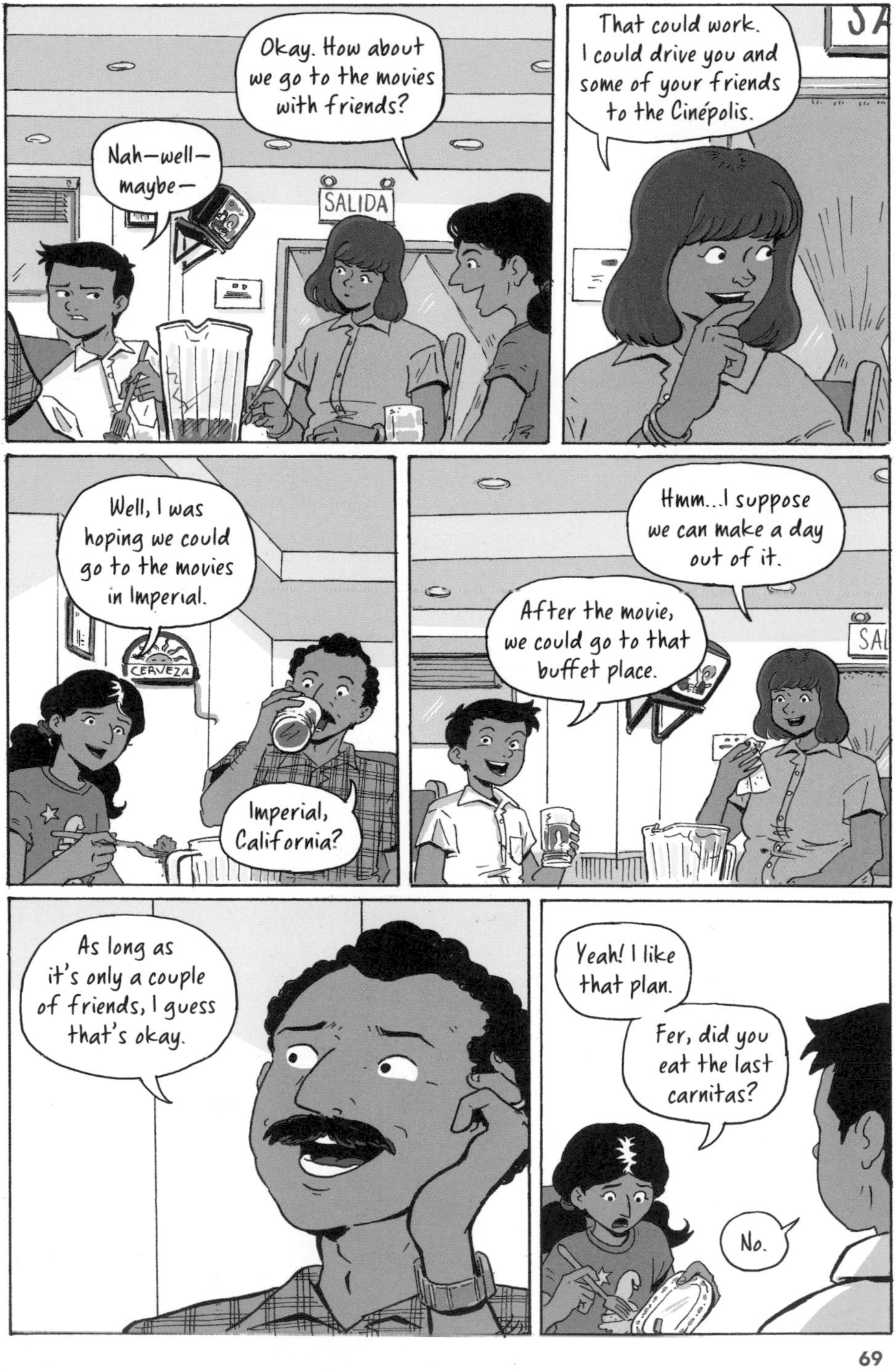
Okay. How about we go to the movies with friends?
Nah—well— maybe—
SALIDA
That could work. I could drive you and some of your friends to the Cinépolis.
Well, I was hoping we could go to the movies in Imperial.
CERVEZA
Imperial, California?
Hmm...I suppose we can make a day out of it.
After the movie, we could go to that buffet place.
As long as it's only a couple of friends, I guess that's okay.
Yeah! I like that plan.
Fer, did you eat the last carnitas?
No.

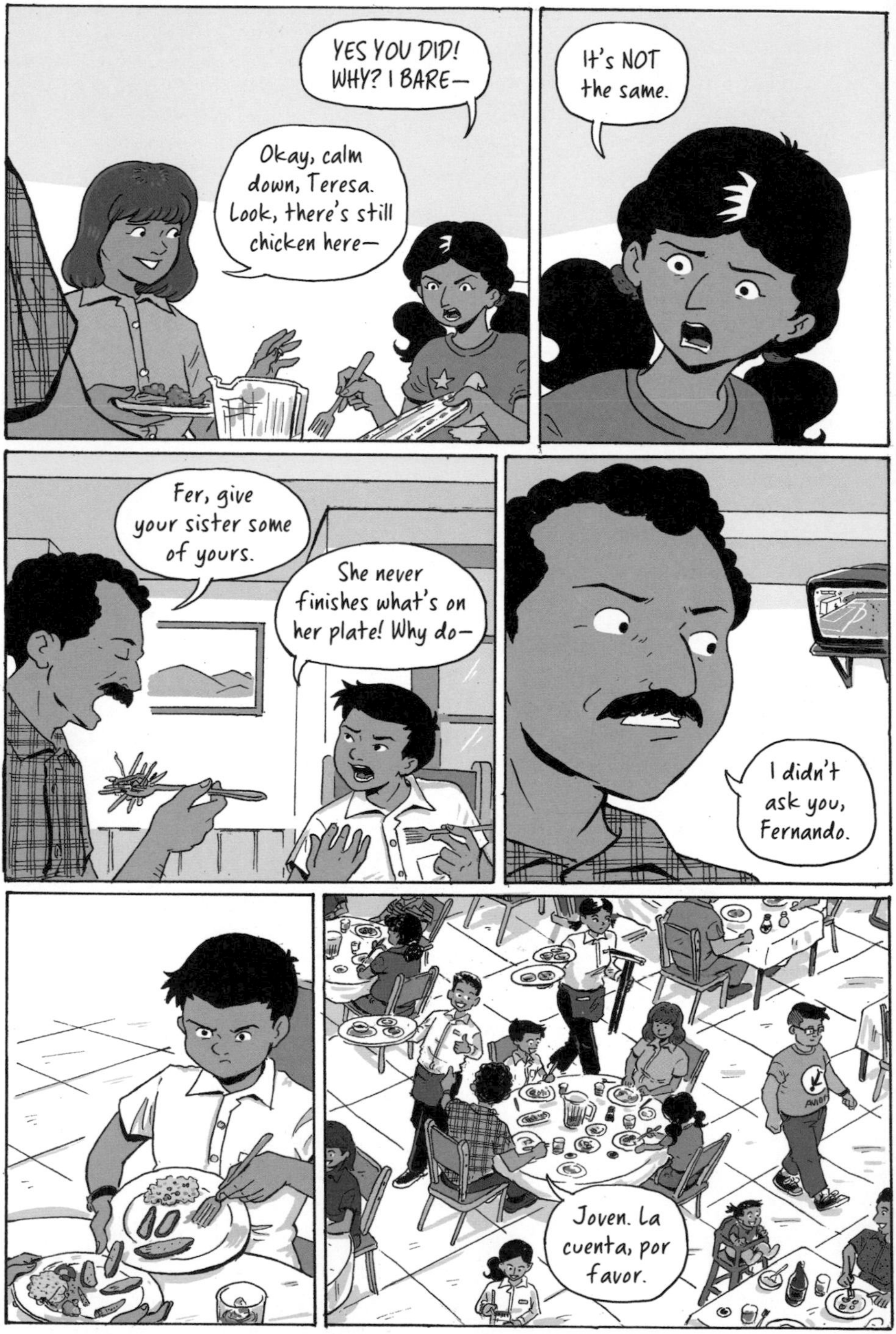
YES YOU DID! WHY? I BARE—
Okay, calm down, Teresa. Look, there's still chicken here—
It's NOT the same.
Fer, give your sister some of yours.
She never finishes what's on her plate! Why do—
I didn't ask you, Fernando.
Joven. La cuenta, por favor.

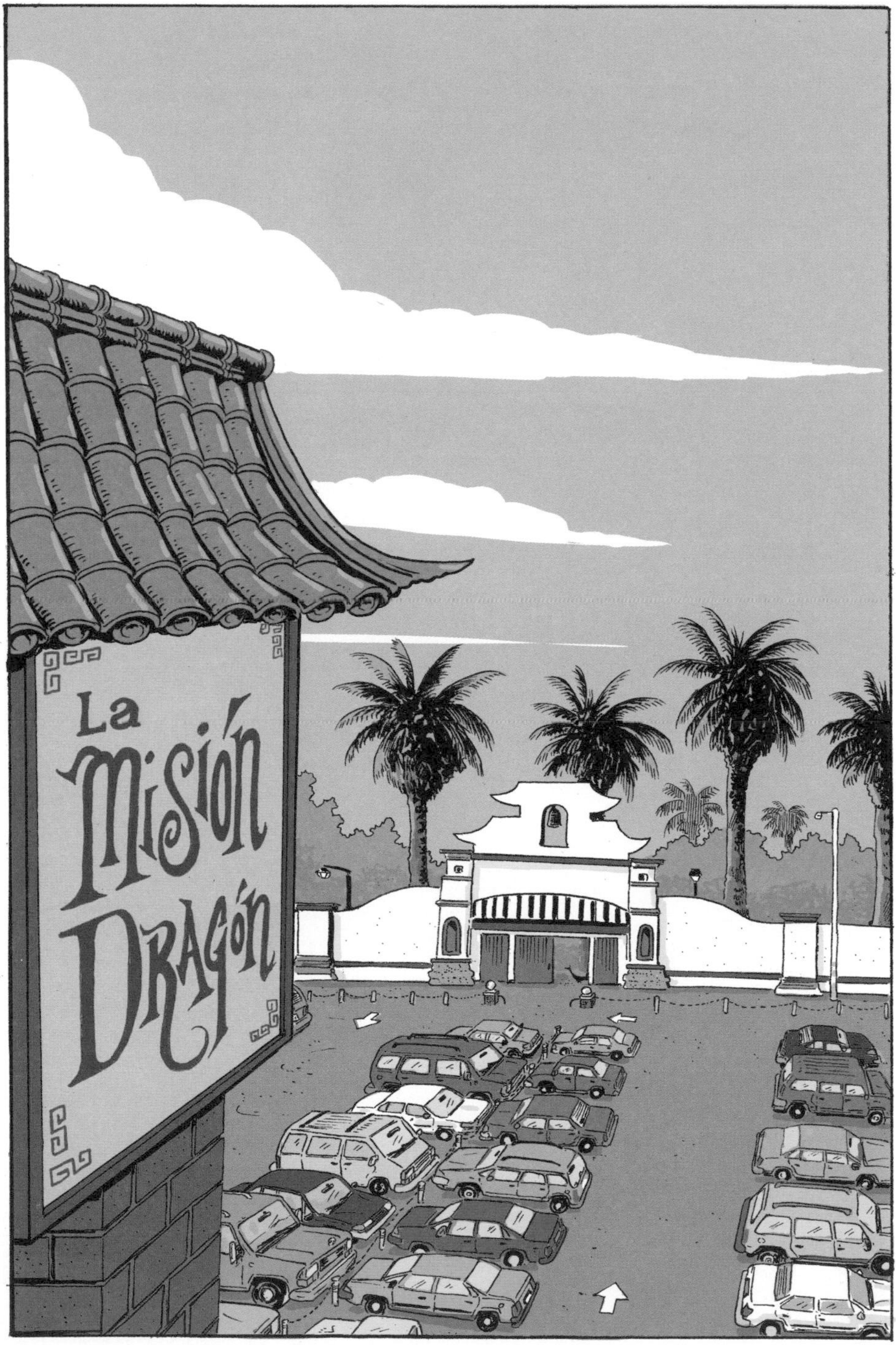
La Misión Dragón

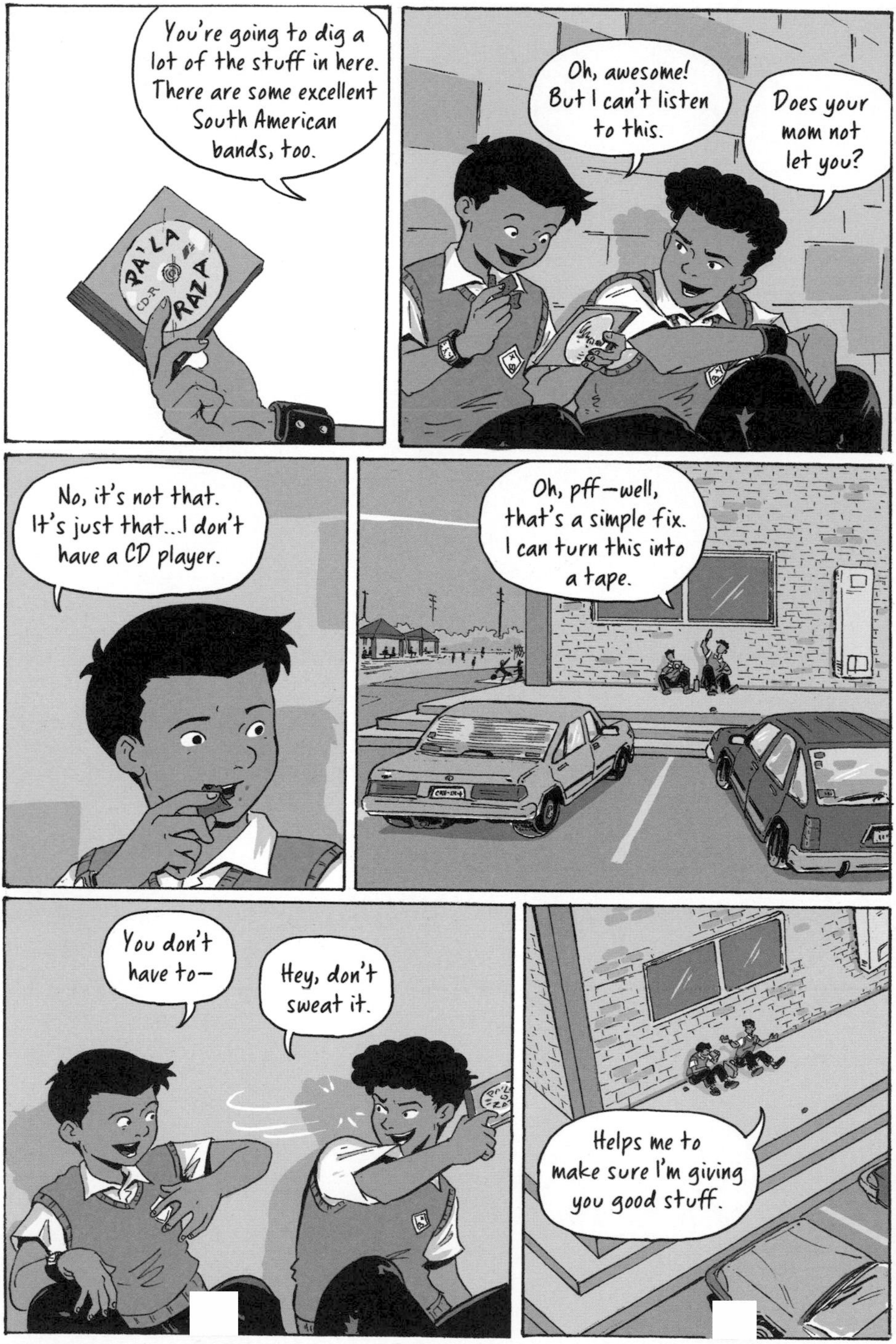
You're going to dig a lot of the stuff in here. There are some excellent South American bands, too.
PA'LA RAZA
CD-R
Oh, awesome! But I can't listen to this.
Does your mom not let you?
No, it's not that. It's just that...I don't have a CD player.
Oh, pff—well, that's a simple fix. I can turn this into a tape.
You don't have to—
Hey, don't sweat it.
Helps me to make sure I'm giving you good stuff.

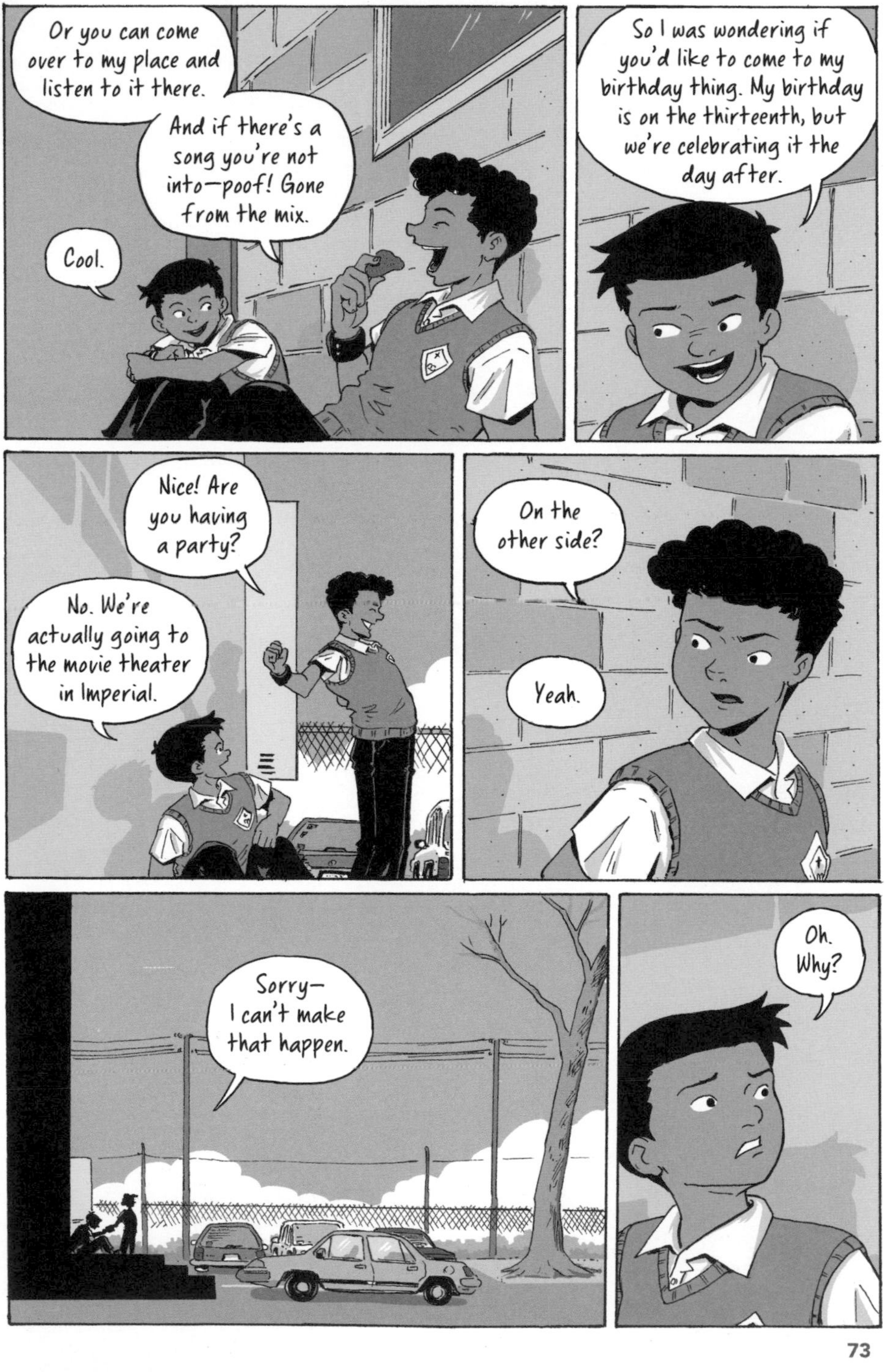
Or you can come over to my place and listen to it there.
And if there's a song you're not into—poof! Gone from the mix.
Cool.
So I was wondering if you'd like to come to my birthday thing. My birthday is on the thirteenth, but we're celebrating it the day after.
Nice! Are you having a party?
No. We're actually going to the movie theater in Imperial.
On the other side?
Yeah.
Sorry— I can't make that happen.
Oh. Why?

77

79

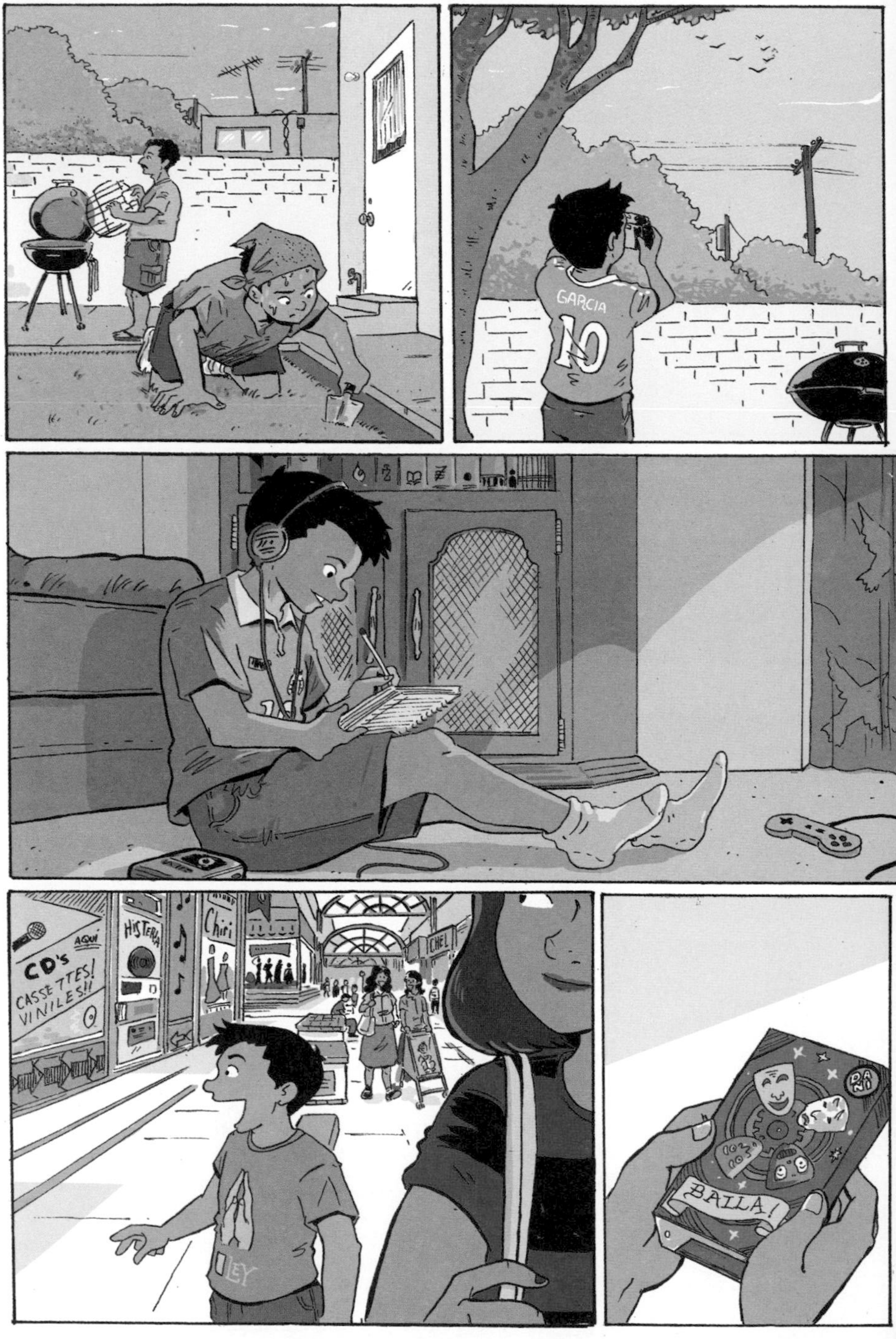
GARCIA
10
CD's
AQUÍ
CASSETTES!
VINILES!!
HISTERIA
Chiri
CHEL
DANI
BAILA!

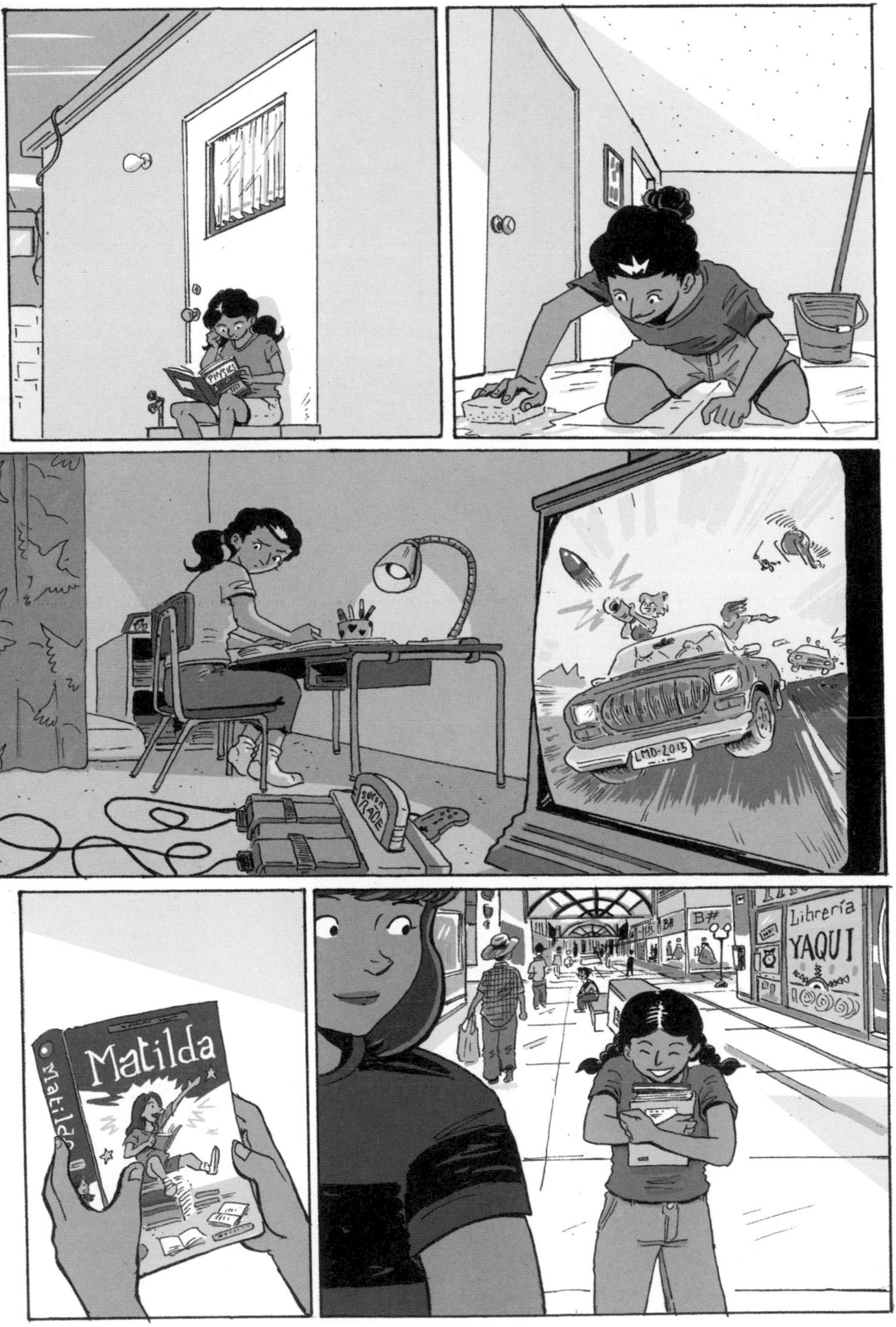
PHYSICS
SUPER RACE
LMD-2013
Matilda
Matilda
B#
Librería
YAQUI

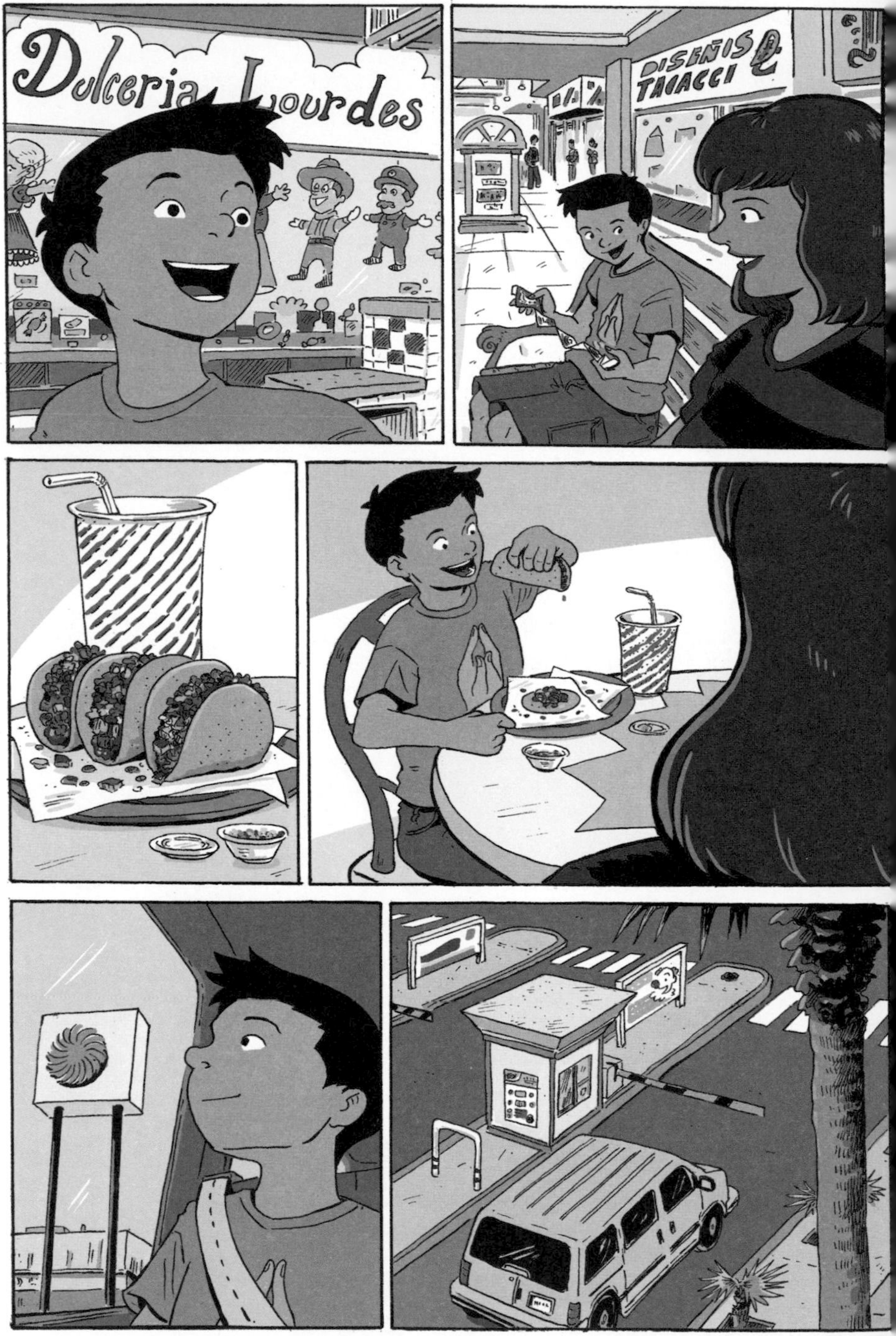
Dulceria Lourdes
DISEÑIS TACACCI

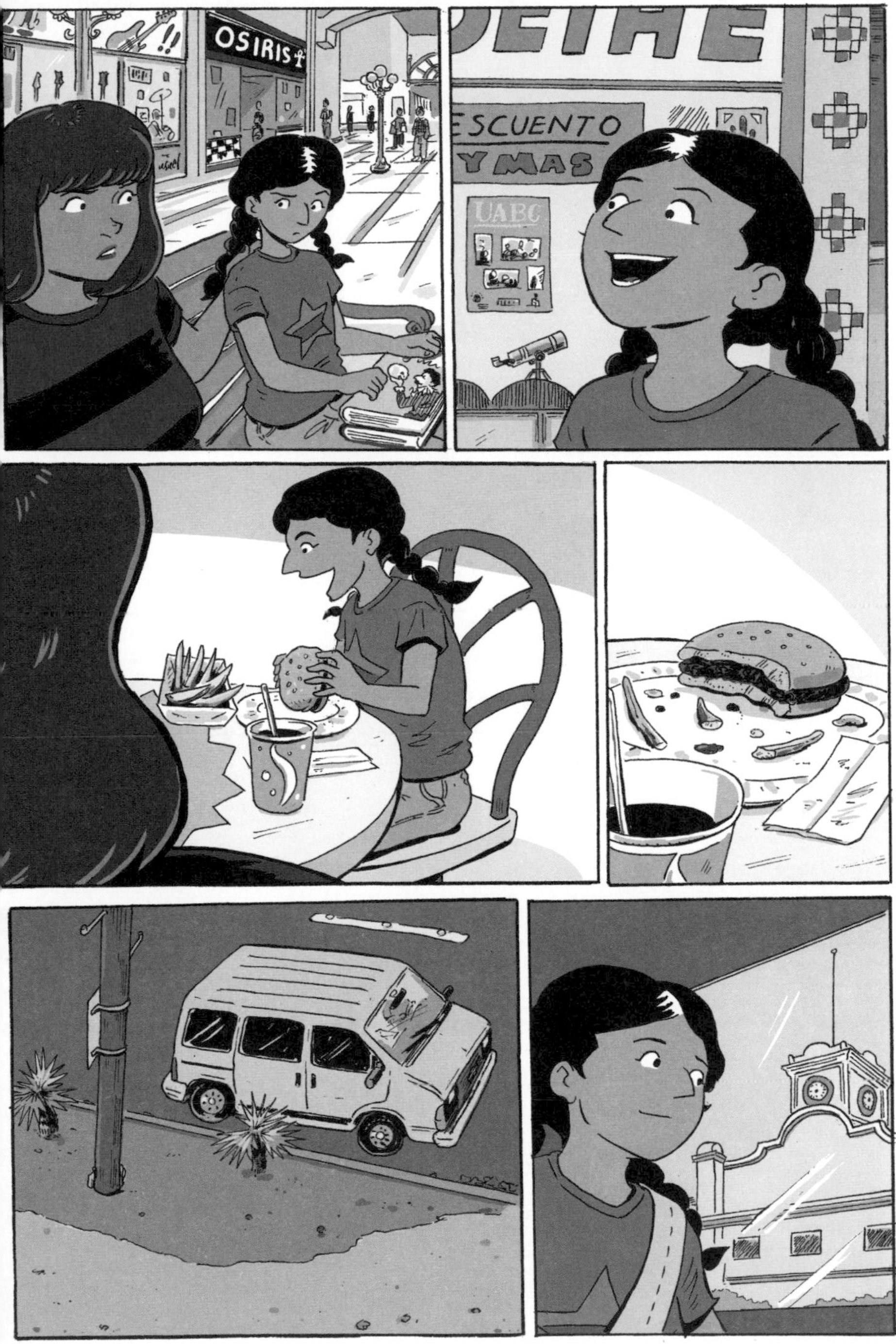
OSIRIS
ESCUENTO
Y MAS
UABC

91

94

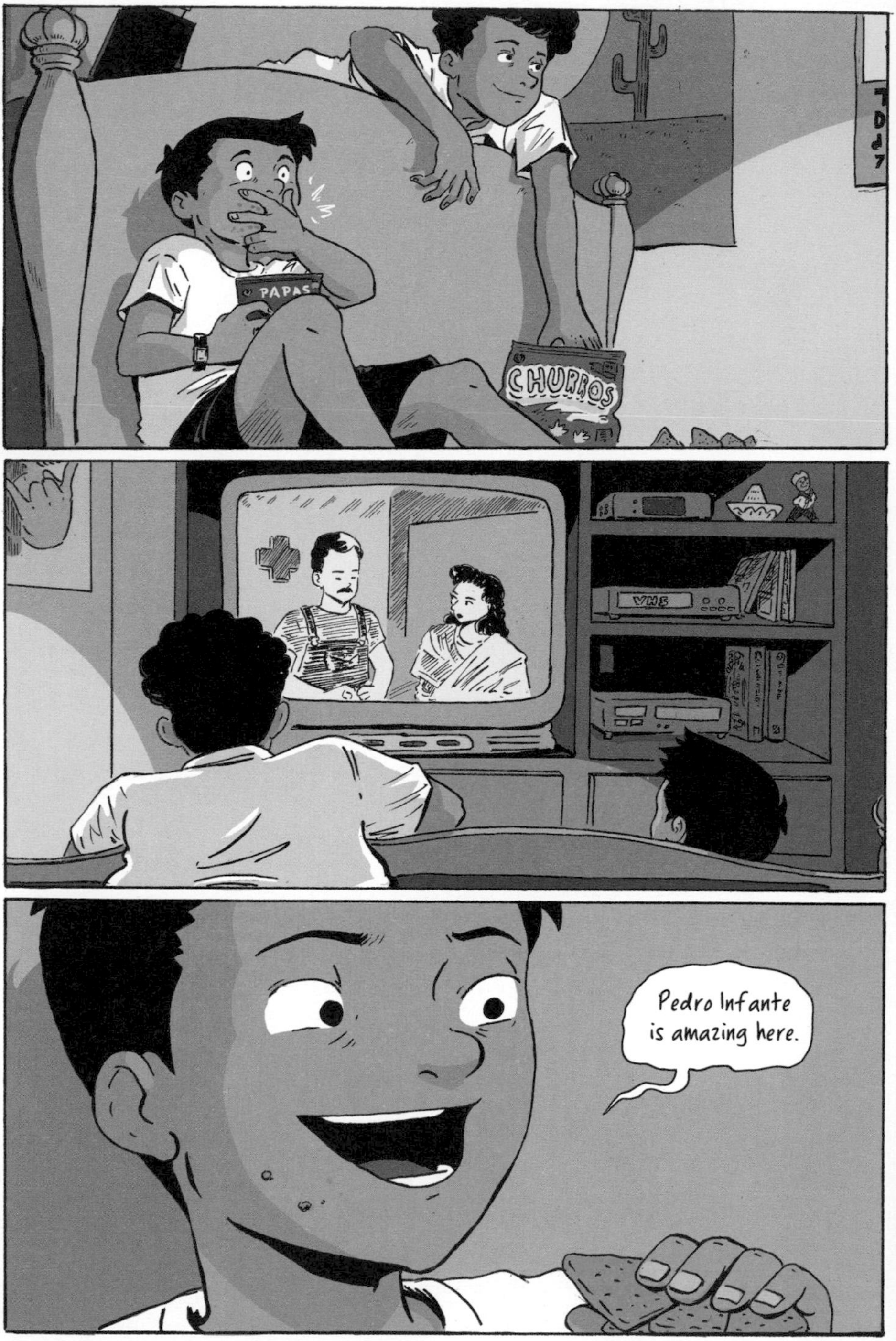
PAPAS
CHURROS
VHS
Pedro Infante is amazing here.

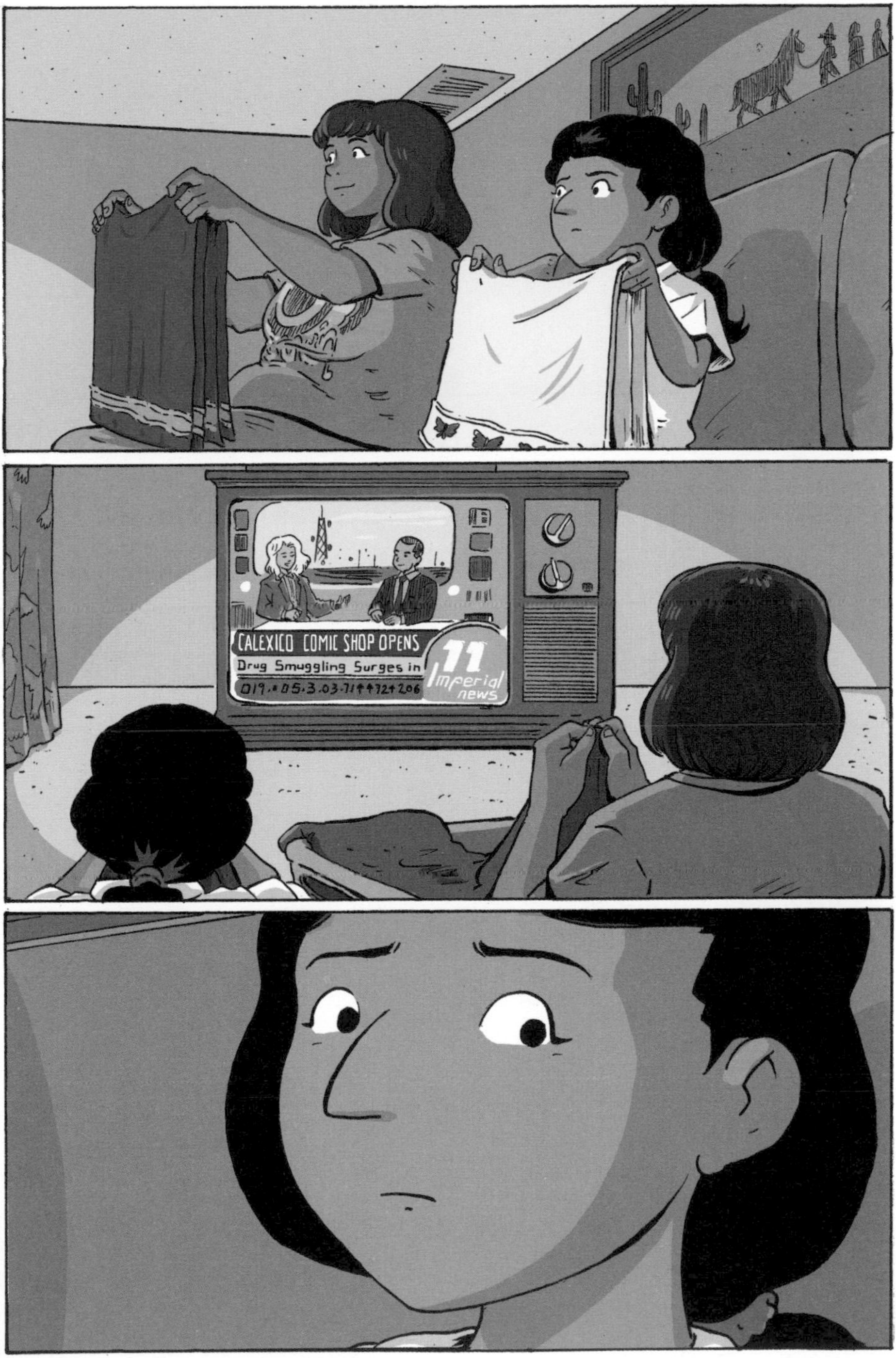
CALEXICO COMIC SHOP OPENS
Drug Smuggling Surges in
11
Imperial
news

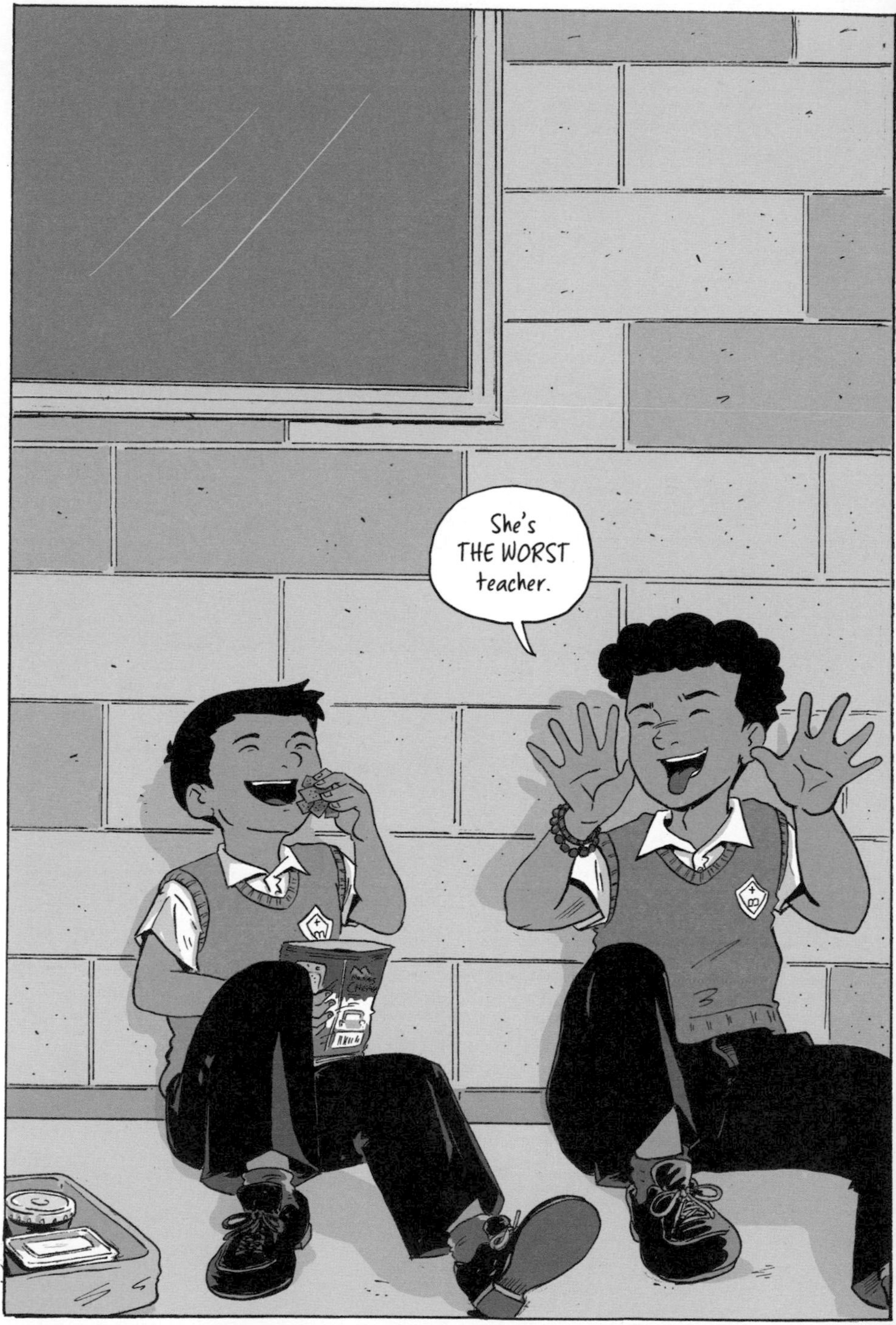
She's THE WORST teacher.

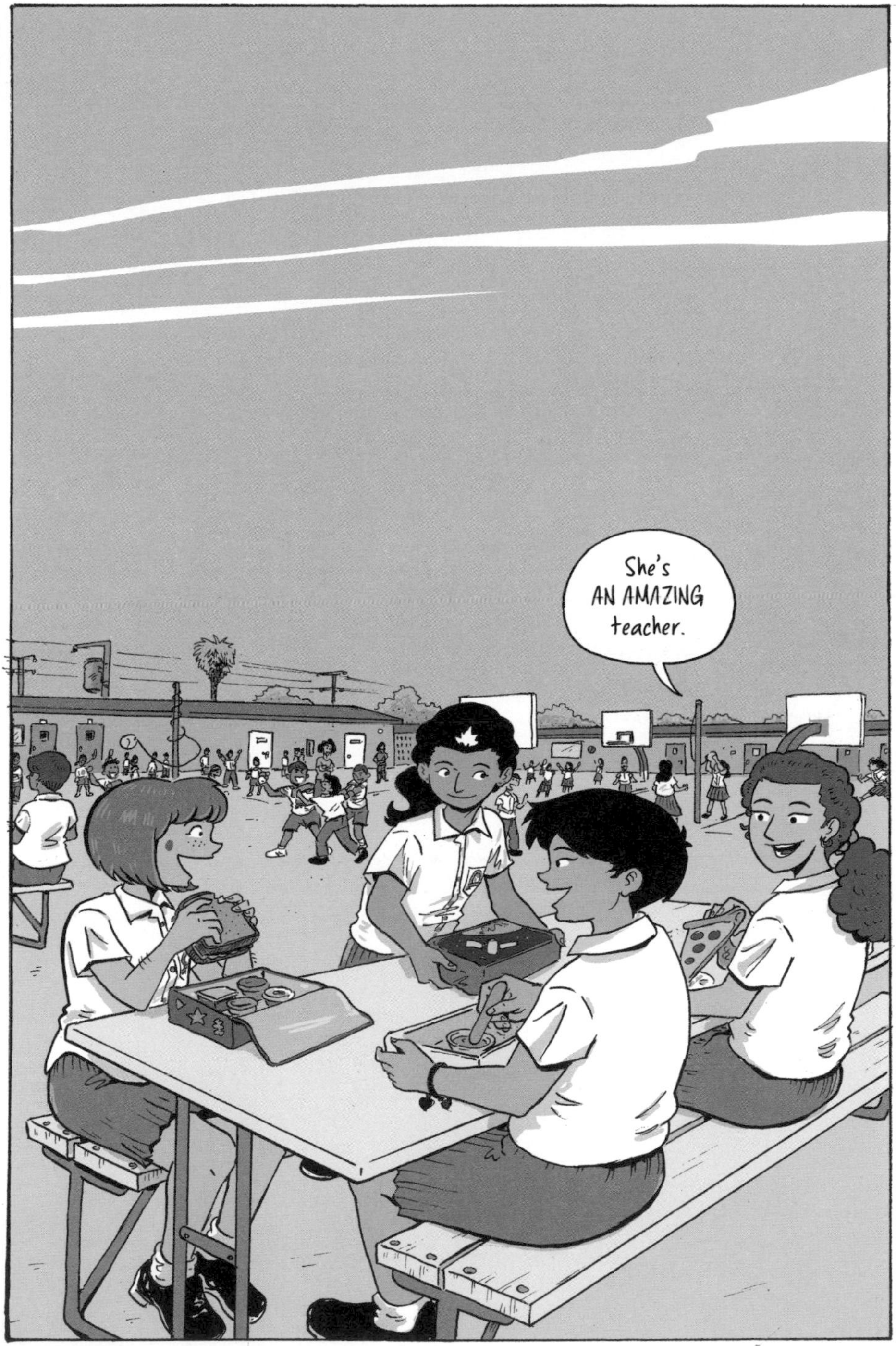
She's AN AMAZING teacher.

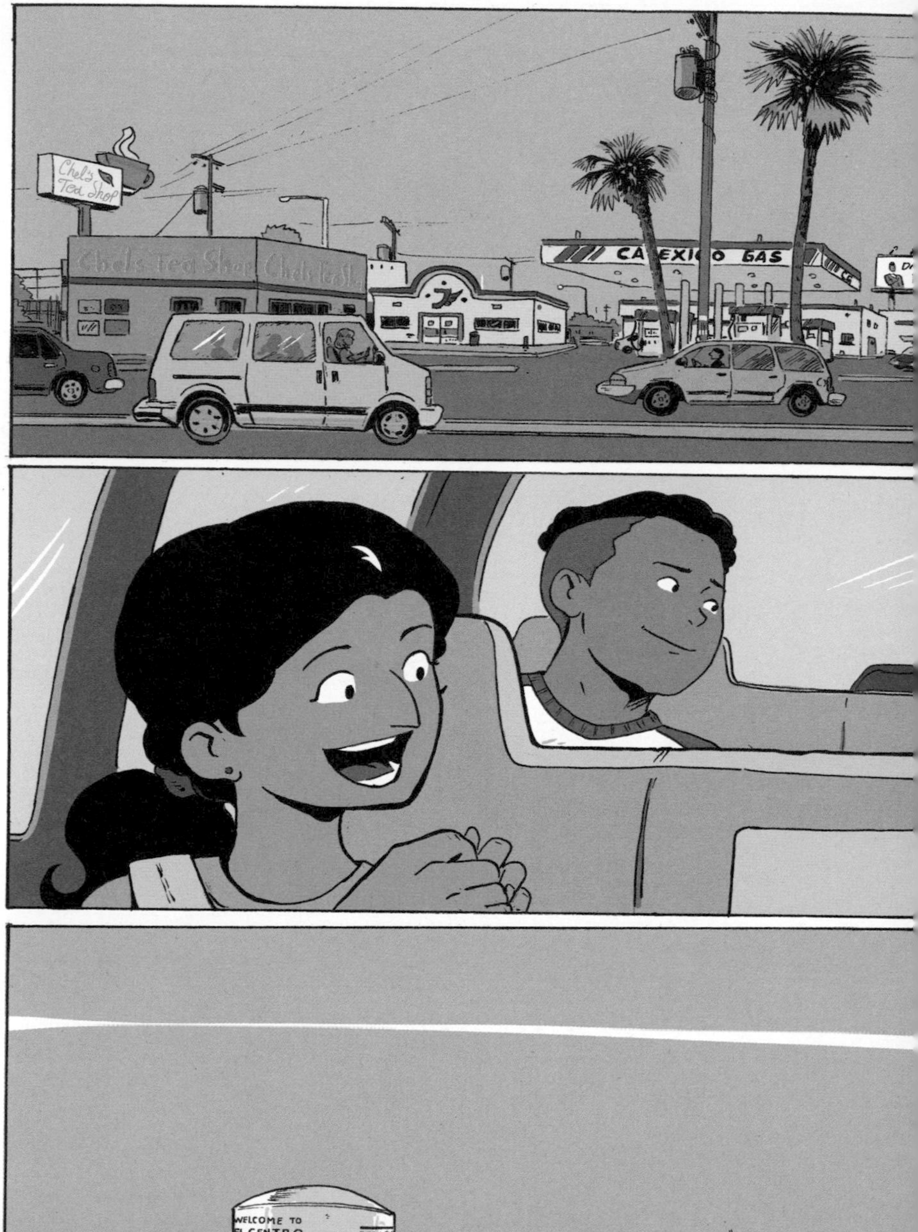
Chel's Tea Shop
CA EXICO GAS
WELCOME TO
EL CENTRO

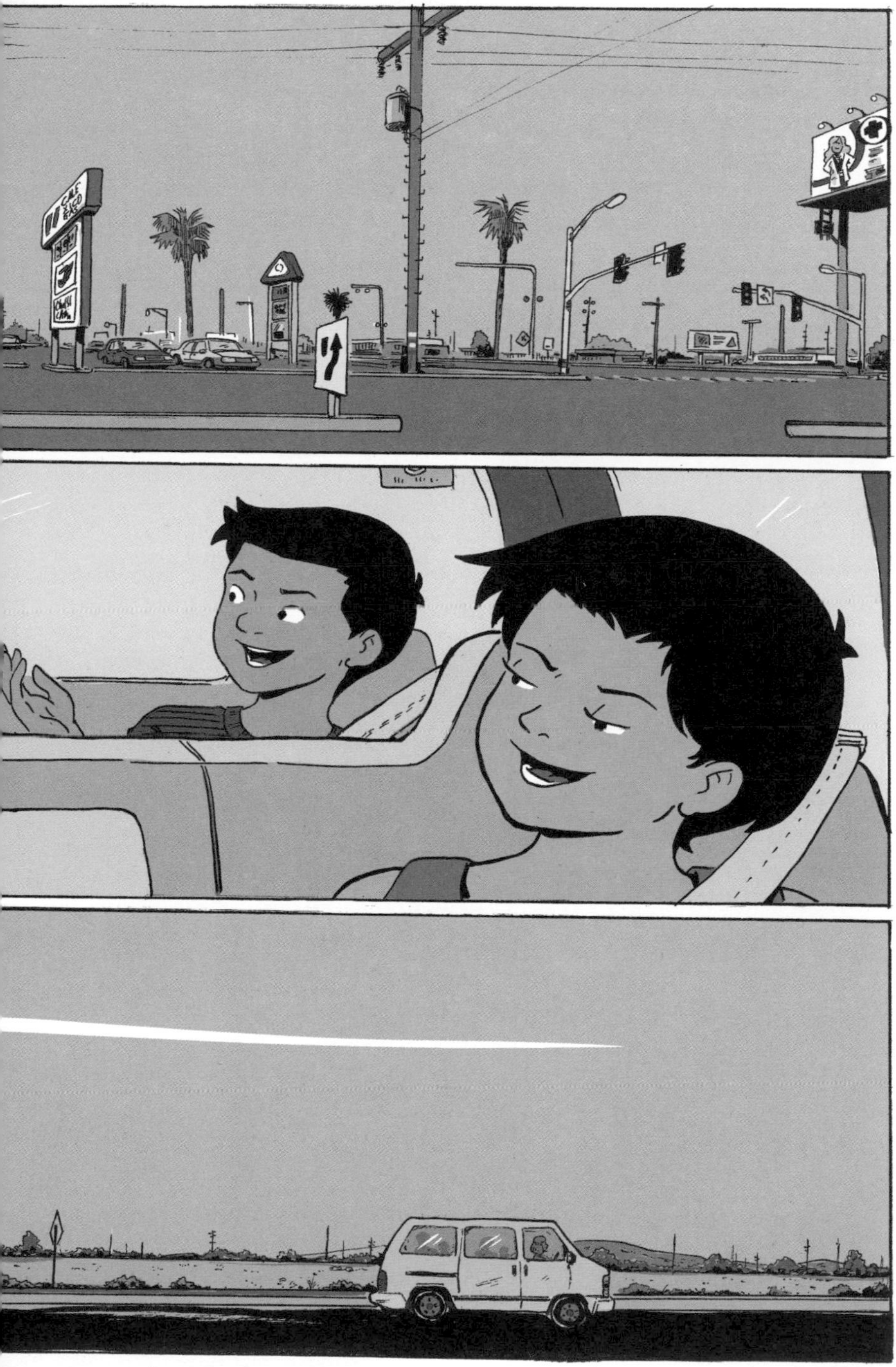

113

115

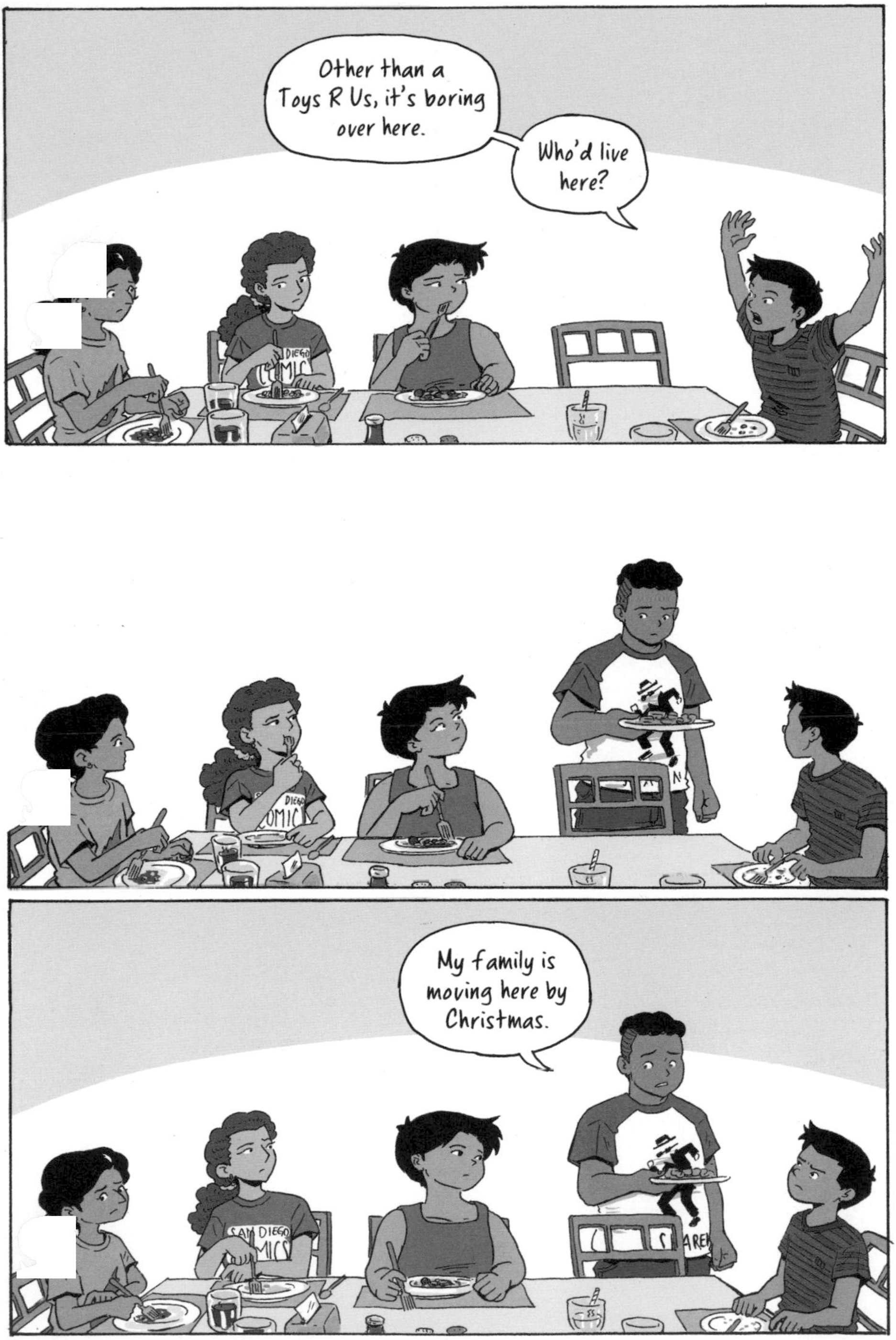
Other than a Toys R Us, it's boring over here.
Who'd live here?
My family is moving here by Christmas.

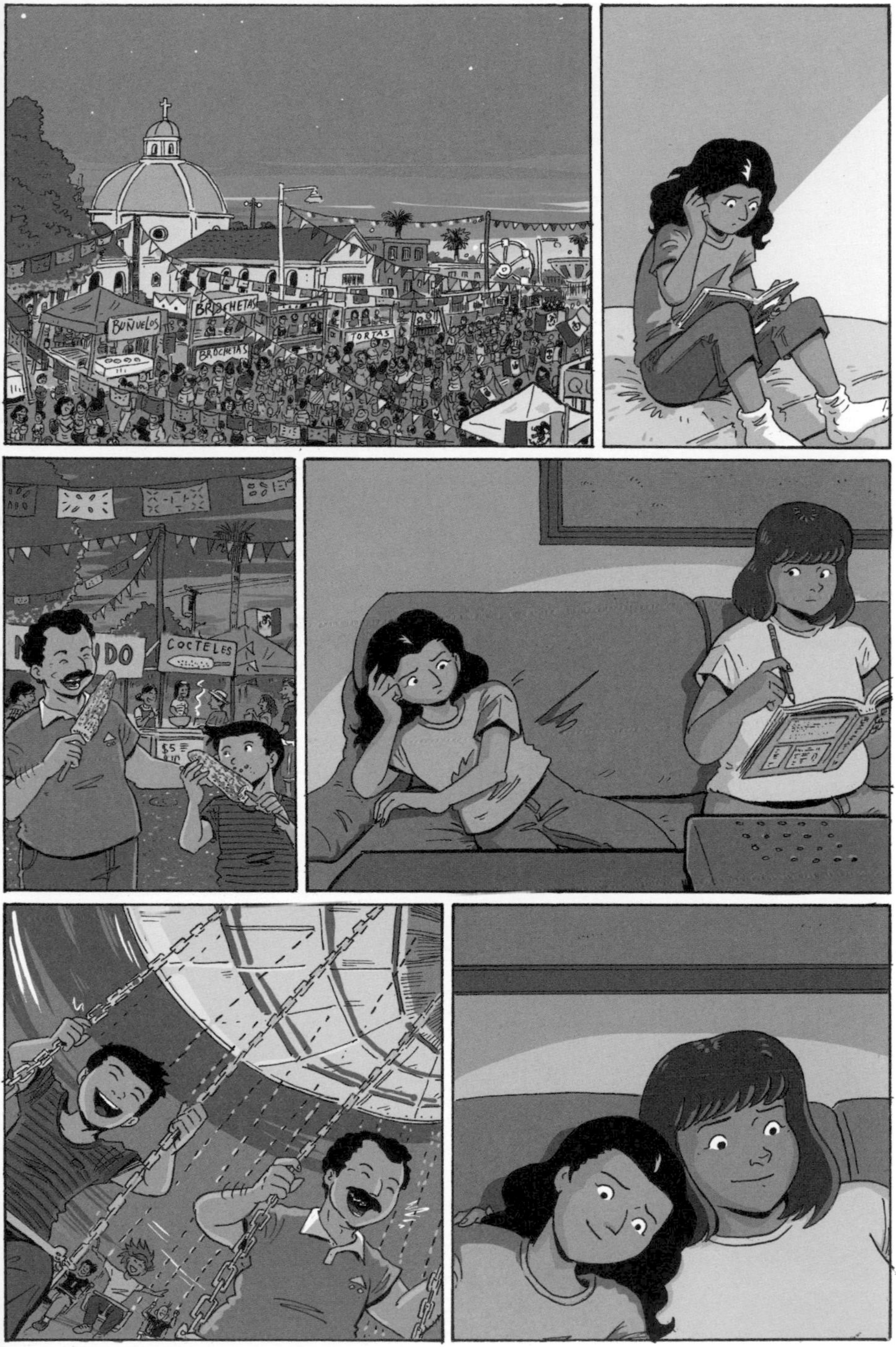
BUÑUELOS
BROCHETAS
TORTAS
BROCHETAS
COCTELES
$5

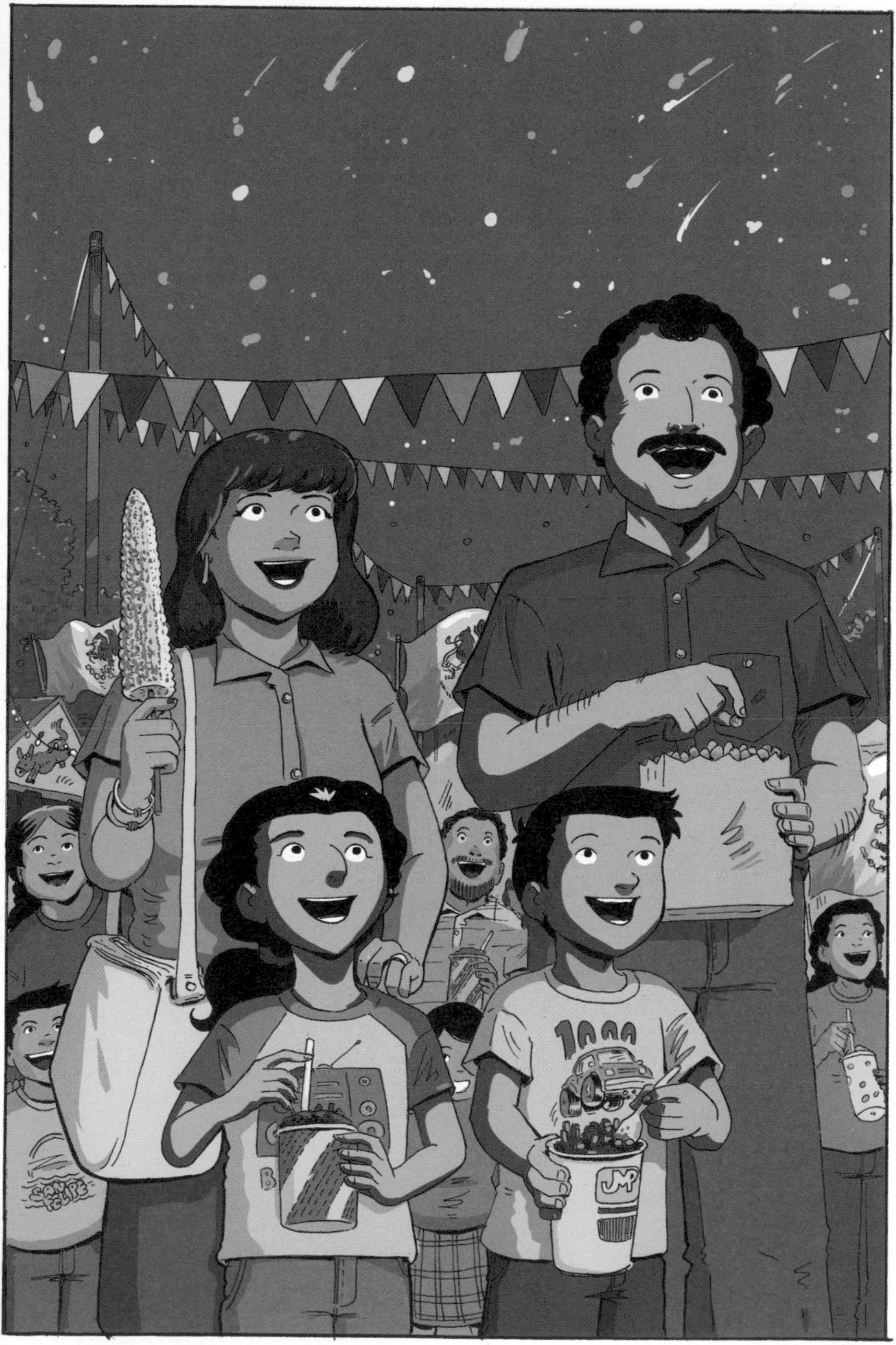

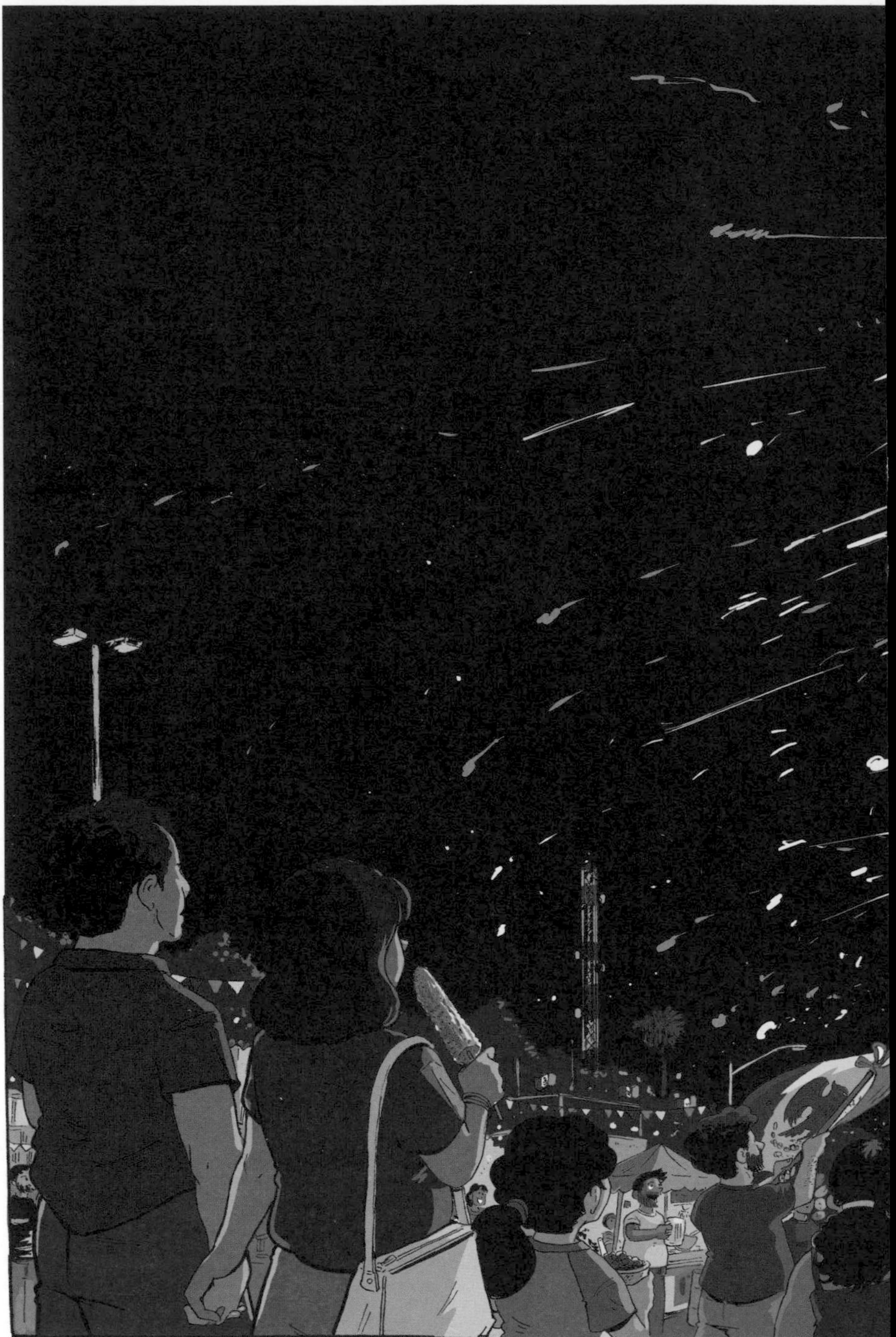

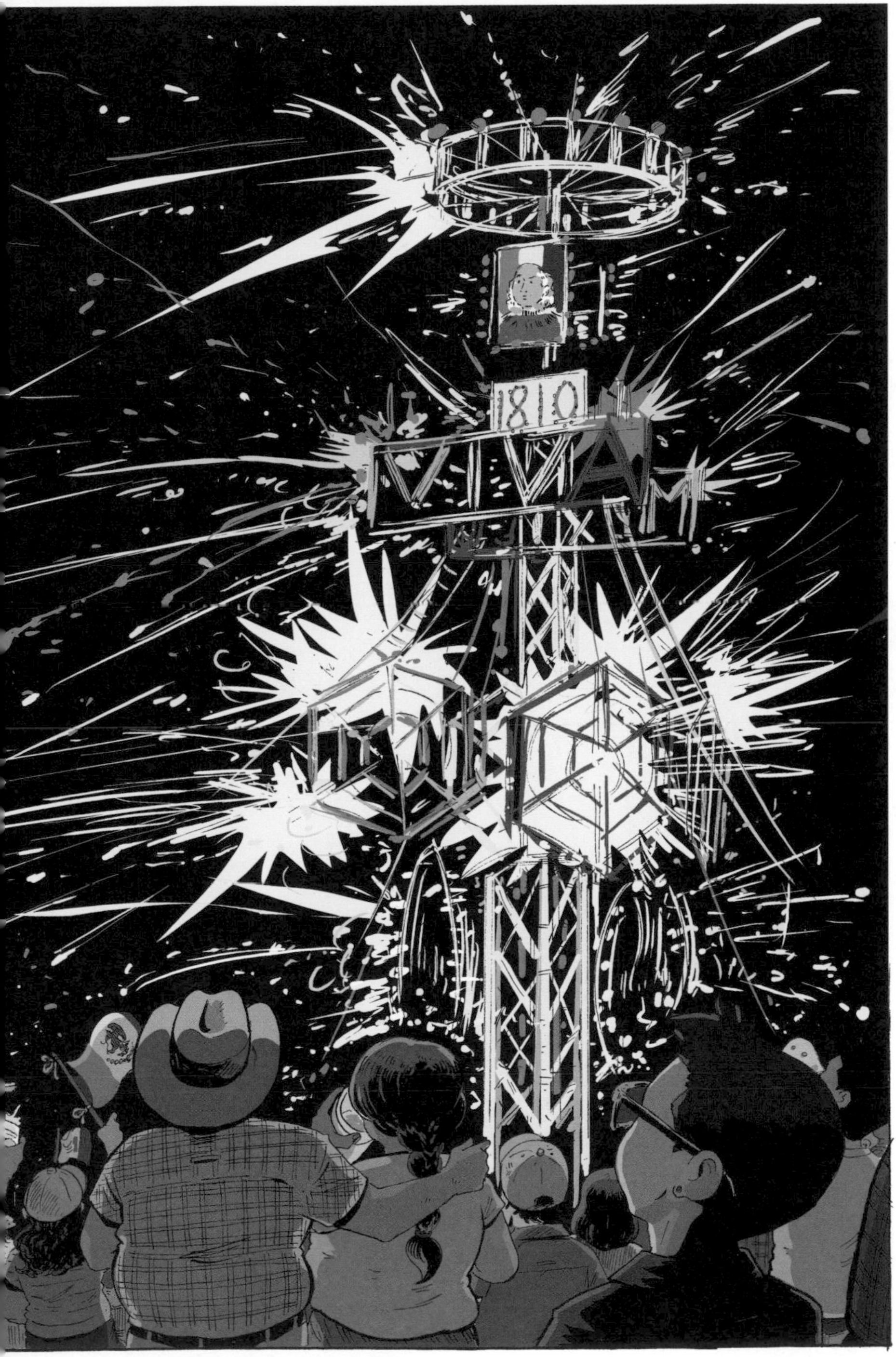
1810
VIVA M

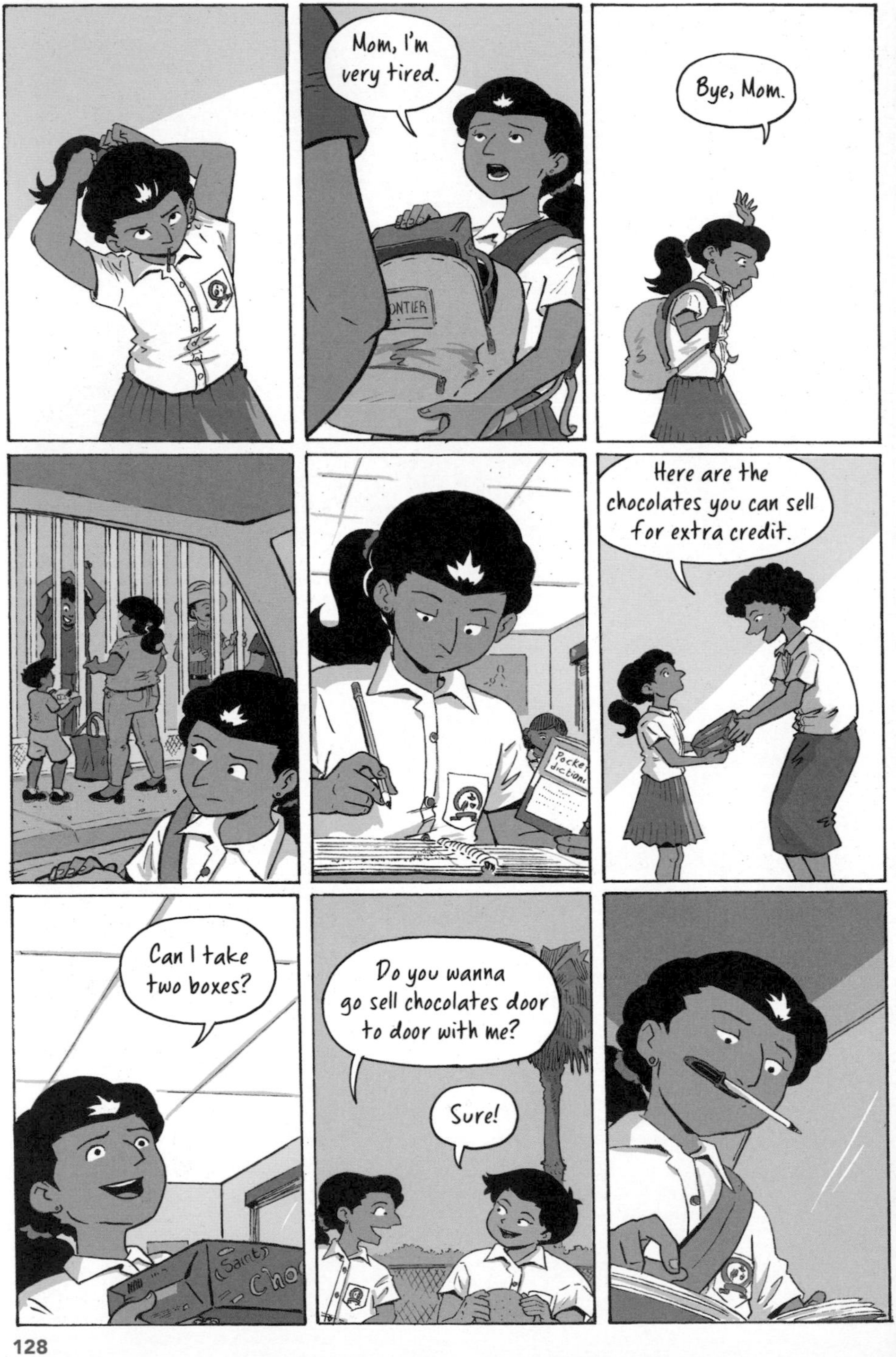
Mom, I'm very tired.
Bye, Mom.
ONTIER
Here are the chocolates you can sell for extra credit.
Can I take two boxes?
Saint
Cho
Do you wanna go sell chocolates door to door with me?
Sure!

131

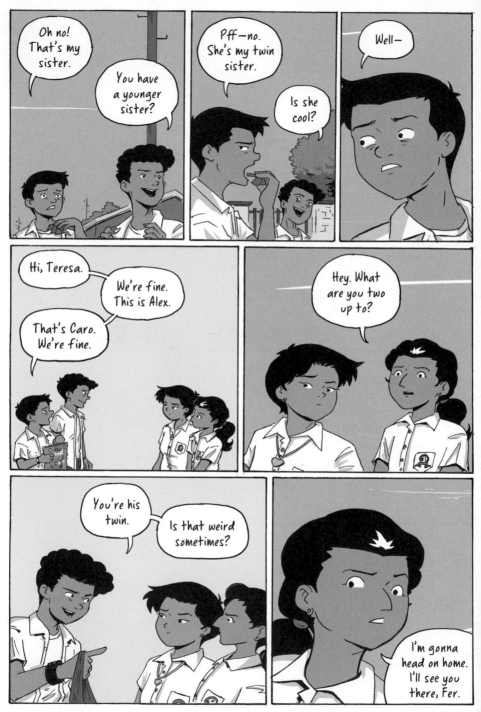

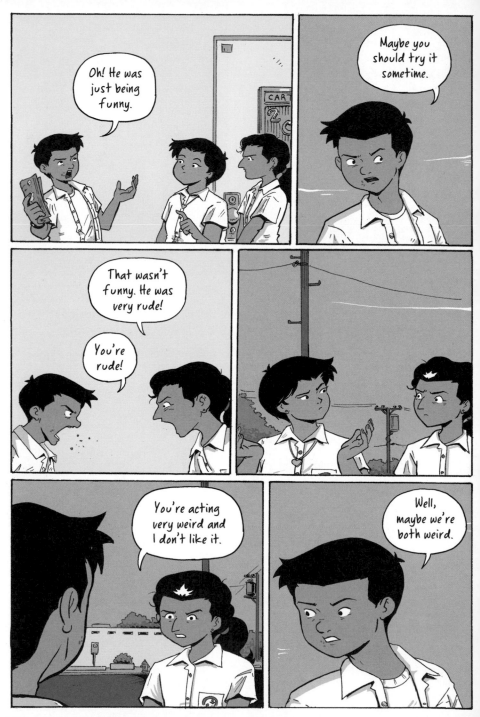

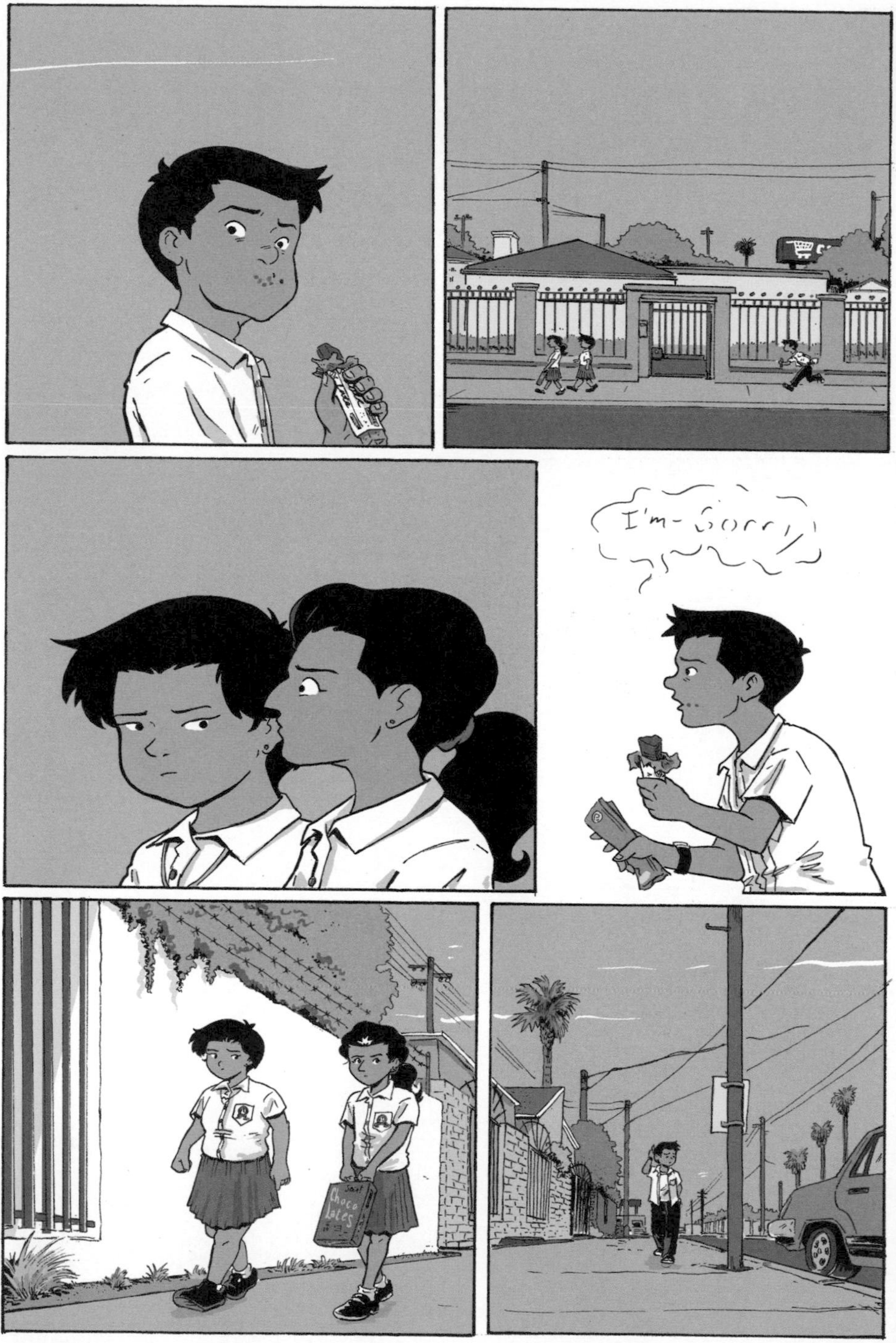
I'm- Sorry

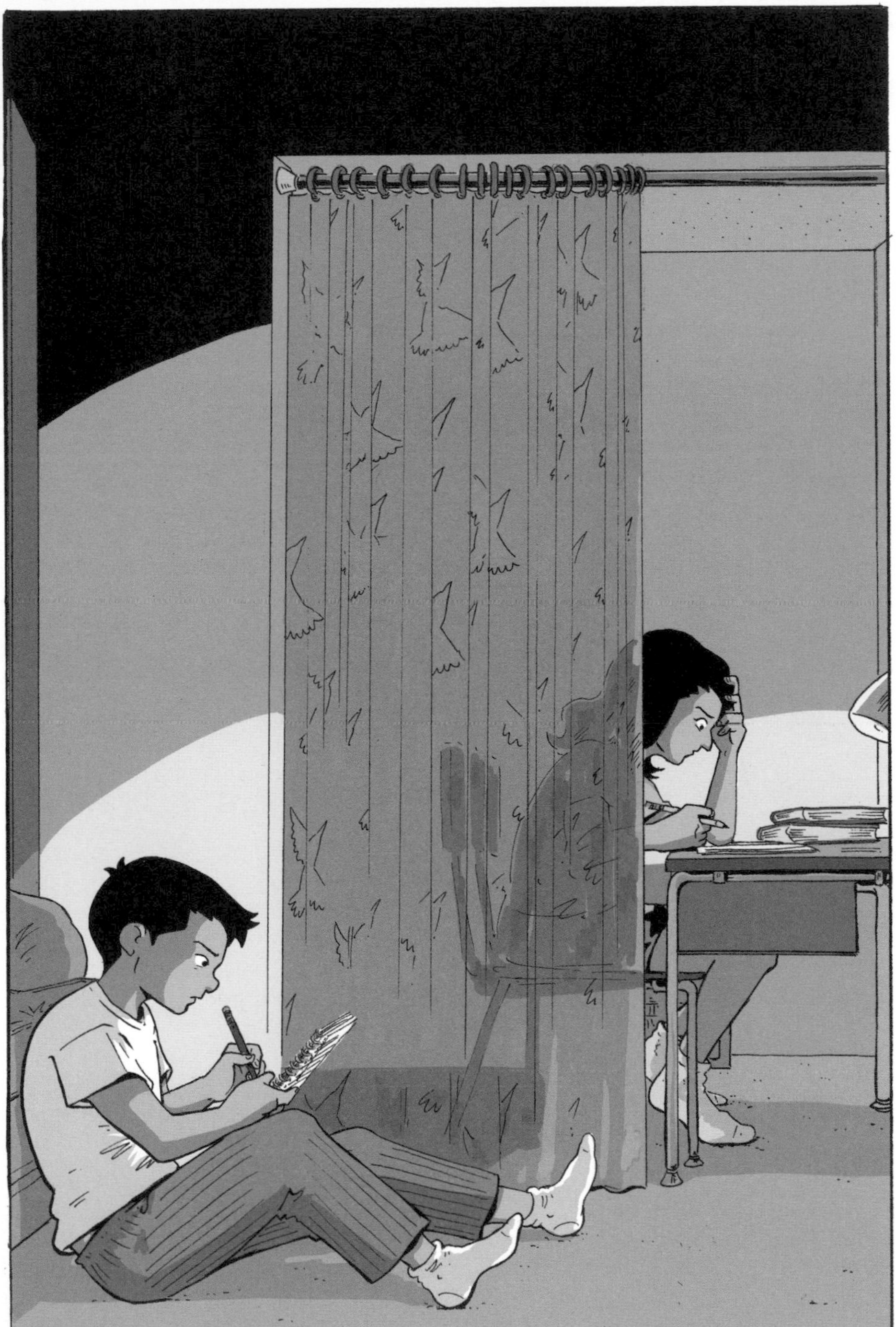

145

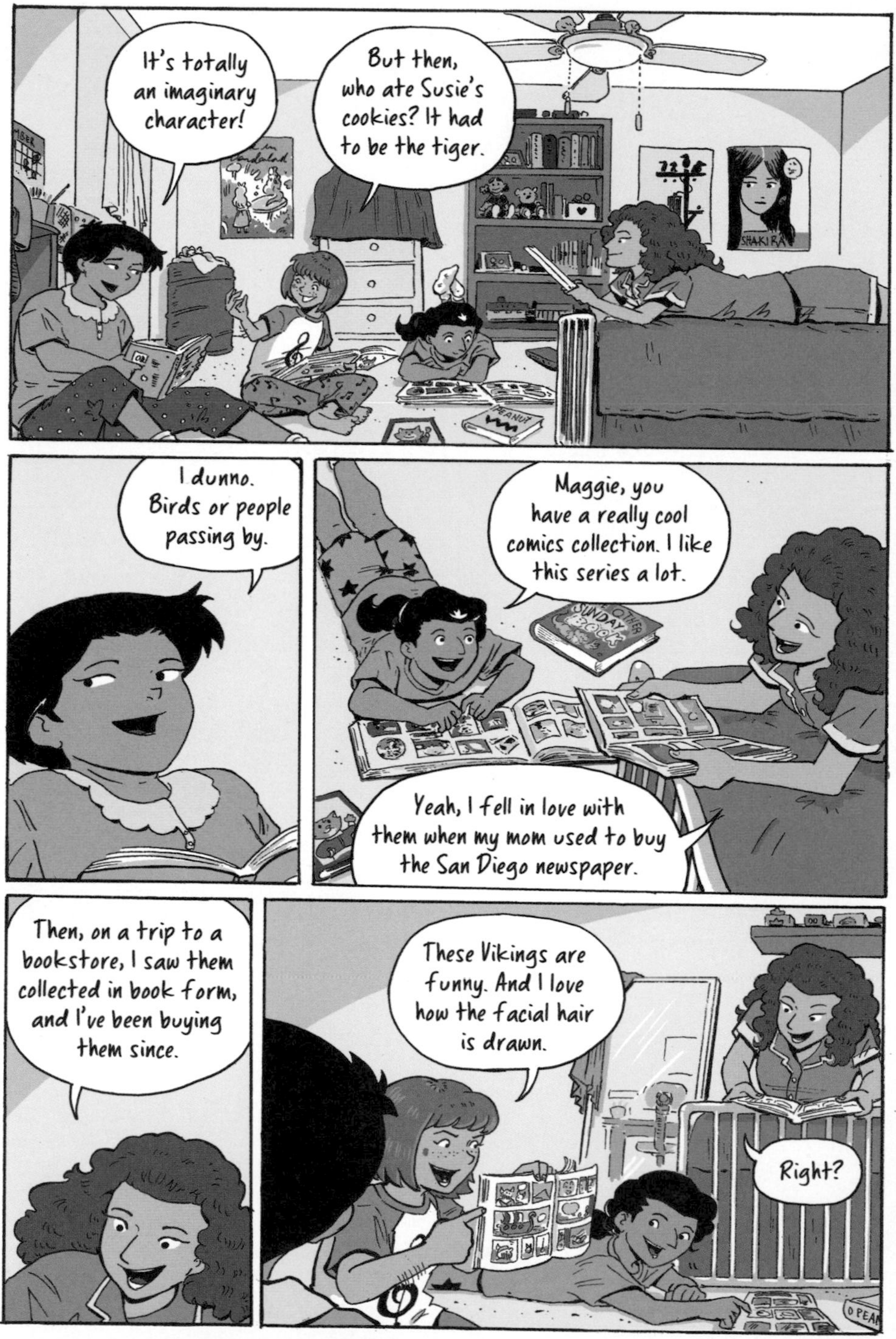
It's totally an imaginary character!
But then, who ate Susie's cookies? It had to be the tiger.
SHAKIRA
PEANUTS
I dunno. Birds or people passing by.
Maggie, you have a really cool comics collection. I like this series a lot.
Yeah, I fell in love with them when my mom used to buy the San Diego newspaper.
Then, on a trip to a bookstore, I saw them collected in book form, and I've been buying them since.
These Vikings are funny. And I love how the facial hair is drawn.
Right?

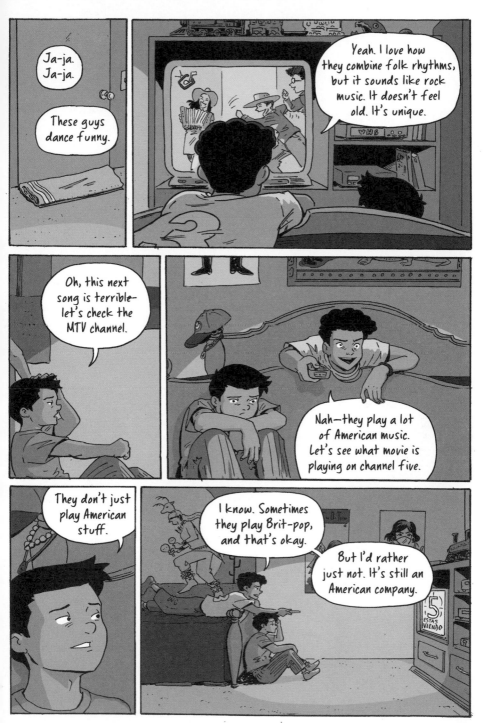

149

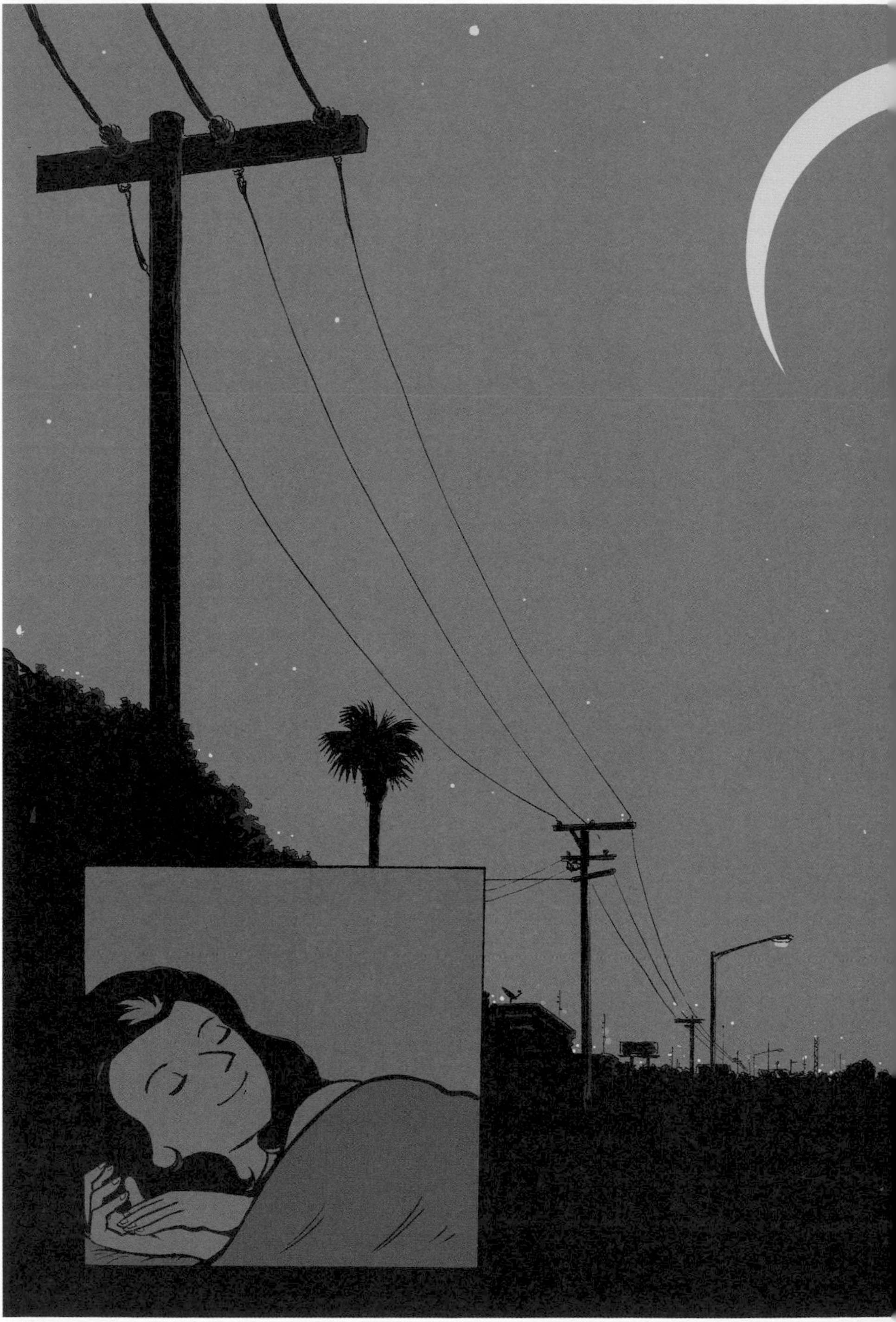

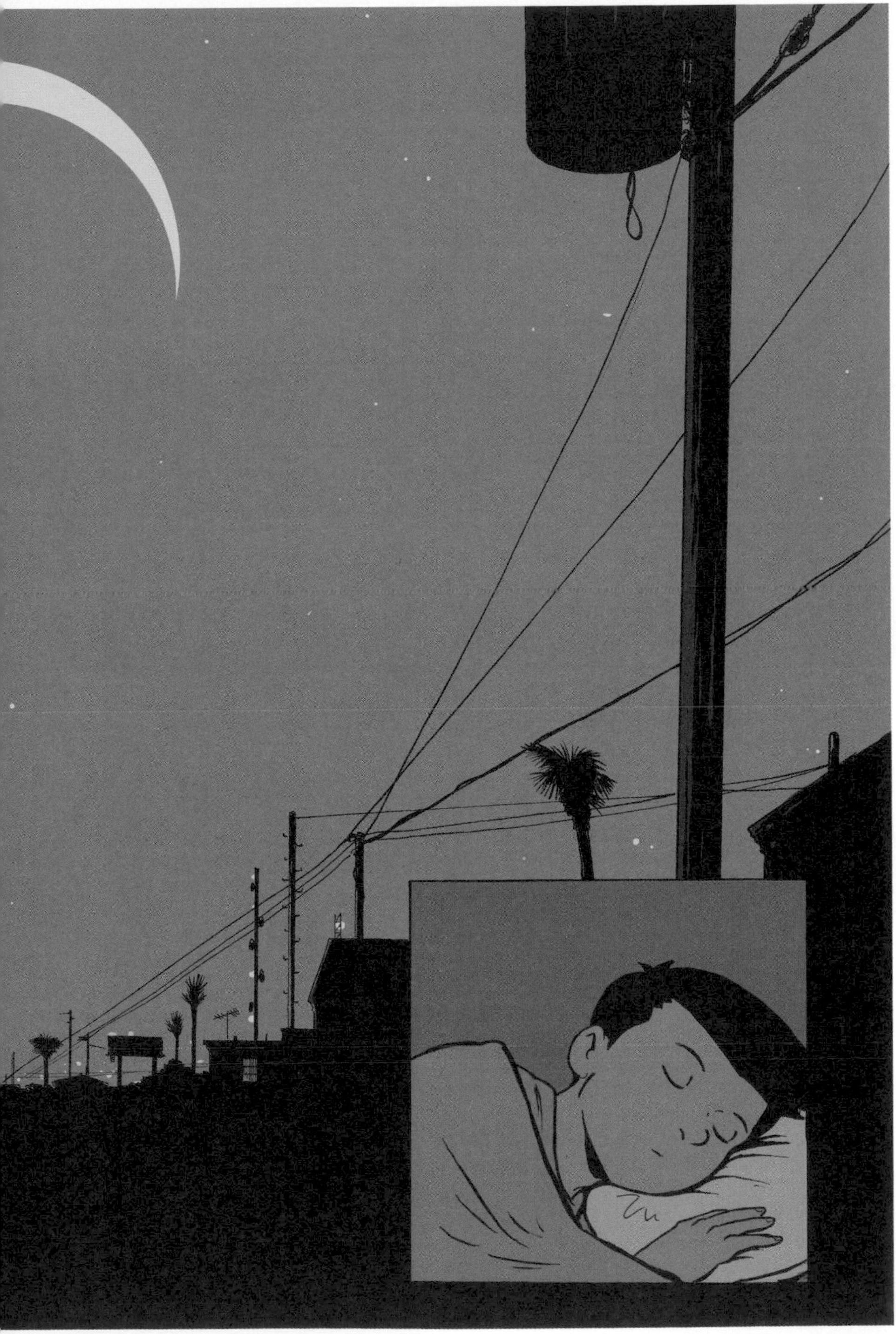

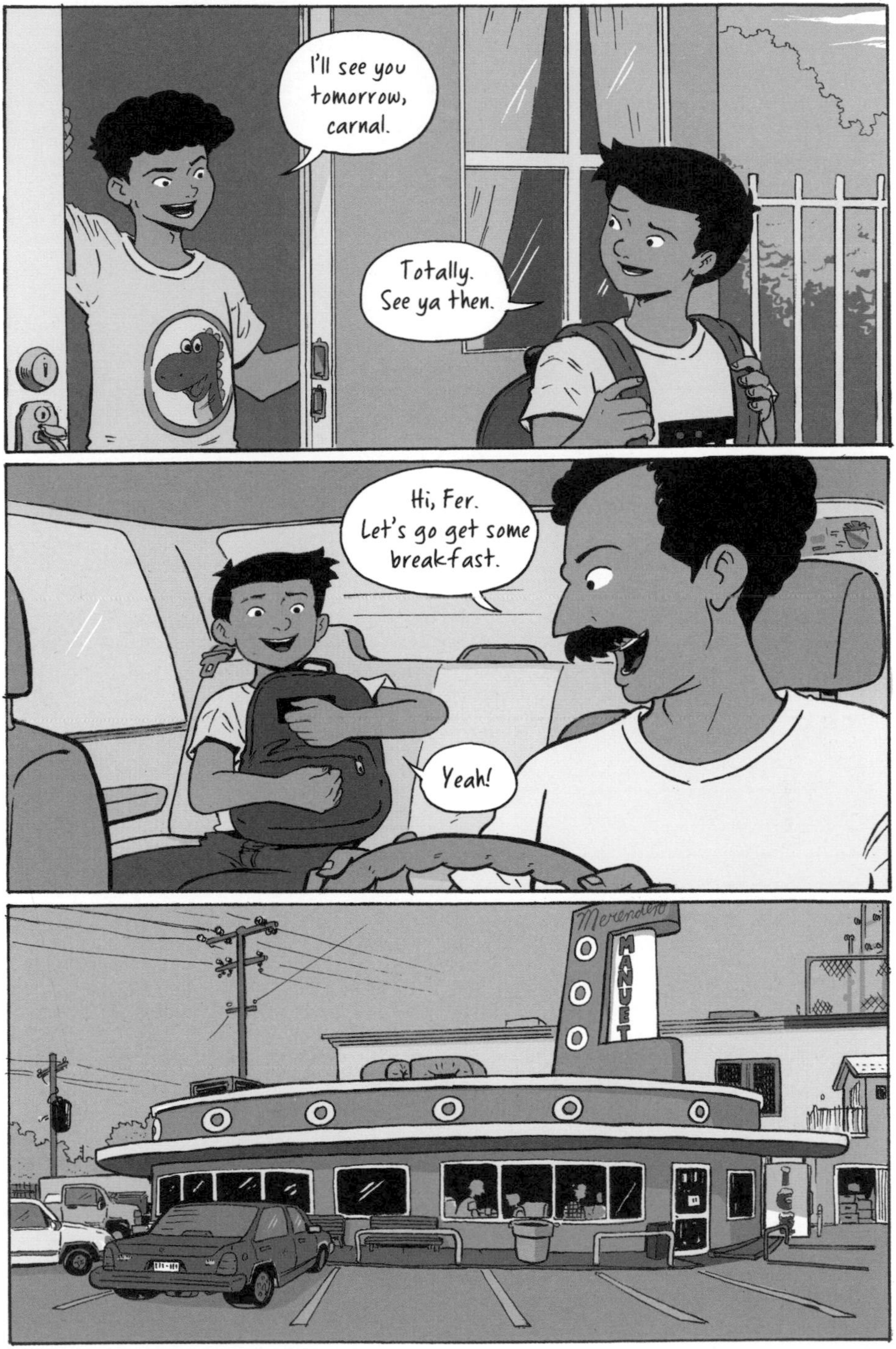
I'll see you tomorrow, carnal.
Totally. See ya then.
Hi, Fer. Let's go get some breakfast.
Yeah!
MANUET

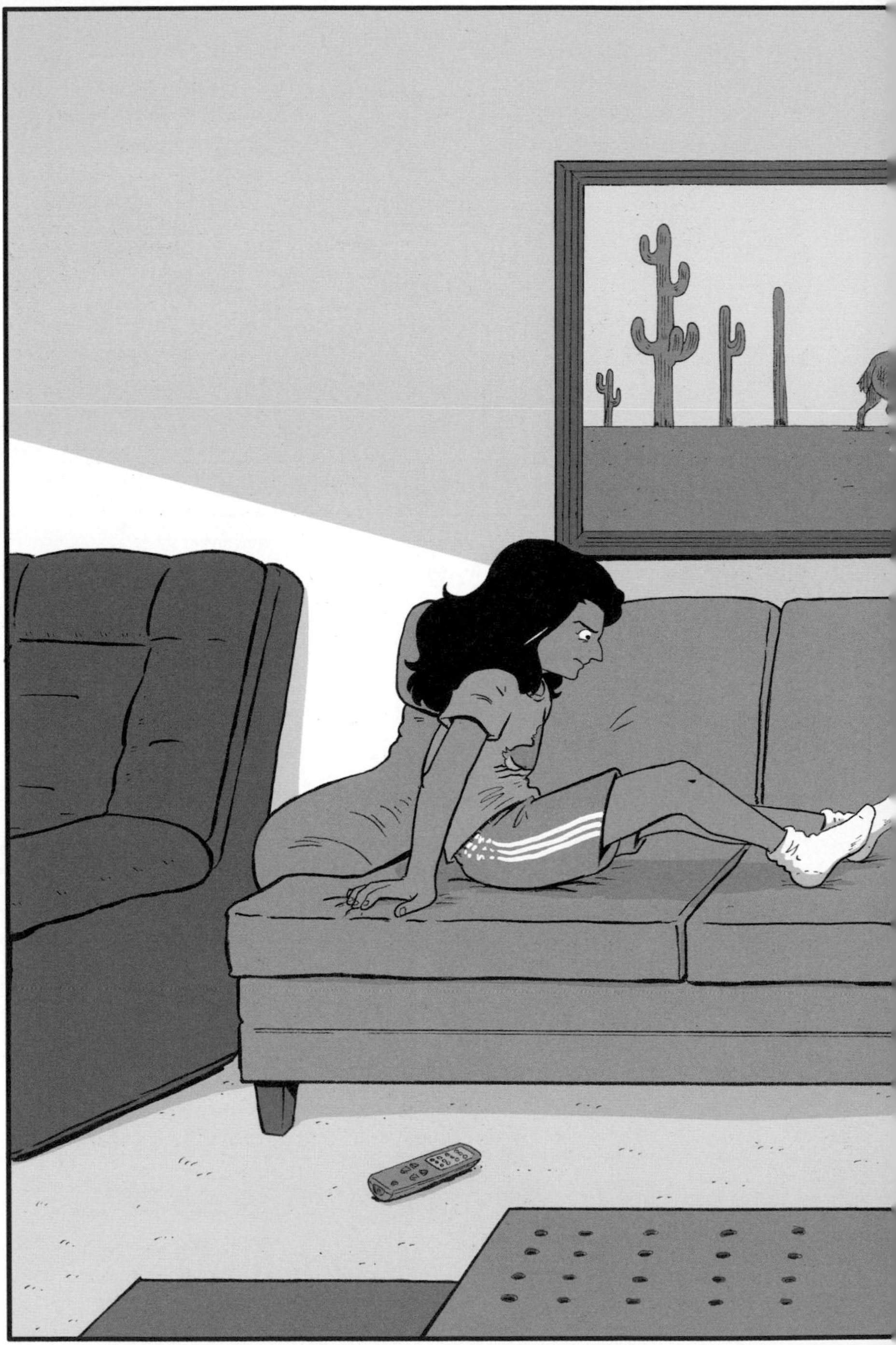

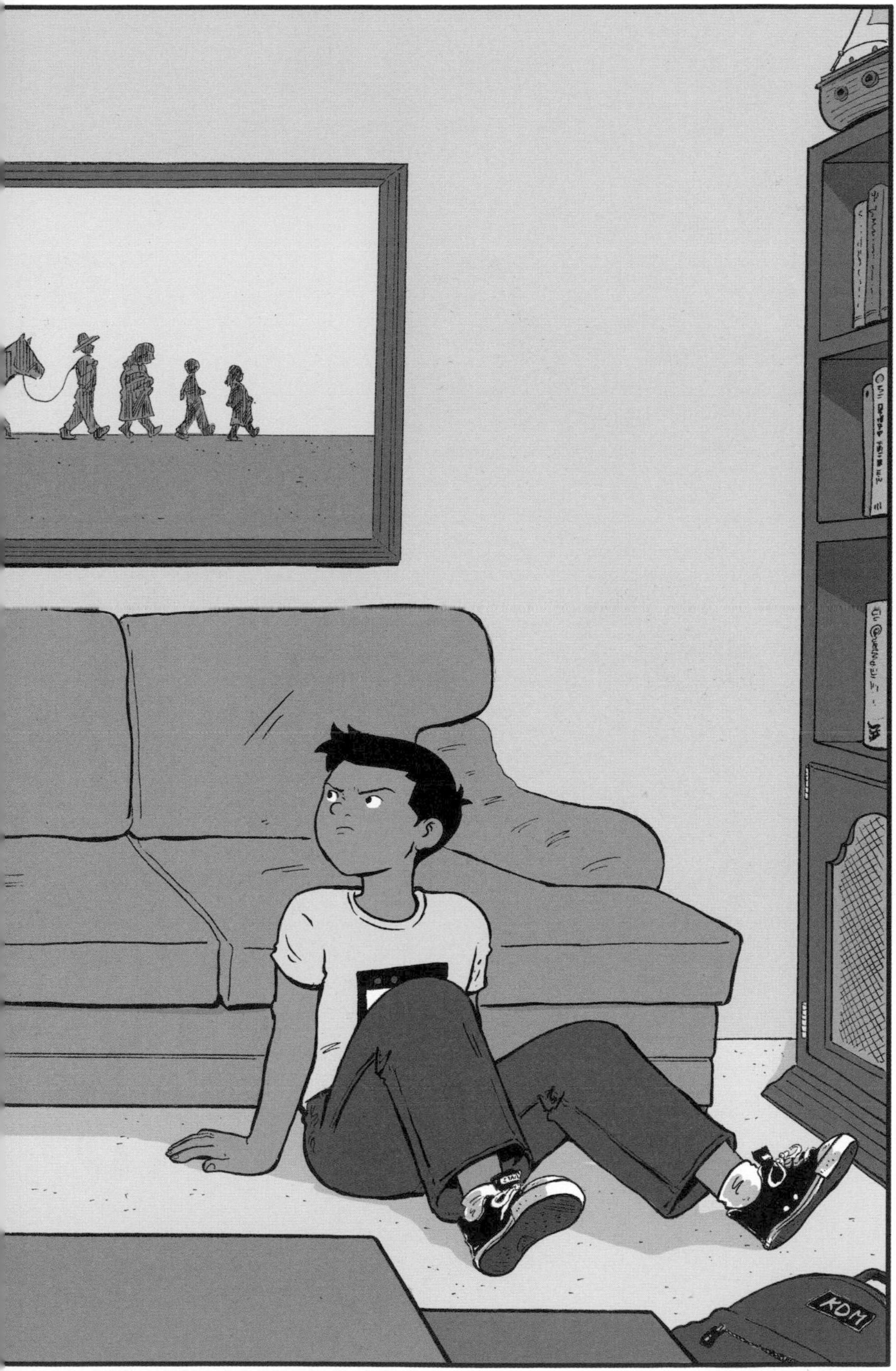
KDM

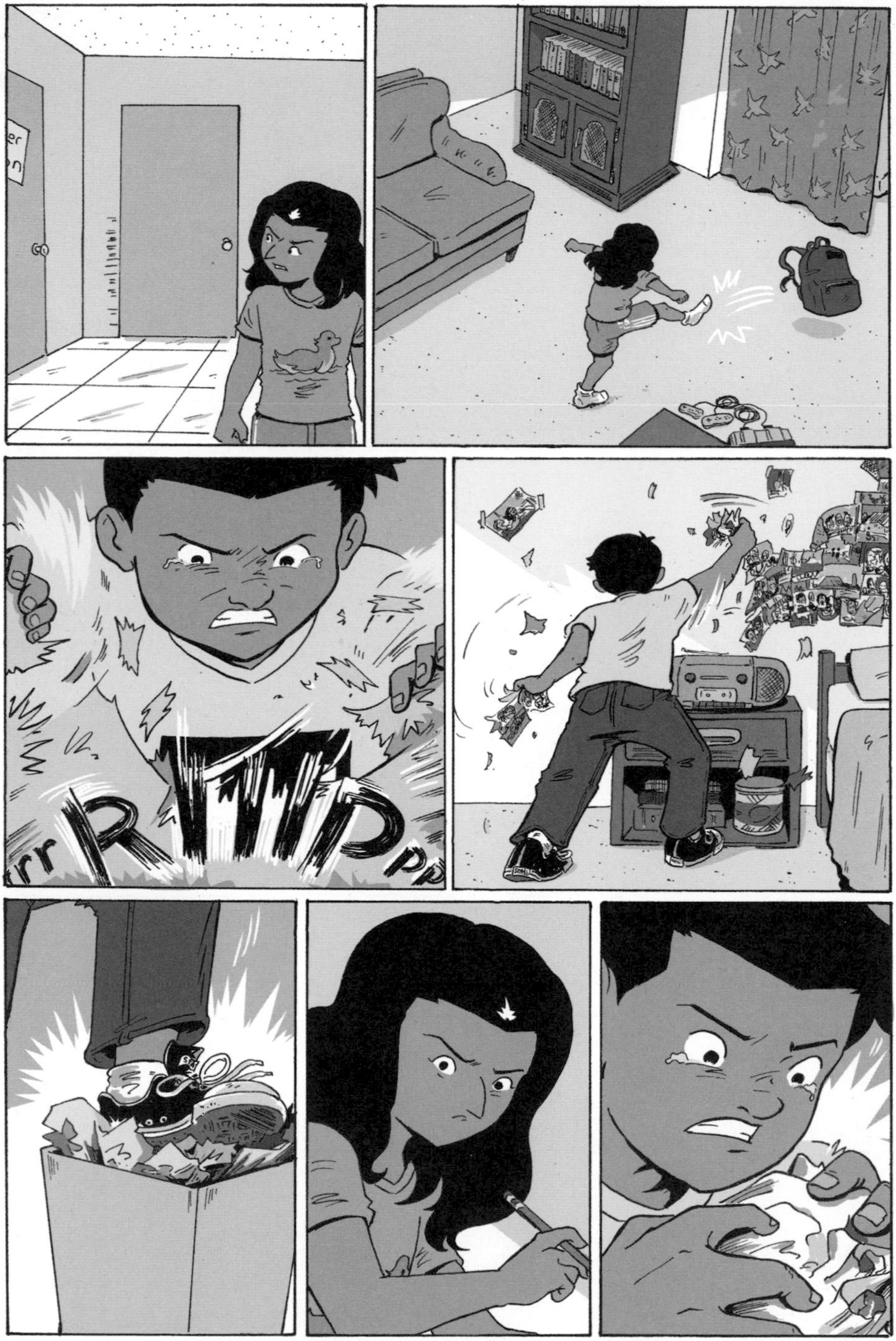
rrRIIIPpp

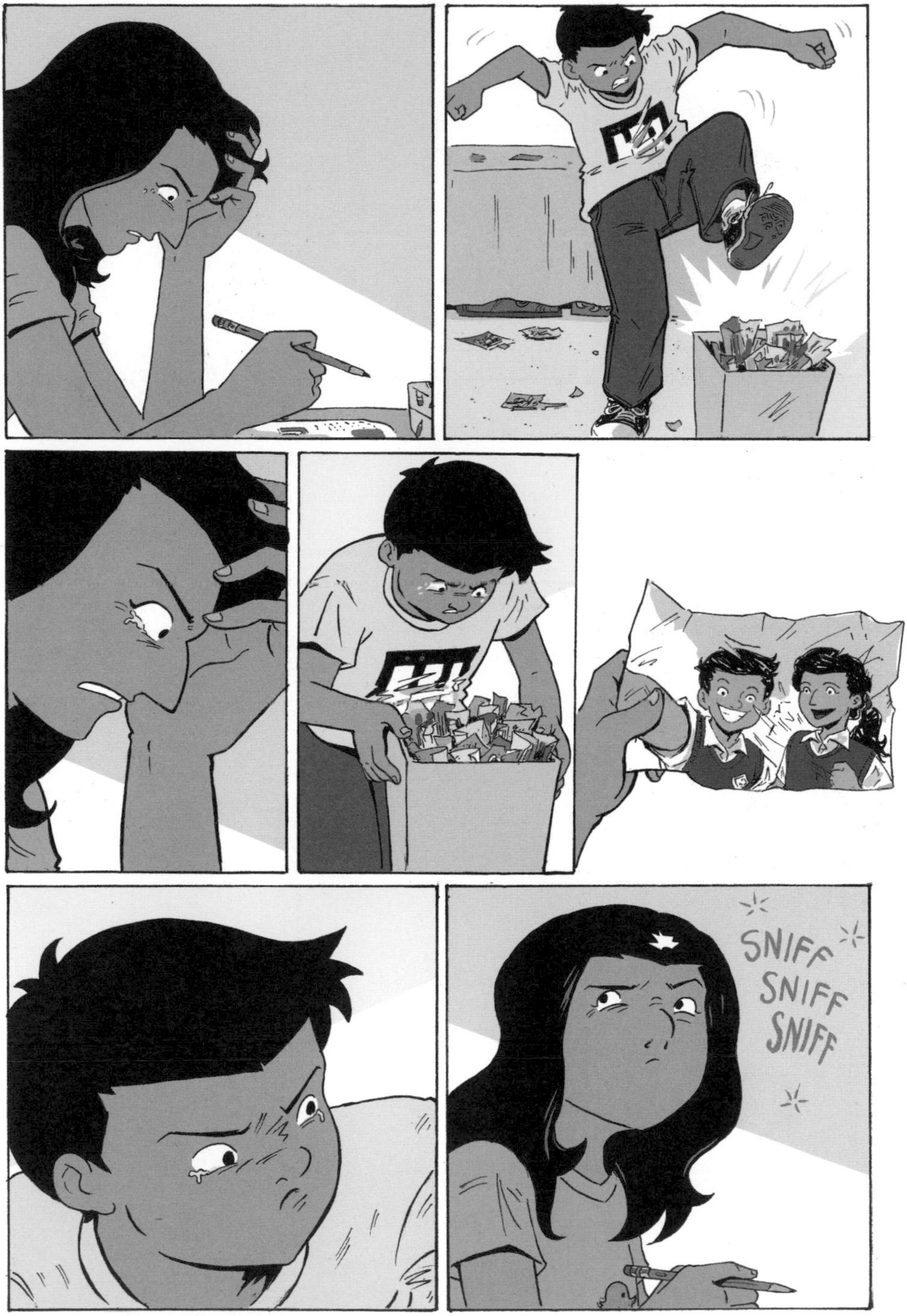
SNIFF
SNIFF
SNIFF

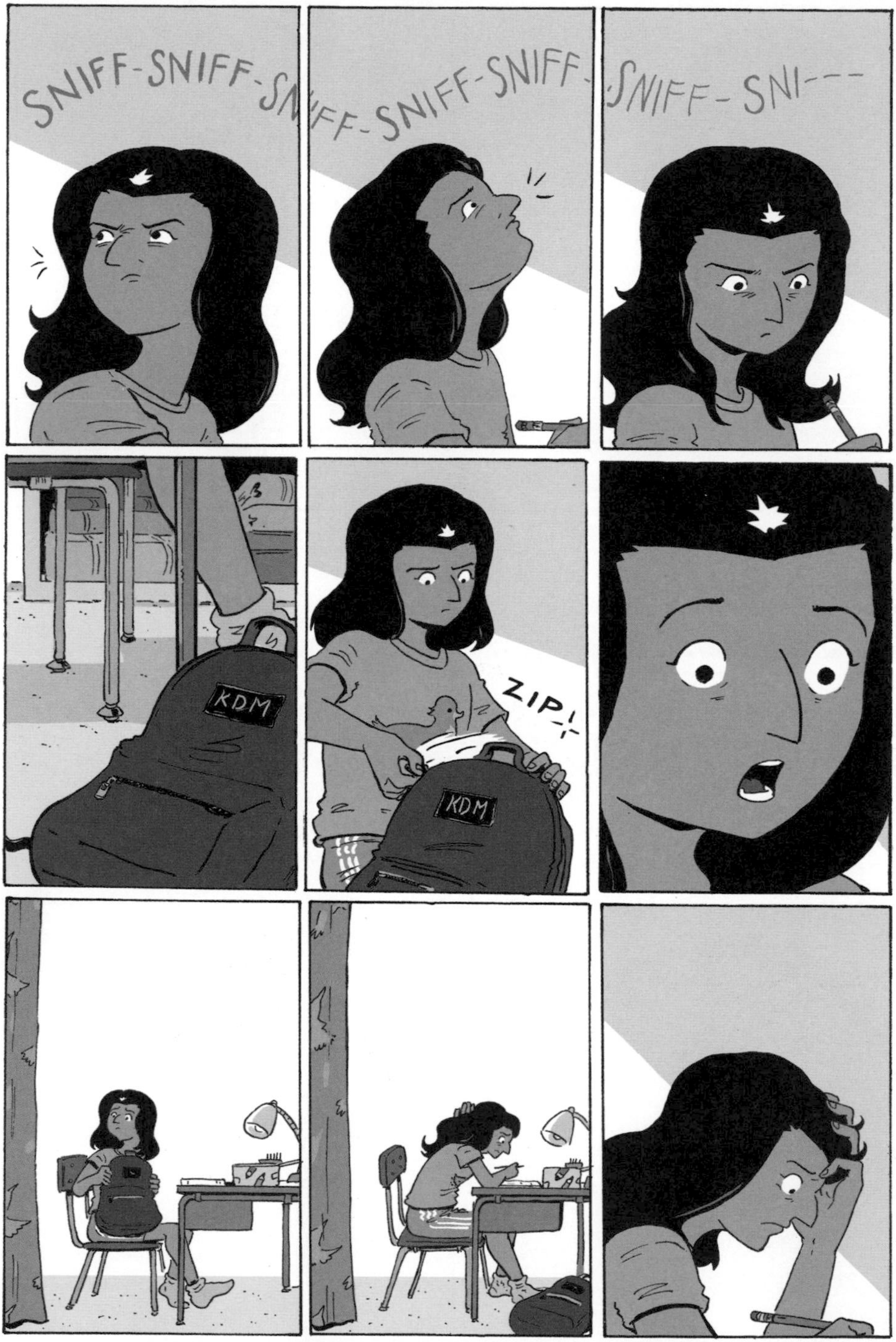
SNIFF-SNIFF-SNIFF-SNIFF-SNIFF-SNIFF-SNI---
KDM
KDM
ZIP!

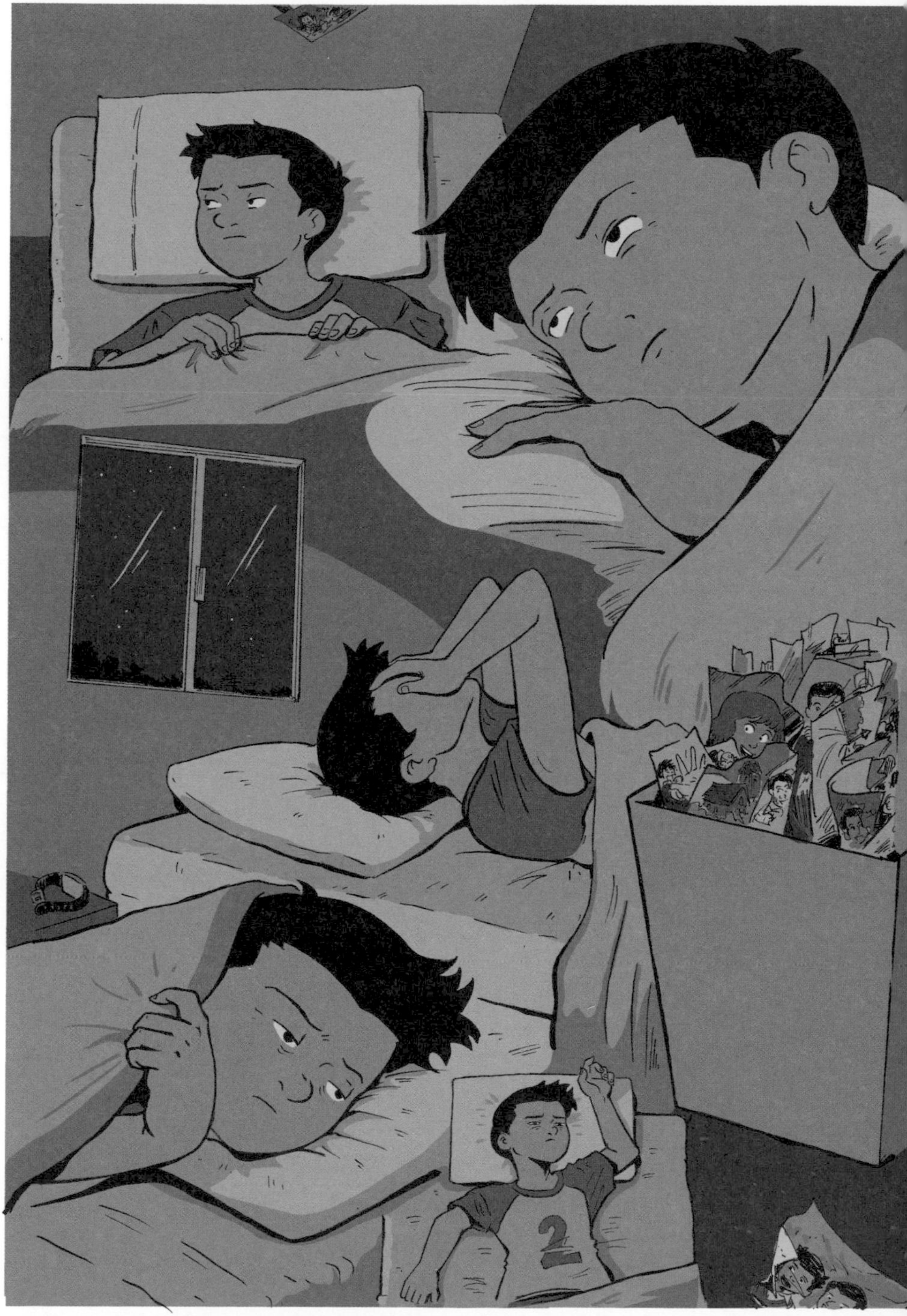

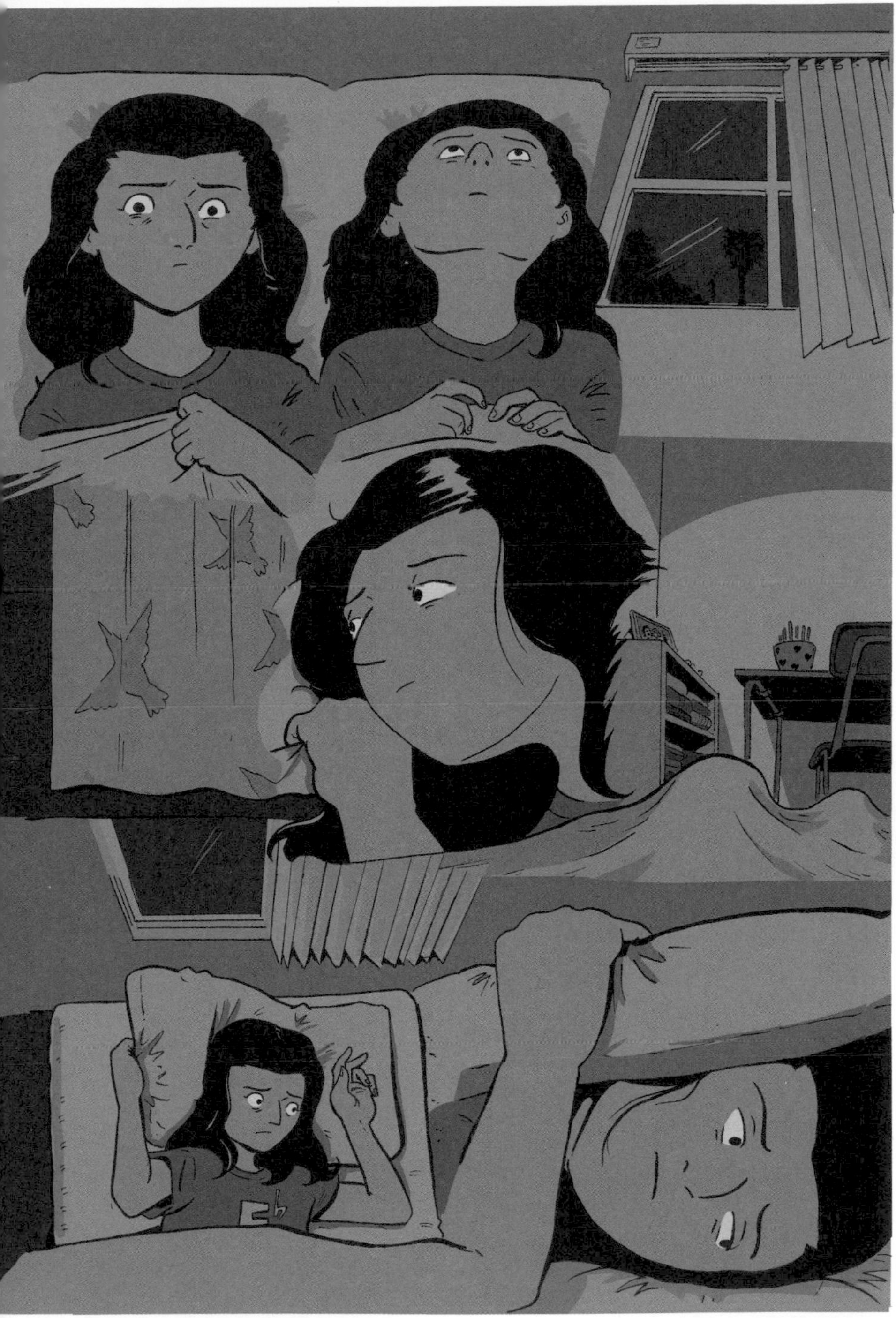

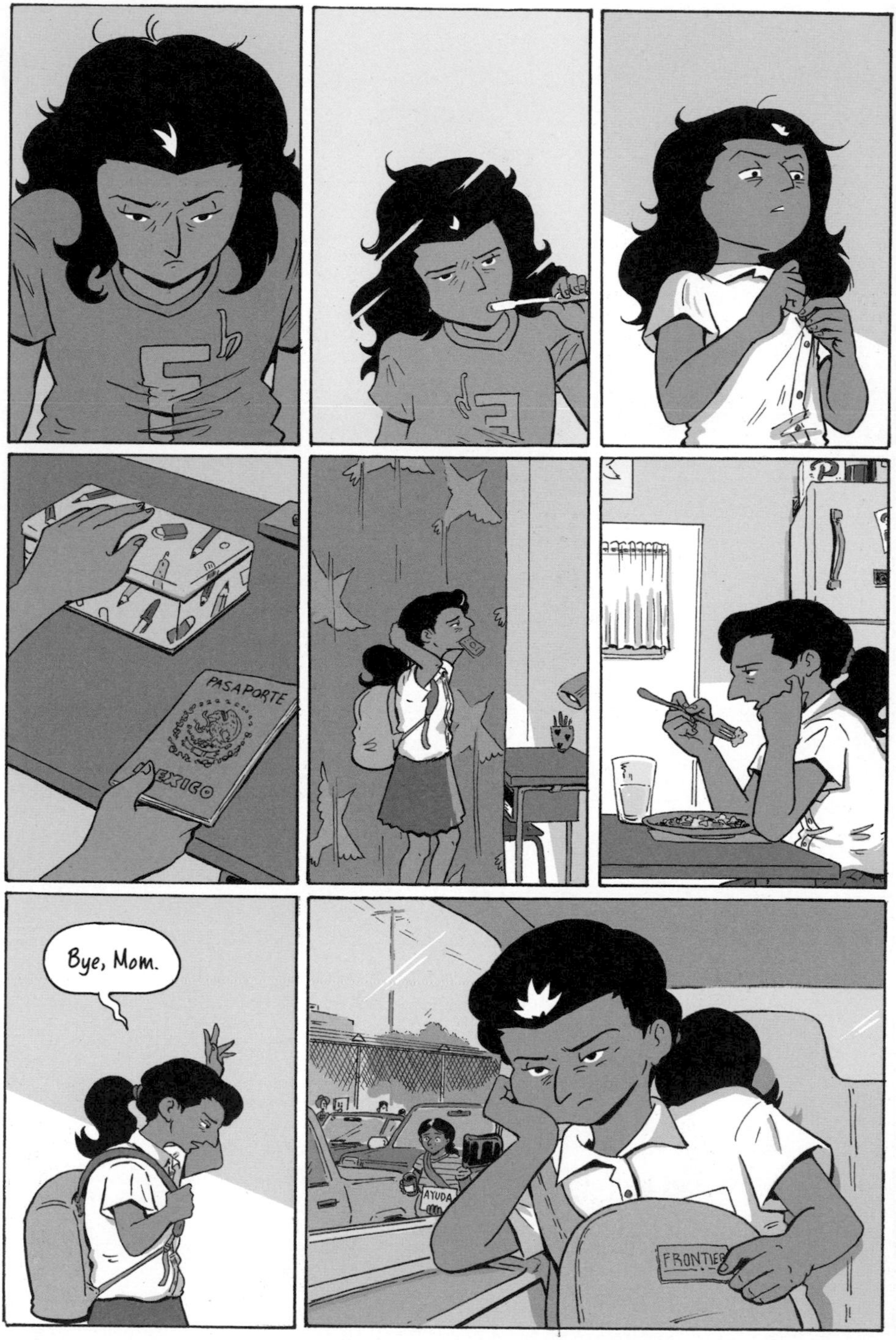

PASAPORTE
MEXICO
Bye, Mom.
AYUDA
FRONTIER

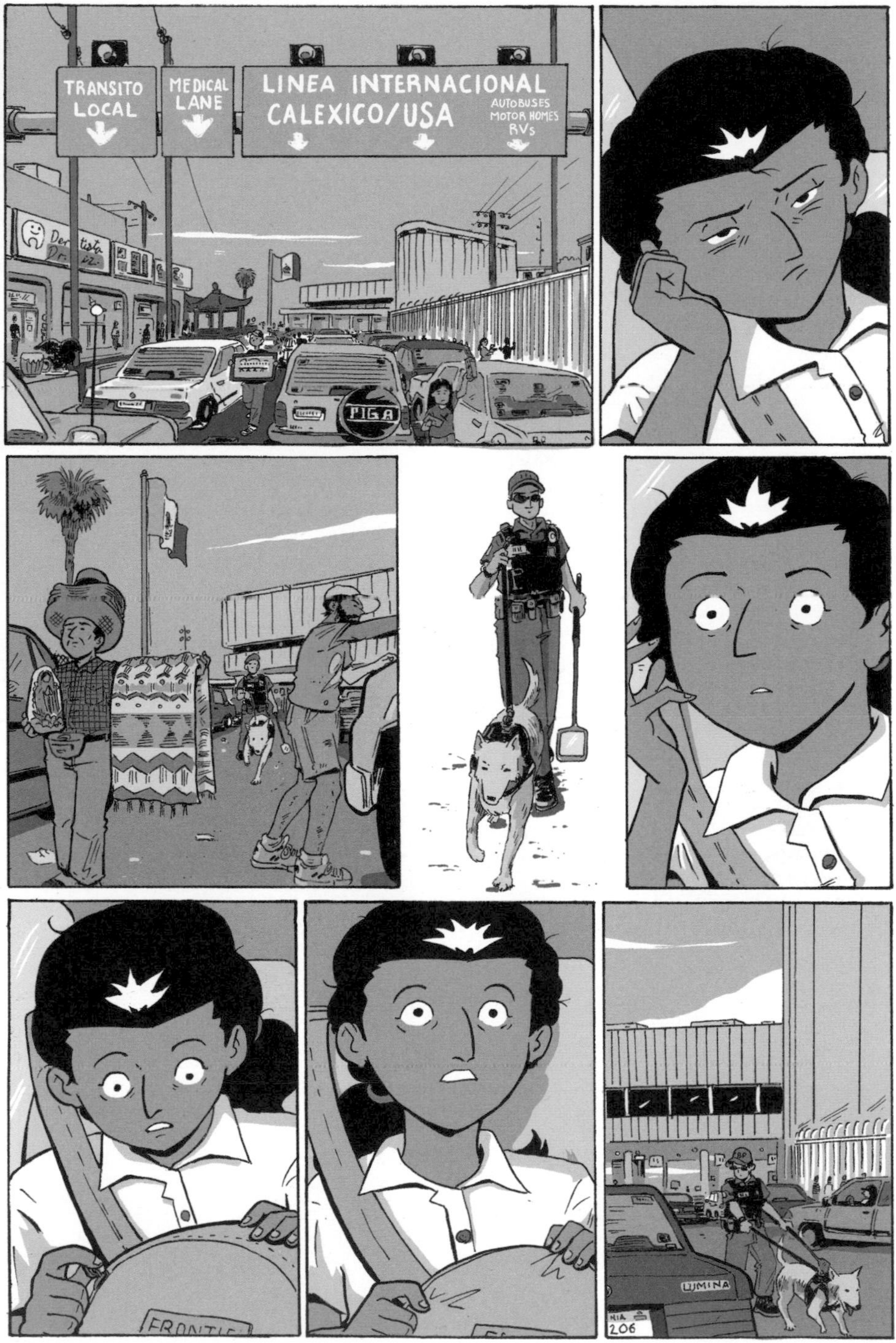
TRANSITO LOCAL
MEDICAL LANE
LINEA INTERNACIONAL
CALEXICO/USA
AUTOBUSES
MOTOR HOMES
RVs

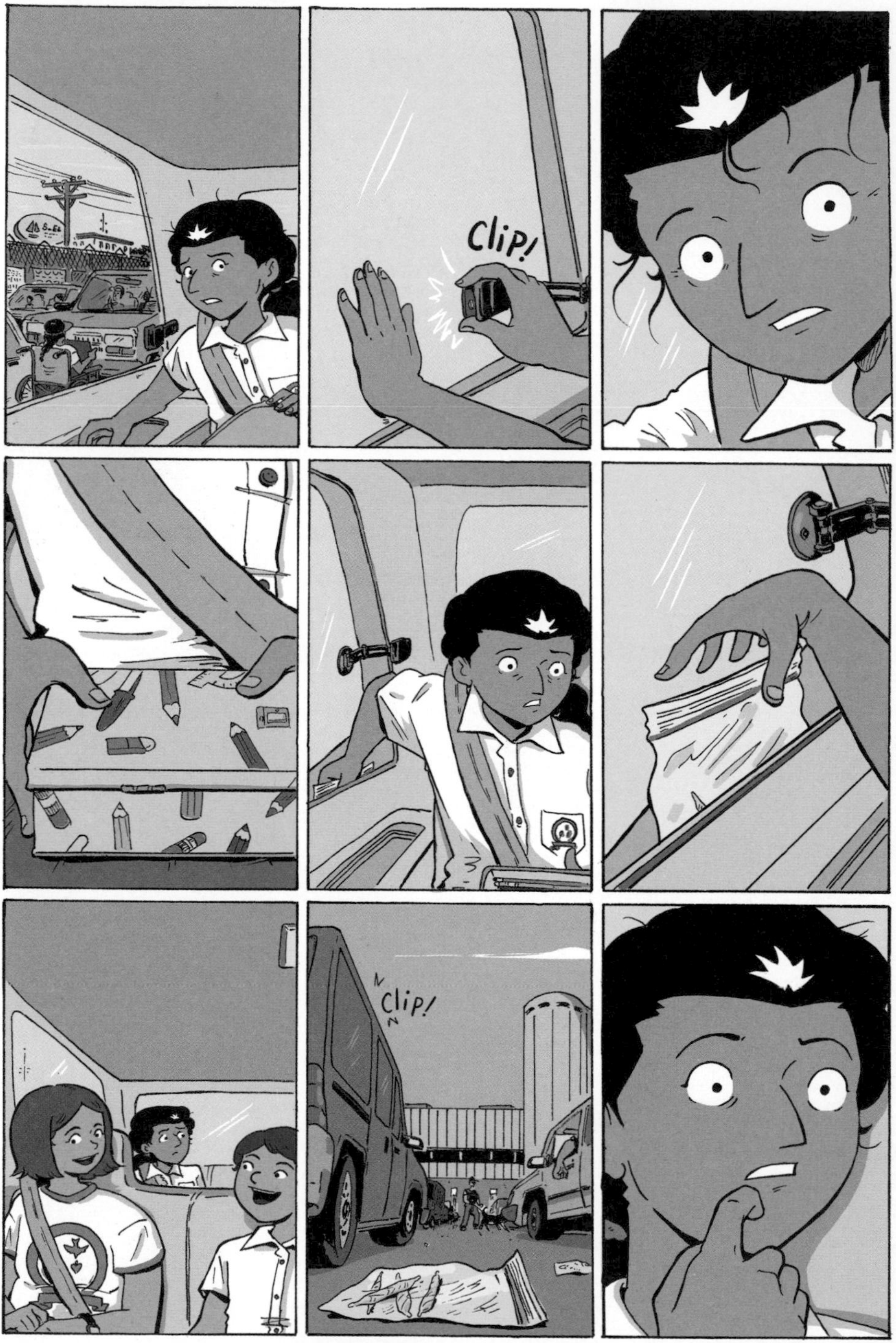
CLIP!
CLIP!

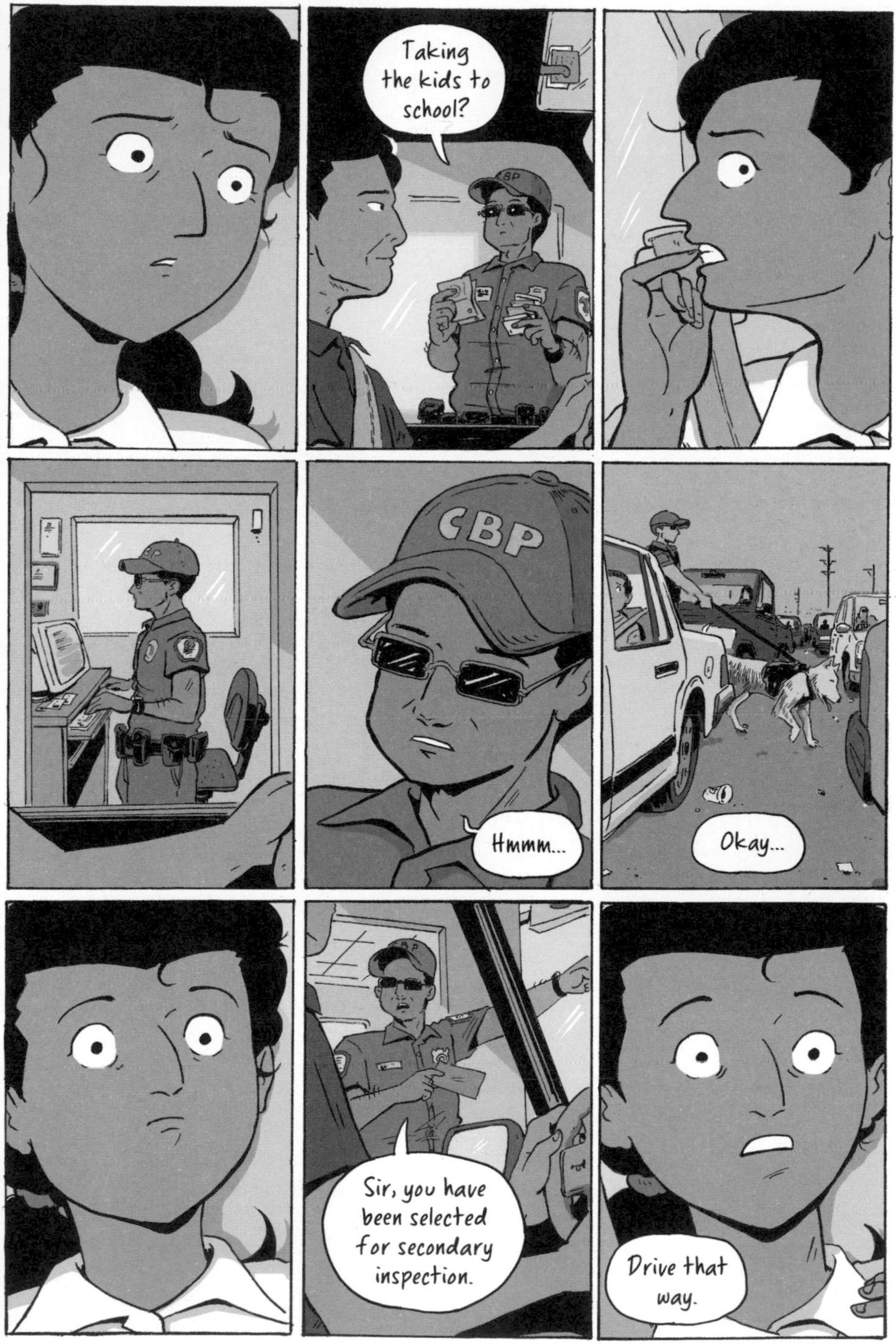
Taking the kids to school?
CBP
Hmmm...
Okay...
Sir, you have been selected for secondary inspection.
Drive that way.

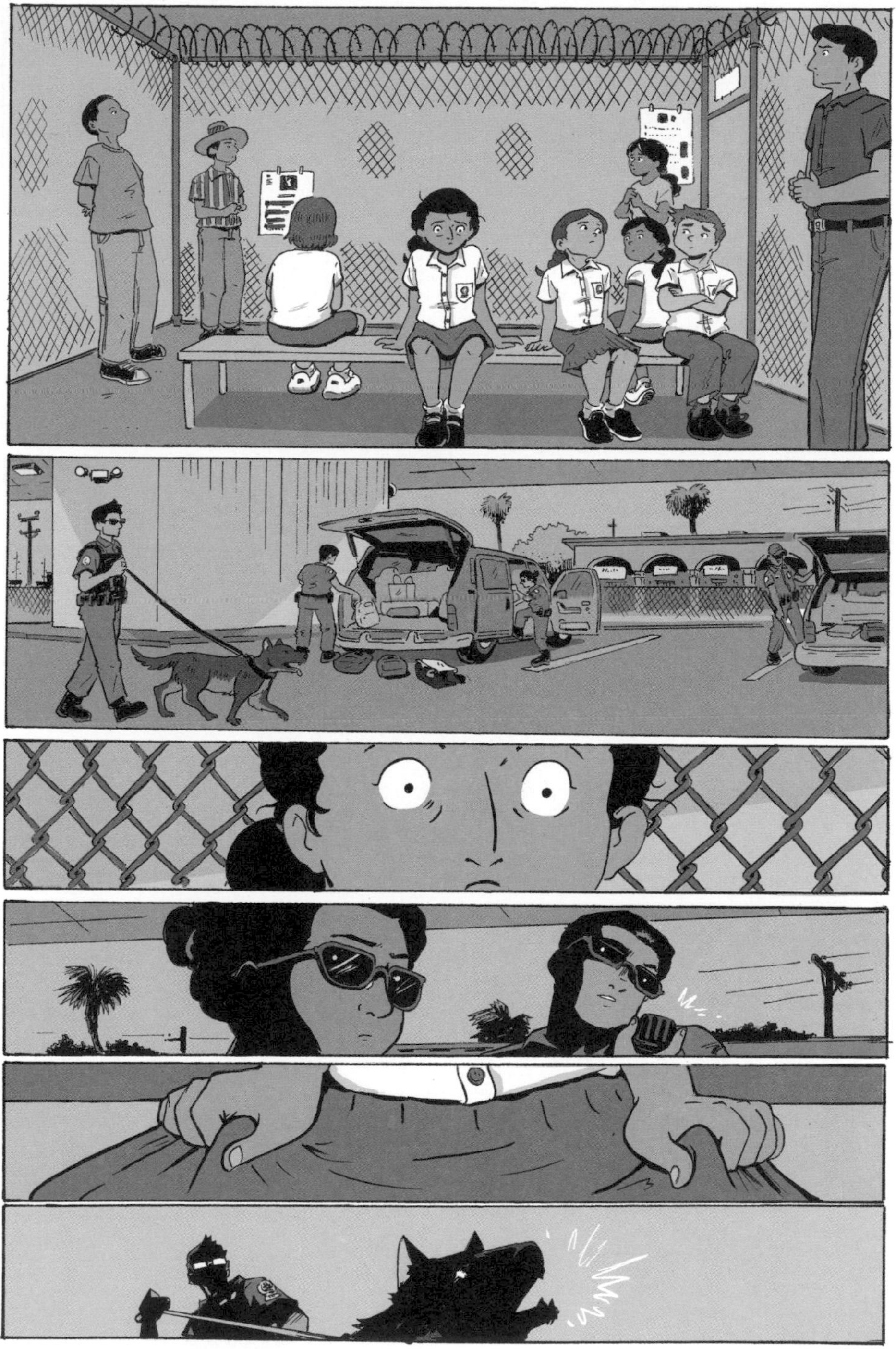

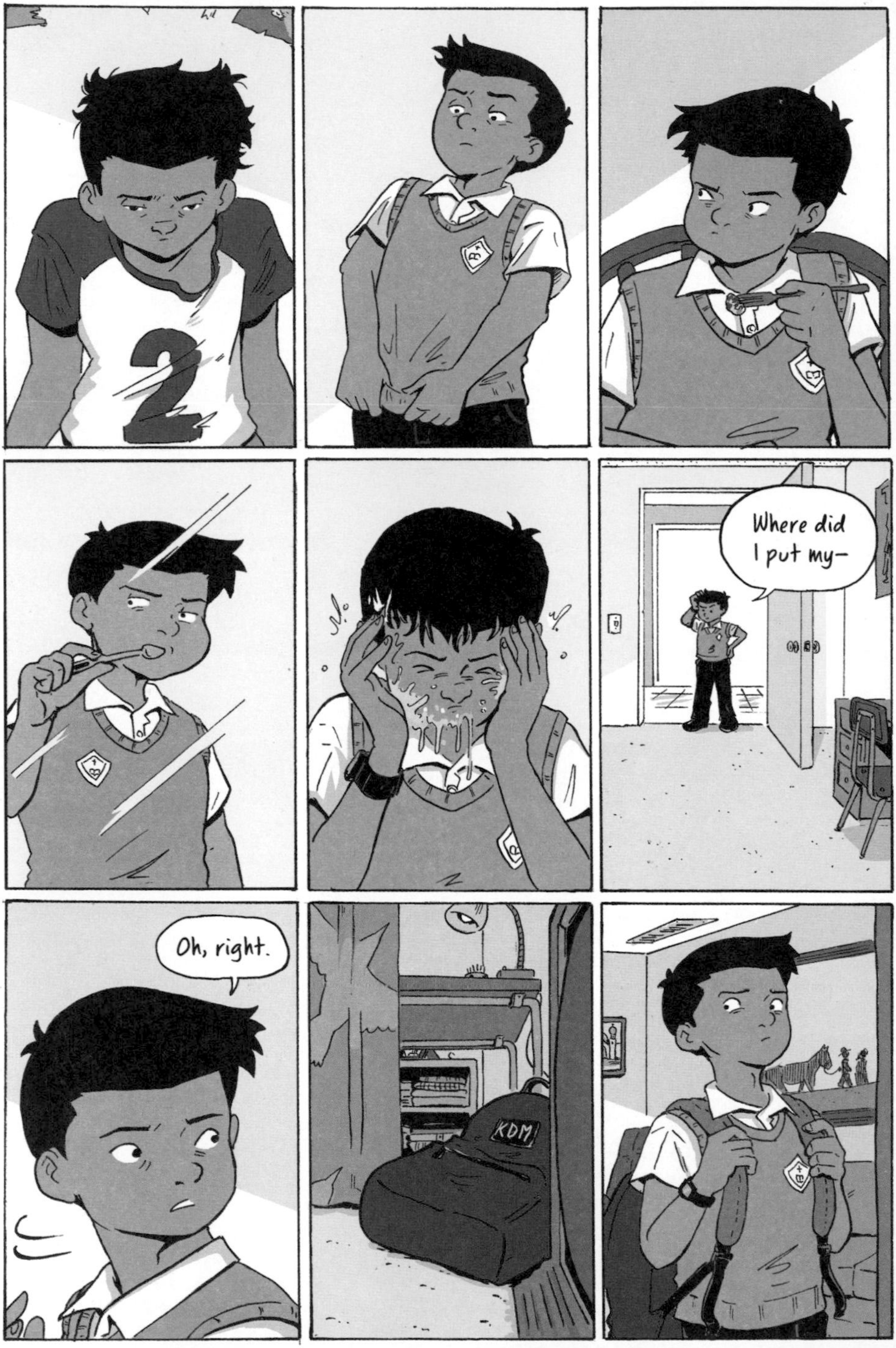
Where did I put my-
Oh, right.
KDM

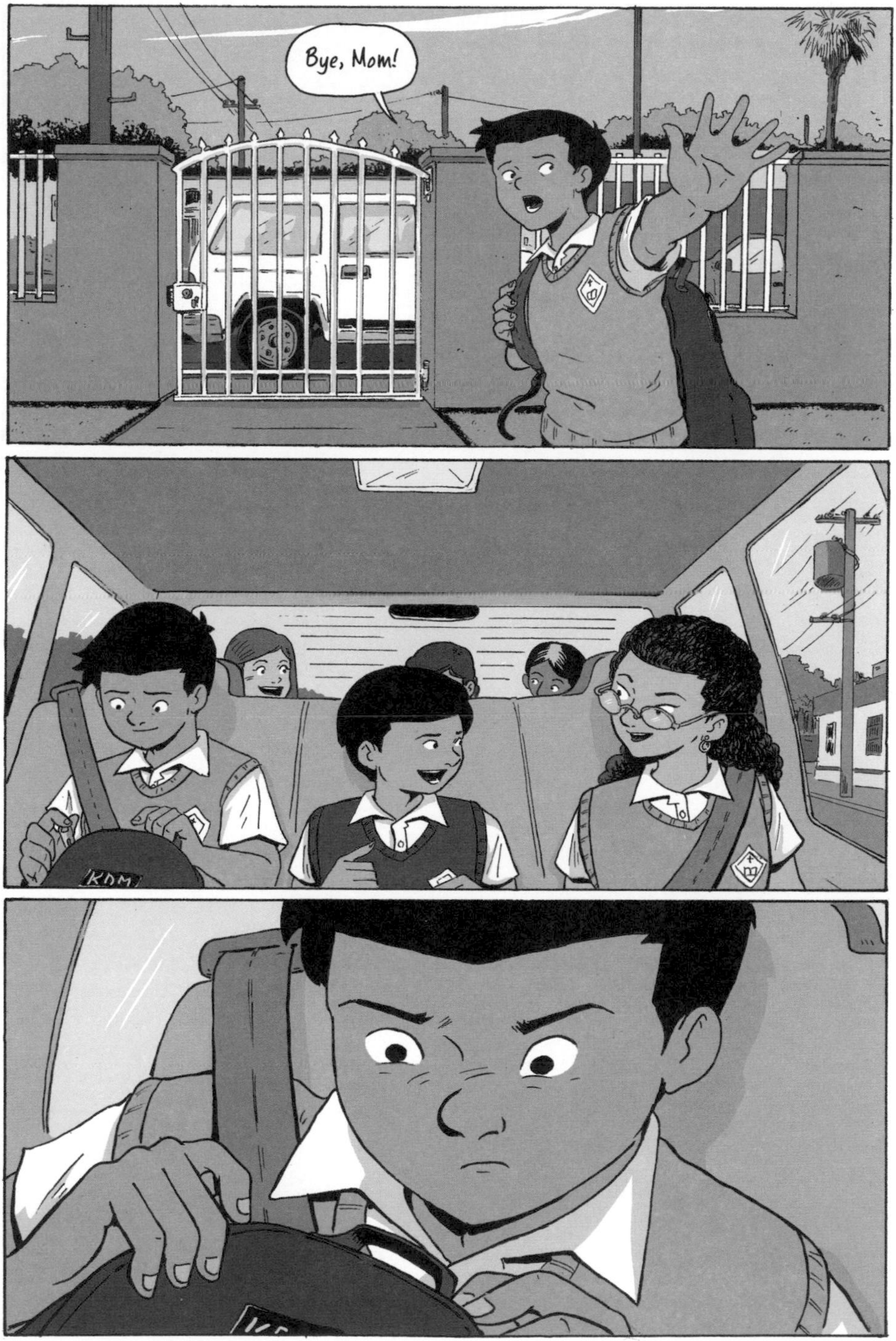
Bye, Mom!
KDM

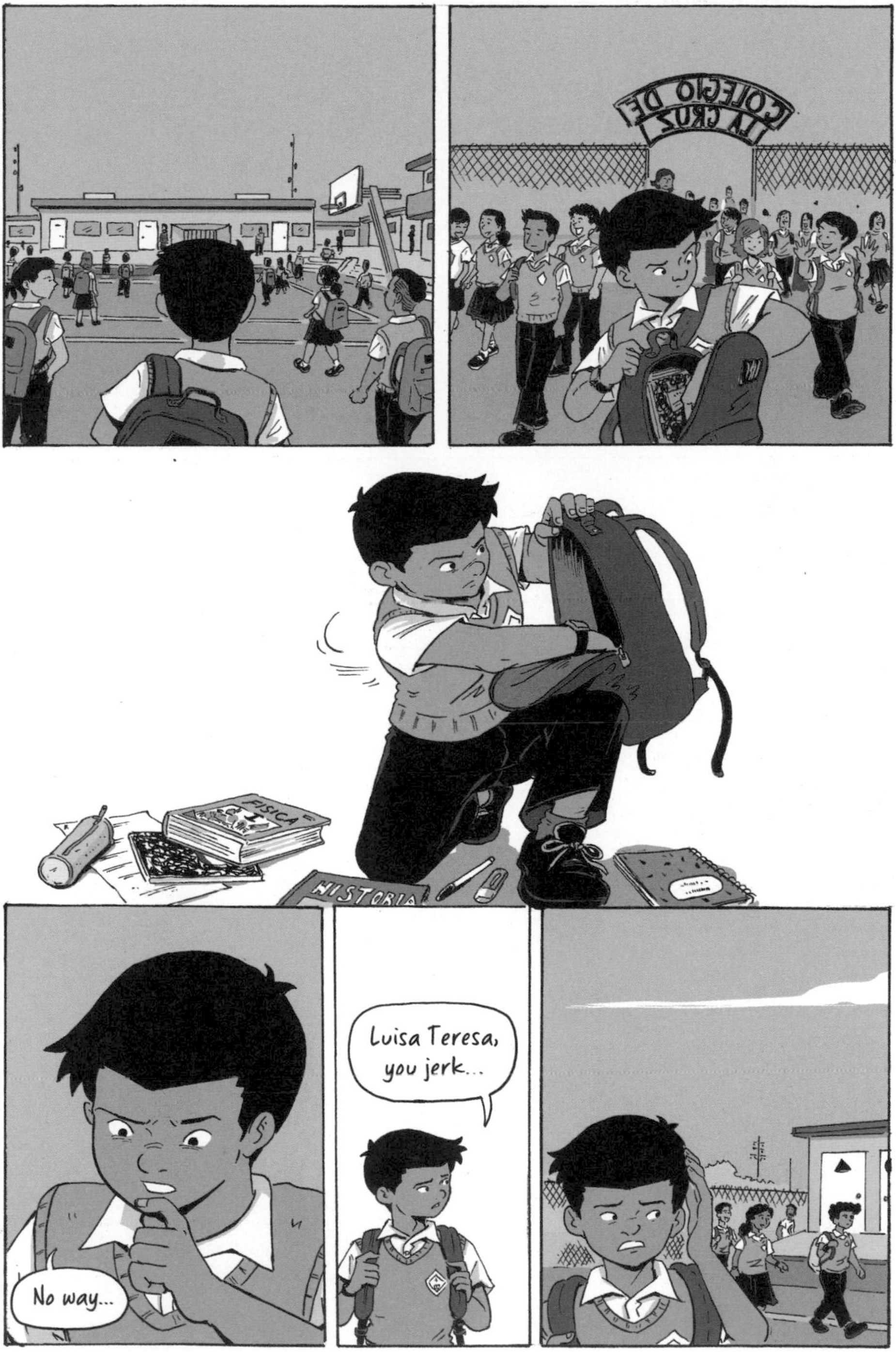
COLEGIO DE LA CRUZ
FISICA
HISTORIA
No way...
Luisa Teresa,
you jerk...

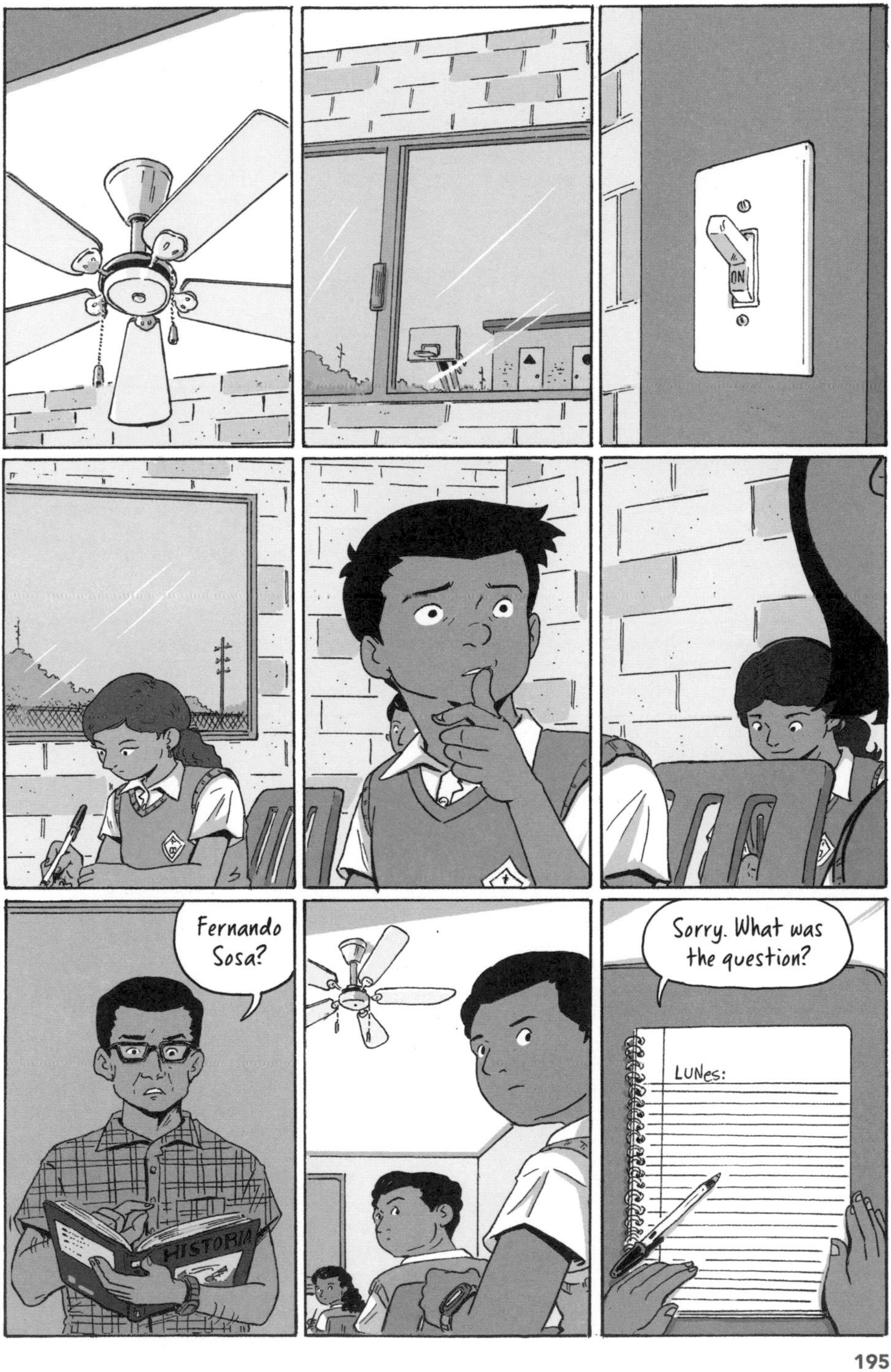
ON
Fernando Sosa?
HISTORIA
Sorry. What was the question?
LUNes:

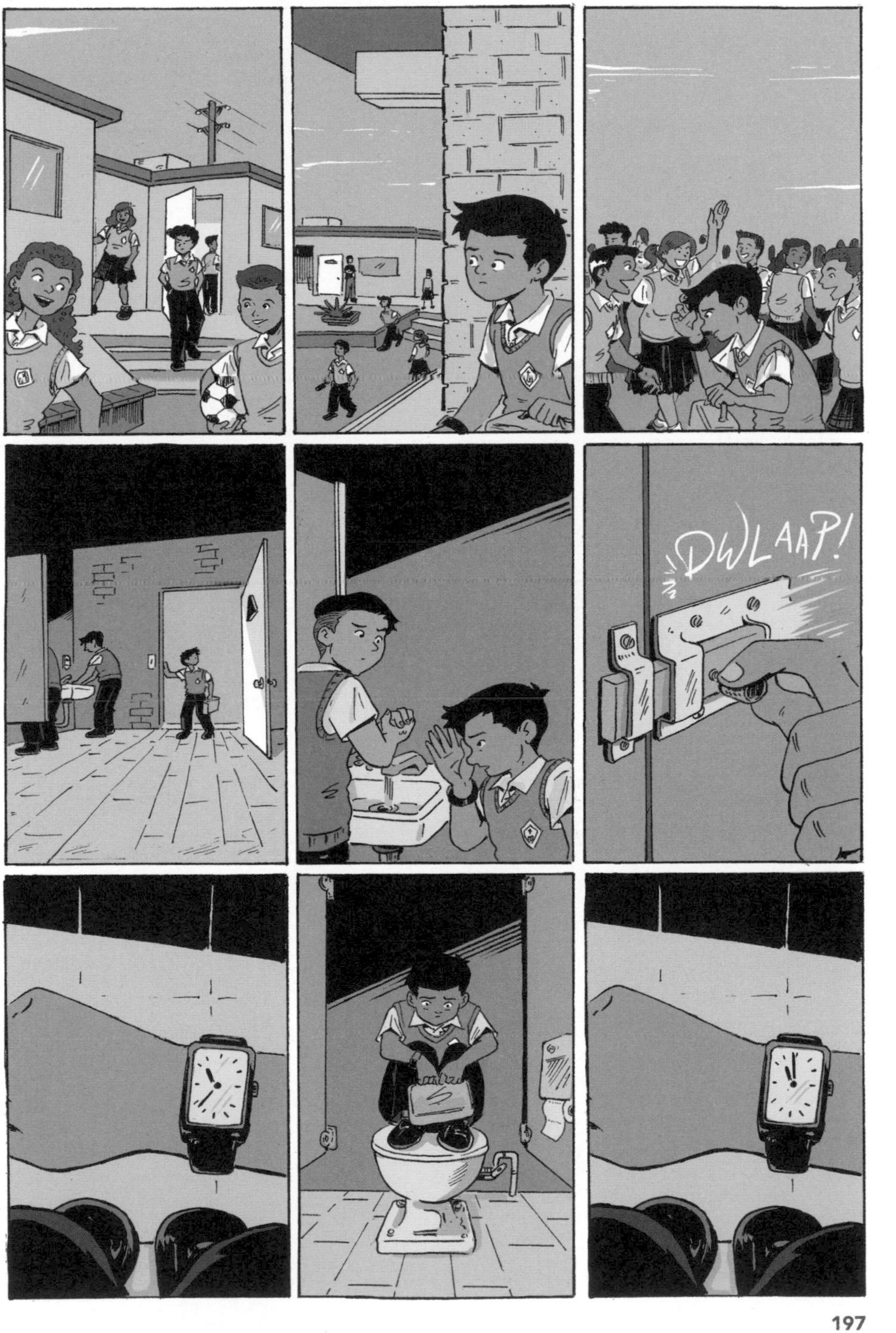
DWLAAP!

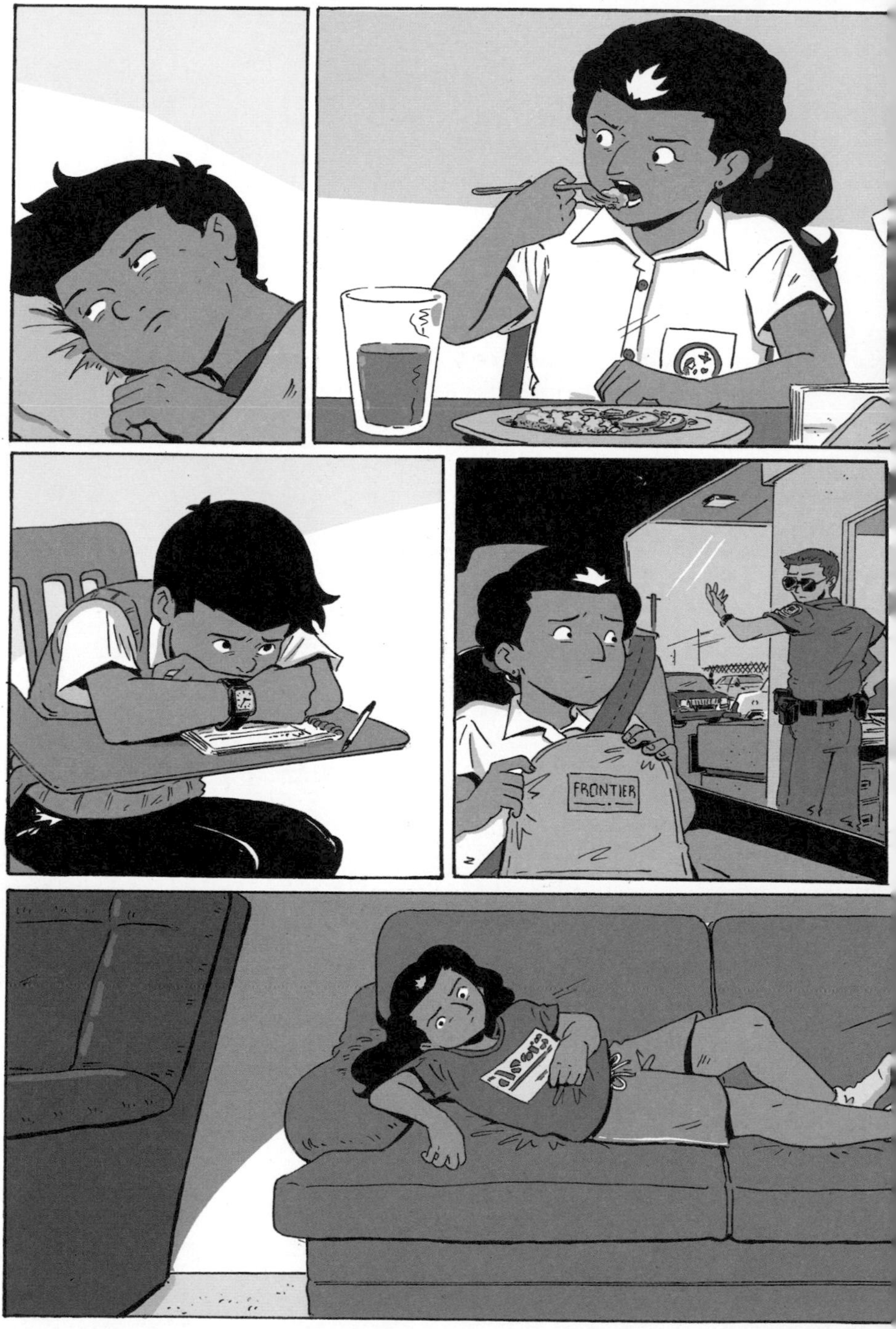
FRONTIER

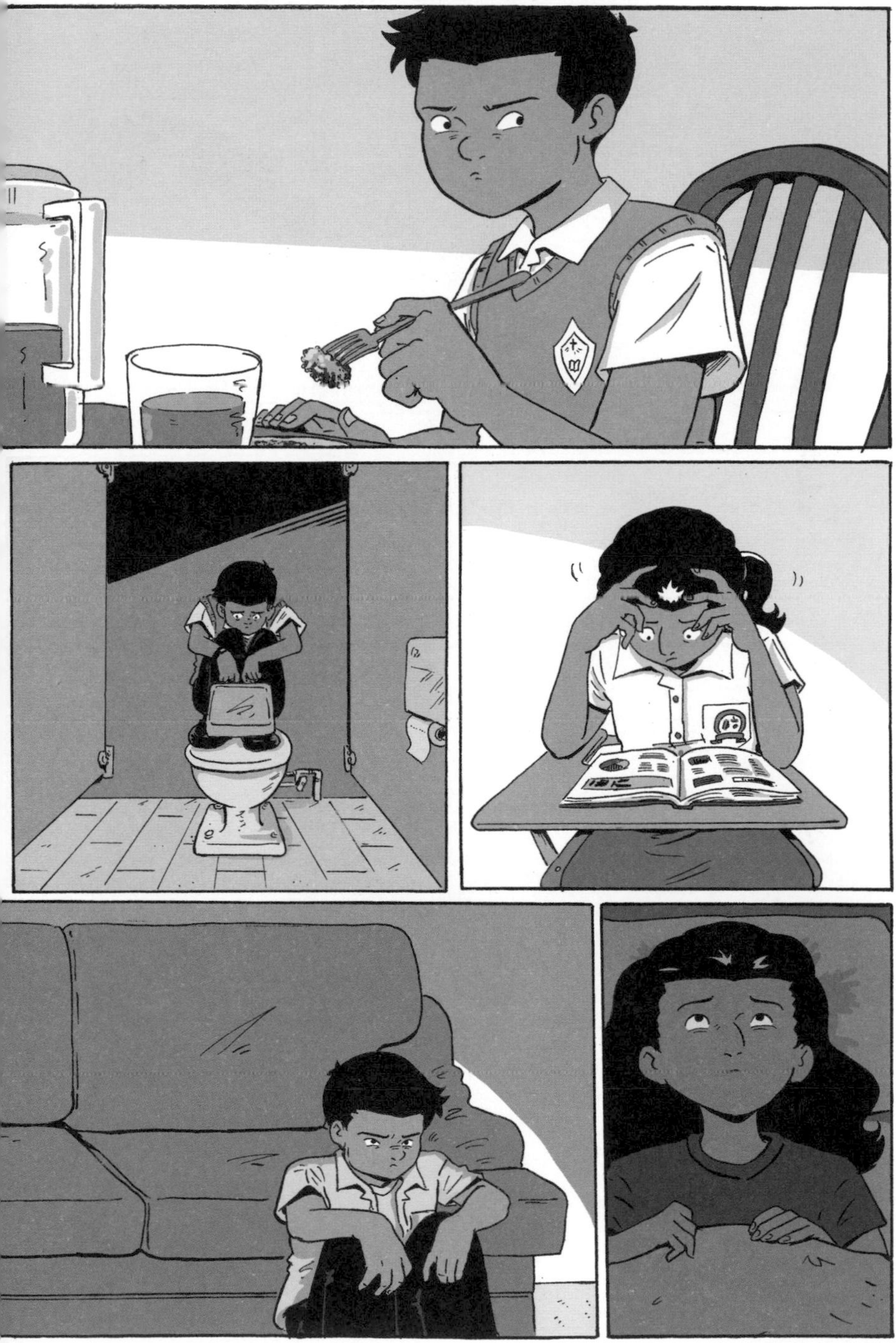

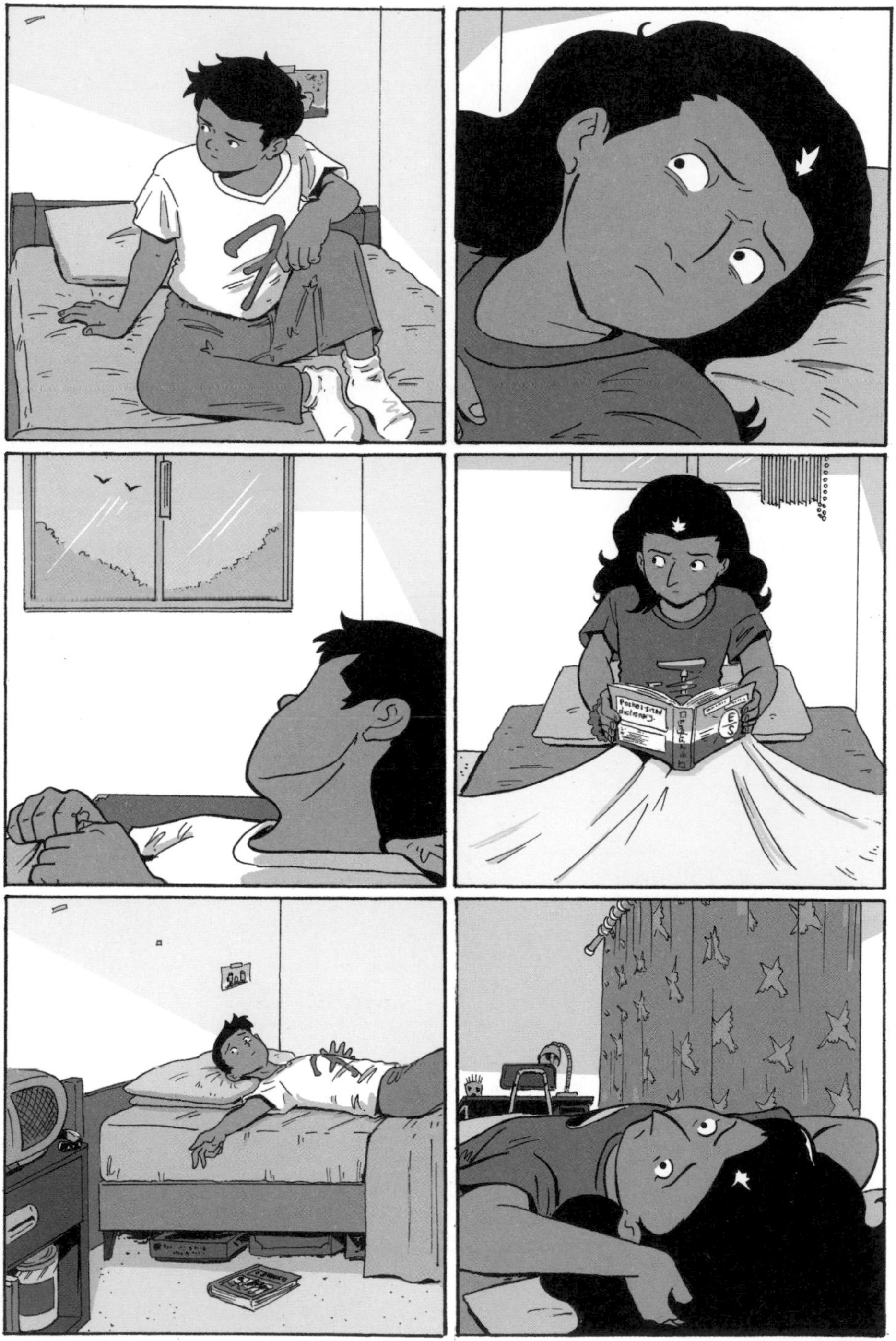
Pocket-sized dictionary.
E
S

It's past two o'clock. Are you feeling any better?
A little better. But I think I don't want to go to school tomorrow, either.
Well, if you're still sick, we'll go to the doctor. But if you're not sick, you have to go.
But what if I'm not sick, but still...don't want to go?
Oh, Teresa, you really
How's your head?
It still hurts.
I thought it was your stomach.
It's both, Mom!

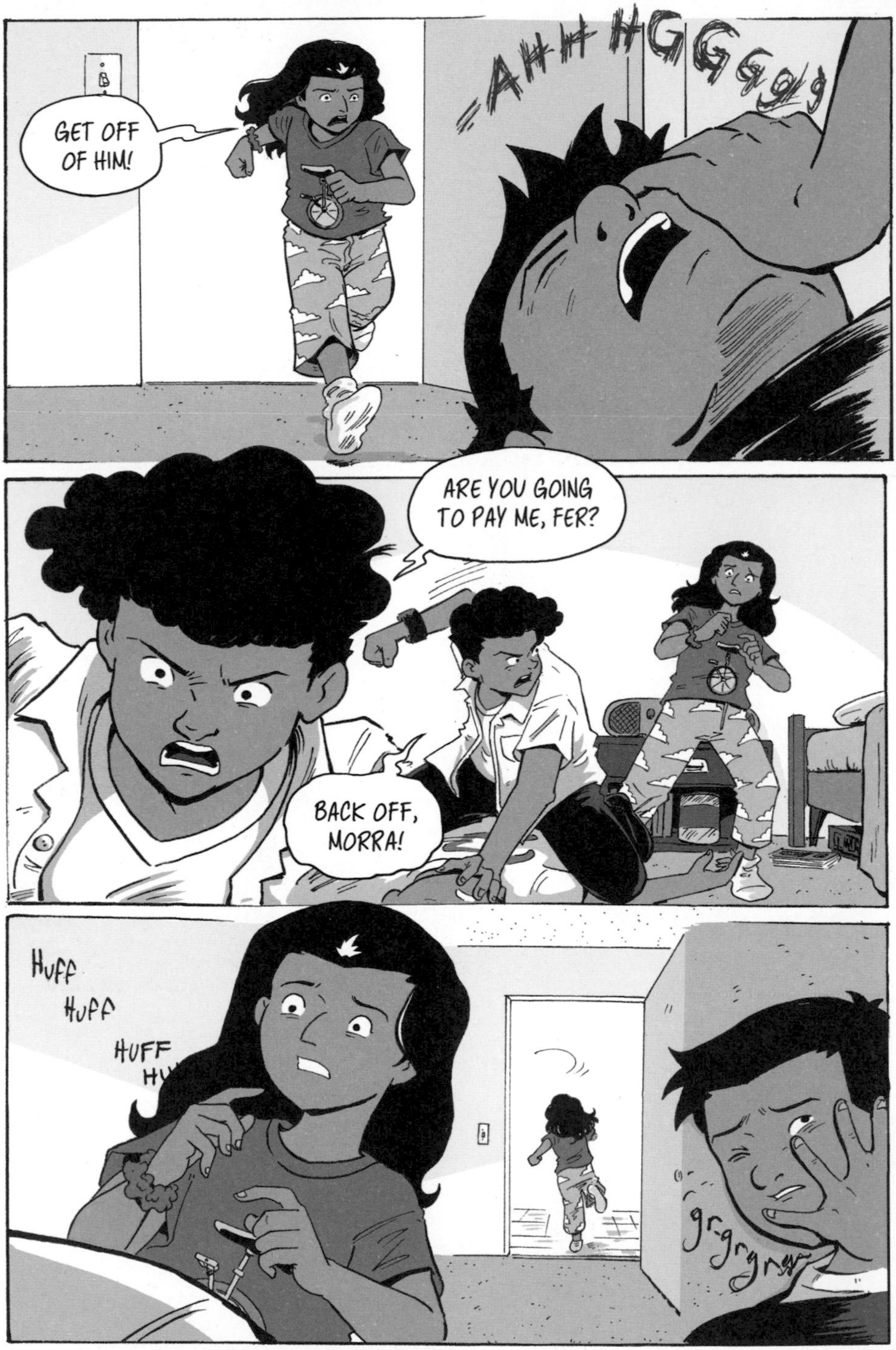
GET OFF
OF HIM!
AHHHGGggg
ARE YOU GOING
TO PAY ME, FER?
BACK OFF,
MORRA!
HUFF
HUFF
HUFF
gr-grgrer

214

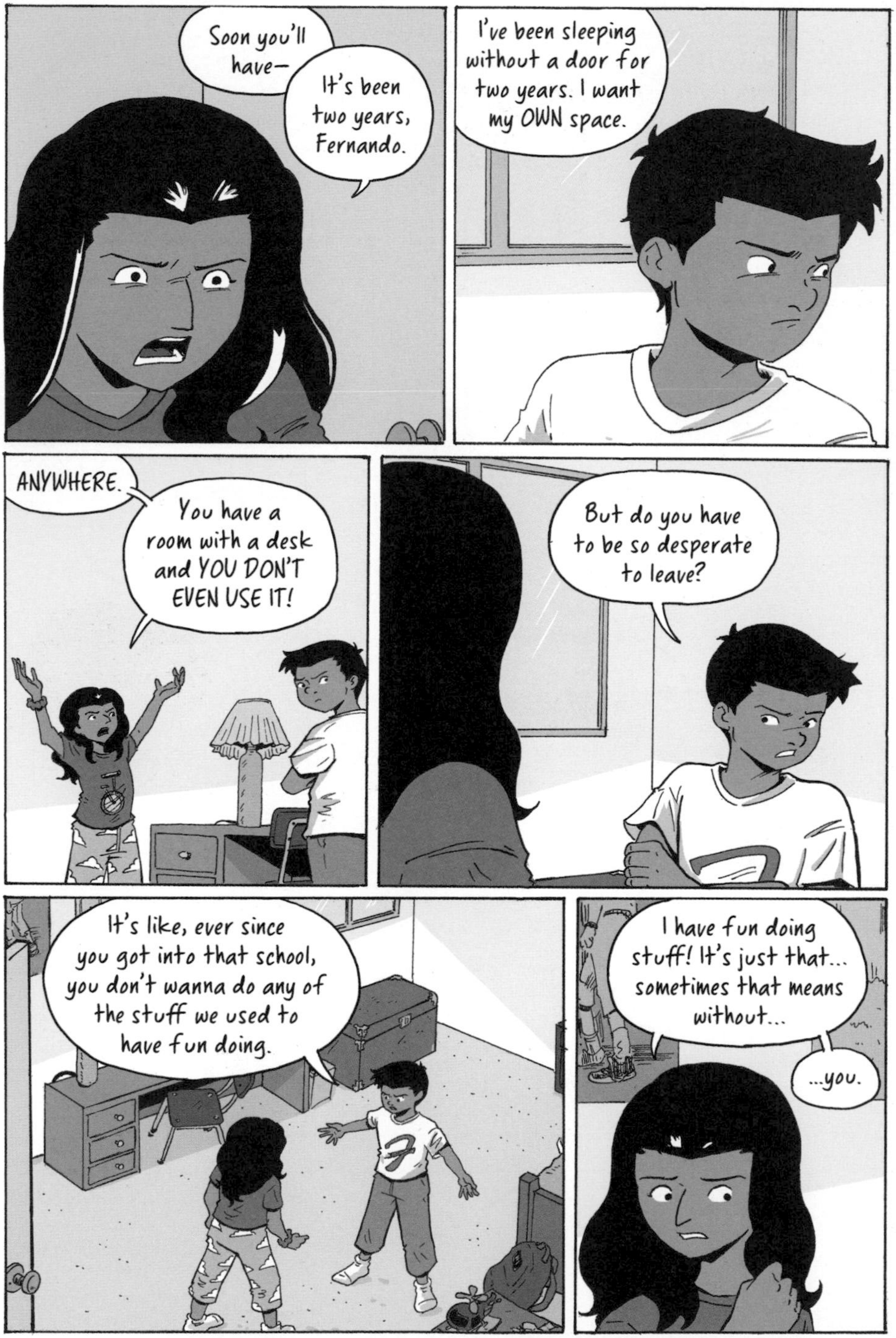
Soon you'll have—
It's been two years, Fernando.
I've been sleeping without a door for two years. I want my OWN space.
ANYWHERE.
You have a room with a desk and YOU DON'T EVEN USE IT!
But do you have to be so desperate to leave?
It's like, ever since you got into that school, you don't wanna do any of the stuff we used to have fun doing.
I have fun doing stuff! It's just that... sometimes that means without...
...you.

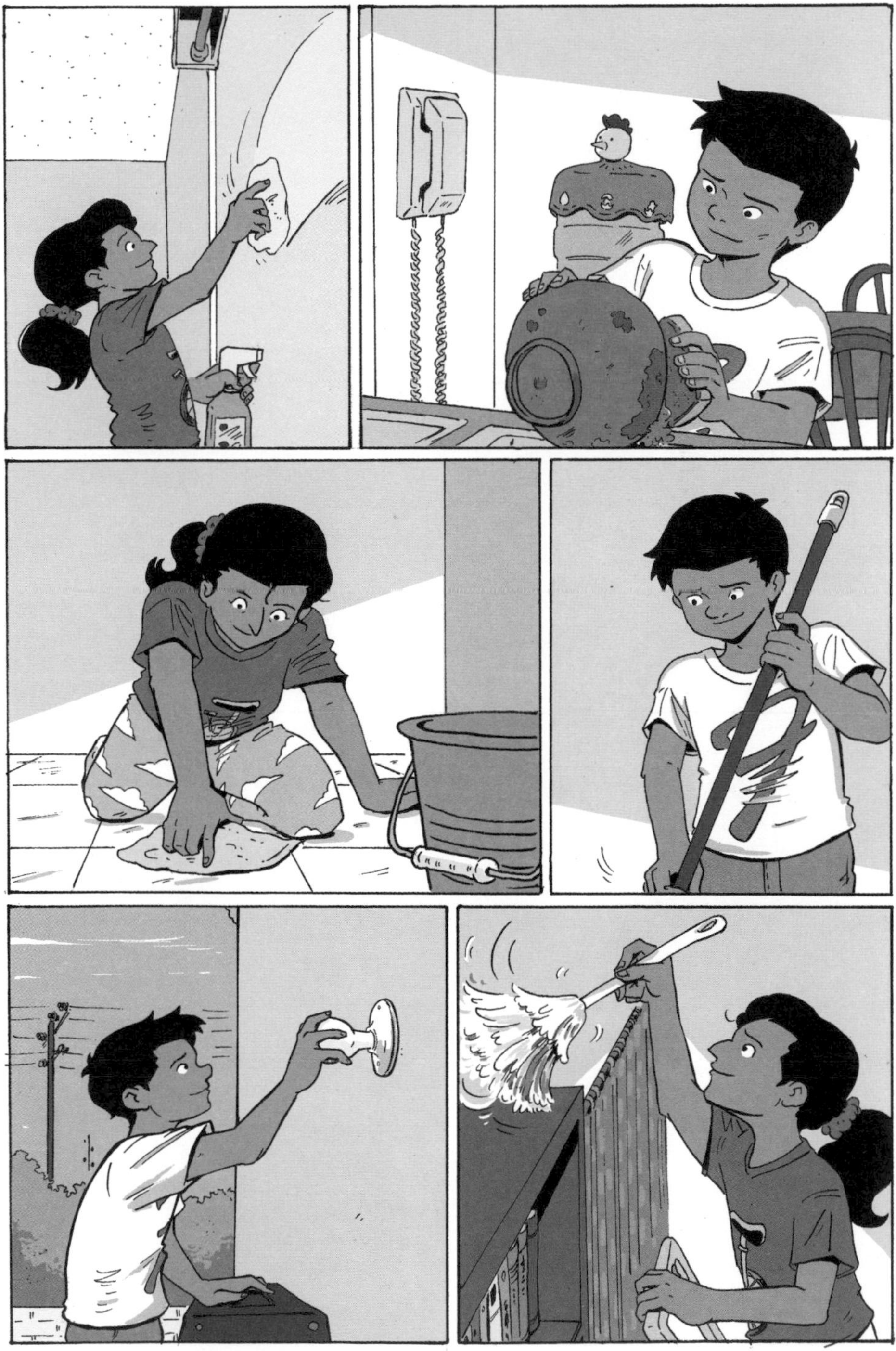

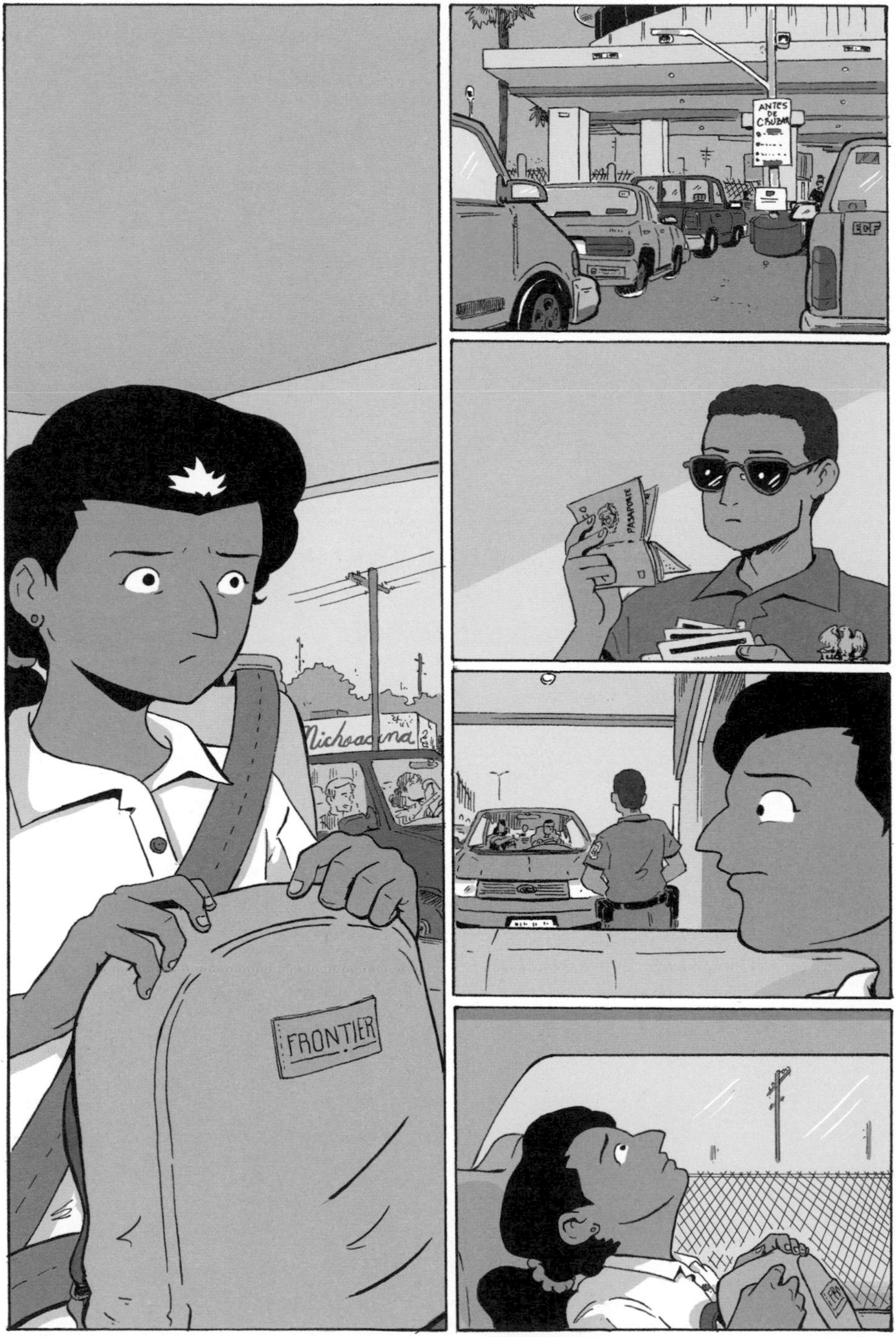
FRONTIER
ANTES DE CRUZAR
ECF
PASAPORTE

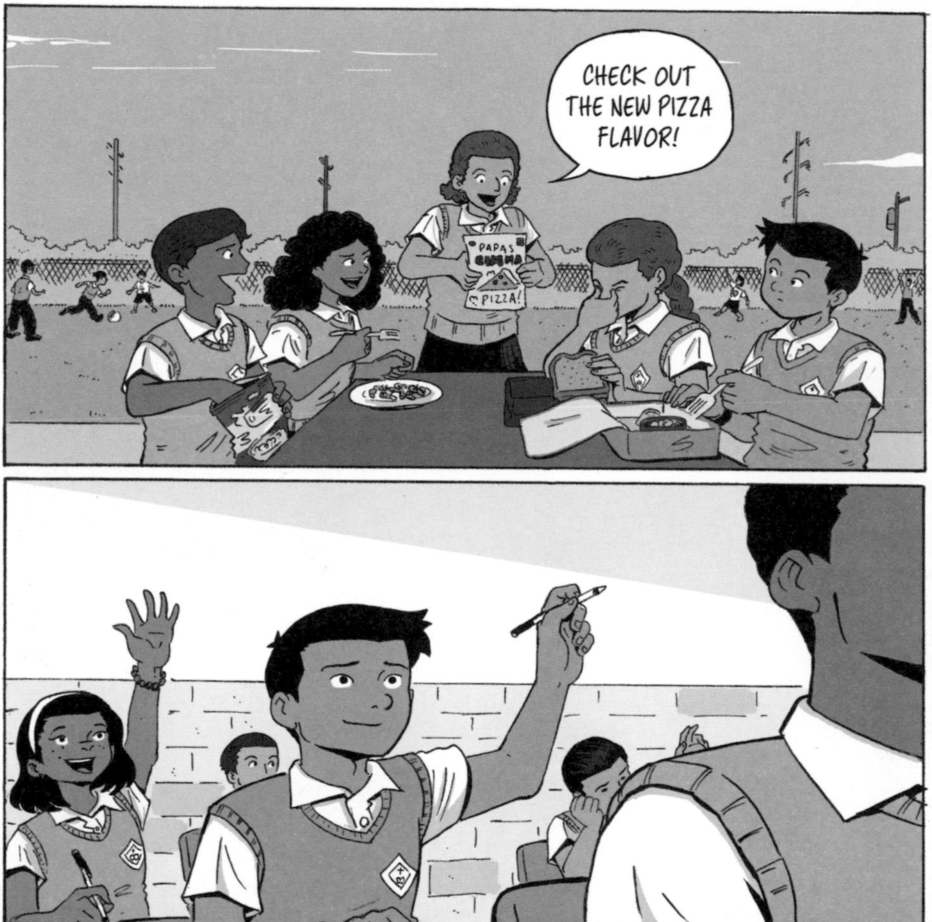
CHECK OUT THE NEW PIZZA FLAVOR!
PAPAS
PIZZA!

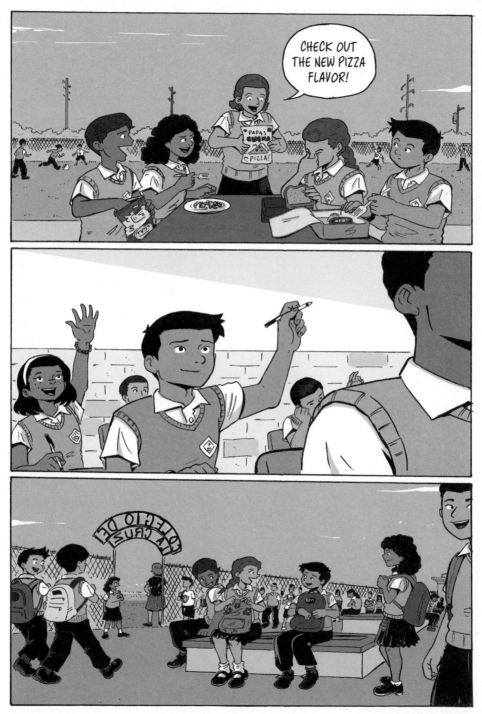

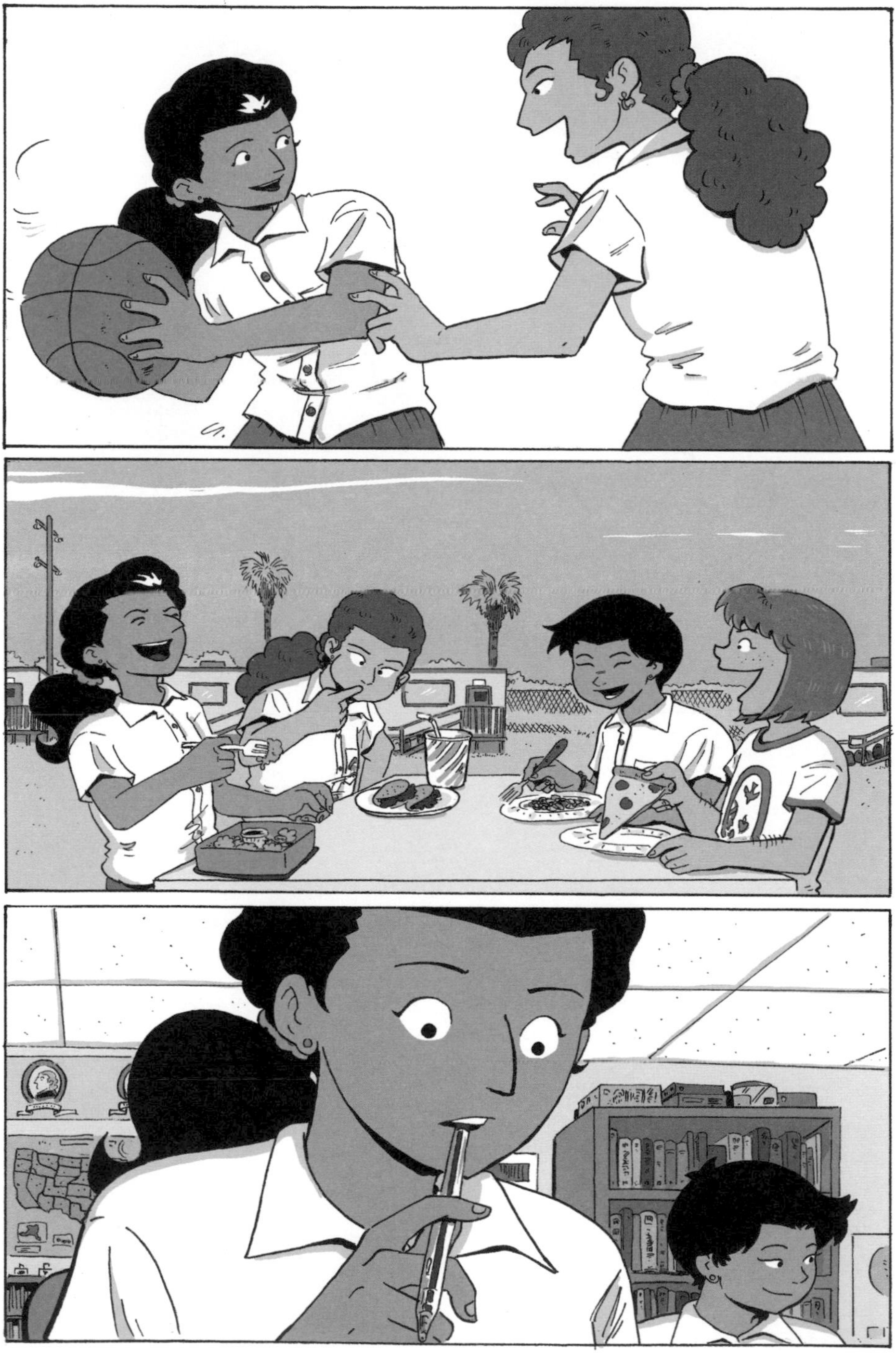

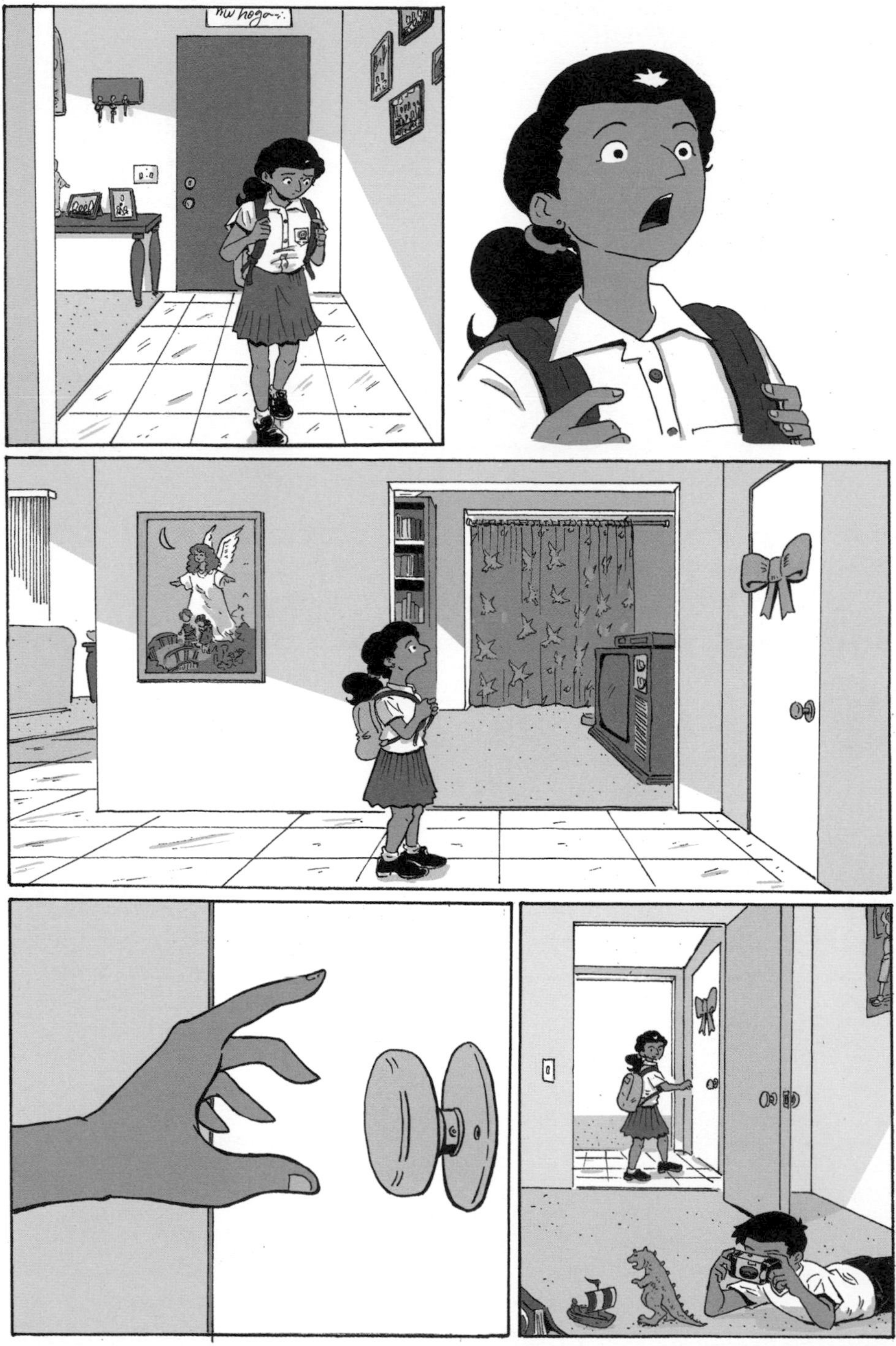

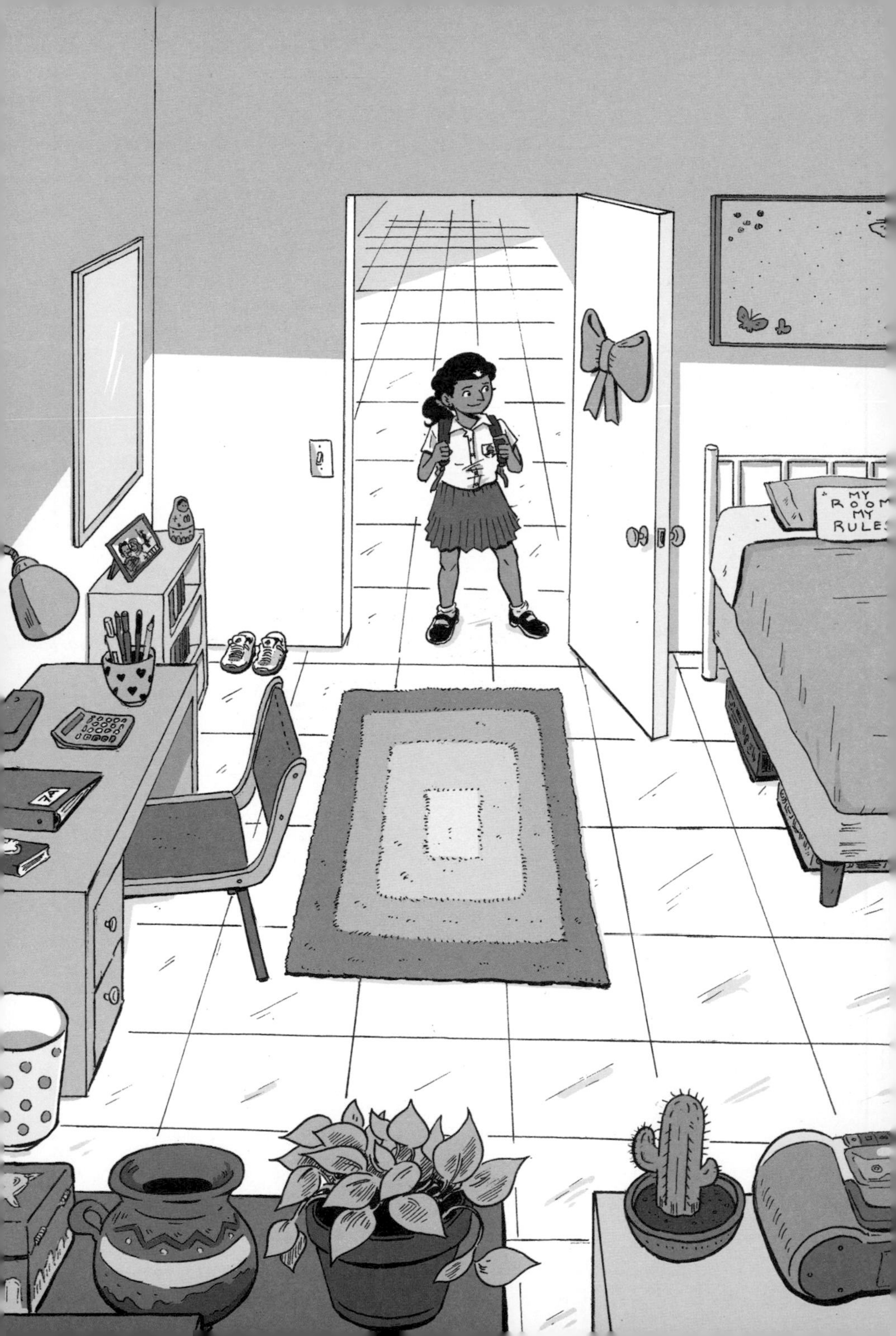
MY ROOM MY RULES

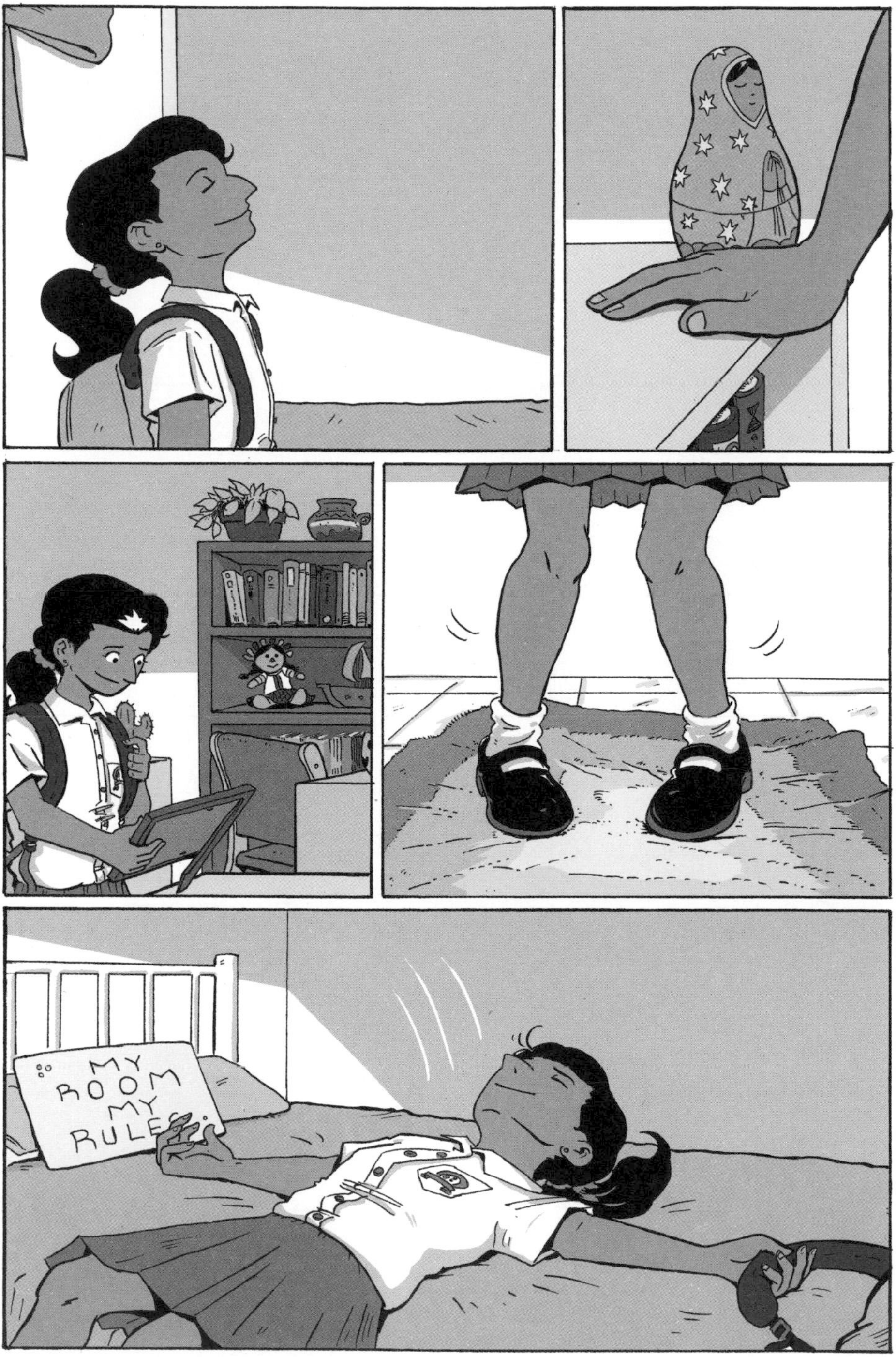
MY ROOM MY RULES

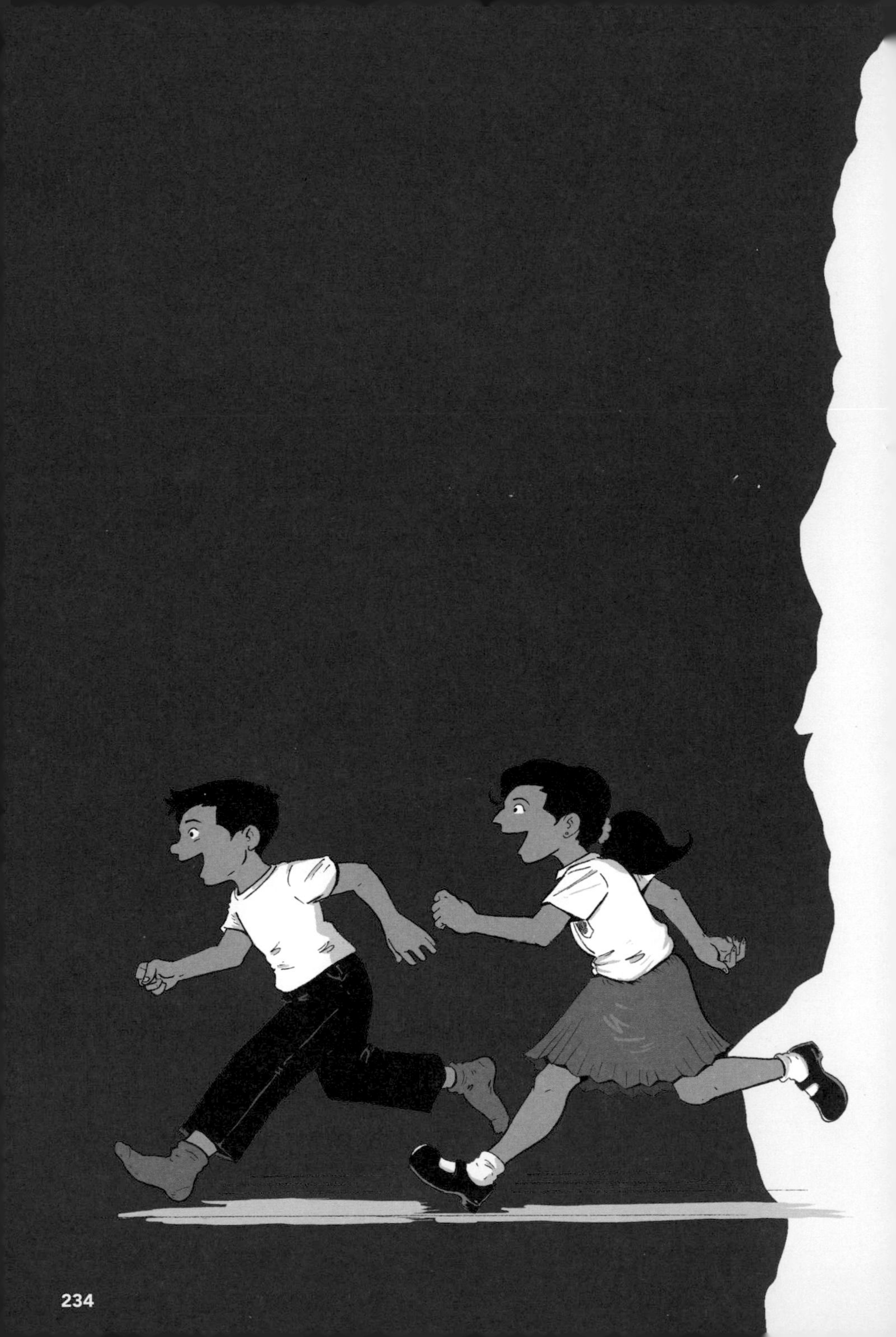

A Very Personal Note

Twin Cities came from a concept so simple that it remains the tagline: Mexicali twins continue their middle school education on opposite sides of the border.

I chose middle schools in Mexicali and Calexico as a setting because I had a similar experience. When I finished sixth grade, my parents presented me with the option of studying in the United States. They told me it would make it easier if I ever wanted to attend high school or college on the American side. If I didn't like it, I could come back to finish middle school. I decided to stay on the Mexican side because my friends were there. But I still wonder what would have happened had I made a different choice.

My siblings had different experiences. My brother went to middle school in Calexico but finished high school in Mexico. My sister spent most of her academic life in Calexico and went to an American college. As siblings do, we often compared notes on the pros and cons of each school. We also compared the Mexican school system with the American one. Without knowing it, we were generalizing two countries to make sense of our day-to-day lives. We shared stories about teachers, parts of the school that we were familiar with, and the advantages of getting up earlier or getting home sooner. A lot of families go through similar situations. As I was writing this book, I wanted to examine some of those moments and figure out what was at the core of them. Little to no surprise, it is a combination of things.

Siblinghood is complex. For many, siblings are the people who watch us grow as they grow alongside us. They live under the same roof, so territoriality can be an unspoken force for peace or downright war. From food to toys to who gets to choose the channel or who gets to ride in the front seat, bargains are made or conflict ensues. Our siblings can be the people in whom we most confide but also the ones who know how we are the most vulnerable. They have a unique position in our lives; we do not choose them, but we can choose to keep them. They are not our ancestry nor our individuality, but they can reflect where we come from— sometimes more bluntly than we'd like. And yet, they can be our rocks. Our champions. They can remind us without effort of what we have gone through and how we could be better. Siblings, especially at a young age, are the people who first show us that we can be different and unique while still sharing traits and worldviews. Siblings grow together, which means they can branch out while remaining tethered.

Writing this book also put me in a position to explore things that I've been dealing with for a very long time. I was born in the Imperial Valley, but I grew up on the Mexican side. I watched American television but listened to Mexican music. I went to American concerts but ate Mexican food. My passport says one thing, but my heritage says another. Even when I was as young as the characters in *Twin Cities*, I had questions but lacked the vocabulary to articulate them. I wanted to explore something I still experience through these characters—not just Teresa and Fernando but their friends and parents as well.

The longer I live in the United States, the more distant I feel from my Mexicali upbringing. Not just because I get older. I love getting older and discovering new interests. But I can't help but notice some things dim in the distance or become unrecognizable. This is for things such as TV shows, music, or a type of humor. But it can also be for deeper matters such as friendships or customs. To consider that my hometown and my language may be among those things sometimes terrifies me, so I have to make efforts to continue cultivating them. I have to make efforts to continue to carry some of those elements I love. *Twin Cities* was one of those efforts. In a way, one of my intentions with *Twin Cities* was to remind myself why Mexicali is special but why I chose to leave. I wanted to express thanks for all the good times, the shortcomings, and the valuable lessons of growing up in a border city with strong people all around. I hope this book gets that point across.

When I was growing up, crossing the border was easy and quick. We even had jokes that one city was the extension of the other, no difference between the two. The other side of that coin was to joke about how we behaved differently as soon as we crossed that border line. Over the past few years, the physical barriers between Mexicali and Calexico have become more rigid. Working on this book was a constant reminder of the growing emphasis on the differences between the two nations instead of the similarities the people share. It's painful. Still, this project was my vessel to visit Mexicali and the Imperial Valley. Despite my unfavorable opinion about the desert's weather, I feel nothing short of pride and praise for Mexicali and Calexico. Mexicali held the world record for the largest taco in the early 2000s; it's the only border city where the Mexican side has a larger city than the American side; and its best feature is the people. I don't visit as frequently as I would like to. However, I stay in touch with relatives and friends who give me updates and recommendations on what to eat or where to go the next time I swing by. And as soon as I'm there, I smile. It's where I'm from, and it's where a lot of wonderful people live.

I should also note that for younger cities, Mexicali and Calexico are abundant with immigrant and native stories. I highlight Chinese food as the regional food, but the history of the Chinese community is a pillar to the region, yet it's not my story to tell. I recommend looking into it since it's also tied to the history of the United States. Likewise, local indigenous communities of the Baja peninsula have a rich culture tied to the land. They are their own storytellers and must have recognition for history through their lens. They have been here the longest and know the land better than most. I rarely touch on the subject but am trying to learn more from them.

CHARACTERS

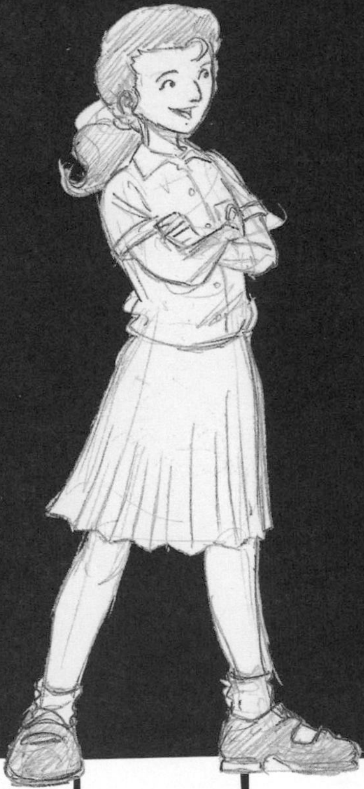

Luisa Teresa Sosa

Born on September 13, she's a girl who has recently developed an interest in studying in the United States. She's not afraid to ask a question when she's feeling uncertain and enjoys talking to her friends during lunch. She loves video games and candy. She also has a tendency to not finish her food. Since Teresa grew up as a twin, she's accustomed to being treated as half of a unit. But she's learning to set boundaries that let people know she wants to be her own person. She's even leaving her old nickname, "Lu-lu Twin," behind in order to claim full autonomy of her identity. Her favorite color is blue, and she loves Mexicali's Chinese food.

TERESA

Luis Fernando Sosa

Born on September 13, he's a bit on the shy side and likes things the way they are. He doesn't enjoy mowing the lawn, which his father makes him do on a regular basis. He prefers to watch television and play video games. He also loves taking photographs and turning them into a collage. Unlike his twin sister, he loves being treated as half of a unit. He may think he's the better half, but he's happy being half of a Lu-lu Twin. His interest in school has less to do with his classes and more to do with seeing his friends. He loves corn chips, Mexicali's Chinese food, and any Mexican candy. Fernando is also left-handed.

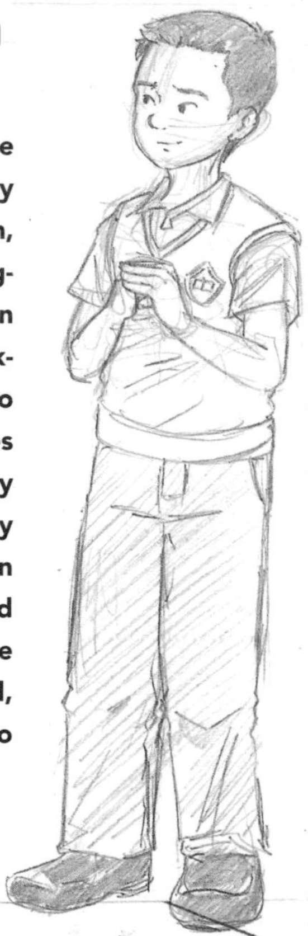

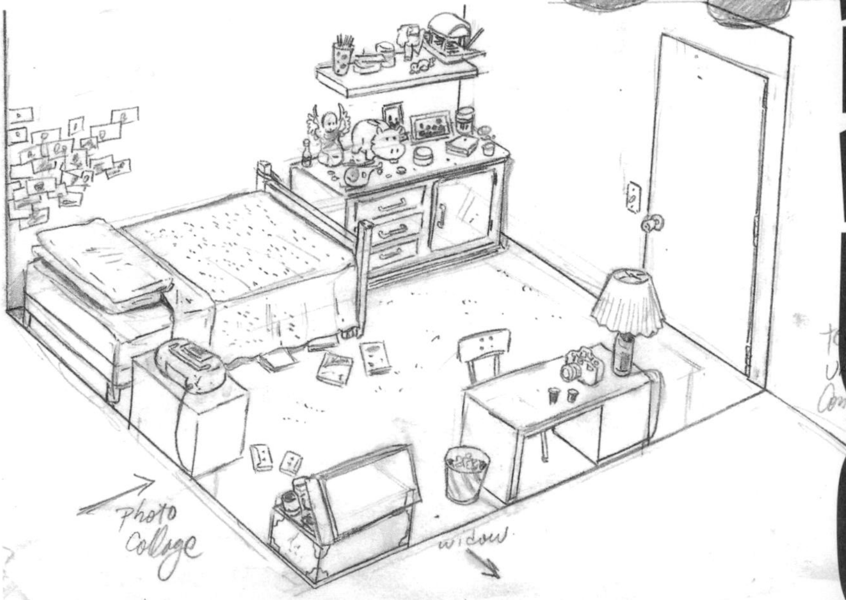
Photo Collage
widow

FERNANDO

SKETCHES

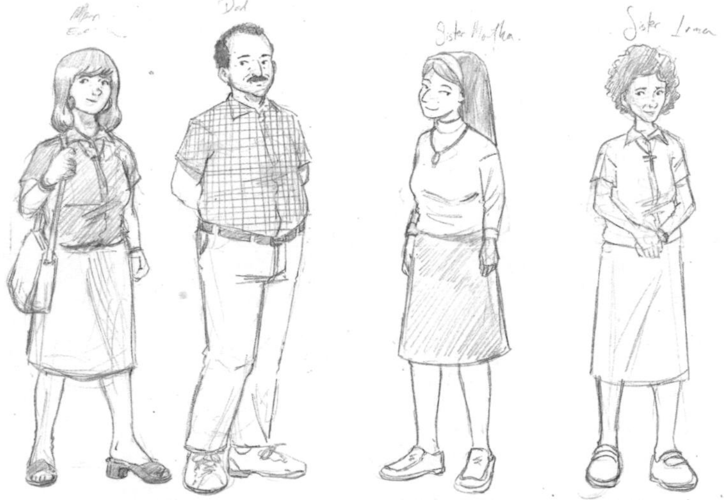
Dad
Sister Martha.

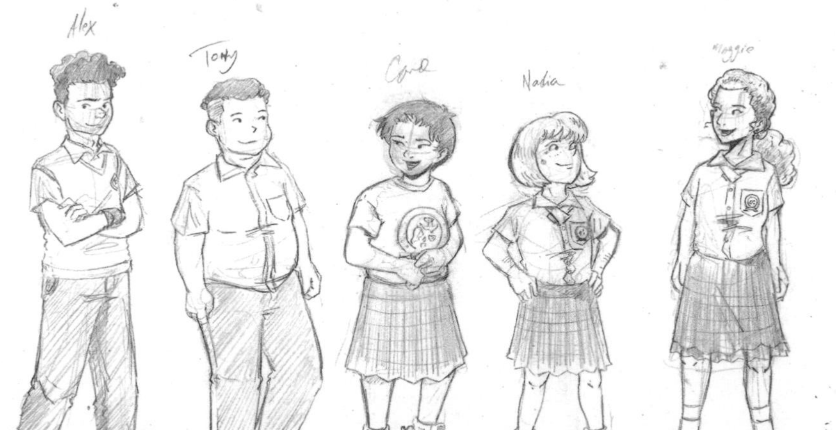
Alex
Tony
Nadia
Maggie

to of
rch
→
tower)

HALLWAY
to
Kitchen
→

wide opening
Arch.

FeR's
Room

Room
under Construction

Power strip

BACK door

HALLWAY

phone

241

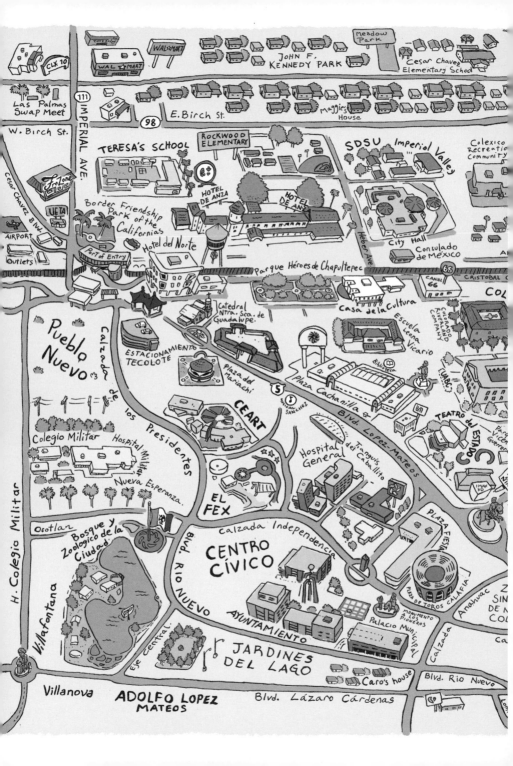

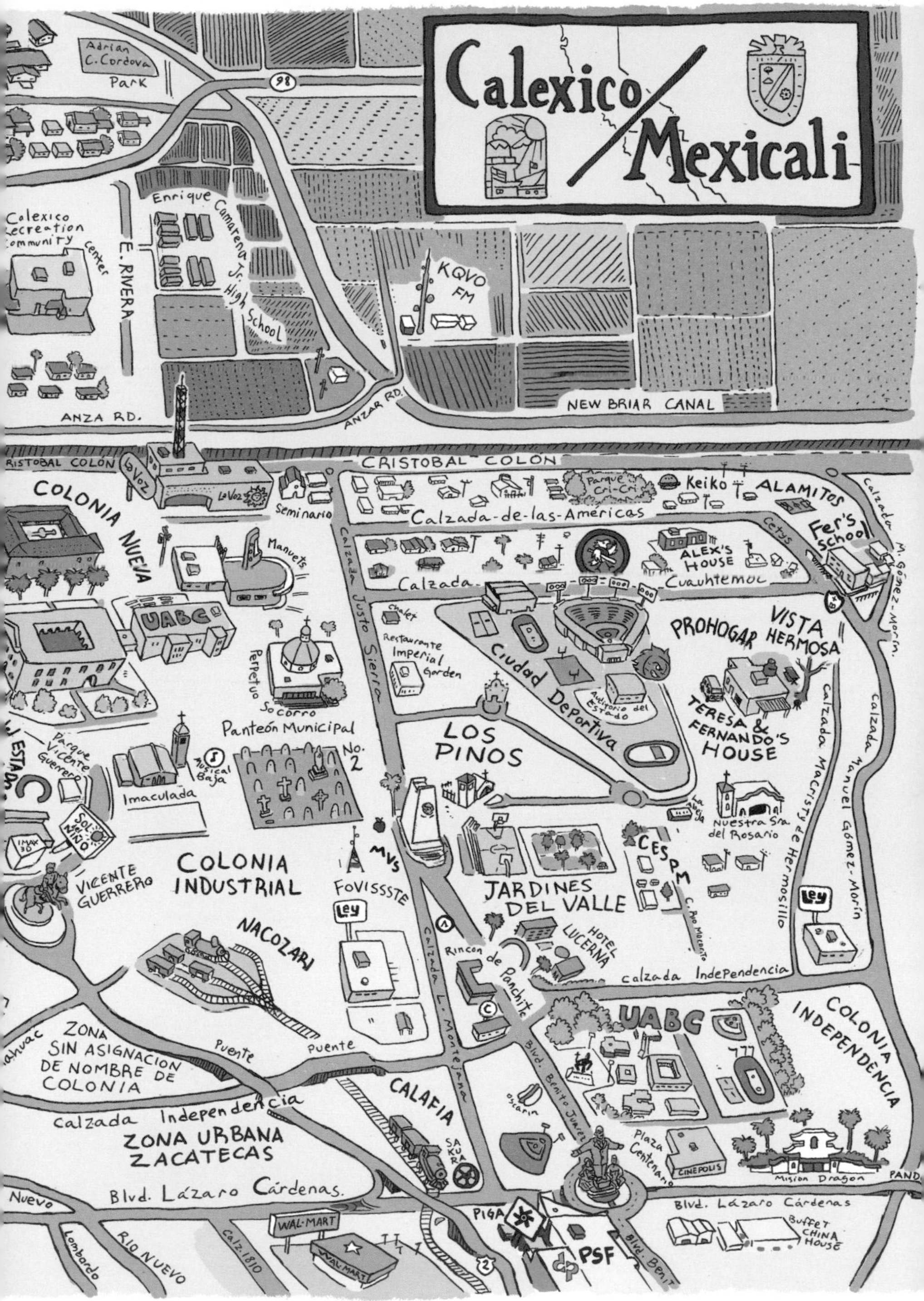
Calexico / Mexicali
Adrian C. Cordova Park
98
Enrique Camarena Jr. High School
Colexico Recreation Community Center
E. RIVERA
KQVO FM
ANZA RD.
ANZAR RD.
NEW BRIAR CANAL
CRISTOBAL COLON
COLONIA NUEVA
La Voz
Seminario
Manuets
UABC
Parque Cri-Cri
Keiko
ALAMITOS
Calzada-de-las-Americas
Cetys
Fer's school
ALEX'S HOUSE
Calzada Cuauhtemoc
Calzada M. Gómez-Morín
Calzada Justo Sierra
Chalet
Restaurante Imperial Garden
Perpetuo Socorro
Ciudad Deportiva
Auditorio del Estado
PROHOGAR
VISTA HERMOSA
TERESA & FERNANDO'S HOUSE
Panteón Municipal No. 2
LOS PINOS
Parque Vicente Guerrero
Musical Baja
Imaculada
SOL del NIÑO
IMAX 3D
La Abeja
Nuestra Sra. del Rosario
Calzada Macristy de Hermosillo
Calzada Manuel Gómez-Morín
CESPM
MVS
COLONIA INDUSTRIAL
VICENTE GUERRERO
FOVISSSTE
Ley
JARDINES DEL VALLE
C. Rio Mocorito
NACOZARI
HOTEL LUCERNA
Rincon de Panchito
Calzada L. Montejano
calzada Independencia
COLONIA INDEPENDENCIA
UABC
Puente
Puente
ZONA SIN ASIGNACION DE NOMBRE DE COLONIA
Calzada Independencia
ZONA URBANA ZACATECAS
CALAFIA
SAKURA
Oscarin
Blvd. Benito Juarez
Plaza Centenario
CINEPOLIS
Mision Dragon
Blvd. Lázaro Cárdenas.
Blvd. Lázaro Cárdenas
Nuevo
Lombardo
RIO NUEVO
Calz. 1810
WAL-MART
PIGA
PSF
Blvd. Benit
Buffet CHINA HOUSE
PAND

Acknowledgments

It's worth mentioning that this book was scripted and drawn through a tough year for many people. I was one of those fortunate enough to keep working, but many weren't. May we hear their stories as soon as possible. May better days follow.

Twin Cities came to life because of the efforts of many talented individuals. Editor Whitney Leopard and my agent, Elizabeth Bennet, were present from the initial proposal all the way through the printed page. Their input always made we wonder if I was telling the best version of the story I wanted to tell. In its final form, thanks to them, the answer is yes. We did it. *Twin Cities* happened because they believed in it from the beginning.

A special thank-you to Kristen Gish. Our mutual support makes our home a wonderful environment. During the creation of this book we both made big adjustments and came out stronger together. To my parents and siblings, I'd like to express tremendous gratitude. A lot of details regarding Mexicali, Calexico, school, and pop culture were inspired by conversations with them. Our upbringing was a source of inspiration. Even though this book is not autobiographical, it is rooted in the personal. Thank you for everything.

While I was growing up, I loved going to school to see friends. Quite a few of them are still important people in my life. Thank you for being there, whether to listen, shake your heads at me, or make helpful suggestions.

Huge thanks to Mabel Meneses for all the input on transborderism, which is a major element in this story. Transborder students cross the border every day to go to school, but "transborder" also applies to people who live in border regions and go back and forth for a number of reasons.

I wasn't aware this was a field of study, but thanks to Mabel and her recommended texts, I got to learn more about an experience I was already familiar with.

Before I started writing the script for *Twin Cities*, I talked with many twins. They shared stories about their favorite moments, tough feelings, and the events that marked their bond as well as their individuality. Thank you for sharing.

The schools that Teresa and Fernando attend are based on real private Catholic schools. The one in Mexicali is inspired by Instituto Felix de Jesus Rougier. Thank you to the principal and staff who allowed me to take photographs for reference.

Last but not least, something I found challenging for *Twin Cities* was how to approach coloring without repeating what I had done in previous comics. During the making of this book, I relied on the advice of my editor as well as peers. They listened to my ideas on color palettes for themes and gave me constructive suggestions. I'm very happy with the results. So to you, Orpheus Collar, Kel McDonald, Joss Martinez, and Bones Leopard: Thank you very much. It made all the difference.

Notes on a Particular Word

Making comics that take place in Mexicali raised a difficult question for me: "Why am I writing this in English if it takes place in Mexico?" I understand the logic and have seen other artists and writers come up with great solutions. Still, it feels like a compromise. But since the dialogue and occasional caption box are in English, I take joy in inserting as many Spanish labels, signs, and interjections as I can. From changing the laughter of "Ha ha" to "Ja ja" to replacing a "Hey!" with an "Eits!" adding any indication that these characters are living in Mexico is an important element. They are small details, but I care deeply about them.

When I was writing *Twin Cities*, Whitney and I had conversations over certain words. The word that took the most attention was "pocho/pocha." For the record, it is pejorative. In this section, I'd like to talk a little bit about it.

I grew up hearing the word as a term for people of Mexican descent who lived in the United States and spoke Spanglish. At the time, Spanglish was not recognized as a formal language by most Mexicans or even Americans. There is also the word "pochismo(s)," which means to modify a word loaned from one language to another. In this case, specifically from English to Spanish or vice versa. For example, instead of saying "estacionar" (the verb "to park"), they will say "parkear," turning the verb "to park" into Spanish. For many on the Mexican side of the border, a "pocho" or "pocha" ("poche" didn't exist yet) was someone who spoke a mix of two languages and was not taking action to become fluent in Spanish. It was someone who, in their eyes, had abandoned their heritage and culture, starting with language. Like I said, it's pejorative, but some Mexican Americans have reclaimed and embraced the term. Some use it to informally mean they speak Spanglish and to signal their dualistic background.

So what's going on here? Is it offensive? Does it make room for a nuanced discussion? Why use it in this book? Like many things involving language and geopolitical circumstances, it has a long history.

First things first. Where does the word come from? It's a Spanish word typically used to describe fruit that is overripe, discolored, or rotten. So right away, it's not a flattering term.

Mexico and the United States are relatively young neighboring countries. Both have a history of colonization from European empires. One of the biggest marks left by those empires is the language. On the border regions, such a mark is vibrant. (I would like to recognize that there are indigenous languages still spoken in these areas, but I will stick to English and Spanish here, since I'm talking about just one word.) Living in this area can bring up difficult questions: What language does a person speak? English or Spanish? If you can speak or understand both, which one is preferred? Why the preference? Because, surely, if a person is proud to be from somewhere, that person must practice its customs. In this case, the custom is language. And what if that person doesn't practice such a custom? What does that imply about them? There aren't simple answers to these questions. They demand personal responsibility over something larger, with a long and violent history. There are many reasons why a person may not speak a language or choose to speak a different one. Calling someone "rotten" because they may not practice a custom is transgressive. It doesn't help anyone.

In *Twin Cities*, Alex is a complicated boy. He has gone through a lot, and his anger has gone unchecked. His bias says that if you're not living in Mexico or if you don't speak Spanish, you're not Mexican. Personally,

I don't agree, but his experience is one that many people can relate to. Moreover, a lot of people don't pause and unpack that bias. Meanwhile, Fernando is at a crossroads in his life and is influenced by Alex. Fernando has always seen himself as part of a duo, and now that his sister is seeking independence, he wants to cling to what he finds familiar—in his case, his Mexican roots. Teresa's interest in the United States feels to him as if she is abandoning her roots. Fernando speaks the term in anger. On the other hand, Teresa is trying to broaden her vocabulary. She and her friends speak a mix of Spanish and English. Their friendship overcomes language barriers, and as long as they understand each other, it doesn't matter which language is dominant. Still, the term is hurtful to Teresa because of how Fernando uses it.

Is it offensive to some people? Yes, absolutely. There are Mexican Americans who have chosen to embrace the term and use it with pride due to their multicultural heritage. That is a personal choice. There are many terms for people with Latin backgrounds living in the United States. Each of those are a mix of cultural history and choice. That said, from my own experience, I have always seen the term "pocho" as mean-spirited. Does it make room for a nuanced conversation? That depends on who is in the conversation and who's driving the discussion. There is always room for more listening.

Why use it at all? In this story, I decided to use it because it gets to one of the ongoing themes of the book. Two siblings are starting to grow apart, and in a heated argument, one goes for the meanest word he can think of. Siblings can be like that. They know each other so well, they know what would hurt the most. Within the story, I wanted to address that it is a word that intends to other someone. It was a big decision—I don't casually use the word, especially since both Spanish and English have a variety of wonderful words that emphasize our similarities and the positive aspects of our differences. To use it, even in fiction, meant being responsible for it.

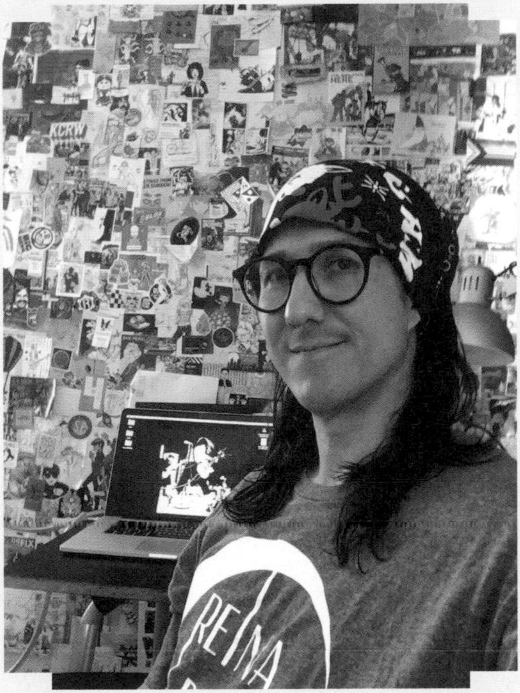
KCRW

About the Creator

Jose Pimienta grew up in Mexicali, Mexico, listening to music, watching movies, and walking around as much as possible. They attended Savannah College of Art and Design, where they studied sequential art and developed an interest in storyboarding. After graduating, they moved to Los Angeles, where they currently reside. Jose makes comics with different writers and publishers and creates storyboards for films and commercials. Their first solo graphic novel, *Suncatcher,* came out in 2020. See more of their work at josepimienta.com.

FIND YOUR VOICE
WITH ONE OF THESE EXCITING GRAPHIC NOVELS